I0780444

SKY KNIGHTS

THE GREATEST ENEMY IS THE DARKNESS WITHIN

James Domenighini

Copyright © 2025 by James Domenighini

All rights reserved. No part of this publication may be reproduced, distributed, or transmitted in any form or by any means, including photocopying, recording, or other electronic or mechanical methods, without the prior written permission of the author, except in the case of brief quotations embodied in critical reviews and certain other noncommercial uses permitted by copyright law.

978-1-965552-51-3 (Paperback)
978-1-965552-50-6 (Hardback)

Library of Congress Control Number: 2025921115

admin@bookwrightshouse.com
☎ (213) 286 6700

CHAPTER ONE

SOMEWHERE BENEATH ME PEOPLE were dying. Their lifeboat had fallen into the turbulent atmosphere of a gas giant, the planet Gargaphia. Even now they might be suffocating as their air ran out, freezing as their power failed, or watching as their lifeboat's hull bent inward, crushing under the severe weight of the planet's tremendous atmosphere.

Meanwhile, my fighter patrolled far above the gas giant's atmosphere, along with five more fighters from the Forty-Second Fighter Squadron, searching inside Gargaphia's shroud for the missing lifeboat. We had searched for two days, all the while knowing that time was running out for the castaways.

The Search and Rescue boats from our carrier, *Soyuz*, waited farther out. They lacked the sophisticated sensor modules that had replaced our main guns for this mission. Their crews waited with impatience while we probed the atmosphere. Saving lives was their business, not ours.

One of Sky Command's highest principle's is to never leave anyone behind, to never give up on a rescue mission.

My father possessed a similar belief. He taught me to feel the same compassion for others that I'd want them to feel for me. So as I flew my patrol pattern, as I thought about the people down there, on the verge of death, I thought about my father, too. He had been the single most important person in my life.

Stupidity had brought the castaways here. The casual handling of their ship had placed them in jeopardy. And for what? For a simple distraction.

Here on the frontier, on the fringe of explored space, people knew better than to pilot their ships with casualness. Behind every distraction lurked danger. The captain of the starliner *Sunrise* had forgotten that danger as he brought his ship into orbit around Gargaphia. He let his crew and himself enjoy Gargaphia's beauties: the atmosphere's exotic greens and blues; the brilliant flashes of lightning; the reddish streaks of meteors decaying in the upper atmosphere; the gorgeous rings encircling it. *Sunrise*'s passengers and crew had been enthralled by Gargaphia's glories. From one of the liner's other lifeboats we learned that the liner's crew had kept sufficient distance from the meteor stream but failed to detect a few scattered meteors further out. Just a millimeter in diameter, these meteors proved large enough to ruin everyone's viewing pleasure.

Had *Sunrise*'s energy screen functioned, these micro-meteors would've disintegrated against it. But the starliner flew through the upper reaches of Gargaphia's ionized atmosphere, which interfered with the screen's proper operation. The screen was down, a meteor struck, and disaster followed.

The damage itself seemed minor: a maneuvering thruster shattered, a power line broken. But the momentary loss of both items reduced *Sunrise*'s agility. Before the starliner could maneuver out of danger, more meteors struck. One blew a hole through an engine and doomed the ship.

One small error, sufficient to plunge *Sunrise* into Gargaphia's atmosphere and scatter its desperate passengers about in lifeboats. Just enough of an error to send seventy souls into a black hell.

"Ice Maker, this is Samurai," my patrol leader, Captain James Gray, called over my comm unit.

"Ice Maker here," I replied.

"I'm spreading us out. We're going to patrol ten thousand kilometers apart, rather than the usual five hundred. *Soyuz* just called. Commodore Peng has decided this will be our final patrol. If we don't find anything now, that lifeboat is officially lost. Everyone will be listed as dead."

"He can't do that. We can't stop just because Peng's tired of spending time looking for them."

"Ice Maker, I feel the same way. But we have to trust in Peng's decision. Besides, it's our duty to the survivors we've rescued to get them to safety."

"We can send them back aboard one of our destroyers. We can't stop searching. How can we give up when there's even the slightest chance of success?"

I heard Gray sigh. I'd flown as his wing mate for four years now. He respected my opinion. We understood each other, depended upon each other.

"It's not my decision. I'm just following orders, as you should be. Besides, one destroyer wouldn't be enough."

"Then send both destroyers. Send the supply ship, too, if that'd help. We can't leave until we're certain they're dead. They might still be alive. If we leave them, it's just as if we killed them ourselves." Our small flotilla, designed for frontier patrols, for fighting piracy and smuggling, and for rescue missions such as this one, consisted of our carrier, *Soyuz*, two destroyers, a supply ship, and a small corvette designed for long range reconnaissance rather than combat.

"We can't send both destroyers away," Gray replied. "We'd be naked."

"But what about those missing people? We've as much of a duty to them as we do to the people we've already rescued."

"We have our orders, Ice Maker. We'll just have to trust that this time we'll find them."

"Trust? Trust what?"

"Trust we'll be lucky. Peng knows what he's doing."

"He knows what he's doing all right. He's condemning those people to death!"

"You don't know that."

"Maybe I don't. I just know we have to find them."

"Affirmative. I'm sending you the patrol coordinates. See you out there. Samurai out."

He patrolled too far away for me to see him vector off, but my sensors revealed it. My canopy was transparent at the moment, my fighter oriented upside down so Gargaphia appeared above me.

"I have received coordinates for our new vector," my A. I. counterpart, Kon, announced.

"Implement." I rolled my bird over so Gargaphia appeared below me. Then I let Kon fly us to our new patrol vector.

We hadn't found anything flying patrols five hundred kilometers apart. Would we at ten thousand? I doubted it.

Gargaphia was two-thirds the size of Saturn. Our sensors reached a few thousand kilometers into its ionized atmosphere before fading away. With fifty thousand kilometers of atmosphere between us and the planet's icy surface, what hope had we of success?

I suspected Captain Shumacher, our squadron's exec, had ordered one final patrol, then a quick return to *Soyuz*. But as the operation's commander, Captain Gray had a say in how things played out. He was making a last, desperate attempt to find that lifeboat.

We all were.

For forty minutes, I flew along my new vector, watching my instruments, without results. Somewhere below, enshrouded in a cold, oppressive prison, waited seventy people.

I felt frightened for them. What a horror, fighting for your sanity, knowing that at any moment you might die. How to hope for life with death all around you?

Perhaps they were already dead. Perhaps their lifeboat had burned up in the atmosphere. Or a lightning strike had blown it apart. Or it had smashed upon the icy surface. Or the stress had overcome them and they had murdered each other.

Who knew?

"Message from *Soyuz*," Kon said. "Return."

"We can't. We have to find them."

"Return has been directed."

"It's too soon."

"We must obey. It comes from Commodore Peng."

"We can't quit now. We're going down for a closer look."

"I cannot allow you to jeopardize yourself, nor this craft. I am returning us to *Soyuz*." Kon took control from me and we began ascending.

"What are you doing? Those people will die if we don't find them soon. Give me control."

"Commodore Peng has decided they are dead. We shall obey our new directive."

"Those people are alive down there. But they won't last long if we don't do something. We have to take a chance. This is no different than when we rammed that Na ship, *Gaeg*."

"Irrelevant. Then none of our weapon systems were effective against *Gaeg*. Ramming it was the only logical alternative. Burning up in Gargaphia's atmosphere chasing a fantasy is neither logical, nor acceptable. We will return to *Soyuz*."

The time for arguments had passed.

"Relinquish control to me or I'll exercise my override option."

"You cannot."

I took a deep breath. "For the record, I, Second Lieutenant Hector Josef Crossman, officially declare an override."

Kon didn't respond.

"Do you accept?" I asked.

No reply.

"Do you accept?" I demanded.

"I shall close down all peripherals," Kon replied. "You will have to fly this craft blind."

"That's mutiny. That goes against all your directives."

While we argued, we drew closer to *Soyuz*. Soon we'd be far from Gargaphia. By arguing, Kon kept us away from the gas giant.

"Final warning. Do you accept?"

"Affirmative."

"And our peripherals?"

"Fully functional."

"Good. Vector the lifeboat's descent into the atmosphere. Then provide me with an intercept vector. I'll bring us around."

"All possible vectors have been previously performed."

"So do it again," I said. Kon provided the information. I turned us back toward Gargaphia, this time moving toward a different patrol route.

"Ice Maker, this is *Soyuz*, what is your situation? Recall has been ordered," a flight controller called.

"Don't respond," I said.

"Ice Maker, this is Samurai. Form up. Recall's been sounded. There's nothing more we can do."

I kept quiet. I couldn't tell him what I intended doing, he'd know soon enough anyway. Besides, if I told him now, he'd have to order me back. Yet the closer I drew to Gargaphia, and the further from Gray, the less power he possessed to keep me from plunging into it.

One of the SAR boats called next. "Ice Maker, this is Birddog Twenty-five Two. Are you in trouble? Do you need assistance? Tell us, Hector."

I almost answered this call. It came from Second Lieutenant Corinna Vernon, co-pilot of Birddog Twenty-five Two, call sign Corrie. Her voice, soft and full of concern, drew me to her. But I dared not respond, no more than I dared answer the flight controller aboard *Soyuz*, or James Gray.

"Ice Maker," Captain Walter Sprague, the birddog's pilot and commander, spoke up. "If you need assistance, reply immediately."

They possessed the power to stop me. Their birddog, while not as fast as my fighter, carried a graviton beam capable of dragging me back.

"Negative," I replied, then shut my comm system down. I didn't want anyone arguing me out my intention.

Instead, I focused on Gargaphia. It loomed before me, a greenish-gray mass, streaked with blue and crimson. Bright flashes of yellow and white lightning rippled through its sky. Probes from our flotilla had already descended into the ionized atmosphere, searching for the lifeboat, finding nothing. Twice before, other members of my squadron had entered it, searching for clues. But the intense winds, great pressures, and lightning strikes had chased them out.

As we descended at a steep angle toward the atmosphere, I morphed my canopy from transparent to opaque. Images of the exterior world appeared upon my canopy. Whereas the world without grew dark and dismal, the virtual view on my canopy remained clear.

My bird, a TF5F tactical fighter, was one of the most advanced spacecraft in the Interstellar Association. The cockpit was so well insulated against radiation and sound that as we descended into Gargaphia's atmosphere at fifteen thousand kilometers per hour, I neither heard the screaming wind outside, nor felt any of the thermal spill-off from friction. Normally, my energy screen would've absorbed the heat, but the ionized atmosphere kept it from functioning. My fighter's kiron hull took the beating without complaint.

Though unable to hear the wind, I felt its presence. Thousand kilometer-per-hour winds slammed into us. It took all of my skill to keep us on course.

The sensor module in my bird's nose, where my main weapon usually sat, seemed useless. The friction and ionization interfered with its operation. I needed to slow below five thousand kph before I might receive any useful information from it. Yet the slower I flew, the more difficult survival would be.

Even while busy flying, I often thought of those people in that lifeboat. I wanted to find them. I didn't want to remain down here any longer than I had to, nor did I want them to, either.

I wanted them safe.

My canopy went berserk, its images flashing and fading. My cockpit darkened; then everything returned to normal. The virtual view resumed.

"What happened?" I asked.

Kon reported that lightning had struck the right trailing edge of our bird, almost wiping out our systems. Our rapid descent into the atmosphere polarized our hull, making us a flying lightning rod.

I slowed down, dropping our velocity to ten thousand kph. A little information started coming from the sensor module in our nose.

Flying became more difficult. At my faster velocity, the crosswinds had been a nuisance; now they became hazardous. When I had cut through the currents of hydrogen and methane at fifteen thousand kph, I hadn't traversed those currents long enough for them to affect my progress. Now, at my lesser velocity, they blasted against me, trying to rip my bird apart.

My antigrav field and lateral maneuvering thrusters compensated for the decreased velocity and increased wind sheer, but the deeper we descended, the stronger the winds became, gusting from four to five thousand kph. The atmosphere also grew thicker and heavier.

Flying along the lifeboat's predicted vector, we failed to find a shred of evidence it existed. Where was it? It had to be somewhere.

"We are receiving transmissions from *Soyuz*. Major Kreski commands our return."

"Burn him."

"Do you desire that transmitted?"

"Negative."

The atmosphere continued thickening as we descended. After forty thousand kilometers of angled descent we reached a layer so thick it was like flying through mud. I slowed below two thousand kph. The crosswinds had also slowed. They averaged about four hundred kph, with gusts up to six hundred.

"This is so damned frustrating," I said.

"Why are you so obsessed?" Kon inquired. "They are dead. We have no evidence to the contrary. Commodore Peng has declared them dead. Why not accept it? Destroying yourself will not change their demise. It will only add to the casualty list."

"Commodore Peng's wrong. They're alive. We are their last chance. We can't desert them."

"You are following a fantasy. You are going to destroy yourself just to prove that you are wrong."

"I'm willing to risk my life for others. That's what I've been doing for the last seven years."

"And upon what do you base your assumption that they live?"

"I can feel it."

"This is what separates man from machine. You desire for those people to live. You desire it so intensely that you make it so in your imagination, even when facts indicate otherwise."

"You're right. Human feelings defy logic. They defy mathematics. That's what separates humans from programs. Intuition is an important quality in a fighter pilot. And my intuition tells me those people are still alive."

"Then we must reach the surface as soon as possible."

"Why?"

"All systems are under great stress. The longer we remain, the greater the stress, until they cease functioning."

"What happens then?"

"We cease functioning."

"I see."

"Is there no manner by which I can dissuade you?"

"None."

"The record will then show that I am against this folly."

We descended deeper. A blast of wind blew us far off course. My bird's systems compensated for the motion. There wasn't any vertigo or sensation of lateral movement. It took us sixty seconds to restore our course.

I changed my canopy from opaque to transparent, but the atmosphere appeared black, colorless. I changed it back.

Several hours passed.

Did my squadron mates wonder if I still lived? Were they even still out there? Had Commodore Peng also listed me as dead? If so, would there be anyone out there to rescue us, if I found any lifeboat survivors, and if we escaped Gargaphia's ugly atmosphere?

I reached the surface. Jagged, icy outcrops pointed upward like giant thorns. The surface was under such great compression that the ice was stronger than my kiron hull. Crashing would be fatal.

I flew a few hundred meters up, well clear of any obstacles, at just a few hundred kilometers per hour. I cruised for several minutes, finding no trace of the lifeboat. No wreckage, not even a radiation signature, existed.

I was frustrated.

"What do you think happened? Did they manage to maneuver their lifeboat? Or did they vanish from the universe altogether?"

"Unknown."

"They must've been blown off course," I said. "That lifeboat couldn't have handled these winds. It could be hundreds of kilometers from here."

"Thousands of kilometers are not unlikely."

"That's a cheerful thought."

"What is your wish?"

I said nothing. Instead, I maneuvered into an ever expanding spiral around the ending point of the lifeboat's calculated vector, at five hundred meters up. Cruising at two hundred kilometers an hour, my bird bounced wildly about in the wind. Each blow, whether head-on or sideways, felt like slamming into a solid wall, shaking my fighter and straining my body with every impact.

As my spiral expanded, as my sensors failed to reveal any evidence of the lifeboat, I doubted the wisdom of my decision. I'd made it to the surface, something no one else had done. With considerable effort and luck, I might make it back to *Soyuz*. But I'd failed to find the lifeboat. If its occupants weren't dead, they soon would be.

My efforts had changed nothing.

"The gravitic generator is overheating," Kon announced.

"Will slowing down help?" I asked.

"Negative. Decreasing velocity will only intensify the stress upon the generator."

"How about if I landed and let the generator cool down?"

"The results would be negligible."

"Then what can I do?"

"Exit the atmosphere as soon as possible."

"How about if I increased velocity?"

"Velocity would have to be increased to six hundred kph. Six thousand would be better. However, the friction at six hundred, owing to atmospheric density at this depth, will be considerable. At that velocity the sensors will have only a few seconds to detect and confirm any target."

"So I might miss the lifeboat."

"Affirmative. Wind sheer will continue straining the gravitic generator, but not as seriously as at the present."

"Understood." I increased my velocity to seven hundred kph. As my spiral's diameter increased, many of my sensors failed. I had to find the lifeboat before all my sensors failed.

I rubbed my eyes. We'd been spiraling for an hour now. The winds weren't much of a problem at this velocity except when I flew into them. The gravitic generator behaved itself, though operating hotter than normal.

"Sensors are detecting increased neutrino activity."

Neutrinos existed everywhere in the universe. However, increased activity might indicate an artificial source.

"Where?" I demanded.

"Neutrino activity has disappeared."

I spun about, my systems straining with the maneuver.

"Activity relocated. Activity lost. Perhaps it is a natural phenomenon."

"Where are they?" I snarled. "We had them. I'm sure of it. Where did they go?"

"Unknown."

"Find out!"

"Several systems, including heat transference and gravitic generator, are nearing critical stages."

I came around again, spiraling tighter. Twice the sensors peaked. I circled lower and slower, wrestling with the wind.

"There!" I cried out as a dark, bread-shaped lump barely appeared before me on Gargaphia's frozen surface. Tears welled in my eyes.

I had found the lifeboat!

It sat against an icy outcrop, its hull crumpled. Was it wrecked? Were its occupants dead?

I dropped to the surface and hovered a few meters from the lifeboat. The stress upon my gravitic generator increased as I fought to remain in place.

"Life signs?" I asked.

"Inconclusive," Kon replied.

"We have to know if anyone's still alive."

"Attempting short range communications."

Nothing happened,

"The lifeboat's power plant barely functions," Kon said.

"Broadcast it's position to the orbiting SAR boats," I said.

"Transmitting. Reception confirmed."

A Search and Rescue boat now had a lock on the lifeboat's position. It's crew also knew I was alive.

"The lifeboat has failed to respond to our broadcasts. It appears lifeless."

"Let's find out." I shot my bird over the lifeboat at fifteen hundred kph. The shockwave rocked it. My stressed inertial dampers released a few gees into the cockpit and I felt myself slammed into my seat, a great weight upon my chest.

Returning to the lifeboat's location, I saw lights on in several viewing ports.

"Thank goodness you found us!" a man's voice sobbed. "We only have a little air left. We're all crammed into the passenger section. We've suffered a hull breach in the control section. Our computer's fried. We're so glad you found us. We didn't think anybody was up there. We thought we were dead. Thank you! Thank you!"

"Your position's been given to Search and Rescue. They're on their way," I said.

"You'll stay nearby until then, won't you?" the man pleaded.

"Negative. My systems are failing. I've got to go."

"Please don't leave us. We've been so alone."

"How soon will the birddog be here?" I said to Kon.

"Birddogs' Twenty-five Eight and Twenty-five Twelve are twenty minutes away," Kon replied.

"We've been here for so long and are so alone, please don't leave us," the man begged. "Please."

I cut the connection. They were safe now. Help was coming.

I lifted away from the surface at a gentle speed. At one kilometer up, I rotated our bird around and caught the wind. It pushed us far away before I cut in my engine and rocketed skyward.

Atmospheric friction overheated our kiron hull. No amount of insulation could protect us from this much friction. Already the interior felt like an oven.

Enclosing myself in my suit, my helmet wrapping around my head, in seconds I was sealed tight. My suit's cooling unit instantly activated.

"Velocity exceeding thirty thousand kilometers per hour. Hull temperatures approaching critical limits. Gravitic generator failure imminent. Sensor module sealed from exterior. Fighter integral sensor systems failing. Systems approaching critical temperatures."

"So am I," I gasped. "Vent the cabin's air. Make it a vacuum in here."

"Affirmative."

"Concentrate the gravitic generator's power into the inertial dampers. Don't worry about maneuvering. The winds won't deflect us at this velocity."

"Affirmative. Altitude ten thousand kilometers."

We continued climbing. My weight increased as gee forces eluded the inertial dampers. Every breath strained, I struggled to keep from suffocating. I couldn't lift my hands. As blood began draining from my head, my suit tightened around my waist and legs, restricting the flow, keeping me from blacking out. The pressure dragged me towards oblivion.

As our systems began failing, Kon cut the engine. I found myself weightless and the sudden release of the strain robbed me of consciousness.

"How do you feel?" Kon asked me.

I blinked. A red mist filled my vision. My suit's first aid system administered a stimulant. My vision cleared as my heart rate increased. I moved an arm and groaned. "Status?"

"Present velocity is fifty thousand kilometers per hour. The hull has surpassed critical temperatures and is molten. However, we are outside the atmosphere and the hull is cooling. I am attempting to vector our thrusters into a stable orbit.

"Inertial dampers have failed. The gravitic generator has failed. Sensors have failed. Communications have failed. Lateral control has failed."

"What hasn't failed?"

"Waste disposal systems are functional."

I laughed. "With so many failures, how are you vectoring our thrust?"

"Engine thruster controls are responding at twelve percent."

"At least we can do something."

"Affirmative."

"Where the hell is everyone?" I wondered aloud.

"Unknown."

A substantial jolt shook us.

"What just happened?"

"Unknown," Kon responded.

Another jolt shook us.

"A micro-probe has penetrated our hull."

My suit's comm system activated.

"Ice Maker, Ice Maker," came Corrie's frantic voice. "Are you okay? You're cherry red. Be okay. Please be okay."

I was too choked to respond.

"Ice Maker, respond," Captain Gray called. "The lifeboat is coming out. Twenty-five Eight and Twenty-five Twelve have retrieved it. I hope you're okay. What you did was a miracle. It'll be an even greater miracle if you're still alive."

"I'm alive," I replied.

"Thank god! We've got you locked up. We'll have you back aboard *Soyuz* in ten minutes. You'll have to eject your cockpit. Your bird's too hot to take back aboard. We'll let you know when to eject."

"Affirmative."

"I'm glad you're alive," Corrie said.

"So am I."

CHAPTER TWO

I RETURNED TO *Soyuz* TO a hero's welcome. People patted me on my back, shook my hands, hugged me, thanked me, shouted for joy, cheered, laughed. Their excitement was infectious. I found it difficult to free myself from them, to reach my mission debriefing, to gain my quarters, to sleep.

Later, after sleeping, a shower, a meal, and a physical, I found myself at a party given in my honor. I'd accomplished something that no one else had. And I'd done it not for personal glory, but to save seventy lives.

I saved those lives because I couldn't have lived with myself if I'd left them behind. I'd had the courage to take the initiative, to disobey orders. In saving those seventy souls, I also saved the souls of the nine hundred people in our flotilla. Instead of hell, we were in heaven.

My heaven was very near, dear, and personal. My heaven contained only one being, not a god, but an angel. And I danced with my angel at the party: I danced with Corinna Vernon. Holding her in my arms meant more than any honors. With Corinna beside me, time stopped.

Corinna's boyfriend, a SAR pilot named Jake McVeen, hated seeing her with me. He glared at me, but kept his distance. We detested each other. We had argued, and thrown punches, over her.

McVeen was far from decent enough for her. But how to tell Corinna this, how to make her believe it, without ruining our friendship? If only she might see his true nature.

Before I had a chance to dance with Corinna again, Captain Gray summoned me to his office. I left the party, wondering why. He knew of my feelings for Corinna. For whatever reason, James Gray needed to see me now. The sooner I reached his office, the sooner I'd dance with my angel again.

A few minutes later, out of breath from rushing, I reached his door. I'd visited his office many times. It was small, with just enough room for a desk with a chair, and two extra chairs before the desk. I announced myself and his door admitted me.

I entered his office. On the wall to my right, I saw a computer-generated image of the Crab Nebula as seen from Earth, with its pale blue center and crimson fringes. The left wall generated a high-orbit view of Gentry, Gray's home world, a blue-green planet, bigger than Earth, but with a similar gravity.

As the door whispered closed behind me, I turned and saw a marsh scene from Gentry appear. Brown marsh plants, straight and tall, with angular green leaves, climbed out of grayish-blue water. Yellowish sunlight twinkled on the water, while the office's computer produced a faint breeze with the sweet scent of green plants. Adding to the illusion, a marsh goof, an amphibian native to Gentry, giggled in the background.

Facing back around, I spied James Gray sitting at his desk, viewing a holo image, invisible from my side except for a slight flicker. Behind Gray, on the wall, several computer-generated tactical displays depicted the individual flight paths of our various search patrols around Gargaphia. I had trouble spotting my path.

I cleared my throat and Gray glanced up. He looked tired. Standing, he switched his holo off and plodded around from behind his desk.

"I see you changed your walls again," I said.

"I grew tired of the seascapes from home. But I didn't want to delete Gentry altogether."

I pointed toward the Crab Nebula.

He shrugged. "It's always been my favorite."

"I didn't know that," I said. "Jim, what's up? I was dancing with Corinna."

"I know. I was at the party for a while."

His tone worried me. You couldn't fly with someone for four years and not know him.

"What's wrong?" I asked.

He cleared his throat. "You."

"Huh?"

"You're what's wrong. Not exactly you. Hector, I'm sorry, but I'm about to make a misery of your life. I don't have a choice. It's my duty."

"What're you talking about?"

"You're being promoted."

I stared at him, then smiled. "You're joking."

"No."

I found it difficult believing him. Promotions in Sky Command were infrequent on the frontier. Few pilots retired. Fewer died in combat against smugglers, pirates, or unfriendly races. Few command slots existed beyond the squadron level. Once a pilot reached a certain rank, he often remained there forever. A promotion only meant that one of my seniors had found a better slot with another squadron. Good for him, better for me.

Grinning, I said, "I knew I had a good record, but I hadn't expected this."

"You should have."

"You don't seem happy for me. What aren't you telling me?"

He sat in one of the two chairs before his desk. He glanced up at me. "You disobeyed orders."

"So? Fighter pilots disobey orders all the time. It's part of our nature. I've done it dozens of times. So have you."

"You embarrassed Major Kreski."

"So?"

"You embarrassed Commodore Peng as well."

"The man declared those people dead. It was inconvenient for him to keep searching. He was ready to abandon them rather than spend any more time looking. I can't help it if he's embarrassed. Those people were more important than his pride."

"I agree with you. Most of us do. You've brought honor and pride to the squadron and the flotilla. But you've angered Peng and Kreski. You can't second-guess your commanders. You have to obey orders."

"They're morons. They shouldn't be in command. How anyone could put such idiots in positions of command amazes me."

Gray shook his head. "That's just the sort of garbage that gets you into trouble. You can't go around disparaging people like that. That's why they're doing this to you."

"Are they going to block my promotion?" I asked.

"No. They're in favor of it."

"Then what's the problem?"

James Gray folded his hands, his eyes sad. "Lieutenant Colonel Daggett and I nominated you for the Scarlet Nova. Kreski concurred. And Peng agreed. A few hours ago word came from Sky Command approving it. With the Nova comes an automatic promotion."

"So? Who do I replace?"

"No one."

I stared at him. "You're not making any sense. Here I've got the chance to hold Corinna in my arms and McVeen can't do a damn thing about it, and you're wasting my time with stupid jokes."

"It's not a joke."

"Then what's going on?"

"You played into their hands. You embarrassed them and now you've given them the opportunity to get even. There's nothing I can do for you. It's done."

I continued staring at him, not knowing what he meant.

Leaning forward, he glared at the deck. "They didn't have the guts to tell you. Instead, they passed the duty to me. Shumacher should have told you. As the exec, it's his duty, not mine. But he's one of them. They're moral cowards. But they're our commanders. They've given me my orders and I have to obey them. Just as you do."

"What are you talking about?"

He looked up at me. "Your promotion is effective immediately. But there aren't any slots for another first lieutenant in our squadron. You're being transferred out. You handed them the best opportunity to get rid of you, and they took it. But you did the right thing. If you hadn't disobeyed orders, those people would've died. But by saving them, you condemned yourself."

"I don't believe it."

"I'm sorry, Hector. It's done."

"But this is my home. I've been aboard this ship, with this squadron, for seven years."

"And now it's time to move onward."

"But I don't want to move onward. I've finally got a chance with Corinna. I think she sees me now as more than just a friend. If I leave, what'll happen? I can't leave her with McVeen. He's wrong for her."

"Who's to say you're right for her?" Gray asked.

"We both know I am."

"I don't know that, Hector," he said, standing. "And neither do you. Just because you're leaving the squadron doesn't mean you won't see her again."

"Get serious. I might be posted back on Earth, a couple of thousand light years away. Or on the far side of the Association. Even if I stayed in this region, it's one thousand light years per side. That's a billion cubic light years! I might never see her again."

"But you might."

"No. This is my home. I'm staying. You'll just have to transfer someone else out."

Gray shook his head. "I can't transfer anyone else out. I don't have that authority. You have to go. You have to make room for someone else now."

"I don't want to make room for anyone else. I'm staying."

My friend placed his hand on my shoulder. "I know how you feel. But you have to go. It's your time."

"How could they do this to me? What kind of creatures are they, that it gives them pleasure to ruin a man's life?"

"Cowards. That's what they are. Petty. Selfish."

"How can I fight this?"

"You can't, Hector. It's done. Your promotion and transfer have been recorded."

"What's Colonel Daggett say about it? He's the Commander, Sky Group. He out-ranks Kreski and has authority over me, not Commodore Peng."

"While you're with this flotilla, Peng has authority over you," Gray reminded me.

"But he doesn't have the power to transfer me. Only the senior Sky Command officer has that authority, and that's Daggett."

"It's a hopeless vector. With the Nova comes the promotion."

"I don't want the promotion. I won't accept it."

"You're losing your perspective. If you don't accept the promotion and the Nova, it could ruin your career. You could be discharged. Then you'd never see Corinna again. You'd ship home."

"Others have received the Scarlet Nova and not been promoted."

"True. But that's been a second or third award. You only receive a promotion on your first awarding of it."

I glared at him. "You're not helping any."

The corners of James Gray's mouth sagged into a frown. "Some duties are easier than others. Getting rid of a friend comes under the heading of the most difficult. There's nothing that can be done."

"You keep saying that."

"Because it's true."

I struggled to contain my anger. "When do I leave?"

"You're to return to Vasalyssa aboard the supply ship."

I stared at him. With the new supply ship and its destroyer escort en route, *Sunrise*'s survivors had already boarded the old supply ship. "But it departs in less than two hours."

"I'm sorry."

"Rescuing those people cost me more than I knew," I said. "This is goodbye, isn't it?"

"I'm afraid so. You've been a good wing man."

We shook hands. "You've been a good leader."

"You did the right thing saving those people. I'm sorry it ended this way. I'm sorry I couldn't do more for you. Next to Colonel Daggett, you're the best pilot I've ever flown with. And the colonel thinks you're better than he ever was."

My throat tightened, my lips and tongue numb as I spoke. "Thanks. I wish I knew what was going to happen next."

"Don't worry, Hector. Everything will work out."

"Like it has?"

"You're bitter now. But it will work out. Be patient."

"But my life's falling apart!"

"I know. See you out there."

"I hope so."

He nodded as I left.

Out in the corridor, as the door hissed closed behind me, I leaned against a wall, not knowing what to think, what to feel, what to do.

I felt abandoned.

I started back for the party. I wanted to tell everyone what had just happened to me. I wanted to make life for Peng and Kreski as much of a hell as they'd just made my life. I wanted *Soyuz*'s crew to hate them. I wanted my squadron to hate them, as I now hated them.

I was several decks from the party. It seemed so far away. I started running, harder and harder, my anger moving my legs. Darting past a few people, I dived into an empty lift. Jabbing at its controls, I sent it speeding toward the party's deck. Pacing back and forth inside the lift, I tried relaxing, tried catching my breath.

Breathing hard, my face flushed and sweaty, my fists pressed together until their knuckles turned white, I brooded over my conversation with James Gray. My life had gone from one extreme to the other in a matter of minutes. I had entered his office a hero. I exited an outcast.

Out in space, in my fighter, I felt invincible. Here, deep inside *Soyuz*, I felt helpless, at the mercy of spiteful, cowardly men who had destroyed my universe. Once my universe consisted of friendship and family, purpose and place, but now only pain and rage filled it.

The lift stopped. Its doors opened. I exited. Down the corridor, the party roared. Its merriment mocked me.

I no longer cared about telling my story, nor about revenge. Seeing Corinna became paramount. I had to tell her of my feelings for her, hold her in my arms, know if she felt the same way. I had to see her eyes, smell her hair, hear her laugh, taste her lips, touch her heart.

But what if her heart denied mine?

Taking a deep breath, I entered the party. Laughter, joy, happiness, wailed in my ears. As I looked for Corinna, bodies pressed against me, people twittered at me, offering cake, ice cream, punch.

Unable to locate her, I questioned several people. I learned she had left earlier with McVeen. I hurried to the nearest comm terminal, inquiring from the ship's computer of her location. She was in *Soyuz*'s library, two decks down.

Entering another lift, I left the party behind. It took but a few moments to reach the library.

The library occupied the equivalent of six crew cabins. The main room consisted of several reading machines, plus a few archaic electronic books. Beyond the main room existed four viewing rooms, each capable of projecting upon its walls ancient films, computer-generated versions of novels, plays, documentaries, biographies, et cetera. Corinna had entered one of these rooms.

As I entered her viewing room, I heard the lovely strains of an ancient Earth symphony by Beethoven. Upon the ceiling floated clouds in a darkening blue sky. On the wall before me an orange oval sun sat low over a rolling prairie. Green grasses full of yellow, purple, pink, and black wild flowers covered the prairie. Green beasts galloped by on the wall to my right, their tangy scent tingling my nostrils. The smell of dust and dew filled the air, along with the stale smell of dry manure. Behind me, where the door had existed, stood a silvery city. The last orange and scarlet rays of the setting sun caught the tops of tall towers. As the sun sank into the prairie, the ceiling-sky grew purple, then black. Stars came out, lights came on in the city, the symphony died, and night creatures began to buzz, chirp and squeak.

It dazzled me. I turned from wall to wall, from image to image, forgetting for the moment my sorrow.

"Hector, what brings you here?" Corinna asked.

"This is Gentry?" I asked.

"How did you know?"

"I know that you and Jim Gray are from the same world. I've seen some of the images he has of home. But I never saw anything like this. It's incredible."

She nodded.

"Where's Jake?" I asked.

"He's on duty now. You shouldn't be here. He won't like it. He didn't like you dancing with me."

"Does that matter to you?" I asked as I stepped closer. Her hair smelled of peaches.

"He's asked me to marry him."

My heart cracked. "Are you going to?" I whispered.

"Are you okay, Hector? You don't sound well."

I cleared my throat, trying to hide my anguish. "Are you going to marry him?"

She turned away to face the visions on the walls. "I come here when I need to figure things out. I miss home so much."

In the increasing darkness, she turned back to me. Yellow light from the city-image behind me reflected in her eyes. I wanted to hold her, to kiss her.

"What are you going to do?" I asked.

"I'm going home. I've resigned. I don't want to ever leave Gentry again."

"Then you're not going to marry McVeen?" My dying heart leaped to life, a phoenix reborn.

"No. We have different futures. Mine is home." She placed her hand, soft and warm, on my arm. "You've been a good friend. Without you, I think I'd have been lost."

"Am I just a friend?"

"The best. So many men have hit on me. A few women, too. I've been grateful for your friendship. You gave me the freedom to be just me."

"Then you never had any romantic feelings for me?" I kept my voice steady, neutral.

"Some. But your friendship meant so much more to me that they slipped away. I so needed a friend like you. But something's troubling you. What's wrong?"

"I'm leaving, too. They gave me the Scarlet Nova for the rescue. I've been promoted."

"That's wonderful, Hector! Where are they sending you?"

"I don't know yet. But I'll miss this ship. And you."

"I'll miss you, too. Friends like you are so rare." She kissed my cheek, then hugged me. I felt her heart beating against my body. I felt her warmth, her softness. We held each other beneath the glittering stars of the ceiling-sky.

We embraced in an empty room, surrounded by the images of another world. A room where my heart died, where my life aboard *Soyuz* ended.

CHAPTER THREE

MY DAD USED TO say that endings were always beginnings, that when one part of your life ended a new part started. That there was always something new ahead. But he never taught me what to do with the interstices, the spaces between the endings and the beginnings, the spaces that crushed your heart and soul.

His business frequently took him away from Earth, away from me. Every time I watched his shuttle disappear into the sky, I felt a great sorrow. Later, as the days drew nearer his return, joy rebounded in my life. But the day he failed to return stretched that particular parting into a painful eternity.

I'd hoped to never again suffer such a day, but as I left *Soyuz* behind I knew yet another such painful day had crept upon me. On *Soyuz*, I left behind a fellowship of friends, my family for the past seven years. I left behind my heart, my joy, my life. I left behind my home, from which I'd been cast out!

Small wonder then that the hundred light-year journey aboard the supply ship bound for Vasalyssa consisted of four days of misery, despair, and emptiness.

Yet misery only lasts so long before it ends in either death or victory, though victory inhabits many forms. My heart was broken, but not crushed. I had survived the death of my father. I had survived the emptiness of my mathematician mother, who cared more for her cold calculations than for me. I had survived combat against the Na. And I had survived Gargaphia's crushing atmosphere. So I would survive my unrequited love for Corinna Vernon and the loss of my squadron, because if I didn't survive, I'd die, and I wasn't ready for death.

Yet my four days of sorrow aboard the supply ship seemed like a prelude to death. My father's death left me with a loneliness only healed when I attended Sky Command's Academy and later when I joined the Forty-Second Squadron. Yet Corinna's admission that she loved me like a brother and not as a lover reminded me that I might always be alone in the universe, without a family of my own. It was a fear that festered deep within me, with which I wrestled daily. But I realized that with Corinna's own departure from *Soyuz*, remaining behind would've crushed me.

Yet Sky Command never lets anything waste away, least of all the pilots in which it has invested thousands of hours of training. I anticipated little time for self-pity, what with all the work I'd receive while at Vasalyssa. Even so, it would take a long time to forget Corinna. And longer still to bury my loneliness.

There would be freedom, the freedom flying brought me. But there would also be pain and sorrow.

If the four days I spent aboard the supply ship seemed endless, then the four months I spent on Vasalyssa seemed like an eternity. An agrarian, Earthlike planet with an industrialized moon, Vasalyssa was the regional capital for this part of the Interstellar Association. On it operated the headquarters for the Navy's Twelfth Fleet, as well as the regional headquarters for Sky Command, for the Ministry of Colonization, and for countless other governmental organizations and offices. Vasalyssa's moon, Babayaga, boasted the only naval shipyards this far from Earth. The corvette serving with my former flotilla came from Babayaga.

Four Colonial Guard fighter squadrons were based on Babayaga, as well as two Sky Command SAR squadrons. On Vasalyssa existed the various ground units of Sky Command's regional headquarters.

Upon arrival, I sent a request off to the personnel officer for an immediate posting to a knew squadron. Every day after, I sent in another urgent request. Often I felt like sending more than one per day, but that would've been rude and might have angered the personnel officer. After a few weeks of waiting with the other forlorn souls in the regional replacement pool, I began wondering if another squadron assignment might ever come. So I wrote a letter to Lieutenant Colonel Daggett, *Soyuz*'s Commander, Sky Group, asking if there was anything he might do for me. I told him I couldn't see myself sitting in the replacement pool forever. I was a fighter pilot, I said, too young to fly a desk.

While I waited for Daggett's reply, I had plenty of work to perform. I was the assistant Training Officer, in charge of creating and maintaining simulations for the active and reserve fighter and SAR squadrons in our region. My first assignment consisted of creating a simulation based upon my dive into Gargaphia's atmosphere.

That proved harder than I'd imagined, for I first had to deal with my emotions about the whole adventure. My Gargaphia flight had been intense, what with hours of difficult maneuvering, doubts of ever finding the missing lifeboat, and frustration and fear.

It took me some weeks to deal with my emotions. When I had, I created a simulation as intense and as real as possible. Then I worked on other simulations based upon the experience of other pilots from our region and from the other eleven regions of the Interstellar Association.

When not writing new sims, I made friends with some of the other pilots biding their time in staff positions. During my first few weeks, I'd remained aloof. Hoping at any moment to be assigned to a new squadron, I avoided growing close to people I might never see again. But I gradually opened up.

One pilot whose company I enjoyed, a second lieutenant named Roberta Sanchez, was aggressive, tough, and brutally honest. We became friends.

I remember the first time she stepped out of my Gargaphia simulation. Sweat spotted her forehead. She looked pale.

"Well?" I asked.

"Shit."

She hated it. No doubt, since she referred to it as excrement. So I spent the rest of the day reprogramming it, making it even more intense. When I saw her at dinner, I asked what she hated about it.

"That it scared the hell out of me," she said.

"I wish you'd said so before. I just made it more intense."

"Then I won't to do it again. Let some other moron do it."

I laughed.

"Was it really that bad?" she asked.

"Worse, but I just can't seem to get it across in the sim."

"I'm glad you did it then and not me. But I'd do it in an instant, if it'd get me into a squadron."

"Me, too."

Every two weeks I got the chance to fly. I took a shuttle to the Command's base on Babayaga, where I got to know members of one of the Colonial Guard squadrons. I flew practice combat operations, known as COPs, with other members of the squadron and with members of other Guard squadrons that were part of Vasalyssa's Planetary Defense Forces.

The Colonial Guard is a conglomerate of forces from various member-worlds of the Association, as well as the unattached colonial worlds. When any world faced long-term trouble the Association called up the Guard and then various worlds would deploy their Guard forces.

Every world possessed its own defensive forces, but not necessarily the resources for sophisticated military technology. Here the Guard stepped in, with Association financing. For every sky squadron or ground battalion dedicated to the Guard, the Association provided the training and the weapon systems for it. The minimum Guard requirement per world was eight battalions or four squadrons, plus supportive personnel.

The Colonial Guard was good, but not as good as Sky Command. I flew against fourteen Guard pilots at one time or another, defeating them all.

With all the practice I received dogfighting with the Guard pilots, and through simulations, I kept my skills sharp. But it wasn't enough. I needed a squadron. I needed a home.

But my home flew far from me. *Soyuz* patrolled the frontier. Not scheduled for a return to Vasalyssa for another six months, I never saw it again.

At first, my friends on Soyuz wrote to me. But soon they stopped, their lives continuing, while I rotted in the replacement pool.

I hated it, being part of the replacement pool, and not having anyone to replace. Yes, I performed a worthy function by developing sims for other pilots. Yet those pilots flew in squadrons, while I sat flying a desk, stuck going nowhere fast.

The Academy graduated three hundred pilots every year. Most joined SAR squadrons. Dozens more filled empty slots in fighter squadrons. Others ended up in replacement pools scattered throughout the Association, waiting for their chance. Their numbers grew year after year as more graduates joined their ranks. Part of a system created for emergencies, as when huge gaps appeared in the ranks during warfare, pilots in replacement pools languished in virtual non-existence.

The system was flawed. It never took into account the incredible efforts Association diplomats made at keeping the peace with hostile neighbors.

As peace prospered the replacement pools grew. Frustrated pilots resigned from the Command and joined the Guard. Or they transferred into the Interstellar Marines, flying gunboats in support of ground troops. But they rarely achieved their goal of flying for the Command.

Unless there was a war.

You see, when you're flying your fighter, you're the master of your universe. You're the captain of your own little spaceship. You decide what maneuvers to make. You decide who to chase, where to aim, whether to shoot or hold your fire. You take orders from others, yes, yet you still command your bird.

That's why waiting for a slot to open up in a squadron depresses you. And if you've already flown with a squadron for several years then waiting for a new home becomes an endless agony, with every homeless day squeezing the life out of you.

Endings might be beginnings, but some beginnings seem an eternity from realization.

Days came and went. The night sky's stars beckoned to me. The weather grew cooler. Winter approached, bringing with it a deep dreariness.

I awoke one morning to find black clouds drifting past my dormitory window. Rain had arrived during the night, scattering broad gray puddles across the beautifully landscaped compound beneath me. The black clouds shrouded the upper floors of the other buildings and covered the tree tops in gloom. Vasalyssa's sun had arisen but darkness engulfed the compound: the street lights still glowed.

I arose and went to my desk. A light flashed at my comm console. "Activate," I said.

The screen remained blank. The message said: "First Lieutenant Hector Josef Crossman, you are instructed to report to the Commandant's Building, fourteenth level, Command Briefing Room. Arrive by Eight Hundred Hours. End of Message."

I glanced at the time. I had an hour to travel the twenty kilometers to the Commandant's Building. I shaved, took a warm shower, dressed, and hastened down to the cafeteria, where I grabbed a meal packet and a carton of milk. Then I hustled to the garage beneath the building. Six other pilots waited there, Roberta Sanchez among them.

"So they called you, too?" she said.

"Guess so," I said, tearing open the meal packet and removing one of the two chocolate breakfast bars.

She stared at me. "How can you eat that crap?"

"I like it."

"It's too dry for me. It's like eating wood, but without any flavor."

"It tastes good to me," I said.

"Yeah, right. Here comes a car."

A transparent car glided into the garage and stopped before us. A door opened and we climbed inside. Two cushioned benches lined the sides of the car. Sanchez and I sat down on the left side with another pilot, while the rest of the pilots sat on the other side. When no one else entered the car, its door closed. After Sanchez mentioned our destination the car sped from beneath our building out onto a busy highway.

As our car pulled out into the dark, dreary day, we all shivered. Warm air circulated around us. Warm light glowed from twin strips along the ceiling. Yet we still shivered. The black clouds above us let loose with rain and hail. Large flecks of ice ricocheted off of the car's curving sides while fat raindrops fell from the sky.

"Ominous," said Hennisee, a blond pilot across from Sanchez. I barely knew him.

"Spooky," replied the pilot next to me. His name was Pender. Long and thin, with a weathered, grayish-white complexion, he looked more like a twisted strand of wire than a man. "Might be a bad omen."

"What's with you people?" I said. "It's just weather."

"You don't have a clue about what's going on, do you?" Hennisee asked.

"What're you talking about?"

"Why we're being called to the Commandant's Building."

I glanced at Hennisee, then at Sanchez.

"Think it through," Sanchez said. "We're being called in because something's up. We're all senior in the replacement pool. Somebody's gotten into trouble and lost a lot of people."

"Maybe," I said. "Or maybe someone's planned a training COP. Or we're being transferred to a newly-formed squadron."

Sanchez nodded. "Yeah. It could be a lot of things. But I think your head's full of shit. We're all assigned to headquarters. We all knew by our second day everything that was going on. Don't you think we'd know if there was a training COP? Or if we're all assigned to a new squadron?"

"Right. And you know every classified thing that's going on, too, huh? So what is going on?" I demanded.

Sanchez glared at me. "Eat your damned breakfast."

Taking another bite of my breakfast, I stared at the sky. "I bet it's blue above all of this."

"What"s it to you?" asked Pender.

I turned to him. "Haven't you ever noticed how on most Earthlike worlds, after this kind of a storm, the air is clean and clear. Storms like this purify the sky. Far above us, right now, float lots of little clouds, white puffs. And above those scoot the thin, higher clouds, collections of ice crystals drifting on the surface of the sky. And above all that is the clear blue sky. kies like that are worth flying through."

We continued toward the Commandant's Building, but I no longer saw the black rain clouds. My heart flew far above the weather, in the clear, cold, blue sky I knew was up there. I remained quiet, lost in thought, far from my mediocre life, until our car eased to a stop in the garage beneath our destination.

A lift took us to the Command Briefing Room. Located on the fourteenth floor, the room's windows revealed the dark heart of the storm. With its view obscured by the weather, the room felt more like the interior of a starship than the inside of a planet-bound building.

Twenty chairs faced a blank viewing screen. We sat and waited. After a few minutes, a tall, thin major, with closely-cropped black hair and brown eyes, entered.

"I'm Major Lao," he announced. "You are all being transferred to the Ilmatar region. A conflict has erupted on Eos, two hundred light years from Ilmatar. Several squadrons in the region are under-strength due to promotions, transfers, and retirements.

"You will journey to Eos courtesy of the Navy. Four fast frigates are being transferred to the forces protecting Eos. You will travel aboard the frigate *Sagacious*. Attend to your personal things. Your shuttle departs in two hours. *Sagacious* departs in three hours. If you fail to board, it still departs. Dismissed."

Major Lao started for the door, then paused. He turned around. "I wish I was going with you. See you out there."

After he left, we stood. "That was quick," I said.

"He could've sent the information to our rooms," Sanchez grouched. "There wasn't any damned reason for us to come all this way for a forty-five-second briefing."

"The Command loves personal contact," Pender said.

"It takes two months by regular transport to get to Ilmatar from here," said Hennisee. "If they're sending us aboard one of the new frigates, it'll probably take less than two weeks."

"They're fast, all right," Pender agreed. "And cramped."

"I'll sleep in a cargo box, if it gets me into a squadron," Sanchez said.

"Affirmative," I said. "I've had enough of the ground. I want to feel the vibration of a carrier's deck beneath my feet again. I love flying through blue skies, but not as much as flying in the blackness of space. I belong out there."

"We all do," Sanchez said.

"That's the truth!" Pender said.

"And another truth is that Hector gets to lead us," Sanchez said. "Isn't that special?"

There was nothing special in commanding our party. We all arrived on time with our belongings, embarked on our shuttle, and flew to the frigate.

Sagacious was cramped. Recreation facilities were an afterthought. Designed for a crew of fifty-four, our seven extra bodies overcrowded it. The frigate was short one middle grade officer so three of us crowded into a cabin meant for one, while our other four bunked with the frigate's junior officers, doubling the number in each two-person cabin.

The crew, though friendly enough, kept busy. So we played games, watched holodramas, read electronic books, and exercised. We slept whenever possible, haunted the officers's ward room when convenient, and stayed out of the crew's way.

We were bored out of our skulls.

But everything ends, including the fifteen-day, one thousand light-year journey to Ilmatar.

From orbit, Ilmatar appeared as a great blue ball, spotted with white clouds. A water world with limited dry land, Ilmatar had a breathable atmosphere. Somewhere on its surface was the Association's headquarters. We weren't destined to visit it. *Sagacious* docked at the Navy's vast orbital complex, remaining in-system only long enough to draw fuel and supplies. While we waited, we received a visit from another Sky Command major. He briefed us in the frigate's cramped ward room.

"Eleven months back," the major began, "the fragile peace between the humans and Gorgons on Eos broke down. Unrest has always existed between our races. Our physical and chemical constitution causes the Gorgons extreme anxiety, driving them to exterminate humans at every opportunity. Their language remains beyond our comprehension. And since they can't stand being around us, all we know of them we've learned from other races."

"Sounds like a screwy world," Sanchez said. "Who'd want to share a world with an alien race driven to kill humans on sight?"

"I hear Eos is a beautiful world," I said.

"Correct," the major continued. "And both races claim it. More than a hundred years ago, we fought a border war with the Gorgons over Eos. Through transmitted maps and symbols a rough peace and division of the planet occurred. Ever since, they've existed uneasily near us.

"There have always been misunderstandings, especially along the equatorial borderlands. Occasionally, the Gorgons made extermination raids into the human zones. Human reprisals followed. But prompt communications, again with symbols and maps, smoothed things out."

"So what went wrong?" Hennisee asked.

"Apparently, they've just had enough. The Gorgons want us gone. Many months back, a massive invasion force crossed the borders and began slaughtering people. Naval Intelligence thinks they've been importing large numbers of regular soldiers to Eos, portraying them as agricultural workers. The same appears true for armored ground and sky vehicles, camouflaged as farming and construction equipment."

The major took a deep breath. "Simultaneous with the ground invasion, Gorgon warships entered the system in tremendous force. The Association's representatives on Eos broadcasted a call for help. That call became frantic when Gorgon battleships vaporized our orbiting Naval station and its two assigned destroyers."

"Sounds like the Gorgons have this well-planned," I said.

"Affirmative."

"How are we involved?" Pender asked.

"Ninth Fleet, based here at Ilmatar, has sent a large task force to Eos. Since the attack on our orbital station, there hasn't been any further engagements between our ships and theirs. Maybe because we have better technology. Given this, we should easily defeat them.

"The situation on the ground is somewhat different. Gorgon ground forces have made rapid gains, while killing every human in sight. The Gorgons are assaulting up the east and west coasts of Titanus, the main continent, and up through the middle as well. They've divided their forces into three armies, which are further divided into three columns.

"Leading their columns are armored ground vehicles and shock troops. They're supported in the sky by armored gunboats. The gunboats have gained sky superiority. Their the shock troops and tanks have slashed through our ground positions. Following these units are clean-up squads, which track down and slaughter every remaining survivor."

"How nice," Sanchez said.

The major continued. "The Eosian Army is giving ground. Thousands are dying every day. Their own sky forces are wrecked.

"Ninth Fleet has sent the carriers *Akagi*, *Resolute* and *Yorktown* to Eos. Marine gunboats from these carriers spend most of their time fighting for sky superiority, as do our fighters. Marine brigades from all across our region have been sent, too. They're also coming from other regions. Volunteers from several colonies and member worlds are arriving every day. The Ministry of Colonization is called has called up the Colonial Guard.

"For our part, all replacement pilots in the region have been called up. Your group will fill gaps in our squadrons aboard the carriers orbiting Eos. The situation is severe and casualties have occurred. Take care of yourselves and good hunting. See you out there."

After the major left, we spent a long time discussing the situation on Eos. We wanted to get there before the fighting ended. We wanted to prove ourselves. We wanted a home.

We also wanted to do our share in defeating the Gorgons.

Discussing what we remembered from our Academy classes concerning the Gorgons, we realized little was known about them.

They seemed similar to humans and the Na. But they differed in that instead of eyes, ears, or tongues, all of their sensory organs covered their heads, where their hair should've been. Hundreds of small, wavy tendrils covered their skulls. Some tendrils contained optical sensors, other tendrils consisted of auditory sensors, while still others were chemical sensors for tasting and smelling the air. Some tendrils allowed the Gorgons to detect local changes in electrical fields. And some seemed for verbal communication.

Besides the hundreds of waving, wormlike tendrils atop a Gorgon's head, its only other features consisted of two horizontal openings: one for eating, one for breathing. They sat one above the other on a Gorgon's face.

Their name came from the first human explorers encountering them. These explorers named them after the gorgons of ancient Earth mythology. That first encounter resulted in the deaths of lots of innocent people.

As our discussion died down and we drifted back to our quarters, *Sagacious* left orbit. In three days we'd reach Eos.

Later, I wandered into the ward room. The frigate was quiet. The crew had changed watches. The somnolent hours after midnight were upon us. I found Roberta Sanchez beside a food dispenser, drinking a cup of coffee.

"Something wrong?" I asked.

"Couldn't sleep. You?"

"Same."

"Want something to drink?" she asked.

"Hot chocolate would be nice. How about vectoring me a raspberry-flavored one?"

"Don't you ever drink anything else?"

"Sometimes." I sat at a table.

She fixed my hot chocolate. Sitting down across from me, she slid over my cup.

"Thanks." I sipped at my steaming drink.

After a moment's silence, Sanchez asked, "Have you ever killed anyone?"

"I'm not sure."

"What do you mean?"

I sighed. "I flew a COP against a Na smuggler. It had kidnaped several people, mostly kids, from Faraway. Its crew intended selling them to a renegade O.

"This smuggler had O technology. When our flotilla's two destroyers grabbed it with graviton beams, the Na neutralized the beams. There was nothing we could do and it was leaving orbit. Two of the pilots in my COP attacked it, and the smuggler vaporized them both. I got angry.

"So I accelerated full power at them, firing my particle cannon and all my missiles at once. That kept the Na too busy to fire at me. My COP leader, and wingmate, Captain Gray, ordered me back, but I ignored him. I'm good at that."

"Go on," Sanchez said.

"I couldn't figure out anything else to do but ram the bastards, so I did. I ejected my control pod just before my bird flew into its engines. The engine room and my bird exploded.

"That's what combat's like. It's desperate. You do what you have to do. What you can do. I was scared they'd get away. I was scared for their captives. And I was mad.

"You know, the O are an intelligent and gentle race. But their renegades, their criminals, are literal monsters. They consider humans a delicacy and they eat their prey live. I couldn't let that happen to those kids. And I couldn't let the Na get away with treating people like cattle.

"You see, I was mad at the Na for killing my friends. And for what they were doing. I had to stop them. And I did. I only worried about getting killed later."

"Did you get a medal for it?"

"A Gallantry Commendation. But sometimes medals aren't worth as much as you think."

"How do you figure that?"

"A medal put me here."

"And that's not good?"

"It took me from my squadron."

"Point taken. How does your story answer my question?"

"I don't know if I killed anyone in that engine room or not. They may have gotten out. No one ever told me."

After a long pause, Sanchez volunteered: "I've killed."

"When?"

"When I was seventeen. My Uncle Colombo taught me how to protect of myself. I come from Uno Mas. If you can't take care of yourself there, then you deserve being a victim. I killed a couple of stupidos trying to rape me. It wasn't what they expected."

"Sounds like a tough place."

"It's a mean world and if you're not meaner, you won't survive. I'm a survivor."

"I can tell. So what's bothering you?"

"What do you mean?"

"Your question. This conversation. Your being up so late. Something's troubling you."

"Nothing's troubling me."

"Have it your way. I got up because I'm nervous about joining a new squadron, especially while its involved in combat. Usually, you get a chance to make friends and prove yourself over several weeks or months. But in a war everything's different. If you fail, that's it, you're done. Your career, even your life, ends."

Roberta took a deep breath. "I don't want to fail. I mean, fighting for your life's one thing, when stupidos are trying to hurt you. But having time to think about it as you fly into a fight while others are depending upon you, well, I don't know how I'll do it. I don't want to let anyone down."

"You won't."

"And what makes you so damned sure?"

"You do. You come from a mean world and you're meaner than it. You're going to a mean place and you'll be meaner still. You're a survivor, Roberta. You've come this far, you'll make it the rest of the way."

"Thanks. Maybe we'll get to fly together."

"Who knows?"

CHAPTER FOUR

As *SAGACIOUS* ENTERED THE Thea star system, bound for Eos, the fourth planet, battle stations sounded. Serving seven years on a warship taught me that whenever a ship entered a hostile system, it went to battle stations. The other pilots, unaware of this, grew frantic as the alarm sounded. They were less afraid of the frigate being attacked than of failing to reach their squadrons and achieving their goals. How ironic, how pathetic, waiting an eternity to join a squadron and then dying just before you arrive!

Yet it was only a routine procedure and so I gathered the others into the ward room, where I calmed them down. Minutes later, we joined Task Force Thirty where it orbited Eos.

The task force was divided into six task groups, each with a specific mission. The battle element, consisting of battle ships, battle cruisers, and heavy cruisers, orbited ten thousand kilometers above Eos, forming a barrier between the Gorgon fleets and the rest of our task force.

Closer to Eos flew the bombardment element, consisting of heavy and light cruisers. Orbiting six thousand kilometers out, it protected the rest of the task force. Its original mission, providing fire support for the ground forces, had changed due to the political nature of the conflict. So the task group positioned itself to keep enemy vessels from vectoring in from low-orbit and attacking our carriers.

Far over the north pole, at an altitude of twelve thousand kilometers, orbited three more task groups: the transport group, of which only part had arrived; the supply group, to which *Sagacious* was assigned; and the command group, including the task force command ship, a science ship, three hospital ships, and eight destroyers.

Between the three groups at the north pole and the bombardment group orbited the ground support element. Our frigate flew toward this group.

The ground support element consisted of one attack carrier, *Akagi*, and two support carriers, *Yorktown* and *Resolute*. Four light cruisers and eight destroyers formed a security screen around the carriers.

While *Sagacious* matched orbits with *Akagi*, we gathered inside the shuttle bay, awaiting transport to the attack carrier. Our shuttle pilot greeted us, saying he felt the Gorgons didn't desire another interstellar war with the Association. At the moment, he explained, the fighting appeared limited to ground combat and sky duels. He said it would soon end, with everyone returning home. Fools that we were, we wanted the conflict to continue until we had tasted it.

As our shuttle approached the carrier, we each activated our individual viewing screens. A beautiful ship, *Akagi* stretched out as a long, flattened-out cylinder with an elliptical cross-section. Four fighter squadrons flew from her, totaling ninety-six fighters. She also fielded two SAR squadrons, each with twelve birddogs, and three Marine gunboat squadrons with twenty-seven gunboats total.

The Marine gunboats consisted of large armed and armored cargo shuttles. With strong energy screens and a fair amount of maneuverability, they matched the powerful Gorgon gunboats. Carrying crews of four, our gunboats sported plasma cannons and large missile bays. Their mission, as artillery platforms for the Marine ground forces, had changed. So far, only our gunboats proved effective against the enemy's gunboats.

While *Akagi* carried three gunboat squadrons, the two support carriers each had five gunboat squadrons but only one SAR squadron and two fighter squadrons. These smaller carriers ran half the size of *Akagi*.

"Her sides bulge," Sanchez said.

"They do," agreed Pender.

"She's very different from the escort carriers in the Twelfth Fleet," I said.

"Why are they different?" Pender asked.

I shrugged. "Someone thought that a spherical design was better for escorts. Less length, better turning ability, better screen coverage, and still plenty of volume for crews. Remember, escorts carry three gunboat squadrons, just like *Akagi*, but only one fighter and one SAR squadron each. We could launch all our fighters and all our gunboats simultaneously, all in different directions."

"Like a seed pod," Sanchez said.

"Affirmative."

"Then why this shape?" she wondered.

"It carries a lot more fighters. I guess the designers wanted to be certain that if one part of the ship was damaged, fighters could still launch from other parts of the ship."

"How about one design comes from one ship builder and another from a different ship builder?" she suggested.

"Could be."

"Sounds more reasonable. Money talks, politicians listen."

"She's a beautiful ship, though," I said, glancing at my view screen again.

"What's that dome for up front?" Pender wondered.

"I have no idea," I said. "But that tower in the middle's called an 'island'. It contains command and control sections, as well as some defensive gunnery."

"Stupid placement, I'd say," Sanchez said.

"You act like you've never seen this ship design before."

"I've never seen anything this big before. Have you?"

"No. Battleships and battle cruisers are big, but they're spherical, like escort carriers, as are all heavy and light cruisers. But I've never seen anything like this before. Certainly nothing this long."

Sanchez nodded. "The warships of the Twelfth Fleet are destroyers, destroyer escorts, frigates, corvettes, and heavy and light cruisers. We don't have any battleships or battle cruisers. We've got escort carriers, but nothing else. Our region is considered too rural for capital ships."

"The Navy considers cruisers capital ships," I reminded her.

"Whatever. The reason we don't have capital ships is we don't border any major power. The Shh'Uruu are too far away. So are the O, as if we could ever beat them. The Gorgons are over here. Pirates and smugglers, that's all we have, and they don't fly big ships."

"Don't forget the Frolians."

"A beaten race, like the Na. They're in Sixth Fleet's jurisdiction anyway."

"And the Jesseneau?"

She glared at me. "Also beaten. They're just merchants now, no threat to anyone."

"That war lasted fifteen years."

"We just needed to learn how to fight them."

"Docking procedures commencing," the shuttle's computer announced.

Slowing, our shuttle approached *Akagi* from the port side. A graviton beam caught the shuttle as it ducked under the carrier. The shuttle shut down its engines and the beam lifted us into a belly hangar. Inside the hangar, a lesser beam took over, guiding the shuttle into an individual bay. The bay's doors closed; atmospheric pressurization began.

"What do you think we'll get?" Sanchez asked, excited.

"I don't know. Any squadron's fine, just so long as I can fly again."

"I'm hoping for the Black Birds."

I stared at her. "First Squadron's here?"

"Has been for two years. Didn't you check the roster to see who was aboard that ship?"

"Negative. Too excited, I guess. The last I heard, the Black Birds were with First Fleet, aboard *Columbia*."

"Not anymore. But I'm just dreaming. They only take the best. You, probably."

"Not me. But it's nice to know they're here."

"Why?"

"My best friend from the Academy's with them. At least, he used to be."

"Probably still is," she said. With the shuttle bay pressurized, the airlock at the rear of the shuttle opened. We exited. "When did he join them?"

"The day we graduated."

"Right. Tell me another false tale."

"I'm not kidding."

"Grads don't go into the First. You've gotta transfer in from another squadron."

Outside the shuttle, a Sky Command sergeant greeted us. Motioning us to follow him, he proceeded from the shuttle bay down a corridor and toward a lift.

"Pedro did," I explained, following the sergeant. "He graduated with the third highest score in the Academy's history and at the top of our class. There was an opening in the First and they picked him. The number one grad traditionally picks his assignment. But Pedro didn't mind."

"I wouldn't have, either. What's his name again?"

"Pedro. Pedro Jose Alvarez." We entered the lift. It ascended through *Akagi*'s various decks.

"A nice name. I'd like to meet him. Where's he from?"

"Earth. From Madrid, in Spain. We practically grew up next to each other. I lived in Valencia. My father moved us from England. He liked the weather in Spain better."

"Did you know each other as children?"

"We met at the Academy."

The lift stopped and its doors opened. The sergeant directed us toward a briefing room. Entering the room, I abruptly realized we'd traveled the entire width of the ship, from the carrier's belly to the island atop it. Located in the aft portion of the island's base, three quarters of the briefing room's bulkheads formed a fantastic curving view port. Before me I saw the carrier's stern, and beyond it a few distant blinking pinpoints: the running lights of other ships in the task group.

"Crossman," Sanchez called. She stood by the curving view port, looking out. As I approached, she pointed down, past the curvature of the ship. Beneath us floated the green and blue ball of Eos, clouds blanketing it.

"Ten-hutt!" the sergeant growled. We snapped to attention. In walked two Sky Command officers: a full colonel, followed by a brigadier general.

"Thank you, sergeant. That will be all," the general said. He faced us as the sergeant left.

"People, this is *Akagi*'s captain's briefing room. He's kindly letting us use it, so remember your manners." He glanced at each of us before continuing.

"I'm Brigadier General Henry Devon, the task force's Commander, Sky Forces. Glad to have you aboard. Usually, on other carriers you'd be briefed by the Commander, Sky Group. But the CSG, Colonel Bradley Wallis here, is letting me indulge my desire to get to know you. Let me welcome you to our family."

I'd never been personally briefed by a CSF before. He surely had enough things to worry about without greeting every new pilot that arrived aboard *Akagi*. For instance, he had the day-to-day flight operations of all the fighter and SAR squadrons in the task group to coordinate, as well as coordinating operations with the Marine gunboat squadrons, with the Eosian Planetary Defense Force squadrons, and with the Colonial Guard squadrons. He also coordinated with whatever ground forces his pilots flew support for. With such a crippling workload, why did he bother performing a task best left to *Akagi*'s CSG?

"I'll get right to it," General Devon said. "We're involved in a very tough situation here. The Association doesn't want an interstellar war. It's not going to let the fighting spread beyond this system. It doesn't even want the fighting to spread beyond Eos. So we're politically limited here. And let me tell you, it stinks.

"So far our COPs have been limited to defensive actions against Gorgon craft entering our skies. The Gorgons only fly gunboats and we're having a helluva time shooting them down.

"You've probably wondered about all the pilots transferred here from Vasalyssa and Ilmatar and what our casualties have been. They aren't as serious as you would think. We've only had a few. Before the conflict, the squadrons aboard *Akagi* and the other carriers transferred pilots back to Earth where new squadrons are being formed. We were under-manned when the fighting started so we called up replacements after arrival.

"But the fighting's getting worse. This is a racial war. The Gorgons want to kill all humans on Eos and they'll stop at nothing to do so. They have ten times as many ground troops, three times as many warships, and maybe fifteen or twenty times as many sky craft."

"Plenty of targets," Sanchez said.

"You bet. And lots of ways to get killed, too. I've been in a war before, so I know. So does Colonel Wallis. So do your squadron commanders.

"Right now only the Marine gunboats are knocking the Gorgons out of the sky with any success. They have a two-to-one success ratio: two Gorgons destroyed for every Marine gunboat. Even though our fighters and weapons are better than the theirs, their gunboats are so heavily armored and screened that it takes several of our fighters firing their plasma cannons and launching all of their missiles together to kill one gunboat."

"How can that be?" Sanchez asked.

The general shook his head. "It just is. This war's getting tougher every day. And the ones that'll be hurt the most are the millions of innocents down on Eos. And let me tell you, after a while their suffering's going to get to you. It'll eat at you. So I'm ordering each of you to talk with whomever you need to about what you're feeling. Talk to your friends, the medics, the surgeons, the chaplains, your superiors, whomever, but talk to them! If you hold it in, it'll eat you alive. And when that happens, you'll become less effective at your job.

"Now, what I'm about to say will sound evil. It'll go against what most of you believe. But it's true. You're in a war now and your job is to kill Gorgons. There's nothing harder on your spirit than treating life as trivial. But killing the enemy is the only way to end this war. So get used to it.

"I wish I could've welcomed you aboard under better circumstances. Yet this is your chance to be part of a squadron. I understand how you feel. It took me thirteen months to get assigned to my first squadron. But in your joy, don't forget that you've a helluva job to perform, a life and death job.

"Colonel Wallis here will give you your assignments. See you out there."

Without another word, the general exited the briefing room.

"Passionate, isn't he?" Sanchez muttered.

"Enough of that," Colonel Wallis snarled. He raised a small electronic notepad. "Mingoro."

One of the pilots stood.

"You're assigned to Fifth Squadron, the Wildcats. Report immediately."

Mingoro hurried out. As he left, I saw both excitement and disappointment on his face. He wanted the Black Birds, as did Sanchez. And, strangely, as did I.

"Hennisee. Seventh Squadron. The Sentinels. Pender..."

Pender, our wiry friend, stood. "Seventh Squadron."

"I hope everything works out," Sanchez whispered.

"Sanchez. Third Squadron. The Rogues."

Standing, she grinned at me. "I've finally made it!"

"Be careful."

"You bet. See you out there."

"What's your call sign? You never told me."

"My instructors picked Vixen. And yours?"

I laughed. "That fits you. Mine's Ice Maker."

"Sanchez. Report to your squadron," Colonel Wallis said.

"Affirmative." She left, smiling.

The remaining two pilots with me found themselves assigned to Third and Seventh squadrons.

Then, without another word, the colonel switched off his notepad and left the briefing room. I watched him leave. What was going on? Had they forgotten me? Why bring me here, if not for a squadron assignment? Standing, I started for the door, ready to find Colonel Wallis, General Devon, or anyone, and drag the answer from them.

But I barely began my quest before the door whistled open and General Devon entered. "Sorry I'm late."

I started to speak, but he raised a hand for silence. Motioning me back into my chair, he swivelled another chair around and sat down across from me.

"I can guess what you were thinking just now, but you're wrong," he said, leaning forward. "I wanted to talk to you alone. I waited until everyone had gone."

"Sir?"

"One of my closest friends, someone I haven't seen in years, wrote to me about you. And let me tell you, I trust him more than anyone else in the Command.

"Fifteen years ago, Claude Daggett was my wingman. We fought together against the Shh'Uruu. He told me about the bad deal you got, how your former commanders used a medal to get rid of you. He asked if I could do anything for you. He told me all about you. He thinks a lot of you, and let me tell you, it's rare when Daggett admires anyone.

"I received his letter before we called up the reserves, so to speak. I thought about it for a long time, how I might help you. When we suffered casualties, I sent for replacements, including from Vasalyssa. Being one of the quietest regions in the Association, the transfers easily worked out. I made a point of asking for you."

"Thank you, sir. But what am I going to do?"

"You're gonna fly with the Black Birds. They ask only for the best and that's what you are, Hector, the best."

"Thank you, sir."

"You're welcome. I know Dag will be happy. He said you reminded him of me. Well, I don't know about that. Personally, you sorta remind me of my brother, Edgar."

Not knowing what to say, I kept silent.

"I'm on your side, Hector. But let me tell you, right now you're gonna have a helluva fight ahead of you. I don't mean just the war. I mean your squadron commander and his exec. They didn't like me pulling rank and putting you in there. Usually, it's their privilege to decide who joins the squadron, but not this time. It's not much different from the situation you just came from, so you'll just have to handle it.

"They're good people. If you get them on your side, they'll stick with you no matter what. But watch out if you turn them against you."

"How do they feel about me now, sir?" I asked.

"They don't trust you. They might not even like you. That's the tough part. You'll have to prove that they can rely on you. I can put you into the First, but I can't order them to like you. You've gotta earn their respect. Just as in any other squadron."

"I'll do my best, sir."

General Devon stood "That's all any of us can do. While you're fighting for your squadron's respect don't forget you'll be fighting the Gorgons, too. Be careful."

"Thank you, sir," I said, standing.

He nodded. "Time to report in. If there's anything I can do for you, let me know. See you out there, Hector."

"See you out there, sir."

CHAPTER FIVE

I FOLLOWED GENERAL DEVON OUT of the briefing room, excited. I had a squadron again, and the Black Birds at that! Every cadet and junior officer dreamt of a posting to the Black Birds, the elite squadron, the first and the best. Success in it guaranteed your career.

Though excited, I still had to report to my new squadron's exec. After that I could exult in my posting while finding my quarters. Then I'd seek out Pedro, if he still flew for the squadron.

Consulting with the ship's directory, I located the office of the exec, Captain Sanura Mboko. It was located, along with the squadron's other offices, just forward of the squadron's hangar and flight decks. These decks, along with ready rooms, equipment bays, repair shops, squadron stores, and munitions, were forward of amidships on *Akagi*'s starboard side.

It took me a few minutes to reach the exec's office. Her door stood open. She wasn't there. I went inside.

Her office consisted of three sections: a waiting room, her office proper, and an inner sanctum, a hiding place, to get away from everyone and everything for a while.

The doors to all three sections stood open while two small janitorial robots cleaned them. Wandering around, I noticed she even had a small food service unit and a private lavatory in her inner sanctum.

Mboko's office had a definite martial theme to it. A battle mural covered a wall in the waiting room. White men in red coats and white pith helmets stood among grassy knolls firing ancient rifles at black warriors in feathered headdresses and wearing loincloths made of animal skins. The warriors carried shields of gray hide and brandished long wooden spears with shiny metal tips. Thousands of these warriors charged the red-coated soldiers. Many of the warriors lay dead, while several of the soldiers appeared dead as well.

Beyond, in her office proper, two spears similar to those of the warriors in the computer mural were crossed on a wall, over a hide shield. I examined them. They seemed authentic.

"It's improper to scrutinize a senior's office while she's absent," a sharp voice reprimanded me.

Turning around, I came to attention. Captain Mboko had returned. Taller than me, she had a definite coolness about her. Her hair was cut short. The sharpness of her eyes matched the sharpness of her voice. Her dark black uniform's shoulders were colored red, a distinction given to Sky Command personnel for exceptional service or heroism. Only a handful of pilots possessed the Red Wings decoration and Captain Mboko was the first officer I'd ever seen wearing them.

"First Lieutenant Crossman reporting for duty, ma'am."

"I recognized you from your file's holo. What are you doing in my office?"

"The doors were open, ma'am. I came in to wait."

"So you felt it acceptable to intrude upon my domain?"

"What are you talking about, ma'am?" I asked, stepping aside as the janitorial robots scurried out.

"Find a seat. Secure." The doors to the corridor, her waiting room, and her inner sanctum hissed closed at her command.

I sat down.

Sitting behind her desk, she said, "Your file reveals your performance on Gargaphia. You disobeyed your orders. I find that unacceptable. This squadron is a team. This team flies together. It fights together. And each member obeys orders. From your record, I see poor performance where teamwork is involved."

I stared at her. "I saved the lives of seventy people. Without me, they'd have died."

"You saved their lives. But you disobeyed orders. It's a consistent pattern with you. An unacceptable pattern.

"You're not the caliber of a pilot we like in this squadron. You're not our choice. Apparently, through connections I'm not cognizant of, you managed to impose yourself upon us. But we do not desire your presence. We're in the midst of a conflict and we need assurance we can rely on every pilot in our squadron."

"You can rely on me, ma'am."

"I doubt it."

"Why?"

Captain Mboko glared at me. "What words did you not comprehend? Your record speaks for itself. You disobey orders. You refuse to operate within established parameters. To put it in simple language that you can comprehend, you're not a team player. We require team players."

"What are you going to do with me, then?"

"Given the option, I would transfer you out. But neither the major nor I have control over the matter. We have decided that you will assume whatever duties we can provide to keep you from combat. We cannot chance your disobeying orders at a crucial moment."

I stood up. "You're going to waste me? You're not even going to see if I have anything to contribute?"

"You have nothing of any value to contribute to us."

"How can you say that? How can you sit there and pass judgement over me without knowing who I am or what I can do?"

"It's my function to decide who can perform for this squadron and who cannot. Your record informs me you cannot."

"Where the hell d'you get off deciding that?"

Captain Mboko stood. "Is that all, lieutenant?"

"Negative. The Command never wastes anyone or anything. But that's just what you're doing with me. You don't like me. You don't want me here. You're not even going to give me a chance to prove my worth. You've passed judgement on me just because you feel like it. What you're doing is wrong, but you don't care. You just want to strike back. You're letting me be the target of your frustrations.

"Well, I won't be your target. I'm a good pilot. My record shows it. It shows that more than anything else. And I'm good enough to be in this squadron. But maybe you're not. Otherwise you wouldn't be so arbitrary in your treatment of me."

She glared at me. "You're scheduled for a physical exam in two hours," she said. "My computer will direct you to your quarters. At zero six hundred tomorrow you will report to Captain Jonkowski, the squadron's training officer. You will assist her developing more sophisticated simulations reflecting the present situation on Eos. You will not be wasted. You will be utilized in the manner best befitting your talents.

"Dismissed."

I was so damned mad at her. But I couldn't think of any arguments that might move her. So I came to attention and left.

A thick kiron bulkhead separated the command offices and pilots' quarters from the flight deck behind them. My quarters were forward of the senior officers' quarters, which were forward of the staff offices.

Finding my quarters, I logged in my name with the door, then entered. In a foul mood, I instructed my cabin's computer not to let anyone disturb me.

Earlier, when I'd had my physical examination, I'd been in a foul mood. This forced the medical robot conducting it to allow for my emotional state while examining me. It had instructed me to calm down, but I found relaxation anything but easy. As soon as my physical ended, I left for my quarters. Now I stood in my cabin and wondered if this was all my life would ever be, the victim of rude and ungracious officers.

My cabin, roomy by comparison with the one I'd had aboard *Soyuz*, seemed alien to me. A long, narrow desk occupied half of one wall. A short distance from the desk a bed folded from the same wall. Several closets and cabinets covered two of the other walls. The last wall was blank. My cabin's computer awaited instructions for projecting any image that I desired upon the wall.

A small table, two comfortable chairs, and a small cozy couch completed the furniture within my cabin.

I took a few uncaring glances around, then noticed one of the closets stood open. Inside I found my belongings. Unpacking, I dwelt more and more on my situation until I grew so furious that I threw my bag across the room.

I had to prove myself to this squadron. My future depended upon it. Failure here meant the end of my career. Once I vectored out of the Black Birds, I'd be out of Sky Command. Even planetary defensive forces wouldn't want me. I might get a job as a shuttle pilot for some beat-up old freighter with a tired, old crew, but little else.

Frustrated, I flopped onto my bed and ordered the lights out. I instructed my cabin's computer to project a night image of the Earth's Summer sky, as seen from the Sierra Nevada Mountains of southern Spain, on the ceiling above me. The computer searched for a few moments before finding the image.

I stared at the Big Dipper and the Milky Way for a long time. They were old friends. My dad and I had camped many times in the Spanish Sierras. I missed him. I missed his stories and his laughter. I missed his wisdom and strength.

I needed his strength now. Thinking about him brought him back to me. I remembered hiking and camping with him. I remembered playing sports and games with him. And I remembered the things he taught me. He taught me more by example than by word, and those examples became part of who I was. Remembering Dad gave me the strength to go on.

The first thought I had upon arising at Oh-Five-Hundred the next day was that I'd find a way to prove myself to my squadron. I had no intention of sitting out the conflict that stormed across Eos far below. Flying mattered to me. Once inside a fighter, I'd prove my worth.

I took a few moments to straighten my bed before folding it back into the wall. I looked forward to meeting Captain Jonkowski today, whatever she might be like. I hoped to make her an ally. Not everyone could be as cold-hearted as Captain Mboko.

My stomach growled. It was hungry. I quickly shaved, showered, dressed and made my way to the pilots' ward room. Located forward of all the hangar decks and bays, the ward room provided meals to all of the Sky Command pilots aboard *Akagi*. I'd had a quick snack there the night before. There had been a few tired-looking pilots from the Seventh Squadron, the Sentinels, present. They hadn't talked to me and I hadn't talked to them. I'd eaten quickly, used the facilities, and left. But that little snack hadn't carried me far.

In the ward room, I ordered steak and eggs, hash browns, toast, and hot tea for breakfast. When my food arrived, I gulped it down. Pilots from the other fighter and SAR squadrons filled the room. Some, recently returned from the fighting over Eos, looked exhausted. Others, fresher looking, prepared to go out.

I caught bits and pieces of their conversations. The situation didn't sound good. The Gorgons had the advantage at every turn.

My own situation seemed so bizarre that I avoided those around me. Until I knew where I stood, I kept to myself.

Finished with my meal, I stood up to leave. A robot cleared my table. As I moved toward the exit, I saw a tired major approaching. Another pilot, a fellow first lieutenant, accompanied him. The lieutenant also appeared tired, but his eyes were sharp and cold.

Letting the two pass, I started out. By accident, I brushed against the major. I excused myself. He nodded. Then he noticed my Black Birds insignia.

"Who the hell are you?" he demanded.

I took a deep breath. Both pilots wore Black Birds insignia. The major must be Anton Garacyk, my squadron commander. "I'm Lieutenant Hector Crossman, sir."

"I see." He said nothing else but just stared at me. Uncomfortable, I excused myself again and started to leave.

Major Garacyk turned to the lieutenant with him. "Johnnie, I've good men and women in my squadron. I need them all."

I relaxed. Maybe he wasn't as judgmental as Captain Mboko.

"But not you," he said, turning back to me. "I know what you are, Crossman. You're a politician, not a pilot. You're more concerned about advancing your career than fighting for your squadron mates and humanity. You're not Black Birds material. You're not even Sky Command material. How you got this far, I can only guess. But you're not going any farther. No one can help you now. Your days are numbered. When the opportunity presents itself, I'm kicking you out."

Words failed me. I felt my face flush under his tirade. I wanted to leave, but couldn't.

Finished with me, the major turned his back and entered the ward room.

Humiliated, I walked away. My life was fast becoming one long ride through hell.

Almost an hour later, I arrived outside of Captain Jonkowski's office, located several doors down from Captain Mboko's office. I announced myself to her door and it admitted me to her outer office.

Like the walls of Mboko's office, the walls of Jonkowski's office were adorned with computer-generated images. But these far out-performed those in the exec's office. Mboko's pictures posed quietly upon her walls, while Jonkowski's images lived.

Dragons flew above my head. On the walls around me, on the door behind me, and on the door leading to Jonkowski's inner office. Unicorns galloped across her walls, grazing, and tended to their young. Among the unicorns danced winged horses. Sometimes these horses leaped from the walls, playing tag with the dragons in the mock sky above.

The whole scene dazzled me. Standing in awe of the images, I forgot to announce myself to the inner office.

The scene before the inner office wiggled, disappearing as the door whispered open. A woman as tall as me came out. Her short white-blonde hair, cut similar to Captain Mboko's, enhanced her lean features and her deeply tanned skin. Passing through the open doorway, she read a small holo-pad in her hand.

When the door closed behind her, the unicorns and flying horses returned. Glancing up, she stopped and smiled: one of the most beautiful, warm, and friendly smiles I'd ever seen.

"You are Crossman?" she asked, her voice friendly and melodic.

I snapped to attention. "Affirmative, ma'am."

"Please, not so formal. I'm Captain Rana Jonkowski."

"Affirmative, ma'am."

She laughed. "No, no, that won't do. Call me Rana. Everyone does. I prefer it."

"Okay."

"And I will call you Hector. Okay?"

I nodded.

"Good. I've been reading your file. You performed beautifully at Gargaphia."

"Thanks. I never thought of it as being beautiful."

"Your performance was. You arrived yesterday?"

"Affirmative."

"So did your Gargaphia simulation. I ran it last night after returning from my COP. I found it as intense as the fighting over Eos. How did you compose it?"

"With difficulty."

She nodded. "That I believe. Was your flight that bad?"

"Worse."

"That I also believe. Your simulation took my breath away. Quite literally. Don't make it any more intense. I couldn't stand it."

I smiled. "I don't intend to. I want to get into the action down below. But Major Garacyk and Captain Mboko have decided this is where I belong. That is until they can get rid of me."

"Why?"

"I think because General Devon assigned me here, rather than letting them pick whoever they wanted."

She sighed, then waved me toward her inner office. Again, the unicorns and winged horses vanished as the door opened. She entered and I followed. Her inner office was huge. Before me, along the far wall, sat five simulators.

A windowed smaller room, located to my left, overlooked the larger room. Rana guided me toward this room, her true office.

The door whisked open. Entering the room, Rana sat down behind a small table. I sat across from her.

"Anton is a hard man. But he is a good man. You must give him a chance. He will do right by you."

"I just left him."

"You don't sound pleased at your first meeting. What happened?"

"He announced to the pilots' ward room that I was unfit for either his squadron or Sky Command. He also let it be known that he was getting rid of me at his earliest opportunity."

She shook her head. "He does this to himself. But don't worry, your time will come. He will see that you are a good pilot."

"How d'you know I'm such a good pilot?"

"From your record."

"The exec thinks I'm unfit. She claims my record says so."

"She's jealous of you."

"Why?"

"Anton retained her as his exec. She's functioned exceedingly well within her slot. She should have been promoted to her own squadron long ago. In the last year, she's been nominated for command to two different squadrons. She doesn't know this. Anton should have let her go. But he doesn't wish to lose her. So he's declined her promotion."

"How d'you know this?" I asked.

"Anton is my lover."

"Oh."

"Do not be embarrassed."

"So why's Captain Mboko jealous of me?"

"Because of your actions at Gargaphia. And also because of your award and promotion."

"She's got the Red Wings. That's far better than the Scarlet Nova."

"And it has trapped her where she is. But I feel she is also jealous of your freedom of action. You are not afraid of disobedience if it means saving lives. She so desires a squadron of her own that she feels trapped by her duties."

"Duty traps us all," I said.

"So it does," Rana agreed.

"How do I get out of this mess?"

Rana shrugged. "I can guarantee you that Anton will not transfer you out."

"Why not? D'you intend to intercede for me?"

"No."

"Then how d'you know he won't?"

"As long as you perform well, he has no reason to transfer you. After running your Gargaphia simulation, I know you will perform well here. And your time will come. You must be patient. And trust."

"Who can I trust? And how can I be patient, with the war below passing me by?"

"There is enough death for everyone. Trust in yourself. And in your friends."

"Such as you?" I asked.

She smiled. "Yes. Now, let us find something to keep your mind from your problems."

CHAPTER SIX

SPENT THE REST OF **my second day aboard** *Akagi* **updating the squadron's various training sims. Rana Jonkowski left at Oh-Eight-Thirty to lead a GORCOP: a Gorgon Combat Operations Patrol. At Eleven-Hundred, I took my midday meal break. I made my way back to the pilot's ward room, where I made certain that neither Major Garacyk, nor Captain Mboko, were present before entering and eating my lunch. I had little desire for another reaming out by either of them.**

While eating, I activated my table's holoviewer. I roamed the different channels until I found the ship's Tactical News. A window appeared displaying a selection of the available information stories. Scanning the selection, I stopped on the one for the Black Birds. I wanted to know how we were doing.

We weren't doing well.

A news recap explained that five days before, Gorgon ground forces had smashed through a defensive perimeter the Eosian Army had established along the western coast of Titanus, the main continent. The Gorgons had slaughtered the troops in three Eosian Army divisions. No one had survived. Our forces had fallen back to a new line on the southern edge of the coastal city of Atlatya.

The Black Birds flew support for the forces forming the new line. *Akagi's* other fighter squadrons, along with its remaining Marine gunboats, fought to slow the Gorgon advance.

Militia and police units assisted the city's defense.

Behind the line, Atlatya's evacuation continued. Two weeks before, the Eosian government had started relocating the city's two million inhabitants. While most had cooperated, a few thousand people remained, reluctant to leave their homes and lives behind. However, the Eosian government, responsible for these rebellious citizens, had diverted ground forces for their forcible relocation. Besides fighting the Gorgons, the Eosian Army fought its own people.

Most of Atlatya's remaining refugees evacuated along highways leading north from the city, but thousands exited through the city's skyport, traveling by shuttle to the Task Force's waiting ships, or skimming the upper atmosphere before dropping back toward the refugee camps further north. Meanwhile, the Gorgon gunboats slashed at them, destroying ground vehicles and blasting shuttles out of the sky. And always, our fighters fought the Gorgons away.

I switched the holoviewer off. So Rana flew over the city right now. And maybe Pedro, too. Perhaps even Roberta Sanchez? I hoped Roberta and the other pilots I'd traveled with here had better luck fitting into their squadrons than I did.

Returning to Rana's office, I scanned through the simulation library. Hundreds of sims, many outdated, filled the files. A few fit the fighting below. Among those

I found Rana's almost completed sim. Curious, I climbed into a simulator and loaded the program.

I found myself flying on a COP low over the equatorial region, skimming fifteen meters above the irregular jungle canopy. At one thousand kilometers per hour, I dodged around an occasional emergent tree.

The sim informed me that a box of seven Gorgon gunboats vectored in on me. My sim wing mate suggested we exit the combat zone. But I wanted to know what combat against the Gorgons felt like, even if only virtually. Calculating an intercept vector, I increased my velocity to fifteen hundred kph.

Vectoring at a sharp angle to my left, I directed my sim wing mate to stay on my six, my tail.

The Gorgon box changed its vector, matching mine. The gunboats kept their formation tight. They appeared disciplined. An enemy like that was hard to defeat.

The Gorgons, who had flown a hundred meters higher than me, climbed to two thousand meters. They wanted more maneuvering room.

So did I.

I pulled my sim bird into a straight-up climb and increased my velocity to two thousand kph. As I did so, I directed one of my eight sim missiles to engage the enemy. It exited from my starboard missile bay. Twisting around, the missile vectored in on the Gorgon box at full velocity, fifteen thousand kilometers per hour.

The Gorgons vaporized my missile, then they pursued me.

My sim wing mate had trouble keeping up with me. He kept pleading that we get out of there, claiming we lacked the firepower to engage a box.

But I wanted to know more. At twenty-five thousand kilometers, in simulated space, I rolled over and dived straight at the seven-gunboat box. I directed my remaining sim missiles against the aft gunboat. I also directed my sim wing mate to target his missiles on the aft gunboat. Then I began firing my fighter's main weapon, a plasma cannon, at the gunboats. My cannon's plasma stream licked at the rearmost gunboat.

My missiles launched. So did my wing mate's missiles. They struck their target without results. The simulation appeared unprepared for this action. Then my wing mate and I were among the enemy.

Each gunboat, with the exception of the center one, carried six plasma cannon, three on each side. The center gunboat carried only four cannon.

The gunboat's cannon occupied turrets capable of rotating a full three-hundred-sixty degrees vertically and forty-five degrees horizontally. At once, thirty-plus plasma streams from the six gunboats struck my bird's screens, collapsing them. I felt on fire, my skin broiling, my body barbecuing. I disconnected myself from the false reality and exited the simulator.

The simulation seemed so real that as I climbed out, I found my body covered in sweat. Rana talked about how intense my Gargaphia sim was, but her sim had as intense an ending as any I'd ever experienced before.

I spent the rest of the day updating training sims, then returned to my cabin, feeling tired and alone. The only friends I'd made so far were Rana Jonkowski and Brigadier General Devon. My squadron commander and his exec hated me. And I had yet to locate Pedro.

I'd left messages with his door the night before, this morning, and when I returned from Captain Jonkowski's office. His cabin was two doors down from mine. I wished he'd reply, and soon. I needed friends right now.

I thought about contacting Roberta Sanchez, but decided against it. She needed time to fit into her squadron. As far as I knew, her squadron wanted her.

I wished mine wanted me.

I'd traveled thousands of light years for a new beginning, only to find myself an outcast. I lived on a ship with twelve hundred other people, yet I felt friendless and frustrated.

Tired of the frustration and anger, I wanted free from it all. But how? Could I run away from my life? Could I run away from the distrusting people I met everywhere?

I unfolded my bed from the wall. I wanted to get out of my uniform, put something casual on, and rest for a while. I stepped over to one of my closets.

Its doors burst open. A screaming figure leaped out at me. Crying out, I stumbled backward over my bed, sprawling on the floor, one leg on the bed. Before I could rise, I heard laughter and a familiar face came into view.

"Pedro! I'm so glad to see you. What the hell were you doing in there?" I demanded.

"Waiting for you to open the doors so I could jump at you."

"How long were you there?"

He shrugged. "Twenty minutes, perhaps."

"Twenty minutes? How'd you get in here?"

"Doors are so stupid, wouldn't you agree, amigo? I coughed and said for it to let me and it assumed I was you."

I stared at him.

"Are you going to lie on the floor all day or get up and offer me a chair?"

I glanced around the room. "Why do you want me to get up? Do you have some other trick waiting for me?"

"No, amigo. You just look so silly on the floor."

"Oh." I stood up and offered my hand to him. He shook it, then pulled me into a solid embrace.

After a moment, he stepped back. "I've missed you, mi hermano."

Reaching behind me, I felt along my back. "Do I have some sort of sign on me now?"

He laughed.

Entering my bathroom, I peered into the mirror and made sure he hadn't placed something on my back.

"There's nothing there," he said.

I glanced out to see if he was setting me up for a surprise for later. He stood where I left him.

"Get in here," I growled.

Pedro came in. "What're you looking for?"

Straining to see my reflection over my shoulder, I looked for some sort of paper or other material on the back of my uniform.

"Something that says kick me, or blast me, or up yours."

"But there's nothing there."

"There sure was on Graduation Day."

"Seven years have passed, amigo. I've changed."

"You jump out of my closet, scaring me, and then expect me to believe you've changed?"

"I wanted to greet you in my own way."

"You did."

"Listen, I've a lot of people I want you to meet. Clean up and come with me."

"Where to?"

"To where the excitement is. To the forward upper lounge, where your future friends await you. You'll like it. It's where we unwind. Its ceiling is a huge transparent dome that looks out into space. The ship's just begun a rollover. Eos will be overhead."

I shook my head. "I'm not in the mood, thank you."

"Get in the mood."

"It's not that simple."

"And why is that?"

"People on this ship don't like me."

"How can that be? People like me. They'll like you. We're friends. You're my brother."

"I feel the same way."

"Then come on. Let's vector, Hector."

I shook my head again.

"Why not, amigo?"

"I don't know. Maybe because Garacyk and Mboko are just waiting to get rid of me."

"You must be mistaken."

"Both have told me so. Garacyk said it in front of several people in the pilot's ward room this morning."

"That was you? I'd heard he shouted at a new pilot today. But I didn't know it was you."

"Does everyone know about this morning?"

"Gossip travels faster than light, amigo."

"Now you understand why I don't want to go out, let alone meet anyone new."

"But that is exactly why you should go out."

"I really don't want to."

"Wash your face. Your future awaits you. I've exceptional people for you to meet. Trust me."

I nodded.

"There's someone I especially want you to meet."

"A woman?" I asked, smiling.

"An exceptional one."

"For you? Or for me?" I wondered who while washing up.

"For me. You'll have to find your own woman."

I stared at him, water dripping from my face. "You sound serious. How can the reincarnation of Don Juan settle for only one woman?"

"She's my heart."

"Then she must be an exceptional woman."

Pedro handed me a towel. "Exactly so."

"What's her name?"

"Lori."

"A lovely name."

"She's more than lovely, amigo, she's..."

"I know. She's exceptional."

"Exactly."

"Do you love her?"

"Si, amigo. I never imagined I'd ever find anyone to love. But I love Lori. I love saying her name. I love her voice, the way she laughs, the way she talks. I..."

"I'm growing nauseated," I said.

"You'll understand when you meet her."

"Because she's exceptional?"

"Exactly."

I changed into casual clothes. Then I approached the door. "Let's vector," I said.

We took a horizontal lift almost to the bow of the ship itself. Then we took a lift upward. Two of *Akagi*'s lounges were forward while the other three were scattered throughout the ship. Besides the lounge we moved towards, a smaller domed lounge was located on the carrier's chin, at the opposite end of the lift line we now traveled.

Pedro explained that the smaller lounge had a reverse gravitic field. The lift rotated while descending so that its passengers actually ascended into the smaller lounge. In fact, it wasn't exactly a lounge but rather a low gravity swimming pool with a shallow dome overhead. It had a small wet bar and a food service area around the pool's rim, just under dome's edge.

I wanted to see that one but Pedro assured me I'd enjoy the one we now traveled towards much better. He explained that it was situated under a large dome on top of the upper curve of the hull. He said it was fantastic.

And it was. The lift stopped just beneath it and we climbed a spiral stairwell, exiting into the center of the lounge. As I saw Eos above me, through the curve of the great dome, I forgot that I flew on a warship in a war zone. It felt like I'd just stepped onto a luxury liner.

The lounge consisted of three rings, each ring raised two steps above the last. The outermost ring, along the edge of the dome, stood highest. It had the best view and the most people sat there. Fewer people sat at the next ring down, which had tables accommodating up to ten people. The inner ring ran around the bar and food service unit, with people sitting on stools before the bar. Lively music jazzed the lounge.

After looking around, I glanced up again. The planet's terminus crossed the middle of the main continent. On one side, the sun rose; on the other side, darkness dwelled. In between existed a pinkish area, with long shadows veiling the landscape.

East of the terminus drifted vast streams of white clouds. Beneath the clouds, blue lakes dotted the surface while silvery rivers meandered through green and brown landscapes amid white-capped mountains. East of the terminus, in the darkness, the golden glow of the cities glorified Eos. Sometimes among the cities, and in the vast spaces between them, lightning flashed.

It was beautiful.

Just as I had to remind myself that I now stood on a warship and not a luxury liner, so I had to remind myself that a war burned the world above me, or rather, beneath me.

"Exceptional, wouldn't you say?" Pedro asked.

"In a word, yes," I whispered. I felt more relaxed and at peace than I had since arriving.

"Come with me. I want to introduce you to your new friends." Pedro guided me halfway around the second ring to a table surrounded by six people. A young woman, with medium length brown hair, stood as we approached.

She offered her hand. "Hello, I'm Lori Clark."

I glanced at Pedro and he nodded. Taking her hand, I gave it a little squeeze. "Hi, I'm Hector Crossman. Glad to meet you. I hope."

"Why do you say that?" she asked. She was lovely.

"I've had problems ever since coming aboard this ship. Some people just don't like me."

Someone at the table grunted. I turned to see who it was, but Lori, still holding my hand, pulled me back. "Not everyone feels that way. We trust Pedro. We know him. We know he wouldn't foster someone of poor repute upon us."

"Some know better than that," a voice quipped from behind her. She dropped my hand and turned around.

"That's a good way do die, mon. Lori might mistake you for a wormie and burn you," someone else said.

"Mi corazon, let's introduce Hector to everyone. They're already making him feel at home," Pedro said.

Lori smiled. Looping her arm around mine, she guided me around the table. First we stopped at a thin man with red hair. "This is Lyle Lem," Lori said. "He's new to our group, coming aboard just before we came to Eos. His call sign's BS and you'll understand why."

"She's a pretty thing, dontcha agree? Himself's proud to make yar acquaintance. Any friend o' Pedro's a friend o' mine."

I glanced at Pedro.

Pedro shrugged. "He just talks that way."

I turned back to Lyle. "Glad to meet you."

"Likewise."

Lori guided me to the next person at the table. A tall, muscular man with hair almost as short and white-blond as Rana Jonkowski's, stood up to greet me. Smiling, he jabbed his open hand at me.

"I'm Vladimir Geys. Happy to meet you. Welcome aboard."

"Thanks. Glad to meet you, too," I said, shaking hands with him. His grip hurt.

Still smiling, he let go of my hand. "I'm Vampire. And you are?"

"Ice Maker." I let my hand fall by my leg, flexing my sore fingers.

His smile became a grin. "Interesting."

Vladimir sat back down as Lori moved me a little more around the table. The man beside Geys appeared almost as tall, though he remained seated. He also wore his hair very short. He had a thin face, very dark skin, and a ready smile.

"This is Jacko," Lori said. "Otherwise known as Jacques DuQuesne."

"Careful, amigo. He thinks he knows everything."

"Hey, mon, do I talk that way about you?"

"You do."

"Glad to meet you, Jacko," I said.

"Jacques will do, mon."

Lori guided me to another person.

"And this is Ava Fabian. Her call sign's Racer."

She looked up at me. Her beautiful, dark brown eyes lacked emotion. "Hi," she said. Without another word, she returned to reading an electronic tablet on the table before her.

"Well," Lori said. "And this is Dancer, Lisa Mauros. Lisa's with the Second SAR Squadron. Everyone else here is a Black Bird."

Lisa smiled at me and I found myself captivated by her. A warmth and friendliness emanated from her blue eyes and bright smile. She wore her lovely, golden-brown hair in a pony tail.

"How do you do?" she said.

I smiled back. "You have such a lovely voice."

She blushed. "Thank you."

"Where are you from?"

"Gentry."

I stared at her.

"What's wrong?"

"I knew someone from Gentry once. A SAR pilot on *Soyuz*. Someone I once cared deeply about."

"Oh. Where's she now?"

"She's gone home," I said.

"You sound sad."

"I cared about her. I've never been good at saying goodbye. In fact, I hate it."

"No one enjoys goodbyes. Was her name Corinna Vernon?"

"D'you know her?" I asked, stunned.

"I know of her. Those of us from Gentry kept close while at the Academy. She was a year behind me."

"Oh."

Lori directed me to a seat, then sat beside me. Pedro sat on the other side of her and winked at me.

"So, how long have you known Pedro?" I asked Lori.

"Two years. I transferred from the Double Sixs."

"And were you friends right away?"

"Not exactly, amigo," Pedro said. "I took a few hits before she came around to my way of seeing things."

I glanced at Pedro, then at Lori. She frowned at Pedro, then said: "We've had our difficulties, just as any couple does. And we still have differences of opinions. But that's all."

"We all have differences of opinions with Pedro," Vladimir Geys said.

"Don't I know it," I said. We all laughed.

"Are you hungry?" Lori asked.

I nodded.

"Good." Lori pressed a button near the center of the table. A small opening appeared and a slim stick microphone rose up. A holoviewer activated beside the microphone, indicating the menu. We ordered dinner.

"It will take about ten minutes," Lori told me.

"We've heard a lot about your days at the Academy with Pedro," Vladimir said. "He's described you as a real go-getter, sort of a wild-man."

"Really?" I glanced at Pedro, who shrugged. Turning back to Vladimir, I asked, "What d'you mean?"

"I thought perhaps you might enlighten us," he replied.

"And how should I do that?"

"You might explain how you got Ice Maker as a call sign."

"My flight instructors gave it to me."

"Oh, come now," Vlad insisted. "I heard it had something to do with wrecking the dining hall's ice making machine."

Turning my head slowly, I glared at Pedro. He smiled uncomfortably and glanced away.

"Vlad," Lori said, "please don't embarrass Hector. We've only known him a few minutes."

"And how are we ever going to know him better if we don't ask him questions?" Geys replied, grinning.

"With better questions," Lori replied.

"Ah, the food has arrived," Jacques said. The center of table opened again. From it floated our trays, each with our dinners and drinks.

"Is it really true that ya broke the ice machine? Himself heard a story 'bout how a cadet from a couple of years before smashed up the cafeteria because he couldn't find any ice for his drink. Was that ya?"

"All right, all right!" I growled, embarrassed. "I'll tell you. It was a hot day. We'd just finished a ten-kilometer run. A dozen of us went into the dining hall to get something to drink. I was fourth in line. Pedro had just finished filling his cup with ice. When I went up to the machine nothing came out. I knew it couldn't be empty. One of our drill instructors was with us and he said to tweak it."

"Tweak it?" Vlad snickered. "Is that a technical term?"

"Maybe. I wouldn't know. Anyways, I struck the side of it. A few cubes came out. The drill instructor said it must be frozen inside and said to hit it again. So I did. Nothing happened. I hit it harder, and it fell off its mounting, crashing against the floor. That's all there is to it, okay?"

"Really? That's not quite how Pedro tells it," Vlad said.

"And how does Pedro put it?" I asked.

"He said that the machine began spitting out ice. And that it continued spitting ice all day long."

"Not exactly," Pedro interrupted. "It was more like ten minutes."

"You said 'all day'," Vlad snickered.

"You're mistaken," Pedro said.

"Himself heard it, too."

"Really?" I said. "And how'd it become a whole day?"

"Perhaps I was caught up in the moment, amigo."

"What moment?" I demanded.

"The moment o' makin' a fool o' yarself," Lyle quipped.

Laughter broke out at our table. Pedro looked helpless. I forgot my own embarrassment as I enjoyed Pedro's.

"We should eat," Lori said. "We never know when our next COP might come."

We turned to our food. Silence, except for the sounds of eating, engulfed our table as Lori's words brought reality back to us all.

While eating, I found myself staring at Lisa Mauros. I couldn't take my eyes off of her. When she had mentioned Corinna's name, my heart had jumped. Now it jumped again. There was something about the way she spoke, the way she laughed, that excited me. I felt as if I could listen to her forever.

At one point, she noticed me looking at her. Our eyes met and she smiled.

"Were you close to Corinna?" she asked.

"Just friends. How long have you been aboard *Akagi*?"

"Since graduating from the Academy."

"So that'd make you about twenty-five?"

"Twenty-four. I entered the Academy a year earlier than most people."

"Oh. And were you a city dweller on Gentry? Or did you live out where the green beasts roam?"

"How do you know about them?" Lisa exclaimed.

"I just do."

"This Corinna told him about them," Vlad said, casting cold eyes my way.

"We never talked about that."

"What else do you know about Gentry?" Lisa asked.

"I know that it has beautiful cities, beautiful prairies, beautiful skies, and the most beautiful women of all the worlds."

She blushed again. "Have you been there?"

"Not yet."

"And not probably ever," Vlad said.

"What do you mean?" Lori asked.

"The major chewed him out in the Ward Room yesterday. I wasn't going to say anything, seeing how he's Pedro's friend. But rumor has it that he'll be leaving soon. In a day or so at the most."

"Not if I can help it," I said.

"You can't. The major doesn't want you. Neither does the exec."

"And neither do you."

"I never said that. You're Pedro's friend."

"Does that make me your friend?"

"Who knows?"

"I'm your friend," Lori said, laying a hand on my arm.

"Thanks," I said.

"We're your friends, too," Lisa said. "If you want us to be."

"I do," I said, smiling at her.

"The question, then," Jacques suggested, "is how can we best help Hector? We need every pilot we have. No one would be here if he or she wasn't First Squadron material. You're here, so you must be fit for us. But how do we help the major and the exec notice your fitness?"

"That's two questions," Vlad said, trying to regain favor with the group.

"Two aspects of the same question," Jacques said.

"If I could fly, I could prove myself," I said.

"This isn't a game," Vlad snarled. "We're losing people all the time. Every day, fighters and gunboats are getting blown out of the sky. What's occurring on the ground is too gruesome to even imagine. We need pilots we can count on, not someone who's going to boost it because he's got buck fever. We need experienced combat pilots."

"I've flown combat," I replied. "Against the Na."

"Oh, I doubt that."

"What's with you today, mon?" Jacques intervened. "Why are you such a down-sayer? If the mon says he flew combat, then he flew combat."

"Mi amigo isn't a liar," Pedro said.

"We all build up our stories to impress each other," Vlad retorted. "You did with your story about how Crossman got his call sign. How do you know he's not building up his story about flying against the Na?

"Maybe he did fly combat. At least he considers what he flew combat. Maybe he flew against an old beat up shuttle. But to impress us all, he claims it was the Na. The Na are good. We all know that. Each of you was impressed when he said he flew against the Na, weren't you? Admit it."

The others nodded.

"That doesn't prove that he did. Only that he said so."

"I flew against them," I said. "It's in my record. I received a Gallantry Commendation for it. That's in my record, too. And I can access that any time and show it to you. But that's not the issue.

"The issue's how can I prove my competence to Garacyk and Mboko? And the only way is by flying a COP against the enemy. Pedro knows I'm competent. If you trust him, then trust me!"

All eyes turned toward Vlad.

"Well?" Lori said. "Do you have anything to ask Pedro?"

Vlad threw his hands up in frustration. "All right! If he claims to have flown against the Na, then so be it."

"Now," Lori said, turning to Jacques and leaning forward, "how can we get Hector into a COP?"

"We can't," Jacques said.

"What do you mean?" she said. "We have to. He's correct that if he doesn't prove himself in combat, they'll dismiss him."

"We can't get him into COP. Only Captain Inagaki can do that." Jacques turned to me. "He's our squadron's operations officer. Or Major Garacyk, Captain Mboko, or even the CSG, Colonel Wallis. But we can't get you assigned."

"I see," I said.

Lori sat back and sighed. "I don't know what we can do for you, Hector."

I patted her arm. "You're doing enough now. Until I met Captain Jonkowski this morning, I hadn't a friend in the squadron. Now I've several. And a friend in the Second SAR," I added, smiling at Lisa. She smiled back and I noticed Vlad frowning.

"Friends mean little while your career slips away," Vlad said.

"Friends are everything," I retorted. "You know, none of you are anything like I expected you to be."

"What do you mean?" Lori asked.

"You're all so relaxed. When my squadron mates and I, back aboard *Soyuz*, flew against the Na ship *Gaeg*, to say we were anxious was an understatement. We knew the Na were kidnaping people and selling them to O renegades for sport. We knew that if we didn't stop the Na, innocent people were going to die.

"But you, you're all so relaxed. I don't understand it. You're in the middle of a horrible war. How can you do it?"

"You have to be relaxed, amigo," Pedro said. "You can't handle it otherwise."

"Mon, when we're in here, then the war's far away," Jacques said. "When we climb out of our flight suits, as they drop to the deck, we let our anxieties drop away with them. As we leave the hangar deck, as we pass through the bulkhead doors, we remind ourselves to leave the war behind. We must. If we don't, we won't survive."

"He's right," Lori agreed. "The moment we pass through those doors, we leave it all behind. It's the only way we can survive."

"That makes my next question harder to ask."

"You want to know what it's like, don't you?" Pedro said.

"Affirmative."

"It's hell," Vlad said, standing up. "And you're not strong enough to face it."

"Vlad!" Lori hissed.

"What? You want me to stay and coddle this loser? Well, I can't. Stay if you want, but I've had it. Anyone want to join me? I'm going for a swim. How about you, Lisa? I'd enjoy your company."

"I'd rather stay. Thank you for asking, Vladimir. Another time, perhaps?"

"Whatever." Without another word, Vlad left.

"He's a wee intense tonight," Lyle said.

"Exactly," Pedro said.

Watching Vlad leave, I wondered if I'd made yet another enemy. But, glancing around the table at my new friends, it didn't much matter. Rana, referring to the war below, had earlier said that there was enough death to go around. There seemed enough hatred to go around, too.

And enough friendship.

CHAPTER SEVEN

AFTER VLAD LEFT, WE finished our dinner. And while we ate, I asked how the war went.

"What do you want to know?" Jacques asked.

"I want to know why we're losing. How is it possible?"

"Simple," Pedro said. "The wormheads are better than us."

"But how can they be better than us? All I heard aboard the frigate *Sagacious* while coming here was how much better our technology is than theirs. I know that our training, tactics, and techniques are superior. If we're so much better, then why are we losing?"

"Good question," Pedro replied. "It baffles me, too."

"You see," Jacques began, "our missiles are useless against them. It takes every missile we carry to vaporize just one gunboat."

"I don't understand," I replied. "How can our missiles be ineffective? Our missiles can almost vaporize a destroyer. A squadron can shoot the hell out of a battle cruiser. Why can't we shoot down their gunboats? What do our probes say?"

"They reveal nothing," Jacques said. "The Gorgons vaporize them as fast as we can launch them. We've launched tens of thousands of microprobes and not a one has told us a thing."

"What about the sensors aboard the Marine gunboats? Or our sensors? Or the destroyers on picket duty over the battle ground? Doesn't anyone have any tactical information?"

My voice kept rising as I asked each question. I felt frustration and it came out as I talked.

"Calm down, mon. We're doing the best we can."

"Listen, amigo," Pedro said, his voice calm, which calmed me, "the enemy's box formations are impregnable. Each of the seven gunboats has six plasma guns. That makes forty-two guns for each formation. With their screens interlaced, and with their exceptional ability to bring to bear twenty to thirty guns in any direction, we can't get through."

"How're the Marines doing it, then?"

"A whole squadron engages a box. They flail away at each other at close quarters," Jacques said. "The Marines fly boat to boat, one on one, matching velocities with them."

"So they can break down the defensive strength of a box, but we can't? We're just not strong enough to slug it out with them, then? How can that be? Our speed and maneuverability are our strength."

"Exactly, amigo."

I shook my head. "Something about all this bothers me."

"How so?" Lori asked.

"I don't know. They shouldn't be able to destroy our missiles, nor all our probes."

"They planned this war to the last detail, mon. They secretly transported hundreds of thousands of ground troops here. They smuggled thousands of grav tanks and gunboats in prior to initiating hostilities. Their gunboats seize the sky over a position, then their ground troops eliminate all resistance; then cleansing forces eliminate all survivors."

I leaned across the table toward Jacques. "Then it's by detail work we have to beat them."

"How?" Jacques asked.

"I'm not sure." I turned to Pedro. "You said that each gunboat fields six plasma cannon. But the center gunboat fields only four."

Pedro shook his head. "No, it has six, like the rest."

"I flew Captain Jonkowski's latest combat sim today. She's structured it around a pair of birds engaging a Gorgon box formation over an equatorial forest. From the feel of it, she's used the latest intel on Gorgon tactics, including ship design. The center boat only has four cannon."

"Then she's wrong," Pedro replied.

"She's too good for that," Jacques said. "Such a detail wouldn't be simulated if it didn't exist."

"How did you do in the sim?" Lisa asked.

"I lost."

"And your point is?" Lori asked.

"Why does the center boat have only four cannon?"

"Why does it matter?"

"I've an idea," I said, ignoring her question. "Do any of you remember Lieutenant Colonel Mahura's 'Ancient Aerial Tactics and Combat' class at the Academy?"

Everyone nodded.

"He talked about how in the Twentieth and Twenty-first centuries sky forces used to fly craft to jam the sensors of ground-based sky defenses so they could enter enemy skies with a reduced threat. D'you remember that?"

"Yes," Jacques said. "Are you suggesting that the center boat is a jamming platform?"

"Could be."

"That would explain much," Jacques said. "They might even control the entire box from the central boat."

"So, if we can figure this out," I said, "why hasn't anyone else? There are hundreds of pilots fighting in these skies. Why hasn't another squadron or pilot figured this out yet?"

"When yar too busy fightin', sometimes ya don't have the time to think," Lyle suggested.

"No," Pedro corrected. "This is exactly what mi amigo's best at, reasoning his way through problems. Listen, Hector, you're the first to fly Rana's sim. You brought a fresh view to the table. What you've done is exceptional."

"An' how do we put this to use?" Lyle asked.

"I fly a shiner into a box," I said.

"An' why ya? Himself's as good a pilot as they come. Himself can do it."

"Because I did what no else ever did: I flew into a gas giant's atmosphere, down to its surface, and found a missing lifeboat. And because I need all of you to guard my six while I fly into Hell."

Lisa reached her hand across the table and touched mine. "What you did at Gargaphia was incredible. Every SAR squadron's heard of it. But what you want to do now is far more dangerous. Be careful."

"I will. Thanks."

Standing, she smiled at me. "If you will all excuse me, I must get some sleep. I've another COP early tomorrow. It was nice meeting you, Hector. Do be careful."

I stood. "It was nice meeting you, too. And I will."

"Thank you." Still smiling, she turned and left the lounge.

I watched her go, watched as her golden-brown hair bounced upon her shoulders as she walked away, until Pedro cleared his throat, bringing me back to the discussion.

Sitting down, I said, "She's very nice."

Pedro grinned. "Exceptional, wouldn't you say?"

"Exactly," I replied, smiling. "So how am I going to get a bird and get into the action?"

"How did you get here to begin with?" Jacques inquired.

"I wrote a letter to my previous CSG, who wrote to an old friend of his. His friend assigned me to the Black Birds."

"Colonel Wallis?"

"General Devon."

"He's got the biggest gun on his side," Lyle said.

"Ah," Jacques said. "Such explains Major Garacyk's and Captain Mboko's ire."

"We still have to go through the proper channels, don't forget," Lori said.

"Exactly," Pedro said, standing up. "We're all finished eating. Let's be away."

"To where?" I asked.

"To face Captain Mboko, amigo. But we'll be with you."

A few minutes later, we faced Captain Mboko in her office, behind her desk

"No!," she cried out. "Absolutely not."

"Why not?" I asked.

"We have neither the time, nor the personnel, to waste on such an implausible concept," she said. The exec looked at Pedro and the others. "You shouldn't waste your time associating with this transient. Get to your quarters and get some rest. You all have COPs tomorrow."

"Excuse me, captain," Lori replied, "but according to regulations our time is our own when we're off-duty."

"There is no such thing as off-duty time in a combat zone," Mboko snarled back.

Lori bristled, but Jacques intervened. "According to Section 42A, subheading Delta, 'Off-duty personnel in any and all combat arenas may utilize their time as they so wish.' According to the regulations, even in a combat zone there's off-duty time."

"Enough! I have work to accomplish. Dismissed."

After her door hissed closed, I said: "Now what?"

"Now we visit Major Garacyk," Jacques said.

"From the lioness to the tiger. Himself may as well be back flying o'er Eos."

"That could be arranged," Ava Farley snapped. We all looked at her, surprised she had spoken.

"Aye, when the silent one speaks, it's time to be cautious."

"Well put," Lori said.

"Himself knows when to be quiet around two she-cats."

"Then why doesn't he?" Lori demanded.

Lyle started to reply, but Pedro intervened. "Wouldn't you say now's a good time to shut up?"

Lyle closed his mouth. I grinned.

We crossed the corridor to Major Garacyk's office and announced ourselves. I hadn't visited his office yet. Of the same size and layout as Captain Mboko's office, it had a different feel to it. The gray, barren walls of his outer office intensified the uneasiness I already felt. The door to his inner office opened, revealing more gray walls. He sat at his desk, which dominated the office. Behind him, on the wall, a small sailboat drifted across a dark sea while bright stars reflected on the water around it.

"Captain Mboko informed me of your impending arrival. My answer is the same. All of you but him are welcome," he said, jabbing a forefinger at me. "Get that him of here."

"Sir," Lori began, "you're being unfair to Hector. He's…"

"That'll be quite enough. All of you, get out."

Though mechanically impossible, it seemed as if the major's door slammed shut as we exited his office.

"That was quick," I said.

"And abrupt," Lori added. "So much for protocol."

"Si, mi corazon. Well, onward to the CSG."

Jacques nodded. "Colonel Wallis is more reasonable. But I feel we should go directly to General Devon's office. He assigned Hector to the Black Birds. He'd be the best one to help our crusade."

"You know," I began, as we all crowded into a lift, "I wanted to make my own way in this squadron. I didn't want to call on General Devon, or anyone else, to help me fit in. But Garacyk and Mboko just won't let me in."

"We're all a team, Hector," Lori said. "That's what makes the Black Birds so strong. That's what makes us the best squadron. We're twenty-four individuals working as a team. Flying as a team. Fighting as a team. And as a team, we help each other."

"But you don't know anything about me."

"I know my lover." She wrapped her arms around one of Pedro's arms. "I believe in him and he believes in you, so I also believe in you. There's nothing else to know."

I looked at Pedro. "You're right, she's special."

Pedro smiled. "It's something I've known for a long time."

The lift opened far beneath our squadron's decks, onto the horizontal travel tube that spanned *Akagi*'s center. We entered the tube and traveled aft.

"Does anyone know if Lieutenant Colonel Mahura still teaches at the Academy?" I asked.

"He retired as a full colonel two years ago," Ava said. "Just after I graduated."

"How long have you been with the Birds?"

"A year."

"Did you graduate near the top of your class?"

"No. Sixteenth."

"How'd you get here, then? I don't mean it the way it sounds. It took me seven years to get here, and I graduated third in my class. I'm just curious about you."

"It's none of your damned business."

"Careful, amigo, she's a mean one. But she's the best gunner of all of us."

"And I'll blast your ass out of the sky, too, if you get in my way!"

"Lovely," Lori murmured. "Well. Here we are."

We exited the tube, taking one of the lifts that ascended into the command island atop the carrier. The admiral commanding the task group, *Akagi*'s captain, Colonel Wallis, and General Devon all had offices located there.

"Who're we going to see first?" I asked.

"Colonel Wallis," Jacques said. "We'll maintain protocol."

"I know nothing about Wallis," I said. "But the general seems okay."

"It takes an exceptional man or woman to juggle all the different squadrons and leaders in a combat zone," Pedro said.

Our lift stopped, opening onto the same corridor where I'd talked with General Devon the day before. As we exited, I saw the entrance to *Akagi*'s captain's briefing room to my right. To my left, the corridor curved around the lift well, which contained three lifts. On the far side of the well lay the entrance to the offices of General Devon and Colonel Wallace.

Large, transparent double doors opened into the command offices. The interior looked more like the reception area of a large corporation than the senior Sky Command offices aboard an attack carrier. Inside sat comfortable-looking couches, with small tables beside them. A large desk in the center manned by a Sky Command sergeant controlled the room.

As the transparent doors hushed open, the sergeant at the desk looked up. "What may I do for you, sirs and ma'ams?"

"We're here to see Colonel Wallis," Pedro said.

"Concerning what, sir?"

"A manner by which we may better incinerate the enemy."

"I see." The sergeant glanced at an electronic tablet on his desk. "The colonel's quite busy right now, sir. May I suggest you come back in a day or two?"

"Listen, you moron," Ava Farley growled. "People are dying by the thousands down there and you're giving us the runaround. That pisses me off. So why don't you take us in right now!"

"I can't do that, ma'am. I have my orders."

"What may those orders be, sergeant?" Lori asked.

The sergeant sighed. "I can't say, ma'am."

"Perhaps you should," Pedro suggested.

"Himself's growin' tired o' yer excuses. Get the colonel for us and be quick about it."

"No, sir."

"What did ya say?"

The sergeant glared at Lyle, but said nothing more.

I stepped forward. "Forgive him. He's just an inexperienced junior officer. We'd like to see the colonel. We've an idea on how to break through the enemy's formations."

The sergeant shrugged. "I wish I could help you, lieutenant, but I can't. Orders are orders."

"Why would anyone order you not to let us in?"

The sergeant took a deep breath. "Your exec called and told Colonel Wallis that'd you be showing up with a ridiculous scheme. He left orders that you should follow your exec's orders. He said that if your seniors didn't believe in it, then he certainly couldn't either."

"But he hasn't heard it," Jacques said. "What kind of a fool denies a plan before even hearing it?"

"Not a fool. An officer who knows how to trust his squadron leaders," a voice boomed. We looked past the sergeant. Beyond lay a short corridor with a door on either side and one at its end. In front of the left door, now open, stood Colonel Wallis.

"At least, sir, hear our plan," I said.

"Yes, let us here it."

We turned around. Behind us, Brigadier General Devon had entered from the corridor outside. The sergeant stood up. "Ten-shun!"

"Relax," Devon said. "Good to see you again, Hector. See you've made some friends. Having problems?"

"Affirmative, sir."

"So I thought. Come along into my office. You, too, Brad," the general said to Colonel Wallis.

Wallis followed the general inside, stepping with Devon behind his desk for a consultation. While they whispered together, and as we filed inside, we took the time to glance around the general's office, trying to contain our nervousness.

The office was broad and spacious. A desk in its center faced the door, several chairs beside it. Behind the desk, a broad window revealed the carrier's curving side. Eos filled the upper half of the window's view. On one side of the office was a small table with two chairs; on the other side, a couch. Behind the couch a broad, pastoral mural portrayed cows grazing in a green pasture split by a small stream.

"Rather homey, isn't it?" Lori whispered.

I nodded. On a shelf by the table, I noticed several large and small models of tractors, some of ancient design. Even from across the office I could make out their meticulous details: tiny seats, tinier controls and steering wheels, miniature headlights, mufflers, batteries, brake and clutch pedals. Some of the tractors were yellow with little patches of red; some, green, with yellow highlights. One was entirely red, with black wheels.

"Tis a lot o' pinkness in this room," Lyle said.

Glancing around, I realized that the walls had a definite pink cast to them, unlike the bluish-gray coloration of most of the corridors and other offices, and of my cabin.

"It's the way the evenings look on the Eastern Plains of Nugaea," Ava said.

"How d'ya know that?" Lyle demanded.

She looked at us. "It's my home. And probably the general's, too."

"Correct, Lieutenant Farley," the general said. "Well, let's hear your plan, people."

Pedro opened his mouth to speak. But Lori, striding in front of us, said, "We're here for a variety of reasons, sir. Paramount is an idea Lieutenants Alvarez, Duquesne, and Crossman have for breaking up the enemy's formations."

"Oh?" The general sat behind his desk. He motioned us to the chairs. There weren't enough for everyone so Ava and I sat on the couch. "Keep talking, lieutenant."

"It's not my plan, sir," Lori said. "It's Lieutenant Crossman's."

"So, Hector? Let me here it."

"Sir, I think the center gunboat might be a jamming platform," I began.

Both the colonel and the general leaned forward. "Where'd you get such an ridiculous notion?" Colonel Wallis asked.

First, I explained about flying Rana Jonkowski's newest combat sim. Then I mentioned Mahura's "Ancient Aerial Tactics and Combat" class, pointing out the commonness of jamming platforms in ancient times, and suggesting that just because we didn't use them now didn't keep other races from using them.

"Even so, lieutenant, that doesn't prove the center boat's a jammer," Colonel Wallis said.

"No, sir, it doesn't. But your argument doesn't prove that it isn't, either. The only way we'll know for certain is if we fly a shiner into one of their formations."

"Our sensors would've informed us if the Gorgons were jamming us," Wallis retorted.

"Not necessarily, Brad," Devon said. "It could be a local effect, limited to within a certain range of each formation. We've seen how each formation keeps out of the way of the others. I think he's onto something.

"But let me ask you, Hector, how do you propose to solve the problem? How're you going to prove that the center gunboat's what you say it is?"

"By flying a shiner into a formation, sir. We've got to get close enough to experience the effect."

"That's insane," Wallis said.

"I knew you were gonna say that," Devon said, turning to Wallis. "Brad, have you studied this boy's record? No? Well, he flew a shiner into a gas giant, down to its surface, to find a lost lifeboat. Nobody's done that before. If he could do that, I'm sure he can get into and out of a Gorgon box."

"If they don't incinerate him."

"Brad, we'll just have to provide him with a helluva lot of cover. But let me also ask you, Hector, why'd you bring it to us? You should've taken it to your exec."

"We did, sir," Lori interrupted. "And to our C.O. But neither of them wanted to listen. They both turned us down without even knowing what we offered."

"And kicked us out!" Ava snarled.

"I see." Devon pressed a button on his desk. "Sergeant, will you please get Major Garacyk and Captain Mboko up here now."

"Sir, I'd like my friends here watching my six, when I fly the RECCOP" I said.

"You don't ask for much, do you, lieutenant?" Wallis said.

"Brad, see that it's arranged. Anything else, Hector?"

"I think I'd better carry a full complement of missiles. So the enemy doesn't suspect anything."

"That's a helluva good point. Brad, I want a couple of our gunboat squadrons ready to help out. And see to it that everyone's got a little time to rest before this COP."

"Affirmative, sir."

"Everyone's dismissed. Except you, Hector."

"Affirmative, sir." I walked with the others to the door.

"See you later," I said to them.

"On the vector, Hector," Pedro said, smiling.

"See ya out there," Lyle said.

Lori gave me a little kiss on the cheek. Then my friends left. I walked back over to General Devon. Colonel Wallis had left while I'd said my goodbyes.

"You're not gonna get much sleep," the general said. "You're gonna have to get to know your new bird. And you'll have to practice a couple of sims, too."

"Affirmative, sir."

"Pushed you around a bit, did they?"

I nodded. "Sir, I wanted to make it on my own in this squadron. I didn't want to ask for help."

"And you're gonna have to do it, too. But everyone needs a little assistance now and again. That's called team work."

"Affirmative, sir."

"You know, you'd think feelings wouldn't get hurt, that everyone would trust everyone else. But let me tell you, people are people. It doesn't matter if we're all dying or not, egos exist and get bruised. But we're runnin' outta time."

"Affirmative, sir."

"General, Captain Mboko and Major Devon are here," the sergeant's voice announced from Devon's desk comm unit.

"Show them in, sergeant. Have a seat, Hector. We'll try to even things out."

The major and the captain came into the office. Noticing me, they both stopped and glared at me.

"I've learned that you're wasting valuable resources," Devon said. "And you both know I'm talking about Lieutenant Crossman here. You feel angry that I assigned him to you. Well, it's my right and you both damned well know it.

"Now, the lieutenant and his friends have come up with an interesting plan. We're going to carry it out. I've ordered Colonel Wallis to make the arrangements. Comments?"

"I resent being told who can fly in my squadron," Major Garacyk said. "I don't know this pilot. Nor has he earned my trust as yet."

"That's because you haven't given him a chance. Daggett recommends this boy. You've flown with Daggett. It was his recommendation that got you this squadron. I know you respect Daggett's opinion. So give Lieutenant Crossman a chance.

"Because if you don't, you're failing Crossman, your squadron, Daggett, and me. Not to mention the Command."

"Who's leading this COP?" Garacyk asked.

"That's still to be arranged. But Crossman's flying the shiner. He's a good pilot and it's time you learned that."

"The lieutenant has been known to disobey orders," Captain Mboko said.

"Who hasn't?" General Devon said. "You've already disobeyed my orders by failing to give him a chance."

Mboko stiffened. "He's hardly appropriate material for this squadron."

"Let me tell you, captain, in case you haven't noticed, we're in the middle of a war. Yes, I know, it's being called a border conflict, but it's still a war. Especially to those hundreds of thousands dying on Eos. We don't have time to worry about crushed egos. We have to find a way to break up the enemy's formations. Crossman and his friends have come up with an idea and we're going to try it. Now, give him a chance. That's an order."

"Is that all, sir?" Captain Mboko demanded.

"You're damn right it is."

Captain Mboko came to attention, then left.

General Devon turned to Major Garacyk. "You should've let her go. She deserves her own squadron. Keeping her here is souring her. When this is over, I'm getting her a squadron."

"That's your privilege, sir."

"It is."

"Are you through with the lieutenant and me, sir?"

"I am."

Major Garacyk looked at me and gave his head a sharp little nod toward the door. He turned and left. Coming to attention, I thanked the general, then followed my squadron commander out.

Garacyk waited for me out in the corridor beside the lifts. I hurried to join him.

"You went over me," he stated, with ice.

"I had to, sir."

"That took fortitude."

"Thanks, sir."

"You get one chance. Don't fail me."

"I won't, sir."

"That remains to be seen. But if you're the right kind of pilot, I'll keep you. And that's a big 'if'."

"I understand, sir."

"I hope to hell you do.

CHAPTER EIGHT

ENERAL DEVON'S PREDICTION PROVED correct: rest eluded me. But I didn't mind. I had a chance to prove myself and to fly again; resting was the last thing I wanted to do. So while my friends retired to their quarters for a night's rest, Major Garacyk sent me to Captain Inagaki, the squadron's operations officer.

Arriving at Inagaki's office, his door directed me to the squadron's ready room, a long gallery overlooking the flight deck. The squadron's flight deck, hangar bays, repair shops, ordinance storage, and gallery were just aft of the squadron's offices and quarters, behind the thick, black, blast-proof kiron bulkhead. To reach the gallery, I passed through an airlock in the heavy bulkhead. Regulations required I put on a flight suit before entering the airlock, but I didn't have one. So I walked into the gallery wearing just my field uniform.

Three rows of eight seats each filled the gallery. In front of the seats were several windows set in kiron, the windows overlooking the flight deck below. Soft yellow light illuminated the deck, revealing eight launching sites, enough to catapult a third of the squadron into space.

Glancing around, I spotted a captain and a second lieutenant in flight suits standing at the far end of the gallery, watching a large holo viewer with a news broadcast from Eos. Both men turned around as I drew nearer.

The captain spoke to me. "Where's your suit?"

"I haven't been issued one yet," I replied.

"You're Crossman?"

"Affirmative, sir. You're Captain Inagaki?"

"Affirmative." He turned to the lieutenant beside him. "We'll talk later, Amal."

The lieutenant nodded and left.

"Major Garacyk informed me of your arrival."

"When's the COP scheduled?" I asked.

"Tomorrow afternoon, ship time. Morning, Eos time."

"What should I do first?"

"Get a suit. Then visit Captain Jonkowski. In nine hours meet me here. Bay Twenty-three has your bird. We'll see what you're made of."

"Affirmative."

"Supply has been notified of your arrival. Dismissed."

"Affirmative." I came to attention and left.

Acquiring a flight suit consisted of simply returning the way I came. Situated on the other side of the bulkhead were the men's and women's dressing rooms. Entering the men's dressing room, I went to the back counter where a robot greeted me. I told the robot my name and it handed me a new flight suit, then pointed me toward my locker. I stowed my suit, then returned to Captain Jonkowski's office.

Rana greeted me as I entered her office. "I've heard of your good news. Congratulations. We've much work to do."

"Thanks. I flew your newest sim today."

"So my record shows. Perhaps in a few days I can write a new one with better hope for the user's survival."

"That'd be good."

"Colonel Wallis, Anton, and Sanura Mboko have all been in here in the last hour. Since their visits I have rewritten my sim. We will fly it together. Come, let us see what strategies we can conceive for your success."

We walked over to two of the simulators. As the doors opened, I asked, "How'd your COP go today?"

"Poorly. I hope we can change that."

"So do I."

She climbed into her simulator.

As I entered my simulator the computer inquired: "Lieutenant Crossman?"

"Affirmative."

"I am your new A.I., Prax. I have transferred myself from your fighter to this sim in order to prepare myself for the upcoming COP."

"Hello, Prax. Call me Hector."

"Affirmative, Hector."

"Sorceress to Ice Maker. Let us begin. We will start as before, flying GORCOP over the equator. Three simulated birds will be part of my COP. You will be our recon bird. Are you ready?"

"Affirmative."

"Simulation beginning."

I flew low over a simulated tropical forest. Ahead of me, at ten kilometers up, approached a Gorgon box formation. Behind me flew four sim fighters, including Rana's. As the formation spotted us, it changed direction, speeding our way. Climbing above the forest, I accelerated, vectoring around in a wide arc and approaching the Gorgons from behind. While the enemy engaged our fighters, I raced straight for the box's middle.

Sim missiles from our sim fighters swarmed around the front of the box, each becoming a brilliant flash of light as simulated plasma streams vaporized it. Within a kilometer of the box, ten streams spit at my screens, collapsing them and vaporizing me.

As the images faded, I leaned my seat back and sighed.

"Sorceress to Ice Maker. Are you okay, Hector?"

"Disappointed," I replied.

"Understood. Are you ready to try again?"

"Give me a moment."

"Of course. Sorceress out."

"Not a very good first experience, was it, Prax?"

"Merely a simulation, Hector. Reality may be different."

"Oh, it'll be different alright. It'll be worse."

"Captain Jonkowski has another simulation loaded," Prax announced.

I sighed. "Okay. Ice Maker to Sorceress. Ready."

Two hours and eight more sims later, the results remained the same: I died every time.

At the end of the last simulation, as I popped the hatch, Prax asked, "Are we through, Hector?"

"Affirmative," I said.

"Then I will transfer back to our fighter."

"I want you to run tests of every system."

"Affirmative, Hector."

I exited my simulator and joined Rana beside hers. "Quite discouraging, isn't it?" I said.

"Not so. We learned much."

I laughed sarcastically. "What did we learn, other than how to make mistakes every time?"

"You didn't make the same mistakes this last simulation."

"No, I made all new ones. I wonder if I'm not making the biggest mistake flying a shiner into a Gorgon box. How can we possibly beat them? We've tried every everything."

"Don't base your expectations on a simulation. We cannot know all the choices the Gorgon pilots will make. My simulation lacks much information about the enemy. The program fills the knowledge gaps with Sky Command tactical information. That information is inconclusive."

"How so?"

"The program drew from the records of every pilot aboard *Akagi* who has flown against the enemy."

"So?"

"No one has succeeded in penetrating an enemy formation. The simulation lacks information for extrapolating a successful outcome."

I grunted. "That doesn't make me any feel better."

"You should rest, Hector. As should I. We'll meet again tomorrow. Good luck."

"See you out there," I said.

"And you also," she replied.

Returning to my quarters, I used the toilet and then showered, washing away a day of ups and downs. Afterwards, toweling off, I put on clean clothes, pulled down my bed, and lay on it. My cabin's lights off, I stared at my simulated night sky above me.

Simulated home, simulated space, simulated memories, simulated death. What gifts technology gave us!

Simulations carried you only so far. Love, friendship, and flying were my reality. And tomorrow's flying might bring dying. Yet what was life, without friendship and flying? Besides, the two hundred and sixty million humans on Eos needed my help.

Soldiers and civilians alike died down there. At every point, the Gorgons defeated the defenders of Eos, murdering everyone they found. The enemy seemed undefeatable.

But defeat them we must. For in the control of the skies lay victory on the surface.

I told my room to wake me in six hours and went to sleep.

I awoke fifteen minutes early. Sleep had come in fits. Dream shadows haunted me with images of death and destruction.

Dressing, I cancelled my room alarm and left my cabin. I needed exercise. I needed to swim.

Akagi had several pools. Besides the inverted pool-lounge at the forward end of the ship, three others existed, including a thirty meter racing pool amidships.

I spent twenty minutes at the racing pool, swimming on the surface and underwater. Refreshed and a little more relaxed, I dried, dressed, and took the lift to the pilot's ward room. I grabbed a couple of chocolate breakfast bars and a carton of milk, then hurried forward to our squadron's men's dressing room, where I ate my breakfast while climbing into my flight suit.

Just as I finished closing my suit, Vladimir Geys walked around from behind a locker row. "Oh. Hello, Hector."

"Hi, Vlad."

"I'm sorry we got off so badly last night. You're new and I should have made allowances for it."

I looked up at him. He stood several centimeters taller than me. "What d'you mean?"

"Lisa. She's my girlfriend. You spent a lot of time staring at her and it bothered me. I was jealous. That's why I behaved so badly. I'm sorry."

I felt a tightness in my chest. "I didn't know."

"Forgive my bad manners."

"Sure."

"I've heard what you're going to do today. It's going to take a lot of courage. I'm sure you have it."

"Thanks."

"Well. Later."

He left. It was a strange meeting. Geys had insulted me while trying to make it look like he apologized. I doubted Lisa was his girl. Pedro would've told me.

I left the dressing room and proceeded to the gallery. Captain Inagaki hadn't arrived yet, so I glanced out the windows over-looking the flight deck. Almost everything about *Akagi* differed from *Soyuz*. Aboard *Soyuz*, every fighter could launch from its hangar bay directly into space. But here the fighters taxied from their bays, located on either side of the flight deck, to their launching sites where antigrav catapults hurled them into space. Though twelve bays sat on either side of the flight deck, only eight birds could launch at any single time. Even though *Akagi* could launch thirty-two birds at once, eight from each of its four fighter squadrons, it seemed to me that *Soyuz*'s ability to simultaneously launch all twenty-four of its fighters at once out-classed the attack carrier's capacity. If I had designed *Akagi*, I'd have made it more like Soyuz.

While I mused over the strengths and weaknesses of attack and escort carriers, Captain Inagaki entered the gallery. His soft footsteps caught me by surprise and I jumped when he spoke.

"Have you seen the planetary news broadcast?" he asked.

"No," I replied.

"You should watch it every day. I do. Our practice flight will be shortened."

"Why?"

"The Gorgons broke through south of Atlatya last night. Their armies are on the city's perimeter."

"What about the evacuation of the city?" I asked.

"Thousands of people are still inside."

"Then we need to find a way to beat the enemy, and fast."

He nodded. "Your bird's been fitted with a laser for our practice flight. It's set it to minimum output."

"Affirmative."

"Your bird's in Twenty-three. Mount up."

I nodded. He went to a circular stairwell that took him down to the twelve fighter bays forward of the flight deck. I found a similar stairwell leading down to the twelve bays aft of the flight deck. A well-lit, narrow corridor stretched before me. Every five meters stood a hatch with bright yellow numbers painted on it. Bay Twenty-three occupied the next-to-last position at the far end of the corridor, near the outside hull.

I walked swiftly toward it.

Reaching the hatch, I told it my name, then waited until it confirmed my voice. The hatch opened and I entered the bay.

The interior, wide and bright, resembled the one I'd flown from while aboard *Soyuz*. Machines and cabinets lined the bulkhead behind me. A large yellow "X" covered the center of the deck. This X indicated the location of the service lift to the maintenance, storage, and ordnance bays beneath my hangar bay. Above this X my new bird floated on its antigrav field.

As I gazed at my beautiful, black bird, all the vehemence and anguish I'd experienced since boarding *Akagi* slipped away. What mattered now was flying this wonderful machine.

Two human techs and two robots busied themselves with last minute adjustments to my bird. From inside my fighter's open canopy I heard a third person calling out further adjustments. One of the human techs stood on an antigrav platform beside the canopy. He noticed me, then bent over the canopy for a moment. A red-haired female tech stood up in the cockpit, climbed onto the antigrav platform, and rode it to the deck. As I approached the platform, I saw her insignia. She was a master technical sergeant.

"Hi. I'm Sergeant Valerie Lincoln, in charge of Section Six's birds," she said, holding out a gloved hand, which I shook. All squadrons were divided into six sections of four fighters each.

"I'm Hector Crossman. Is it ready?" I asked, walking over and running my gloved hand along its smooth kiron hull.

"It's ready. Your counter-part helped us make the final adjustments. ou have a full fuel load. Your power plant and engine check out thoroughly. You have a training laser which emits low energy pulses. You can tag Captain Inagaki's bird, which I doubt. But you can't harm him."

I nodded.

"Take good care of it."

"I will," I said, climbing onto the antigrav platform and directing it toward the cockpit.

"Kwan. Cortez. Get the robots and let's get out of here," Sergeant Lincoln said.

As my ground crew scurried away, I settled into my cockpit. My helmet unfolded from between my shoulder blades, climbing up my back molding to fit my head. It sealed itself.

"Hello, Hector."

"Good morning, Prax," I replied. "Ready for some adventure?"

"Affirmative. May I close up and send the platform away?"

"Is the bay empty and secured?"

"Affirmative."

"Then do so." The canopy closed around me, sealing me in darkness. Then the canopy morphed transparent.

"Beginning bay depressurization," Prax announced.

"Let's begin pre-flight."

"I have performed pre-flight, Hector."

I paused before speaking. Every pilot liked performing his own pre-flight. But I'd always let Kon perform our pre-flight inspections. I decided to let Prax do the same.

"Display pre-flight information on the canopy."

"Affirmative."

The information appeared. "Looks good," I said.

"Thank-you, Hector. Bay atmosphere cycled out. Opening flight deck doors." Because of the continual nature of combat operations, the flight deck remained in a vacuum. An energy net kept unwanted objects out, but otherwise the deck opened into space.

The bay doors parted before me, revealing the broad flight deck. On the far side of the deck, in the number three launch slot, floated Captain Inagaki's bird.

Taking control from Prax, I guided us out. A simulator's one thing, but nothing beats the feel of a real bird. I directed us across the deck, gliding into a slot beside Inagaki's bird.

"Guardian to Ice Maker," Captain Inagaki called.

"Ice Maker here."

"Ready?"

"Affirmative."

"Wait for the go-ahead from our controller. She'll refer to us as BARCOP One. We're not on Barrier Patrol. We'll keep close to *Akagi*. The flight won't last long."

"Understood." Behind my bird, a pole rose from the deck. From the top of the pole a broad fan unfolded. Twisting sidesway, it pointed directly toward the rear of my bird. The antigrav catapult began charging itself.

After a few seconds, a female flight technician in the carrier's Combat Information Center contacted us. "BARCOP One, you are cleared to departure."

"Affirmative," Captain Inagaki said.

Prax cut our antigrav field. Instead of settling to the deck, we lifted a little higher as the catapult's field cradled us. The field's intensity increased through two times the negative value of Earth's gravity. Then three times. Then five. When it reach twenty negative gees, it catapulted us into space. My inertial dampers absorbed the acceleration. I felt little motion at all.

The side of *Akagi* blurred past. Fifty meters beyond, Prax reactivated our antigrav field.

Barely a hundred meters from the ship, Guardian activated his energy screen, fired his engine up, rolled onto his back, and dived beneath *Akagi*.

Prax brought our engine to life. Engaging my maneuvering thrusters, I rolled us onto our back and followed Inagaki.

"Catch me," Guardian called. "If you can."

Diving under the carrier, I flew barely fifty meters from the ship's hull. I visually located Inagaki as he approached the ship's engines. He held a tight, fast course. I gently increased my velocity, not wanting to overshoot him.

Pulling to his right, he disappeared from view around and up the port side of the ship.

"Watch out for a double-back, or a left or right break," I informed Prax.

"Affirmative. Energy screen activated."

I followed, pulling into a steep climb up along the carrier's curving hull. And there he was, diving for us. He'd doubled back. I broke hard to the right. We were too close to *Akagi* for loose tagging: someone aboard the carrier might think we were firing at the ship.

Guardian raced under the ship. I climbed over the top, rolled my bird over, and dived down the other side. I spotted Guardian coming out from beneath *Akagi*. He performed a tight-Gee turn, looping back to catch me, supposing I would've come about and followed him along his vector. But I wasn't there.

I fired a burst at him, but his sensors spotted me as I appeared from behind the hull and he dodged my shot. Turning sharp, just avoiding impacting against the carrier's hull, he climbed straight at me.

I broke right again, looping back along my previous course, and accelerated away from *Akagi*, letting him follow me, jinking left, right, up, and down randomly, making it hard for him to hit me. Two of his shots glanced the outer edges of my screen. Only a clean, direct hit counted as a kill.

"Guardian to Ice Maker. You know your basic maneuvering. But your timing's poor. You're dead."

We were far from the carrier now. I'd accelerated to ten thousand kph. Now I broke left, coming about in a high-Gee turn that tasked my inertial dampers to the limit, and fired off a burst at him as I rocketed past. He looped over, rolled from an inverted position, and followed me, firing several bursts.

I managed to avoid any direct hits. But he scored several more glancing shots. He was good.

"What now, Hector?" Prax asked.

There were only so many kinds of maneuvers you could perform in open space. I directed us toward *Akagi* again, slowing, aiming straight for the carrier's engines.

"Guardian to Ice Maker. Surrender now."

"Negative," I replied.

We closed with the carrier. I cut our velocity by a third. Guardian closed the gap. Utlizing our maneuvering thrusters, I dived beneath the carrier and broke hard to the left. Pulling around in another tight turn, I oriented dead on him and fired, scoring a direct hit: a clean kill! At the last moment, he broke right, avoiding a head-on collision with me.

"BARCOP One, this is *Akagi*. Return to your flight deck."

"Affirmative," Inagaki replied. "Guardian to Ice Maker. Back to the bays."

"Affirmative."

"Interesting maneuver, Ice Maker," Guardian said.

"Thanks." Without my maneuvering thrusters, directional engine nozzle, and antigrav generator, the maneuver would've been impossible. Ancient aircraft depended upon maneuvering surfaces: rudders, aerilons, and elevators, to control a sky craft's direction. But beyond an atmosphere such surfaces were useless. Only modern technology allowed me to maneuver in space.

"Any problems?" I inquired of Prax.

"Negative."

"Perform a quick diagnostic."

"Performing. Completed. All systems nominal."

"Good."

Prax deactivated our energy screen. As we closed with the carrier, a graviton beam caught our bird, towing and slowing us as we approached our flight deck. We switched our engine off, letting space cool it down. From inside the flight deck, a separate graviton beam acquired us, pulling us back inside.

As we entered the flight deck, Prax assumed control, guiding our bird back to its bay on its antigrav field. Inside our bay, he rotated us around, facing our nose toward the flight deck once more. The doors remained open while our engine cooled down.

"You performed well," Prax said.

"As did you."

"Engine cooling completed. Closing doors."

"Guardian to Ice Maker. Meet me in the gallery."

"Affirmative." The doors sealed and Prax began cycling the atmosphere back into our bay.

"Continue running diagnostics. We'll need peak performance soon, I imagine," I said.

"Affirmative. Cycling completed."

I opened the canopy. Prax guided the antigrav platform over to me. I stepped onto it.

The platform drifted to the deck. My helmet opened, folded and returned to its place behind my back. After stepping off the platform, I glanced at my fighter.

It was perfect.

I hurried to the gallery. Inagaki awaited me.

"You're better than I anticipated."

"Thank you, sir."

"Now the real trial begins."

CHAPTER NINE

I T HAD BEEN GREAT to fly again. To be free from the ship. To be one with the stars. And to defeat Captain Inagaki. But no sooner had I returned to my cabin than I received word that my Recon COP had been rescheduled to within less than an hour.

I made my way back to the men's dressing room. Arriving, I found several pilots already changing into their flight suits, including Pedro and Jacques.

"Amigo! Good to see you again. A good day for flying, wouldn't you say?"

I smiled. "You're in good a mood today."

"And what's not to be in a good mood about? I get to fly with mi hermano again."

"Your what, mon?"

"My brother," Pedro explained to Jacques.

"Brother?"

"As close as I will ever get to having one."

"Ah."

Pedro turned to me. "How was your practice COP?"

"Successful."

Pedro laughed. "Good. But be careful out there. I don't want to lose you."

"Just keep my six clear."

"Count on it, amigo."

"Come on, or we'll be late for the briefing," Jacques said, leading us to the gallery. The seats, normally turned toward the flight deck, now faced right. Up front sat Major Garacyk, Captain Inagaki, Captain Mboko, and Colonel Wallis, facing those members of the squadron flying in this COP.

Pedro guided me to where Lori saved seats for us.

As we eased into our chairs, Colonel Wallis stood up.

"Ladies and gentlemen," the colonel began, "we have to find a weakness in the enemy's formations. They have broken through to Atlatya. Last night, several Eosian companies, as well as additional units, were slaughtered, with more than three thousand dead. Marine forces on the ground suffered heavy losses as well. The Gorgons are winning."

"Three thousand dead in one battle?" I muttered to Jacques.

"There have been worse casualties," he whispered back.

"As of this moment," the colonel continued, "Gorgon forces are pushing up the center of the continent. Divided into three columns, they are encircling the defenders of Belden, south of the Auster Mountains. The squadrons from *Resolute* and *Yorktown* have suffered heavy losses, trying to keep the enemy from controlling the skies.

"On the east coast, one Gorgon column has successfully crossed the Morz desert. Five hundred thousand enemy troops are attacking the city of Napei. It's expected to fall today. The majority of the cities and human populace are on the eastern side of Titanus. You all know this. And that's exactly why the majority of the Eosian Army and its militia forces fight there. All of the Colonial Guard squadrons fight there, as well as what's left of the Eosian sky forces.

"The other two columns belonging to the enemy's eastern force seem to be resting now. But they'll be moving again soon.

"Here in our sector, one enemy column is maneuvering far to the east, apparently resting from the fighting. Another column is pushing around Calydon Bay and will reach the city tonight. Major elements of the third column have entered Atlatya.

"Naval Intelligence reports that dozens of enemy ships ferrying equipment, supplies and troops are entering the system every day.

"That, people, is the strategic overview. If we don't find a weakness, and I mean today, we are going to lose a lot of people. The Eosian Army can hold out maybe two more months, maybe three. Our Marines and other reinforcements can't attack until we control the skies. And then the Marines need their gunboats to provide close support. That's their purpose. Ours is to control the skies. And we don't."

Lori raised her hand. When the colonel pointed to her, she said, "May I ask, sir, what is being done about all the enemy vessels entering the Thea system?"

"That's the Navy's problem. They'll take care of it."

"If the politicians will let them," someone said.

Vlad asked, "Why can't we attack the enemy ground forces? For that matter, why aren't we striking the southern continent, where they live? Kill a few thousand enemy families and they'll stop killing us."

"There are several reasons why we cannot do that," Colonel Wallis said. "Including that the enemy has a strong sky defense system, that they control their skies with large numbers of box formations, and that the Association Council is still pressing for a diplomatic solution. We're not allowed across the border."

"We're running out of time, sir," Major Garacyk reminded.

Nodding, the colonel sat down and Captain Inagaki stood.

"We'll fly three COPs," Inagaki said. "The shiner will fly with the FORCECOP. I will lead it. Major Garacyk leads the HICOP. Captain Mboko leads the GORCOP. Seven birds, including the shiner, fly in the FORCECOP. Four in each of the others.

"All COPs will vector straight in over the city. The enemy has picket ships orbiting south of the city. All birds will carry eight missiles, even the shiner. In addition, each bird will carry two canisters of microprobes, six hundred probes per canister. The shiner will carry a thousand probes per canister. Launch probes upon engaging the enemy. Success is imperative.

"No matter what happens, the FORCECOP must protect the shiner. Lieutenant Crossman's bird must survive."

"If a box breaks up, can we pursue and engage individual boats?" Vlad asked.

"Protection of the shiner is your primary concern."

As Captain Inagaki sat down, Captain Mboko stood.

"The adversary currently fields seven formations over the battlefield," Mboko explained. "When these seven retire, seven other formations replace them.

"Fifth and Seventh squadrons currently fly GORCOPs of twelve birds each. Their designations are GORCOP Five and GORCOP Seven. Third Squadron is tasked with the RESCUE COP for the Search and Rescue COP. Nine of *Akagi*'s Marine gunboats remain. Five gunboats fly a constant COP over the battlefield.

"The Eosian Army has moved five sky defense batteries into Atlatya. Contact them through Ground Command. They've been designated as Pepper One through Pepper Five. Beware of them. They're inexperienced."

As Captain Mboko sat down, Lori stood up.

"Where's she going?" I asked Pedro.

"She's our weapons officer," he explained.

"I didn't know that."

Up front, Lori faced us. "The enemy continues to field only plasma weapons on its gunboats. A few Sky Defense Units are situated among its ground troops. These SDUs are back among the support forces. The enemy's SDUs also field plasma weapons. But they also have high energy lasers, similar to ours. So far, the enemy has not used missiles of any sort. Because of this you won't need to task any of your missiles for anti-missile interception. I know you all know this. I promise to let you know if the situation changes."

Lori returned to her seat.

Major Garacyk stepped forward. "No speeches or pep talks. You know what's at stake. See you out there."

Standing, we began exiting the gallery. Jacques joined me. "That's the first strategic briefing in weeks," he said.

"How d'you know what's going on, then?" I asked.

"From the ship's news net."

As we climbed down the stairwell, I said, "So many dead. It's unbelievable."

"I know what you mean, mon, but believe it. Thousands are dying every day and we've been unable to stop the wormies.

"You see, according to the old treaty, each side could maintain an active army of eight hundred thousand troops. The Eosian colony got around that with reserves, militia forces, border security, and border police. But most of the real strength is in the Army, and the Army's being slaughtered. More than a third of the Army has been destroyed.

"Not only that, but more than a quarter of the two million militia, border security, and border police troops have died. No one knows how many Gorgons have been wiped out, but they're bringing in thousands of replacements every day."

I stopped with him at his bay door. "How can this be?"

"Overconfidence. Stupidity. Bad planning. The enemy has brought in millions of regular troops disguised as workers. No one believed a war possible. Each side has enough ships to turn the planet into molten rock. But who would want that? Who could live here, then?"

"Not us."

"Not anyone. Not even the enemy. Instead they slaughter us. And if we can't stop them, well, then maybe we'll have to turn Eos into a molten rock after all." Jacques sighed. "See you out there."

"And you." I walked down to my door, paused before entering, and glanced back up the long, narrow corridor. Everyone else had entered their bays. I stood alone. Maybe, after today, I'd stand shoulder to shoulder with my squadron mates, never alone again.

Entering my bay, I found intense activity within. My ground crew chief, several robots, and three other techs, fussed with my bird, loading missiles into their recessed bays and inspecting the shiner package in my fighter's nose.

"Looks like you're gonna see some action," Sergeant Lincoln said, approaching me.

"Affirmative."

"We're with you one hundred percent. Take care of your bird. I don't like getting new birds out of storage every time someone gets careless and gets killed. Good luck."

"Thanks. See you out there."

"Not me. I'm an engineer, not a pilot. You can have it."

I laughed. "Everything ready?"

"Should be. Cortez! You done yet?"

One of her techs came from around the far side of my fighter. "Yep. Everything's go," he said.

"Then get everybody out." She poked a finger into my chest. "Be careful."

"I will."

While I waited for everyone to exit, I walked around my bird, inspecting its smooth surfaces. Its missiles and microprobe canisters were well hidden inside its smooth hull. After Sergeant Lincoln and her crew had left, and the door to the outside corridor was secured, I rode the antigrav platform up to my cockpit.

"Hello, Prax," I said, settling into my cockpit's seat. "Send the platform away, close up, and begin depressurization."

"Affirmative. Would you prefer to pre-flight us?"

"I trust you for the systems pre-flight. How're the missiles and microprobes? Everything operational?"

"Affirmative. Pre-flight completed. All systems nominal."

"Very good." I pulled up a quick diagnostic of the shiner package on my canopy. All its sensors appeared functional.

"How d'you feel about our mission?" I asked Prax.

"Success is mandatory."

"Why?"

"We're losing."

"We are. People are dying down there. No one wants to die. I don't know how it is for a cyber creature such as yourself, but no human wants to die. For us, it's an end to life. Some people believe that life goes on, that there's a higher, spiritual existence after death. I don't know if there is, but I'm not ready to find out yet.

"You see, part of me wants to believe there's more to existence than what I can see or touch. My dad died when I was younger. I still love him and I hope he exists somewhere else and that I might meet up with him again someday. But part of me fears that when you die, that's it, you're dead. That part fears that there's only nothingness beyond life.

"When I see my friends, my only real family, and I think of them dying, I get a cold and empty feeling inside me. I can't dwell on it. It frightens me. Not my own death, but the deaths of those I love.

"So you see that's what makes me want to succeed. People are dying down there. Families are dying. People are being robbed of those they love. And if there's nothing after death but oblivion, then people are being robbed of their loved ones forever.

"So I agree with you. We've gotta succeed. There's no other choice."

"Your feelings are strong, Hector. I am programmed to protect and serve. I will serve you as effectively as possible."

"Thanks. Do you believe in an afterlife?"

"Only what is programmed into me. A copy of me exists inside *Akagi*'s mainframe. But that copy isn't the original. I have sophisticated programs, with extensive encoding. What I am from moment to moment is as unique as what you are from moment to moment. But I have no prior experience with an afterlife. I hope, as you do, that if there is a Grand Creator, a being greater than my human creators, that I am as important to It as you are."

"I hope so, too." I had no idea why I expressed these feelings to Prax. Maybe because of the circumstances down on Eos. Maybe because now that I had a family again, I didn't want to lose it. Or maybe because, as I sat in my bird in my otherwise empty bay, I felt alone.

The bay's atmosphere finished cycling out. The doors opened to reveal the six birds of the FORCECOP maneuvering into their gravitic catapults. I let Prax maneuver us into ours.

"Ice Maker, Guardian. Launch is imminent," Captain Inagaki called.

"Affirmative, Guardian."

"Black Angel to Ice Maker. How're you doing, amigo?"

"Fine, Black Angel."

"Stay close. We can't cover you otherwise."

"I'll be right behind you."

"Ice Maker, this is Diamond." I recognized Lori's voice. "See you out there."

"See you out there, Diamond."

"FORCECOP One," one of *Akagi*'s controllers called. "You are cleared for launch."

After the catapults had built up negative gravs, we launched from the flight deck, one fighter after another, from left to right. Prax and I floated last in line. Just before we launched, I glanced back through my transparent canopy. The eight fighters of the GORCOP and HICOP began moving into position behind us. A moment later, our catapult spit us into space.

As our forward motion pushed me into my seat, my suit tightened to keep the blood from rushing from my head into my legs. My helmet closed. Prax cut in our engine and antigrav generator. With the antigrav generator online, the inertial dampers activated. As the Gee forces on my body dissipated, my suit loosened and my helmet opened again.

I came around and formed up with the FORCECOP.

"Glad you could make it," Vlad said as I pulled up behind him. He was Captain Inagaki's wingmate.

"Glad to be here, Vampire."

"Cut the chatter," Inagaki said.

We flew a tight formation away from *Akagi*. Five hundred meters to my right, and three hundred meters down, flew Lori Clark and Ava Farley. Six hundred meters to my left, and two hundred up, flew Pedro, with Lyle Lem as his wing mate. And I flew half a kilometer behind Inagaki and Geys, and about two hundred meters beneath them.

My sensors showed the GORCOP flew about fifty kilometers behind us, with the HICOP following at five times that distance.

After exiting *Akagi*, we had rolled our fighters over to orient Eos beneath us. Now we scooted three thousand kilometers down range, descending from *Akagi*'s ten thousand kilometer-orbit as we vectored toward our picket destroyers, *Sahara* and *Andes*, orbiting Eos at two hundred kilometers.

"FORCECOP One, this is *Sahara*. There's a lot of activity over Calydon Bay. Recommend vectoring to two-six-five until you are over Atlatya, then drop straight down."

"Affirmative, *Sahara*," Captain Inagaki said. "Vectoring to two hundred sixty-five degrees."

"Very good, FORCECOP One. Our captain wishes you good hunting. *Sahara* out."

"FORCECOP One," Captain Inagaki called, "disperse."

Following Inagaki onto our new vector, we spread out, the distances between each of us increasing. We continued our gradual descent, our screens snapping on, countering the atmospheric friction. As we descended, we cut our engines. We let gravity pull is into the atmosphere.

The sun, Thea, lay hidden behind Eos. Darkness covered the warring world below. We glided toward the terminus between darkness and daylight, beyond which streamed the first rays of the dawn.

Crossing the termibus, we reconfigured our antigrav fields and started our engines, then dived toward Atlatya. Atmospheric friction turned our screens crimson. We became seven fireballs descending into the hell below.

Dawn bathed the city. Scattered puffy white clouds drifted in from the ocean. Black, greasy smoke from thousands of fires plumed high into the sky, drifting over the great, green plains east of the city as Gorgon gunboats and grav tanks swept super-hot energy streams from their plasma cannons across the metropolis, turning it into an inferno. The smoke dirtied the clouds, blackening them with death from below.

"Opaque," I commanded Prax. He darkened my canopy, projecting a virtual image of the exterior world upon its darkened interior. As both my bird's sensors, and those of the shiner module, provided more tactical information than I could assimilate, Prax split his duties between helping me fly and processing the incoming data.

The evacuation of Atlatya continued. GORCOPs from Fifth and Seventh squadrons swarmed around the city's sky port, trying to safeguard departing shuttles from the enemy. *Akagi*'s remaining Marine gunboats flew among these GORCOPs.

I watched as three shuttles boosted away from the skyport, each shuttle carrying more than a hundred people. Three enemy formations attacked them. Our fighters inserted themselves between the Gorgon formations and the shuttles. Blue-white plasma streams streaked the sky, raking against the protective screens of shuttles and fighters alike. Dozens of expanding balls of white-hot gas revealed where our missiles had exploded.

But the Gorgon gunboats got past the fighters. Two shuttles exploded as dozens of plasma streams struck them. The third, damaged, returned to the ground.

I felt sickened. This happened every day, every hour, all across Eos. The Gorgons ruled the skies. And we were powerless against them!

This had to change. We had to be successful today. We had to be! I had to be. Not just for me. Not just for my career, my friends, or Sky Command, but for the people on Eos, for their loved ones, for their children.

As enemy formations swarmed in the sky over the city, we began pulling out of our steep dive. We converged on a lone enemy formation firing upon one of our ground defense batteries by the waterfront.

Contacting Ground Command, we learned that the defensive battery, Pepper Three, had received heavy damage, two of its five large caliber lasers were incinerated. All six of its missile launching vehicles were also destroyed.

"Guardian to FORCECOP and shiner," Inagaki called. "GORCOP One is vectoring over the city. HICOP will assist us. Vector toward the formation engaging Pepper Three. Concentrate all fire on the closet gunboat. HICOP will bounce from above. Shiner, remain close.

"All FORCECOP will release one probe canister upon first pass. Upon return, target nearest gunboat again and release remaining microprobes."

We confirmed our orders. I watched as the engines of the six fighters before me, projected upon the opaque interior of my curving canopy, glowed white with power. As the fighters sped away, I accelerated towards them.

"Guardian to Ice Maker. We're counting on you."

"Affirmative."

"Watch your six, amigo."

"You too," I replied.

The FORCECOP's first past caught the enemy by surprise. My shiner's sensors revealed that our plasma cannons contacted with the nearest gunboat's defensive screen, almost collapsing it. Additional information from the thirty-six hundred microprobes released by the FORCECOP's initial pass reported that the other gunboats extended their screens around their threatened member, strengthening and protecting it. Energy from the central gunboat further backed up the formation's screens.

The FORCECOP pulled up and over the box, drawing more than two dozen blue-white plasma streams. I flew through the firestorm, my screen burning bright blue as the streams, like great searchlights, swung back and forth, brushing against my protective energy field, trying to fry me. I darted left and right, avoiding the beams as much as possible and came out on the far side, more than a hundred kilometers out over the brightening sea.

The enemy followed closely.

The Gorgon formation was less a box or a cube, and more like an irregular sphere. To have been a box would have required eight gunboats occupying each corner of the cube, with a ninth gunboat in the central point. Instead, each gunboat occupied the center of an imaginary wall or side of the cube. Calling it a box was a misnomer, but it was easier to refer to than a sphere.

"Shiner to FORCECOP. The box is flying up my six."

"Break right," Guardian instructed.

I pulled hard to the right, faster than the enemy formation could follow. As I turned, the FORCECOP blasted past, back on target for the box. They blew by it again, releasing the remainder of their microprobes as well as concentrating fire on the closest of the approaching gunboats.

This time my sensors revealed no effect from our cannons. However, the enemy swept the sky with their plasma streams, vaporizing thousands of the microprobes swarming about them.

Coming about, I dived for the deck, the ocean's surface. I pulled up hard, skimming over the water at four thousand kph, swept beneath the box, and pulled out behind the Gorgons, realigning myself behind the FORCECOP. The box arced around for interception.

As I climbed beyond the turning box, the HICOP hit it from above. Sixteen of their missiles and all four of their plasma cannons struck at the uppermost gunboat. Several microprobes disclosed the ineffectiveness of the HICOP's attack.

"Shiner to FORCECOP and HICOP. The center gunboat's directing the formation's screens. It's also boosting energy to any gunboat under attack."

"Affirmative, shiner," Major Garacyk, Kingslayer, said. He led the HICOP down to the deck, where it flattened out and flew west over the sea, just meters above its surface. The FORCECOP, flying before me, broke left and came about again, all six birds maneuvering as if controlled by a single mind. I endeavored to stay with them, keeping just far enough back to avoid most of the action, yet close enough for my shiner to gather information.

"Seventy microprobes still function. They penetrated the enemy's formation during the first attack, when the Number Four gunboat's screen weakened," Prax announced.

"Locations?" I inquired. For accuracy's sake, all seven gunboats in each and every formation were numbered. The uppermost gunboat was Number One. To the port, or left, and down, was Number Two. Three occupied the bottom, or belly, position. Four flew to the right, or starboard. Five lead while Six followed. The central gunboat was always Number Seven.

"Fifteen probes have attached themselves to Number Four. Six have reached Number Seven. The rest are attached to other targets."

"Good. Continue monitoring them." I hesitated to release any of my microprobes, having seen the massacre of the FORCECOP's probes.

"Affirmative."

The imagery upon my canopy revealed bright flashes over the city as the ground defensive forces and our fighters and gunboats vainly fought the enemy. In moments, we'd be back among them, bringing yet another box to the battle.

"Lead to FORCECOP," Guardian called. "Come about. Engage the enemy. Drive them back over the ocean. Shiner, remain behind the box."

"Affirmative," I replied.

The FORCECOP separated into three flights, or pairs, of fighters, each vectoring a different way. They came about, striking the enemy high, low, and in-between. Then they twisted around the box, escaping. Energy streams swept back and forth in every direction, some beams colliding with each other.

The Gorgons pursued.

The FORCECOP flew beyond the box, boosting back out over the ocean. The HICOP had circled far around behind the enemy. Now it rocketed past me, striking the enemy, then hopping over the box and joining up with the FORCECOP. The box dashed after both groups, ignoring me.

I followed the box, all the while receiving telemetry from the microprobes inside the enemy's formation. The probes revealed that the FORCECOP and HICOP plasma cannons and missiles had been ineffective, as before.

That made me mad.

We possessed better technology than the enemy. That wasn't arrogance, but fact. Our AIs, our weapons, our propulsion systems were all at least several generations ahead of theirs. They couldn't have made such a big breakthrough in such a short time. How the hell were they defeating us?

"Prax, have you detected any anomalies in the Gorgons's operations?"

"Negative, Hector."

"There has to be something. Create a chart of the information gathered by the probes during our last two attacks."

"Affirmative."

A chart appeared on my canopy. Its vertical axis represented energy output by the enemy while the horizontal axis represented time. Interspersed among the lines were numbers revealing the wavelength frequencies of the various energies. Something about several of the frequencies looked familiar.

"Shiner to FORCECOP Lead. I need you to attack again. But don't fire all your missiles. Concentrate on the Number Four gunboat. Some microprobes have attached themselves to it."

"Affirmative, shiner."

The HICOP continued forward, slowing to allow the Gorgons to close within firing range. Meanwhile, the FORCECOP broke into two sections. The sections split in different directions, converging behind me and to my right. As the Gorgons fired upon Major Garacyk's HICOP, the FORCECOP bounced the Number Four gunboat, launching a few missiles and firing cannons.

Immediately, all my shiner's passive sensors spiked. New data filled my canopy.

The box, surprised, swung hard to its left, all plasma streams sweeping after the FORCECOP birds as they sailed over the gunboats. Several plasma streams found their marks. The two birds in the trailing section became engulfed in bright fire.

I sucked in my breath. Had I just killed two of my friends?

The two birds, belonging to Lori and Ava, pulled straight up, climbing towards orbit. "Diamond to Lead," Lori called. "Our screens are down. We are exiting the arena."

"Affirmative," Captain Inagaki replied.

"Smooth move, Ice Maker," Vampire called. "You going to try to flame anyone else?"

"Close that hole on your face, Vampire," Kingslayer called.

It felt good to have the major defend me but I didn't have time to feel too elated. I glanced at Prax's chart. Things had happened exactly as I expected. But just what was going on?

"Prax, from this data, it looks like our missiles detonated prematurely. Is that how you interpret it?"

"Affirmative."

"How is that possible?"

"There is insufficient data available for a conclusion."

"Then we have to gather more data. I'm going to fly close past the box and release all our microprobes. Are you ready?"

"Affirmative."

"Shiner to HICOP Lead. I need a repeat of the last attack. I'm closing and releasing both of my canisters."

"Affirmative, Shiner."

The Gorgons pursued the remaining four birds of the FORCECOP. They swept their plasma streams back and forth like giant scythes wielded by Death, with each gunboat one of Death's cohorts. I accelerated toward the enemy's rear. Seven streams of superheated metallic ions swept away from the FORCECOP and towards me. I jinked left and right, avoiding these dangerous spurts. As I maneuvered, the missile bays containing my microprobe canisters opened. Hundreds of microprobes escaped, expanding into twin clouds of miniaturized machines.

At once, the Gorgons discontinued firing upon me and began vaporizing my probes. But the probes took evasive action, flying away from each other while still pursuing the enemy. Fewer and fewer probes blazed out of existence as they successfully evaded the superheated ions hunting them.

Having released my probes, I looped high and wide over the enemy, returning to a position far behind them. Dropping near the surface of the sea, I boosted back toward the box. Every second, the microprobes transmitted megabytes of information to my shiner.

As I looped around, the HICOP, flying parallel to the enemy, vectored sharply inward. They fired their plasma cannons while releasing half of their remaining missiles, targeting them all on the Number Four gunboat. All of the missiles detonated prior to contacting the gunboat's screens.

The HICOP swung away from the enemy, climbing far above the action. "I hope we accomplished something, Ice Maker," the major growled at me.

"You did, Kingslayer." I inspected the new data. "They're using O technology, Prax. The last time I saw such a similar signature was a few years back, flying against a Na smuggler."

"The O are a benign race. Why would they sell technology to aggressive races such as the Na and Gorgons?" Prax inquired.

"They wouldn't. Not usually. But every race has renegades. The O are no exception. And their renegades are like pirates, in a sense. They're unorganized, fortunately, and loners. You never find more than one to a ship. And they're not above selling technology for prey."

"I have just scanned current data concerning the O renegades. I understand. They prefer intelligent species for food, consuming them alive. A disgusting race."

"Just their renegades eat people. But, even with O technology, how are the Gorgons destroying our missiles?"

"I have sorted through the data," Prax stated. "They use a cognizant probing beam that acquires a missile's self-termination code. The beam then analyzes the information and activates the code. The missile vaporizes itself without releasing its deadly energy against the enemy."

I nodded. Our missiles were designed to self-destruct without releasing their destructive force. "But how can a light beam behave like a computer?"

"The technology is many of generations ahead of ours."

"I'd say so."

"FORCECOP Lead to Shiner. The Gorgons are turning back toward Atlatya."

"FORCECOP and HICOP leads, Shiner. We need to destroy the Number Seven gunboat. With the center gone, the box should fall apart."

"And how do we do that?" Major Garacyk demanded.

"I'm working on that, Kingslayer."

"Work faster."

"Affirmative." I had followed the Gorgon box as it pursued the FORCECOP across the ocean and away from Atlatia. Now I followed it back towards the city. As it accelerated, its combined energy screens pushed through the atmosphere like a great ball of fire, creating intense turbulence that bounced my fighter about. So I eased back from them and climbed higher, avoiding their turbulence.

The two COPs followed my example, forming up on either side of me as we pursued the enemy.

"Prax, we have to delete our missile termination codes."

"I do not recommended that, Hector. We would not be able to terminate errant missiles."

"I understand that, Prax, but stray missiles are the least of our worries right now. Somehow the Gorgons know the importance of the termination codes. Without the codes, the Gorgons won't know what to do. We've got to get that central gunboat. All our data indicates it carries the O technology. Vape it and the box disintegrates."

"Concur. Deleting codes. Approaching Calydon Bay."

I glanced at my canopy's imagery. We closed with the city.

"Shiner to FORCECOP and HICOP. Bounce the Number Four gunboat. Hit it with your cannons only. Save your missiles."

"Affirmative, shiner," Garacyk and Inagaki replied.

"Prax, direct all our remaining probes to attack the box. That'll give them something else to think about. Lock two missiles onto the Number Six gunboat. When its screens weaken, direct four other missiles at the center boat."

"Affirmative."

The microprobes, their tiny engines struggling to keep up with the box, attacked it. The Gorgons began vaporizing them.

The combined birds of the FORCECOP and HICOP bounced the Gorgons's right flank, firing upon the strained energy screen of the Number Four gunboat. As they attacked, Prax launched two of our missiles at the Number Six boat. Our shiner recorded the probing energy beam from the central gunboat touching our two missiles.

Our missiles were destroyed, but not by the enemy. They detonated with their full energy yield against the Number Six gunboat's screen! The gunboat exploded.

Before Prax could launch our missiles, I launched them myself. Four missiles leaped from their bays. They raced through the hole created by the missing gunboat. Plasma streams from the other gunboats lanced at the missiles, vaporizing two of them. But the other two reached their prey, turning it into an expanding, brilliant-white flaming gas ball.

The Gorgon formation fell apart.

"Hot damn!" I exclaimed. I activated the general broadcast frequency. "Shiner to Kingslayer and Guardian. The Gorgons are using O technology to self-destruct our missiles. Delete your missiles' self-termination codes and you can vape them."

Without a reply, the eight fighters of the two COPs dived after the enemy. I climbed out of the way as the FORCECOP and HICOP incinerated the five disoriented remaining Gorgon gunboats.

It ended faster than it began.

"*Sahara* to First Squadron. You are directed to return to *Akagi* immediately. Do you copy?"

"Affirmative," came our chorused replies.

CHAPTER TEN

THE RETURN TO *AKAGI,* though no longer than the flight out from the carrier, seemed to take forever. Now that we'd finally found a weakness in the enemy, we wanted to return as soon as possible. We wanted to re-arm and resume combat over Atlatya, vaporizing many more Gorgon gunboats. No more would we be helpless in the skies. No more would we watch innocent civilians die. We were ready to reclaim the skies that rightfully belonged to us!

Yet the flight back sobered us as *Akagi* reported heavy losses among the Eosian ground forces and in the ranks of our Marines fighting with them. Civilian casualties also mounted. And while the enemy gunboats had retreated, cowed by our blasting an entire formation from the sky, their ground forces continued pressing into the city.

Added to our ground casualties, *Akagi* had lost another Marine gunboat. That reduced the number of gunboats aboard the carrier to eight. It had started out with twenty-seven.

However, while such somber news ate away at our elation, it failed to devour it.

As my bird floated back inside the carrier on a graviton beam, my thoughts were far from the fighting below. I wanted to see Lisa again. I wanted to bask in the warmth of her friendship, her beauty, and her smiles. Who cared whether Vlad thought she belonged to him or not? No one owned her. Her heart was free for the giving. Friendship and love couldn't be stolen, but rather given.

Once inside our hangar deck, Prax guided our bird back into our bay on its antigrav field. He rotated us around so we pointed towards the flight deck once more. Our engine, long since shut down, had cooled in space. After our hangar bay had pressurized, Chief Lincoln, two of her techs, and some robots, hurried inside.

While my ground crew began inspecting my bird, I finished writing my after action report and instructed Prax to send it along with his report and with the sensor download from the shiner. Then I opened my canopy. Standing and stretching, I opened my flight suit.

Sergeant Lincoln floated up beside me on the antigrav platform. She glanced up and down the length of my fighter, then said, "I'm glad you brought it back in one piece."

"I did my best," I replied.

"So I see."

"How long will it take?"

"What?"

"How long before my bird can fight again?"

"As soon as we can get your shiner out and a gun pod inside, and a few missiles loaded, you'll be ready to go."

"Good," I said, climbing onto the platform.

She nodded and climbed into the cockpit. "Cortez, start with the shiner. See what condition it's in. Then get it out and down into ordnance."

I watched her while she inspected my cockpit and talked with Prax. Then I lowered the platform. I had a mission debriefing to attend.

As the platform settled, I hopped off of it and hurried for the exit. Sergeant Lincoln called to me. "Hey!"

Turning around, I looked up at her.

"You did good," she said and gave me two thumbs up.

"Thanks."

A few minutes later, in the men's dressing room, I ran into Pedro and Lyle, who'd just changed out of their flight suits.

"Amigo, you flew well today. I knew you could do it. This idiot didn't believe me, but I knew better. I'm proud of you."

"You did good, too," I said. "You guys were on top of those gunboats so quickly after the box broke apart it was like watching sharks at feeding time."

"It was a feeding frenzy," Pedro agreed.

"And you were chief among the sharks. My sensors showed you were the first to drop among them. You got the first one."

"No, you did. But I couldn't let you get ahead of me."

I laughed. "Like that might happen."

"The two o' ya sound like yer married. Bickerin' an' all. How did anyone stand the two o' ya back at the Academy?"

We stared at Lyle, then laughed. Lyle shook his head. "Come on, we have a debriefin' ta attend."

Normally, either the exec, Captain Mboko, or the operations officer, Captain Inagaki, conducted after action debriefings. But the nature of our mission, and its spectacular results, required a special debriefing by Colonel Wallis and Brigadier General Devon. So we proceeded through the ship until we reached the command island amidships, where we took the lift to Brigadier General Devon's offices.

Coming around from behind the lift well, I found the foyer filled with people. As we three entered, applause and cheering broke out. Jacques strode over to us. "A fine performance, Hector. You should be proud. We've been waiting for you."

Before I could reply, the sergeant at the desk stood up and motioned me toward him. "Lieutenant Crossman? General Devon asked me to send you and the others right inside. He's in the conference room at the end of the hall behind me. There'll be only enough room for you and a few others. He's there with Colonel Wallis. The task group commander, *Akagi*'s captain, and some other officers are also present."

"Thanks, sergeant." I led our pack down the hallway.

Before entering the briefing room, I turned to Pedro. "Every time I've done something like this in the last couple of years, I've had a party thrown for me. During the last party, I was promoted, awarded a medal, and kicked out of my squadron. I wonder what evil thing's going to happen this time."

"You'll be fine. Only a fool would expect the worse now."

"Call me a fool, then."

The door whistled open. Before us lay a long, narrow room, with a large table dominating its center. A broad window beyond the table looked forward, down the carrier's long hull, the bright lights of the forward lounge's dome visible up near the bow. Chairs surrounded the table, while a few others lined the walls to either side of the entrance.

A rear admiral sat at the head of the table, in front of the window. To her left sat Brigadier General Devon and Colonel Wallis. On her right sat a Navy captain, a Marine Lieutenant Colonel, and a Navy lieutenant, whose Sky Command rank equivalent was that of a captain. Beside Colonel Wallis sat Major Garacyk and captains Mboko and Inagaki.

"Please, sit down. I'm Admiral Greely," the gray-haired woman said.

As we found seats and sat down, I whispered to Pedro, "Maybe I'm not such a fool. I've a bad feeling about this."

"That's just gas, amigo. It'll pass."

"Very funny."

"Something wrong, lieutenant?" Admiral Greely asked.

"No, ma'am. My friend was only encouraging me."

"Good."

Jacques sat beside Pedro, while Lyle and some of the others stood behind us, against the wall. Lori and Ava plummeted down beside Jacques, with Rana Jonkowski and Vlad sitting beside Captain Inagaki. I nodded to Rana, who smiled back.

Admiral Greely began the meeting. "We've reviewed the recordings made by the various fighters involved in the recent attack on the enemy formation. We believe, that is to say, my staff and I believe, that you were extremely lucky, Lieutenant Crossman. You managed to break through the enemy's formation and destroy the command vessel.

"But we all must realize that this was a unique event. The enemy will no doubt be prepared for our next encounter. Other fighters won't be able to break through the enemy's shielding and destroy the command vessel. We commend you on your daring and initiative. Major Garacyk and

General Devon have recommended you for a Gallantry Commendation, and I concur."

"Thank-you, ma'am," I said. "However, I respectfully disagree with your assessment of the situation."

"Crossman," Major Garacyk said, "remember your place."

"Let the man speak," the Marine lieutenant colonel said.

"I agreed with Lieutenant Colonel Barzani. Let's hear what he has to say," Colonel Wallis added.

"Now you've done it, eh?" Pedro whispered.

"Shut up," I whispered back.

Admiral Greely's eyes locked onto mine. "Well, lieutenant?"

"Sorry, ma'am, but you don't know what you're talking about. This wasn't a one-time event. Didn't you study the reports that my counterpart sent in? Or my shiner's data?"

"Pardon my density, lieutenant. I'm not used to junior officers telling me that I don't know what I'm talking about."

I paused and glanced around the table. Major Garacyk fumed. Captain Mboko stared at me with icy eyes. Rana Jonkowski listened intently, and when she caught my glance, gave me an encouraging smile. Vlad smirked.

Glancing at my friends, I saw only encouragement. So I continued. "I'm sorry, admiral. I don't mean to imply anything. Yet I know this is more than just a lucky break. My shiner picked up a signal from the central gunboat instructing our missiles to self-destruct. That's no accident."

The admiral turned to the Navy lieutenant. "Do you agree with that assessment, Mr. Vang?"

"No, ma'am. That information is in error."

"How can that be?" I demanded.

"The Gorgons don't possess that kind of technology. Therefore your sensors recorded in error."

"But you must've seen my sensor logs by now. The Gorgons possess the technology now. And they got it from the O."

"No, they didn't," Lieutenant Vang snarled. "The Gorgons don't trade with the O. So if they don't trade with the O, then they don't have O technology. Intelligent energy probes are still beyond us. And they're beyond the Gorgons as well.

"Think about it, Crossman. If the enemy had made such a break-through, would they bother fighting us as they have so far? I don't think so. And neither does anyone else in this room. So if they haven't made such a breakthrough, and they don't trade with the only race possessing such technology, then they don't have it!"

"Perhaps there's another race with such technology," Jacques suggested, coming to my aid.

"One that we don't know about yet?" Vang said. "Oh, I doubt that. No, Lieutenant Crossman, for all your diligent efforts, you've gained us nothing. Your information is in error."

"How can you be so blind?" I replied. "People are being butchered on Eos and you sit here telling me that the information I gathered, that my instruments gathered, is in error because you can't accept any other possibility than what your limited view of reality allows you to!"

"Young man!" the admiral snapped.

"I'm sorry, ma'am, but the facts are before your faces and you people aren't willing to accept them."

Lieutenant Vang smirked. "That's all right, admiral. He just doesn't understand. He's young and impetuous.

When he's matured a little more, he'll come to realize that the universe isn't what you want it to be but rather is just what it is. He'll learn."

I glared at Vang. "I'm the same age as you, you ass. We just aren't promoted as fast as the Navy. We have to earn our positions."

"That'll be enough, Crossman!" Major Garacyk said.

"No, sir, it won't be," I countered. "They're trying to hamstring us. They're going to make us fight exactly the way we have before today. And we're going to lose. We're going to lose all our gunboats. And we're going to lose all our fighters. And then we'll watch helplessly as everyone on Eos is slaughtered. All because they don't want to change their limited views!"

"You're a passionate man, Crossman," Vang said. "But in the field of military intelligence you have to be cold and logical. Passion gets you into trouble. We've examined all the facts and the information you've provided doesn't correlate with what we know about the Gorgons. We know they don't trade with the O. And we know their technology is inferior to ours. We don't know how they're defending their gunboats so well, but eventually we will.

"I'm sorry, but your efforts today, dedicated as they were, have led us to a dead end. The Gorgons don't have the capability that you claim. It is you that must accept reality. You have to learn to reason without emotion."

Now Lieutenant Colonel Barzani entered the argument. "You're the one that needs to grow up, Lieutenant Vang. I've had enough of your stupidity. Lieutenant Crossman's right. The enemy's just going to roll over us. There won't be anyone left alive down there after they're done. And you, with all your negative thinking, will be guilty of mass murder. Why, you ask? Because you weren't willing to believe that someone else's ideas might be right."

Vang stared at Barzani. "And your point is, sir?"

"My point is that Crossman's right: you're an ass."

"Colonel, that's uncalled for," Admiral Greely said.

"Perhaps it is, ma'am, but I've worked in Intelligence and I know our thinking can become very narrow-minded. We look for certain results and if they're not present, we continue looking for them. Sometimes the information, as now, is so off-base that we can't accept it. So we ignore it and instead continue looking for the results we expect and wish to find, rather than accept what's right in front of our faces."

"So, colonel, you feel Crossman's on the right track?"

"He is, admiral. I've examined his sensor logs. And I've just spent the last few minutes researching what we know about O technology."

"Sir, are you suggesting you now know everything there is to know about O tech?" Lieutenant Vang asked.

"Not exactly. Look, every race's technology has certain things that are unique to that race. Call them fingerprints, if you wish. Whenever a race develops something similar to what another race has already developed, their fingerprints are different, even if the development is similar."

"So what you're saying, sir," I interrupted, "is that the O signature I recognized in the enemy's energy probe is legitimate?"

"It is." Lieutenant Colonel Barzani turned to Admiral Greely. "There's no mistake. They're using O technology."

"But the O and the Gorgons don't trade with each other!" Lieutenant Vang insisted.

"Do the Gorgons trade with the Na?" I asked.

"They do, but what's that have to do with anything?"

"Well, I know for a fact that the Na trade with the O. If you look at my personal record, you'll see I earned my first kill against a Na smuggler which used O technology. So if one group of Na trade with them, then others will, too. Are those solid enough facts for you, sir?"

Vang glared at me.

"Admiral," General Devon said, "I agree with Lieutenant Crossman that it is possible the Gorgons have gotten O tech from the Na."

"That's all fine and good, general," Admiral Greely said. "But why would the Na give such technology, which must have cost them dearly, to the Gorgons?"

"Because they hate us," Major Garacyk explained. "We conquered them in a war. We've occupied their home world. We've scattered them throughout the galaxy. In all the universe we're their only targets. They want to punish us, destroy us."

"So what?" Vang said. "A few smugglers, a few pirates, an odd terrorist or two. They're nothing to us. Why would they help the Gorgons?"

Jacques shook his head. "Because, mon, the more ships we pour into this system, the weaker our frontiers become. And that's where they strike at us. That's where they live, on our frontiers."

"Whatever." Vang looked tired and defeated.

"Lieutenant Duquesne's right," Major Garacyk said. "Anything that weakens us strengthens them. The more we fight, bleed, and die here, the weaker we are out there. I think Crossman's got it right, too, the Na have bought O technology for the Gorgons. The sooner we wake up to that, the sooner we'll win this war."

Admiral Greely glanced around the room. Her gaze ended at General Devon. "What do you recommend, then?"

"May I add one thing, ma'am?" I asked.

The admiral sighed. "If you must."

"If they can decipher our missile codes, can't they do it for yours as well? If your battleships ever encounter them, how d'you know that your missiles will work any better than ours?"

"He's got a good point," General Devon said. "You want my ideas? Delete all self-destruct codes from all Sky Command and naval missiles immediately. And start figuring out if the Gorgons have any other tricks we don't know about, like maybe O shielding. It might not just be our missiles that won't get in."

"What about errant missiles?" the admiral asked.

"That won't happen. But even if it does, it's a small price considering the alternative we have in front of us right now. And let me tell you, given the choice between helplessness and a wandering missile now and again, I'll take the wandering missile every time."

The admiral nodded. "So be it. What do you want of me?"

"Do whatever it takes to make sure the Task Force isn't compromised. And let me throw as many fighters as I can, as often as I can, at the enemy."

"It's your command. But obey the rules of engagement. Don't cross into Gorgon territory."

"Affirmative."

"Good." Admiral Greely stood and sighed. "This meeting's adjourned."

We stood to attention. The admiral nodded to us all, then began talking with General Devon and Colonel Wallis.

"Let's vector," Pedro said.

I turned to go.

"Lieutenant Crossman," the admiral called to me. "Wait one moment, please."

"Here it comes," I whispered to Pedro. I turned around and replied to the admiral, "Affirmative, ma'am."

"Be strong, amigo," Pedro whispered.

"I'll catch you later," I replied.

I waited while the admiral made her way over to me.

"You're an impertinent young man, but I'm glad you're on our side," she said. "You're courageous and willing to take risks. Not necessarily the best qualities when mixed together, but today you mixed them well. Both out there and in here. I doubt that a Gallantry Commendation says enough about you."

"Thank you, ma'am."

"See that you take care of yourself. Dismissed."

I again came to attention. She nodded and I exited the briefing room. In the narrow corridor outside, I moved along with the herd, looking for Pedro and Lori. I couldn't find them. But I spotted Jacques. He waved me over.

"That was quite a performance today. I'm impressed."

"You know, I didn't realize until just now how close I came to getting into real trouble."

"You were in no trouble. We were with you. It was just fortunate for all of us that Colonel Barzani agreed with you. He saved us all much hard work."

"Why did you stand up for me?"

"You're family now."

"All fighter pilots are family. That doesn't mean we have to like each other, let alone stand up for each other."

"You should let a mon finish speaking," Jacques said. "When I first met you, I wasn't certain about you. Pedro had talked about you. But his view is prejudiced. Just because you were friends and he and I are friends didn't mean I'd like you. But I do like you. You're passionate about your work and your friends. I'm glad to be your friend, mon. And friends stand up for each other."

He held out his hand. I took it and we shook. "Thanks. I need all the friends I can get."

"We all do, mon. Let's go find the others."

"That sounds like a good idea."

CHAPTER ELEVEN

JACQUES AND I EXITED the foyer and proceeded around the lift well. We stood in line while several people filed into a lift. It filled to capacity so we waited for the next lift. We were alone in the corridor, but not for long.

"Crossman!" Major Garacyk growled as he marched up to me, stopping just centimeters from my face. "Remember your place."

"I don't understand, sir."

"You're a junior officer. If you confront flag officers too often, you'll never get a squadron of your own, and if anybody deserves one, you do. You did well today. Against the Gorgons and against that idiot from Naval Intelligence. Even after our COP, even after its fantastic results, I was ready to believe that little shit in there. But I'm glad you held your wind and didn't let any of us stray from the true course. Just don't let it go to your head. Understand?"

"Affirmative, sir."

"Good." A lift opened and the major ducked inside. We waited for the next one.

"That was strange," I said.

"He approves of you. You're one of us now. Be proud."

Another lift opened. Pedro stood in it, arm-in-arm with Lori, and with Lyle and several others. "Amigo! Here you are. We were just coming back to look for you. Listen, we're scheduled for another COP in the morning. We'll blow the wormheads out of the sky. Tomorrow, you and I will be aces."

"And I'm already ahead of you," I said.

"How d'you figure that, mi hermano?"

"What's your score so far?"

"He shot down two gunboats today," Lori said. "As did you."

"D'you have any other kills, from any other actions, to your credit?" I asked.

"No. But what would that matter unless... you do, don't you!"

I smiled. "Ramming *Gaeg* counts as my first kill."

"I'll still make ace before you do."

"We'll see."

"But you know I will."

"Maybe."

Pedro laughed. "What's it matter? Now's a time for celebration, not argument. We're going to the forward lounge. And you're our guest of honor. Let's vector, Hector."

Laughing, I entered the lift. Jacques followed. The lift's doors whistled close and it descended.

"I saw five of you attack the box as it fell apart. If you got two, who got the others? Major Garacyk?"

"Vlad did," Lyle said. "An' he's full o' himself, too."

"All three?" I exclaimed.

"Two and a bit," Lori explained. "We all shot at the last one."

"Himself hit it first."

"You sound jealous," I said

"Wouldn't that be a change?" Ava quipped.

"An' what does that mean?" Lyle replied.

"Sometimes people just have to express their feelings, mon."

"What do ya mean?"

"Vlad's not the only one who's full of crap," Ava said.

Lyle's face reddened.

We all laughed, except for Lyle.

"Come on," I said. "We're proud of you. Almost as much as you are of yourself."

"Himself feels insulted."

"Don't be. We're all family here, aren't we?"

"Yes," Lori agreed, smiling at me. "We are."

Through *Akagi*'s transport system we made our way forward. As the lift opened we heard a jazzy Latin tune playing above us in the lounge. Following the others up the spiral stairs, I found myself amid a wild party. Navy, Marine, and Sky Command personnel whooped it up.

"What's all this?" I asked Pedro.

"This is our first victory in the skies. We deserve a little joy, don't you think?"

"I think so."

Lori and Ava took me by the arms. They glided across the deck, towing me. People I didn't even know came over to congratulate me.

I'd been in several parties such as this. Some in my honor, many more honoring others. But after my initial reception upon boarding *Akagi*, and knowing how badly a victory, even a small one such as today's, counted, this party meant more to me than all the previous ones I'd attended.

Hundreds of people packed the lounge. As we pushed through the crowd, I searched for Lisa. Unless she was out on a COP, she'd be here. But I failed to find her.

Lori loosened her grip on my arm. Turning, I saw her dancing away with Pedro. Glancing behind me, I noticed that Lyle and Jacques had disappeared into the crowd behind us. Even Ava disappeared, pulled away by someone else.

I stood in a sea of people. Sexy music filled the air, increasing the crowd's excitement. Voices soft, loud, hard, and brittle breezed around me. People pushed against me, laughing, smiling, shouting.

I felt dizzy.

As I scanned around, I saw a small hand rise above the crowd. A familiar hand, though whose I didn't know. I vectored toward it, plowing the crowd.

"There you are! Where did you get to?" Lori asked. She and some of the others had managed to reach a table.

"Me? Where'd you and Pedro run off to?" I replied, squeezing in beside Pedro.

"Here," Pedro said.

"Then how'd you get here?"

Pedro smiled. "We danced."

"For a few steps," Lori said, raising her voice to be heard over the crowd. "As much as we could."

"I'm thirsty. Can we get anything to drink?" I shouted. We seemed at the center of the party, where so many bodies gathered that the crowd created its own gravity. And this gravity seemed to draw the voices closer, making them louder.

"No," Pedro replied. "Everything's dry."

"There is water and fruit punch," Lori said.

Pedro made a sour face, as if sucking on a lemon.

"Tis no drink for a man," Lyle said, joining us from out of the swirling crowd.

"I'll take anything. Water's good," I said.

"Why not some punch?" a voice behind me said.

I turned. Lisa smiled at me, two cups of punch in her hands. She offered me one and I took it, smiling back.

Before either of us could speak Vlad pushed himself between us. "You did all right today. But I sure thought you had vectored yourself into a black hole back at the debriefing."

"I'd have flown into hell just so as they listened to me."

"What happened?" Lisa asked.

"Not much," Vlad replied. "The Ice Machine here just tried to make a fool of himself."

"That's not true and you know it, you ass!" Ava snapped. She stood up. "You're just jealous you didn't have the guts to stand up to the admiral the way Hector did."

"What?" Lisa asked.

"Our new lieutenant made even himself proud today," Lyle said. "He told the admiral an' her toadies just what he thought o' fools who kept their heads stuck in the sand."

Lisa glanced from one to another of us, a puzzled look on her face. "I don't understand."

"There's nothing to understand," Vlad said, starting to draw Lisa away. "They're just exhaling hot air."

Standing, I stepped beside Lisa and Vlad and gently pried her from his hold. He glared at me, but I ignored him.

"Join us. Please," I said to Lisa.

"Only if you tell me what everyone's talking about."

I shrugged. "There's not much to tell."

"Just as I said. Hot air." Vlad moved toward me.

But Jacques, now on his also feet, intercepted him. "Hey, mon, we're all friends here, right?"

Vlad glared at me. "Maybe not."

"But what happened?" Lisa persisted. So I told her, though others embellished my bland tale.

"You could have gotten into trouble," Lisa said.

"And should've, too," Vlad said.

"Oh, Vlad," Lisa said, turning to him. "Don't be jealous. You're both good men. And your squadron needs both of you. Remember, you shot down two gunboats today."

"Very true," Vlad said, a cold glare beaming from his eyes toward me. Then his gaze lightened. "Soon I'll make ace. Let Crossman just try to keep up with me."

"He already has," Ava said.

Vlad guffawed. "I've twice as many kills as him."

"He had one already to his credit," Ava informed him. "And he got two gunboats today."

"I don't believe it."

"It's true. That Na smuggler he mentioned, he knocked it out. He's ahead of you," Jacques said.

Vlad's face reddened. He stepped closer to me, towering above me by several centimeters. He thumped my chest with a forefinger. "I'll kill more wormies than you can ever imagine. I'll beat you. One way or another."

"Vlad, there's no reason for this," Lisa said.

He turned to her. "I'm leaving. Are you coming?"

"No."

"Suit yourself."

As Vlad stomped off, Ava shouted at him. "You'll never get as many as Hector. You're not good enough!"

As we sat down, we all stared at her. Turning back to us, she blushed.

"Where'd that come from?" Lori asked.

"I don't know," Ava whispered.

"Himself thinks ya have some feelings for Hector."

Ava struck Lyle's shoulder with the back of her hand. He yelped. "Of course I do. I mean, after all, he's our friend. And he's done more for Eos in one day than everyone else combined. Who wouldn't be proud of him?"

"If that's all yer feelin', then that's fine."

"And what else would I be feeling?" Ava demanded.

A mischievous look filled Lyle's eyes. "A bit o' romance, perhaps?"

I cleared my throat. "Don't forget I'm still here."

"Himself means no disrespect. But the more lasses ya have interested in ya, the better. Pedro agrees."

I turned to Pedro. "Is that your opinion?"

"Yes," Lori said, turning to Pedro as well. "What is your opinion about 'lasses'?"

Pedro cleared his throat. He looked uncomfortable. "It would take an exceptional man to draw a lot of senoritas to him, wouldn't you agree?"

Before I could answer, Lori spoke up. "Yes, it would take an exceptional man. But what he did with those 'senoritas' might change my opinion of him."

Pedro smiled weakly at Lori.

"I'm waiting for the right answer," she said.

Pedro placed his arm around Lori's shoulders. "I have the only senorita I want right here. Lyle and Hector can have all the other senoritas. I have who I want, which is enough."

Lori smiled at Pedro and then kissed him. "The right answer from the right man."

"Don't I get any lasses?" Jacques asked.

We laughed. "You can have all you want," I said.

"This has been all fine an' good," Lyle remarked. "But the lass still hasn't answered himself's question."

"And what question was that?" Lisa asked, coming to Ava's rescue. "Whether she likes Hector or not? She explained all that any woman needs to explain."

Ava jabbed Lyle in the ribs. "Yeah!"

Lyle grunted and scooted away from Ava. "Himself knows when to retreat from overwhelmin' odds."

"Himself isn't as stupid as he looks," I said, grinning.

"Ya could git yerself inta trouble talkin' that way."

"And who would start it?" Ava demanded.

"Yes, who?" Lisa added.

Lyle started to speak, but Jacques cut him off. "One does need to learn to keep one's mouth closed."

We laughed again. It felt good to laugh, to relax, to wash away the day's tensions.

"A smart man should keep a safe distance from danger," I said to Lyle.

He shrugged. "Himself likes a little danger."

Ava glared at him.

"Behave yourself," Lori ordered Ava.

I turned to Lisa. "Were you on a COP today?"

She nodded. Her face hardened. "We flew Rescue COP over Atlatya's skyport. We couldn't save half the people trying to get out."

"Before we engaged the enemy," I said, "I watched the battle for the skyport. It looked bad."

"It was much worse. I joined Sky Command both because I wanted to fly and because I wanted to make a difference. I thought by flying Search and Rescue I would be able to save lives. But today I watched, unable to do anything, while those poor people died."

"That'll change now," Lori said.

"Will it?" Lisa whispered. "Will anything change?"

Jacques nodded. "Everything has changed."

"What do you mean?" Lori asked.

"The real work begins now. Now we have to win, even if it means our dying," he said.

"We haven't had many casualties before," Ava said. "Why should we now?"

"Before we weren't much of a threat to the wormies. Now we are. Before, we hardly harmed them, so they ignored us. We were like bugs before them; a nuisance, but not dangerous. But now we're dangerous. And, mon, we will suffer for that. We're going to die for the power to defeat them." Jacques stared at us. His eyes were both cold and sad.

"Himself will kill a lot o' them before he goes."

"Maybe so, mon, but many of us won't survive."

"And not many of them," Pedro said. "I can think of worse ways to go. Wouldn't you agree, amigos and amigas?"

Lori spoke up. "You're so wrong. The best way to die is when your old, lying in bed, holding the hand of the mate you've loved. I want that to be your hand in mine. So don't go getting yourself killed, my love. I couldn't bear it."

Pedro took her hand. "I will always be here for you."

"Men always make promises they can't keep," Lori said. "Be careful out there. I'll never find anyone else like you."

"What if you have no one hand's to hold?" I asked.

"Then find someone. Find that someone for yourself and for her." Lori glanced at me, then at Lisa. "After all, time is too precious to waste on formalities."

I shifted uncomfortably, as did Lisa.

"I don't understand why fighter pilots are so fixated with all the 'kills' they've made," Lisa said, changing the subject.

"What do ya mean? Didn't ya take Combat Sky Tactics? That's required for all freshman at the Academy," Lyle said. "How can ya not understand it? Tis how we keep score!"

"But why keep score? Why keep track of the beings you've killed?"

"You're calling the wormheads equal to us?" Ava asked. "You've seen what they've done to humans. You've seen how they turn their plasma weapons even on children. How can you talk like that!"

"They have families, too," Lisa said. "We know that from information gathered from other races. How they can do what they're doing to us is well beyond my imagination, though."

"It should be," Ava snarled.

"That was uncalled for," Lori said.

"Ladies, please," I interrupted, anxious to distract Lisa and Ava from letting the violence down on Eos escape from their memories and crush their hearts. "Don't let yourselves vector the wrong tangent. The conversation's about keeping score."

"Maybe it is and maybe it isn't," Ava growled.

"Hector's right," Lori said. She turned to Lisa. "I don't agree with the system. But the better the fighter pilot you are, the better your chances for advancement. And it keeps your mind off other things."

"Tis a fine system. Himself approves o' it."

"You would," Ava snapped.

"But why do it at all?" Lisa asked.

"From a historical perspective," Jacques said, "it's really quite simple."

"Here we go, amigo," Pedro whispered to me.

Jacques continued. "The very first military pilots counted the number of skycraft they shot down. Rarely did they consider the lives they took. Rather, it was a way of keeping track of their ability. Five shoot-downs meant acedom. The more shoot-downs, the more valuable a pilot, the more skill and experience acquired. And really, who wouldn't want to fly alongside whomever would get you back home safest?"

"It's really about keeping score," I said.

"What do you mean?" Lisa asked.

"Well, I know from the years I spent aboard *Soyuz* that most SAR crews keep track of their successful rescues. Maybe not all do, but most do. Whether its imitating fighter pilots or something more personal, I don't know.

"You see, we keep track of our successes in combat, because that's who and what we are: fighter pilots. We're knights."

"How so?" Lori asked.

"Well, more than a thousand and a half years ago, knights kept track of the opponents they defeated. Whether they defeated them in personal combat or at competitions. Centuries later, the first fighter pilots, flying flimsy little sky planes of fabric and wire, thought of themselves as the last remnants of knighthood. They had a code. They were considerate of their opponents. They even saluted them as they fell from the sky. They thought of themselves as knights of the air. And we're just like them. We're knights of the sky."

"Sky knights," Pedro said. "I like that. Amigo, you should be a poet."

"And just like the knights of long ago," Jacques explained, "we're fighting monsters in a glorious crusade."

"Exactly," Pedro agreed.

"It doesn't matter whether we're knights or just fighter pilots," Ava growled, standing. "They're not intelligent beings. They're monsters, just like Jacques says. It's our job to kill them. We shouldn't respect them or wonder whether they have families. We just need to destroy them.

"I know what they're doing to the people down there. I've seen the holos. We've all seen them. The tiny, blackened lumps of charcoal that once were children. Our people can't even surrender. Anyone left behind, anyone who gives up, anyone caught shot down behind the lines, they just burn them! How can you talk about those things out there like they're human? Like they're glorious and honorable? They're monsters. They hate us and we hate them. They don't deserve life or respect. They just deserve death."

We stared at Ava.

"I didn't know you felt like this," Lori said.

"How can you not feel like this after seeing what they do to people?" Ava exclaimed. She turned to Lisa. "I like keeping track of the ones I kill. And I'm going to kill lots of them. You're a fool if you don't hate them, too."

"You need some rest, dear," Lori said, standing. "Excuse me, love, but I need to tend to my partner."

Pedro stood as Lori and Ava left. "In the Botanical Gardens, later, mi corazon?" he called to Lori.

Lori nodded. Then, to Ava, she said, "Come, dear. I think you need a little rest."

"You're not my mother."

"But I am your wing mate. And I do need you fresh for our next flight." Lori put her arm around Ava's shoulders. "Let's go, dear."

"I'm sorry about taking you away from Pedro," Ava said.

"Don't worry about it."

Their conversation drowned in the crowd as they moved away. Pedro watched Lori disappear. He sat back down, his eyes sad.

"Himself thinks the lass is a wee bit angry. She'll be different after some rest."

"I didn't know she felt that way," Lisa said.

"How can any of us not feel that way?" Jacques wondered.

"This war stresses us all," Pedro said. "But you have to put it behind yourself after you come back from each COP or it'll kill your soul. And once your soul is gone you're not any better than the wormheads are."

Lisa nodded. "You're right. But it's so difficult to let go. There's so much suffering down there and so little we can do."

"But that's always the case," Pedro said. "The universe is full of suffering. Plants are eaten by animals and animals are eaten by other animals. Someone is always either lacking something they need or wanting something they don't need. And wanting or lacking makes them suffer. It's stupid, wouldn't you agree? But it's the way people are, whether they're human or alien.

"There's broken hearts and broken bodies, lust and anger and hatred and fear and resentment and revenge and none of it makes you happy and all of it makes you suffer. And we can only do so much to help. Only God can help all those sufferers and only when they want to be helped.

"Listen, amiga, war makes it all the worse. We do what we can. But we have to let go of what we can't do. If we don't, we become like the stupid ones who suffer because they choose to suffer. But they don't know they choose to suffer, do they? And that makes them suffer even more."

"You're right, I suppose," Lisa said.

"Yes, he is," Jacques said.

"I'm sorry I've been so hard on all of you," Lisa said. "It's just so easy to get caught up in the war and so difficult to let go of it."

"But you have to let go," Pedro explained. "If you don't you won't be much good after a while. But you haven't been hard on us, at least not on our eyes. Mi hermano can agree to that. His eyes have hardly left you since you've arrived."

I glared at Pedro, but he only laughed.

"Have you visited the botanical gardens, amigo? They're quite exceptional. You should visit them with Lisa. She spends much of her free time there."

"Himself feels like taking a stroll through them. Would ya care for some company, lass. Ouch!"

"Oh, excuse me, mon. I didn't mean to kick you. I was merely stretching."

"Think nothin' o' it. Himself doesn't. As himself was sayin', would ya care for a little stroll through the gardens?"

Pedro shot Lyle a cold look.

"On the other hand, himself could do wi' a wee bit o' exercise. Anyone care to join himself in the gym?"

"Sounds like a good plan. Shall we go?" Jacques said, standing. He and Lyle said goodbye and left.

"I think I'll see if mi corazon needs any help. See you out there," Pedro said, then left.

I turned to Lisa. "Looks like it's just us."

"So it seems."

"Would you like to show me these gardens?"

"Another time, perhaps. What I'd really prefer is a swim. Care to join me?"

"Sounds good. Shall we vector?

She smiled at me. "Yes."

CHAPTER TWELVE

"**G**OOD MORNING, HECTOR."

"Hello, Prax," I said, climbing into my cockpit. It was Oh-eight-hundred and I prepared for my first COP of the day. I had another one scheduled for mid-afternoon.

"Did you rest well?"

"I did," I said, as the cockpit's canopy closed. "Have you pre-flighted us?"

"Affirmative. All systems are nominal."

"How many missiles in our bays?"

"Twelve."

"That'll do."

"You seem in good spirits today."

"I am. I spent the evening with a wonderful woman. She's a second lieutenant in the Second SAR Squadron. Her voice is soft and kind. We went swimming last night. And after we swam, we spent several hours just talking. It was all I could do to leave her and return to my cabin to get some sleep before today's COP."

"Is it not the custom for males and females to sleep together?"

"Usually. But we're not to that point yet."

"Shouldn't it happen soon after first contact?"

I cleared my throat, embarrassed. "Not exactly. People don't always sleep together after first meeting each other. Human relationships are complex. When you care about someone, you take your time."

"Why?"

"Well, you want to make certain the other person cares as much for you as you care for her. At least, I do. And I'm beginning to care deeply for Lisa Mauros. That's her name, by the way. Anyway, I want our relationship to start out right."

Prax began depressurizing our bay. The ground crew had long since left. "I may be in error, but isn't the purpose of human relations for the replication of more humans?"

"You're not in error. But it's not always about that."

Depressurization completed, Prax opened our bay doors. Out on the flight deck, the other seven birds in our COP jockeyed into position. Prax guided us out.

"I am not in error and yet I am. How can that be, Hector?"

I laughed. "You're not in error. You just don't have enough information."

"Would you please explain?"

"I'll do my best. You see, human relationships involve many factors. And the most complex of all relationships involves romantic love."

"An example, please."

"I don't know if I can give you an example. People have tried to explain and define romantic love for thousands of years. You see, everyone is an expert and yet no one is an expert."

"That is a paradox."

"That's what makes it so hard to explain. So the best I can do is to try and explain why you weren't in error but just lacked sufficient information.

"You see, in human relationships, patience is the operative word. Some people hit it off with one another right away, while for others it takes time. From events in my recent past, I've become wary. There was another young woman that I cared for who, like Lisa, came from Gentry and flew in a SAR squadron. But while I loved her a certain way, she had different feelings for me. When I discovered that she wasn't in love with me but loved me only as a friend, it crushed me. It took time to get over her and I'm not sure I'm entirely over her yet."

"Then I suppose that you are wary of being hurt again by mistaking Lieutenant Mauros's feelings for you?" Prax asked.

"Affirmative. I don't want there to be any error on my part this time."

"Then patience seems the appropriate path for you."

"Very much so. But in the meantime we're enjoying each other's company."

"Good." Prax maneuvered us into our gravitic catapult. He cut our antigrav field and we settled a little before the catapult's field caught and supported us.

"GORCOP One, you will be cleared for launch in two minutes," one of *Akagi*'s flight controllers announced.

"Affirmative, *Akagi*," I heard Captain Mboko reply.

"How long do you estimate before you might be ready to replicate?" Prax asked.

"You're certainly interested in this subject."

"I am fascinated by biological replication. It is a mystery I wish to master."

"Well, in my case it'll have to remain a mystery to you, because it's none of your business."

"Is there no way I can convince you otherwise?"

"Nope. We best concentrate on the mission."

"Understood."

I glanced out of my transparent canopy and over at the bird to my left. It contained my new wing mate, Second Lieutenant Gregory Brattano, who I'd met only twenty minutes ago. He'd joined the squadron a couple of weeks before me, arriving from Ilmatar's replacement pool. His personality fit his call sign: Brat. I didn't like him, but I was responsible for him.

"Thirty seconds, GORCOP One," Captain Mboko announced.

As our catapult began building up negative gravs, the COP's fighters began launching, starting with Captain Mboko, call sign Zulu, on the far left. Each fighter launched one and a half seconds apart. Our bird occupied the last slot.

Right after Brat's bird launched, our catapult hurled us into space. I felt a momentary crushing weight on my chest as we accelerated out of our flight deck. Then Prax cut in our antigrav field and its inertial dampers took the pressure away.

I applied acceleration and caught up with Brat and the rest of the COP in seconds. Pulling ahead of my wing mate, I took the lead. Our COP consisted of four flights, each of two birds.

Each flight flew in echelon, its leader slightly ahead of and to the left of the wing mate. My flight brought up the rear.

Ahead of us flew Captain Mboko and her wing mate, First Lieutenant Angela Fortuno, call sign Lucky. I didn't know her too well, just enough to nod "hello." She was our supply officer.

Behind Mboko and Fortuno flew Pedro and Lyle. Behind them flew Lori and Ava. And behind them, flew Brattano and me.

At our mission briefing Mboko had quickly outlined our COP. During the night, the enemy had resumed aerial activity around Atlatya. In reaction to our shooting down an entire box yesterday the Gorgons had apparently ceased sky operations in order to assess the situation. During this time the evacuation of Atlatya had raced ahead. Most of the remaining inhabitants exited the city. Even so, several shuttles continued withdrawing injured ground troops and those few people too slow to exit with the rest of the city's populace.

However, Gorgon ground forces had continued their vicious assaults. Enemy forces occupied more than half of the city. And now the enemy's sky forces had returned.

In response to the loss of an entire box, the Gorgons had increased the number of sky formations by seven-fold. Instead of forty-nine gunboats in seven formations, three hundred forty-three gunboats in forty-nine formations filled the sky.

Our task, of course, consisted of vaporizing as many gunboats as possible. But for every gunboat destroyed, another formation replaced it. The last two COPs, from Fifth and Seventh squadrons, had shot down fifty gunboats, for the loss of five birds. While this ten-to-one ratio immensely beat the previous ratio of zero kills for an occasional loss, at this rate we'd run out of fighters before the enemy ran out of gunboats.

"Approaching picket ships," Prax announced.

Through my transparent canopy I spotted the running lights of the destroyers *Andes* and *Sahara*. Their blips appeared on the lower right part of my canopy. Not far past them I noticed the blips of five more pickets.

Before the Gorgons hadn't posted any ships opposite our pickets. But since yesterday's sky defeat, they'd moved five destroyers up to shadow our ships. Captain Mboko had briefed us to stay well up-range of all enemy ships upon exiting from space over Atlatya. We'd already lost one careless pilot from Third Squadron who flew too close to the Gorgon destroyers.

"GORCOP One, *Sahara*. Begin your descent now. The wormheads have already fired a few shots past us at approaching COPs. We are unauthorized to respond in such a situation."

"Lovely," Lori said.

"Affirmative, *Sahara*," Zulu replied. "GORCOP One, implement alternative vector toward Atlatya. Maintain communications silence."

Obeying our communications directive, we rolled our birds over and vectored toward the city, several thousand kilometers beneath us. Through my canopy Eos appeared dark. Though morning aboard *Akagi*, night still festered over Atlatya.

As we descended into the atmosphere, Prax activated our energy screen. It flared a slight orange-red from atmospheric friction. Soon the atmosphere, burning against our screen, would engulf us in flames, masking our view. Then we'd have to darken our canopy, with Prax projecting imagery upon it. Until then, I enjoyed looking upon the world with my own eyes, rather than viewing it through my bird's sensors.

As we drew nearer Atlatya, I saw brilliant white flashes over the city. At first, I thought they resulted from the vaporization of gunboats and fighters. But, calling up a sensor display upon my canopy, I saw evidence of an intense electrical storm over the city. Most of the flashes came from lightning, though missiles and energy weapons also accounted for many bright bursts.

The superheated air molecules burning around my screen filled my cockpit with brilliant orange and red flashes. Visibility degraded to such a point that I had Prax darken the canopy. He covered the canopy's interior curve with virtual images of the outside world.

"Traverse left," Zulu called. We followed Captain Mboko into a tight roll to the left. Our goal was Atlatia's skyport, located thirty kilometers northeast of the city and connected to it by roads and travel tubes.

As the Eosian Army tried pulling out, most of its traffic, along with the remaining civilian traffic moved up the highways leading to the skyport and beyond. Two Eosian divisions, nearly twenty thousand troops, filled defensive positions along the highways. But five divisions within the city continued fighting as they withdrew. Two InterStellar Marine brigades fought alongside them.

Our task, as well as that of the COPs from *Akagi*'s other three fighter squadrons, was to clear the skies above the withdrawing troops.

"Multiple targets ahead," Prax informed me.

"So I noticed."

"Black Angel to Ice Maker," Pedro called. "Watch your six, mi hermano."

"Affirmative. You do the same."

"GORCOP One, Zulu. Engage the enemy."

A chorus of "affirmatives" replied to Captain Mboko. Being the tail-end flight, Brattano and I watched as the other three flights broke off and pursued different goals.

Mboko and her wingmate, Fortuno, flew toward the skyport, engaging a box already battling two Marine gunboats.

Pedro and Lyle attacked another box hosing down ground forces with its plasma cannons. Lori and Ava made a pass at that same box. When Pedro vaporized two of its gunboats, the box flew apart. Lori picked off a third gunboat, while Ava got a fourth. The remaining three gunboats ran for it, roaring out over the vast farmland east of the city, barely a hundred meters up.

"Ice Maker to Black Angel," I called. "We'll take them."

"Affirmative, Ice Maker."

"Heads up, Brat," I called to my wingmate. Our bird leaped forward as Prax accelerated us to three thousand kph, our inertial dampers absorbing the bucking from the atmosphere as we crossed the sound barrier. We rocketed eastward, following the fleeing gunboats, racing over fields and occasional homesteads. Some of the homes were intact, but most had been demolished as the Gorgon ground forces destroyed everything human in their path. Checking my sensors, I saw Brattano close behind me.

"Targets are vectoring left and right," Prax said. Two of the gunboats pulled to the left, climbing two kilometers skyward, while the third twisted right and down, barely skimming fifty meters above the surface. Whatever other abilities the wormheads had, they knew how to fly.

"Brat, take the climbers."

"Affirmative."

Brattano and I split apart. Dropping down on the deck, I followed the fleeing gunboat. I weaved around tall trees as we left the cultivated lands far behind. Now we sailed over clumps of giant trees scattered amongst undisturbed plains.

"Prax, contact our picket ships. Make sure we're not flying into a trap."

"Affirmative, Hector."

The target in front of me jerked and bucked, as if crewed by crazed creatures. I had trouble lining it up for a plasma burst; I wanted to save my missiles for the fighting over Atlatya. It took four missiles to blow apart a box. Our plasma cannon wasn't strong enough to damage gunboats when in formation, not with the extra energy their screens received from the center gunboat. But with our missiles now almost invulnerable to them, all we had to do was incinerate an outer boat, then launch a pair of missiles at the central boat. With the center gone, our cannons easily picked off the other gunboats.

Which is why I wanted to use my cannon. A couple of shots from it would knock the gunboat down. But the boat ahead moved too wildly for a clean shot.

"Prax, have you contacted our destroyers?"

"Contact confirmed. Gorgon ground forces ahead, two hundred kilometers distant. No enemy ships or sky forces. But the enemy does possess sky defense batteries."

"Great." I might fly into a trap after all. "Launch a missile."

"Missile away."

Slowing, I curved around, re-orienting toward Atlatya again. I didn't need to watch my missile. With its termination codes erased, it had little trouble reaching the gunboat.

As I vectored toward Brattano, a brilliant flash brightened the sky behind me. Prax informed me the gunboat was gone.

By the time I caught up to my wingmate, he'd vaped one of his targets. The other gunboat had escaped.

"Shoulda had him," Brattano said, as I pulled alongside him.

"You did find," I said.

"Thanks, oh glorious one."

"What?"

"Exalted leader, let's get back to the fighting so I can kill some more. I wanna be just like you."

I kept quiet. I couldn't tell if he kidded me or had something against me. We slowed to eight hundred kph and two minutes later reached the city.

Turning, I switched to our COP's tactical com channel.

"Diamond, two targets to your left. Eliminate them."

"Affirmative, Zulu."

Prax presented part of the battle on the left side of my canopy. I watched as Lori and Ava peeled away from Mboko and her wing mate. They zipped in behind two Gorgon gunboats hosing down Eosian ground troops. Lori vaporized her target with a missile, while Ava fired her plasma cannon twice, burning her target from the sky.

"Ice Maker," Brattano called. "There's a box over by the bay. Let's get 'em."

"Negative. We'll support whoever needs us."

"As you say, manure man."

"D'you have a problem with me?" I demanded.

"No problem, oh glorious ice machine."

"Zulu to Ice Maker. Assist us."

"Affirmative." I sighed as I brought my bird around. Brattano followed.

"Is there a problem, Hector?" Prax asked.

"Too many people don't like me right now."

"I like you."

"Thanks."

Racing toward the skyport, I spotted Zulu and Lucky trying to shield a departing shuttle carrying either civilians or wounded soldiers, or both. They spiraled around the shuttle, crisscrossing over each other's path in a classic flying-scissors formation. By so maneuvering, they protected the shuttle from a Gorgon box trying to vaporize it. Dozens of plasma streams spit at them, turning their energy screens bright blue. Much more of this and their screens would fail. Then in seconds they'd be vaporized, along with the shuttle they protected.

"We're going in," I informed Brattano. "Protect my tail."

"I'll be flying up your ass, oh holy one."

I hated this guy.

Zulu and her wing mate had climbed with the shuttle high into the sky, the box tight to their right. Brattano and I closed upon the box. The Gorgons noticed us too late. As they broke contact with the shuttle and its defenders, already four of my missiles raced toward them.

Two of the gunboats burst into bright white fireballs. A moment later, the center gunboat exploded as well, hit by two of Brattano's missiles. Then Zulu and Lucky broke formation from the fleeing shuttle and completed the job, each vaping two gunboats apiece.

Satisfied with my success, I turned and dived back toward Atlatya. Dropping down to less than a kilometer over the city, I flew back toward the sky port. But before I reached it, I tilted my bird hard on its left side to avoid colliding with a fighter from GORCOP Three zooming skyward, homing in on a running Gorgon gunboat.

"The sky's too crowded here," I told Prax.

"Affirmative."

"Where's Black Angel?"

"Near the city center," Prax replied.

I brought our bird back around, Brattano heeling behind me. I increased my velocity, while Prax awakened two more missiles. As we vectored toward Pedro, my missiles tracked hundreds of enemy targets.

"Black Angel has four gunboats after him. Two others pursue BS," Prax announced.

"Affirmative. Brat, help BS out."

"As you wish, shit brain."

I shook my head. Where'd this guy come from and why had he been assigned to me? Obviously, Mboko still wanted to punish me. She hated me. So she gave me the foulest mouth in the squadron as a wing mate. How nice of her.

As I closed upon Pedro's pursuers, he looped over, coming around and down behind one of them. Three quick bursts from his cannon knocked it out of the sky. Then a missile dropped from his bird. Arcing around, it slammed into another of his previous pursuers, now his prey, vaporizing it.

"Loose missiles now!" I exclaimed. I wanted those other two boats before Pedro got them. His score was well beyond mine already.

"Affirmative."

As our missiles raced away, as the two remaining gunboats closed with Pedro, hosing his screens with all twelve of their combined plasma cannons. But before my missiles even reached their targets, Pedro looped again and blasted another gunboat from the sky.

Having lost one of their targets, both missiles sped for the remaining gunboat and their collective destiny. Pedro's fourth pursuer burst into a brief, brilliant fireball.

"Ice Maker! Glad to have you around, amigo. But I had things under control."

"So I saw."

"Did you see what I saw?" Pedro quipped.

"Funny."

"BS just called. Your companero just cleared his six. Puts him even with you today, wouldn't you say?"

"No, I wouldn't," I said, switching channels. "Brat, form up."

I heard panting over the comm channel, followed by: "Coming, master!"

I sighed in exasperation.

"Ice Maker, Zulu. Return here immediately."

"Who's on a leash now?" Brattano said.

"Shut up."

I heard laughter over the com. I switched back to Pedro.

"Where'd we get this guy?" I asked him.

"Perhaps he's not his best today."

"Maybe."

"Let's vector," Pedro suggested. Circling around, he and Lyle sped back toward the skyport.

Brattano and I followed, flying wide out over the south side of the city and coming back behind Pedro and Lyle.

Plasma fire from ground-based batteries licked at our screens. But as we raced along at three thousand kph, the Gorgon gunners couldn't keep us in their computer-assisted sights long enough.

As we rejoined them, Pedro and Lyle blew through yet another box. The top and center gunboats disappeared from the sky, victims of Pedro's missiles. Lyle damaged a third gunboat, while Brattano finished off a fourth, whooping as he killed it.

I launched a missile and vaporized the fifth gunboat.

With five of its seven members gone, the box disintegrated. Lori and Ava, flying cleanup, chased the survivors back over the city. Lori finished one with her last missile, while Ava burned the other from the sky with her plasma cannon.

"Zulu to GORCOP. Missile count."

"Out," Lori replied.

"Out," Pedro and Lyle announced.

"Out," Fortuno, Mboko's wingmate, said.

"As am I," Mboko replied.

"Two," Ava said.

"Four," I replied.

"Three," Brattano said.

"Reform and return to *Akagi*," Mboko commanded.

"Zulu, Ice Maker. I've still got a good load."

"You had a multitude of opportunities, Ice Maker. Obey my command. Return to *Akagi*."

"Affirmative," I replied.

Before any of us could reform on Zulu, Racer called from somewhere over Atlatya. "Racer to Zulu. Diamond is down. Repeat, Diamond is down. Gorgon box pursuing me. Where's that dammed SARCOP at?"

"Amigo," Pedro pleaded. "I've no missiles."

"I've got it. Protect Zulu."

"Save her, mi hermano."

"Count on it."

"Brattano, form up."

"Negative. I'm following Zulu."

"One of ours is down. We're the only ones available to protect her."

"Zulu to Ice Maker. Reform. SARCOP will rescue Diamond."

"Negative. My sensors show SARCOP is busy."

"I demand you form up."

"Negative."

"You're grounded, mister."

"Diamond's down," I replied. Then, switching off my comm unit, I turned back toward the city.

CHAPTER THIRTEEN

BOOSTING BACK TOWARD ATLATYA, I located Racer on my sensors. She twisted and turned far above the city's center while a Gorgon formation pecked at her. I had four missiles left, enough to blow the box apart. But after I blew it apart what would I do if another box bounced us? Without missiles how would I protect myself, let alone Lori?

However, Racer needed help now. I'd contend with the other attackers later, if I survived long enough.

I switched my comm unit back on, intending to contact Racer. But Captain Mboko, leading the rest of GORCOP One back to *Akagi*, continued to rant and rave at me. I couldn't contact Racer with all that noise on the channel.

"Prax, redirect our broadcast over the GORCOP One channel so that it's localized to within fifty kilometers. Then signal Racer's AI to switch to an alternative frequency."

"Which frequency would you prefer, Hector?"

"I don't care. Pick one without a lot of traffic, and be quick about it."

"Done. Racer is now on channel eight-seven-seven."

"Thanks. Racer, Ice Maker here. Vector out over the eastern plains just above the deck."

"Affirmative, Ice Maker," Ava replied.

Racer pulled into a sharp climb, then rolled over and dived for the city. The Gorgons kept on her tail, all forty of their plasma cannons reaching for her screen, some finding it, most missing it. Yellow and orange flames streaked across her energy screen, but it held.

Upon reaching the city, Racer darted down between the tallest buildings, slowing and weaving among them. Stray shots from her pursuers' cannons struck the buildings, sending showers of molten glass, concrete, and metal into the streets below. I hoped that Lori, if now on the ground, had shelter from this lethal rain.

Exiting the city, Racer accelerated out over the plains, flying just a few meters above the ground. Thea, Eos's sun, was near the horizon. The pinkish-blue light of pre-dawn covered the landscape. Racer's flight raised a dark cloud of dust and debris behind her.

The Gorgons tried keeping up with her. They sought to match velocities with her, seeking a position above her where their cannons could cleave her screen apart, vaporizing her.

As I pursued Racer and her predators, I wondered why they ignored me. They had to know I was behind them. Were they so single-minded in their desire to kill a fleeing human pilot that they disregarded the danger behind them?

I couldn't figure them out. But as they closed upon Racer, I closed upon them.

"Lock two missiles onto the aft gunboat and the other two onto the center gunboat. Launch them one second apart."

"Affirmative. Missiles locked. Launching."

I watched as my missiles streaked away. The first pair reached the rear-most gunboat, turning it into a glowing cloud of super-heated gas. The second pair flew through this cloud and less than a heartbeat later turned the central gunboat into a white fireball.

"Racer, come about."

Climbing sharply, Ava looped backward, rolled over, and began firing at her opponents. The Gorgon formation, its command boat vaporized, dissolved.

As Ava attacked the wormheads, I locked onto the left gunboat and fired my cannon. My first two shots disabled its screen. My third shot knocked it out of the sky. It plowed into the soft soil of the plain, uprooting two magnificent trees.

The Gorgons scattered in every direction now. They no longer sought our lives, but rather thought only of escaping our wrath. Ava knocked another one out of the sky. It exploded as it collided with the surface, sending an ugly black and yellow fireball skyward. I caught one other, sending it to a similar doom. The last two got away.

"Racer, go find the SARCOP. I'll find Diamond. And watch your six."

"Affirmative. See you out there."

Racer shot off toward the sky port as the first morning rays of Thea gleamed off her bird's black body. Meanwhile, I vectored back toward the burning hell of Atlatya.

As I approached the city, I dropped low and slowed. I entered the jumble of buildings near the city's center, where I knew Lori had gone down, maneuvering between the broken and blasted structures. I asked Prax to morph my canopy transparent so I could see for myself just how bad the destruction was.

It was beyond imagination.

Smoke engulfed much of Atlatya. A black cloud gathered overhead. Brown and gray wisps hugged the buildings, drifting in and out of broken windows and shattered doorways like specters of the recent departed. Many structures had great gaps where walls had been and from these emerged flames, orange and yellow, little demons dancing on the bones of the city.

Rubble covered the streets. Blackened, burned-out vehicles, some containing charred corpses, lay scattered about.

Here and there I saw the gory remains of a Marine in his or her battle armor. Burned arms and legs poked from beneath piles of broken concrete, belonging to the civilians and soldiers caught in the path of the advancing Gorgon ground forces.

Occasionally, I flew over a Gorgon corpse. Every single one was headless. The Gorgons wore armor similar to the Marines, but their helmets were shaped like ancient fish bowls, narrow near the neck and widening out to encompass the entire head. Their helmets were transparent, I knew this from the intelligence images gathered from ground units engaging the enemy, so the wearer might better see with its sensory tendrils.

Our Marines purposely aimed at the enemy's head. They knew the Gorgons fried every human they found. They wanted to instill the same fear and hatred in the enemy that we felt toward them by vaporizing their heads.

Through my transparent canopy I saw it all while wending my way through the wasted city at just a few kilometers an hour.

"Have you located Diamond's emergency beacon yet?"

"Negative," Prax replied. "Perhaps she would not broadcast, knowing the Gorgons might detect her."

"Good point. How are we going to find her?"

"There are still some microprobes from previous patrols operating in the area. I am picking up their recognition signals. They are faint. I can contact them and see if they are available to help us."

"Do it."

I continued on, keeping an eye on my sensors. I didn't want an enemy box bouncing me from above. Cramped as these streets were, I'd be vaporized before I could escape.

As I came around a corner, I cut my engine and settled on my antigrav field. Ahead of me I saw a group of clear light bulbs bobbing up and down behind a pile of rubble. They might be walking. They might be dancing. Or they might be killing someone. I hoped it wasn't Lori.

"Seventeen microprobes have replied. Ten are too damaged to be of help. Two are too low on power. But the remaining five will do what they can. I've sent them out to locate Diamond."

"Good. Prax, do you know what's going on behind that rubble pile ten degrees to the right of our bow?"

"I suspect enemy soldiers are located there."

"So do I. Can you tell what they're doing?"

"Negative."

"Are any of those damaged microprobes in a position to look?"

"Inquiring. Affirmative. Two are sending telemetry."

"Let me see it."

"I don't think you should, Hector."

"What d'you mean?"

"It is disturbing."

"Display it."

"Not advisable."

"Do it. I'm worried about Lori. This city's scaring the hell out of me. I have to know what's going on over there."

"Very well." It almost sounded like Prax sighed.

A dark and grainy image appeared upon the lower right of my canopy. It was sent by a severely damaged probe. I had trouble making out the scene. I saw several Gorgons, their tendrils waving wildly in their fish-bowl helmets. Each had what looked like a long stick with a triangular-shaped metal blade at the end. The Gorgons held the axe-like objects in their arms, their claw-like fingers wrapped around the axes's handles. They seemed busy chopping something. But what?

"What're they doing? You said you were receiving signals from a second probe. Let me see it."

"Negative."

"Show me."

"Very well. I warned you."

The image from the second probe appeared clear and colorful. I suddenly realized the point of Prax's reluctance. It was all I could do to keep from vomiting in my flight suit.

The Gorgons busied themselves mutilating two human corpses. They had been human at one time, anyways. I couldn't tell if they were male or female, or whether they were Eosian soldiers, InterStellar Marines, or civilians.

I watched, unable to turn away from the horrific scene.

Their axes rose and fell with such an awkwardness. Blood gleamed on the blades.

Hatred, fear and rage filled my heart. I had known what this war was doing to the people of Eos. But until I had drifted along these streets, until I saw this evil before me,

I'd removed my feelings from it. Now all I wanted was to kill those things out there!

But I couldn't. If I fired on them, then every Gorgon in Atlatia would know a fighter was on the deck. They'd know where I was. Gunboats would come for me. How could I save Lori then?

Yet I wanted to kill them. I had to kill them. They weren't intelligent beings, but things. Monsters. Nightmares.

They didn't deserve to live.

As I watched, my sensors picked up an enemy gunboat formation darting past overhead. I turned from the horrid image before me and watched my sensor display as it revealed the presence of the box. It drifted back and forth in my vicinity, hosing the nearby streets with its plasma cannons. Abruptly, one of the box's seven blips on my canopy disappeared. Then another. The box flew apart as two fighters from one of *Akagi*'s other squadrons jumped it.

"Hector."

"What?" I snapped.

"Something's happening."

I returned to looking at the microprobe's visual feed.

Two glassed-enclosed Gorgons were dragging a struggling victim out from a blackened doorway. It was woman in an Eosian army uniform. One of her legs appeared badly burned from a plasma weapon. The pain from her wound, along with the fear of what these monsters intended for her, showed on her face.

"Hector, one of the other microprobes has located Lieutenant Clark. She's eight blocks ahead and fifty meters to our left. Another microprobe indicates an enemy patrol is headed her way."

I didn't hear him. I couldn't hear him. I watched, frightened horrified, fascinated. The Gorgons tossed the poor woman onto the bloody pile of human remains. Their axes rose. They fell. They rose again, blood gleaming on them. The Gorgons didn't try killing her, but rather began dismembering her bit by bloody bit.

I knew she was in great agony as her face contorted in horror and pain, her mouth open, screaming. I couldn't hear her screams, but I felt them. Her screams tormented me, sending shivers and shudders through me.

Her mouth moved, soundlessly, in the image. Her face contorted. Blood blossomed from multiple wounds.

I couldn't take it anymore!

I screamed. I screamed rage and hatred at the wormheads. My bird leaped forward and upward. Angling over, my nose aimed at the startled Gorgons, my engine held in check, my antigrav field keeping me stationary, I fired at the enemy and their victim. The superheated metallic stream from my plasma cannon vaporized the Gorgons and their prey.

I fired again. And again. And again.

I fired until Prax disabled my cannon.

"Give it back!" I screamed.

"Hector. I have located Lieutenant Clark."

"Give it back!"

"Hector! The enemy's advancing on Lieutenant Clark. Do you wish her to suffer the same as this woman did?"

With an effort, I calmed down. Just a little. "No. Give me a vector. Are they all dead?" I asked, referring to the monsters I'd just fired upon.

"Affirmative."

"And their victim?"

"Mercifully vaporized."

"Enemy contacts?"

"Nothing nearby."

"Good. Contact Ground Command. Relay a copy of what we just saw and then ask if anyone's around to help Lori. And then find out where that SARCOP is."

"Affirmative."

I took a deep breath. Following Prax's vector, I popped up among the rooftops. Up and down, as quick as that, scooting to my left with my starboard thrusters. I took cover among the rubble on the next street over.

"Is she on the emergency channel?" I asked.

"Negative. She is not broadcasting."

"Then how d'you know it's her?"

"A microprobe floats behind her."

"Move it slowly in front of her so as not to frighten her. She'll know it's ours."

"Affirmative."

"Hello, is anyone there? This is First Lieutenant Lori Clark of First Squadron. I see your probe."

"Diamond, Ice Maker. I'm nearby."

"What kept you?"

"Monsters."

"Are you okay, Hector? You don't sound good."

"I'm not. But I'll be okay. Lori, I want you to hide yourself really good. My sensors indicate an enemy unit's coming right up your street. It's about a kilometer away. Looks like ground troops and grav tanks."

"I'll hide."

"Don't let them find you. I just saw what they do to prisoners."

"They don't take prisoners."

"They do now. But they're not vaporizing them. They're chopping them to pieces with axes, while they're still alive."

"Oh, my god! Where's that damned SARCOP at?"

"I have no idea. But I'm not going to let them near you. Now, hide."

"Affirmative."

"Hector," Prax said, "Ground Command has put me in contact with a Marine company. They are pulling back."

"Where are they?"

"Two and a half kilometers up the street from Lieutenant Clark. They have taken heavy casualties and have just disengaged from a superior enemy force. They are also recovering from an attack by an enemy gunboat formation."

"Tell them we need help."

"I have told them. They say they are unable to help."

"Give me vocal. This is First Lieutenant Hector Crossman. Who am I talking to?"

"This is Gunnery Sergeant Wilson. I told your counterpart we can't come. We've taken heavy casualties. You skyboys ain't doin' your job!"

"We're doing the best we can. Look, I've a downed pilot near me, an enemy column coming up the street, and Search and Rescue seems to be lost. I need help."

"You ain't gettin' it from us, boy. My lieutenant's dead. My captain's almost dead. We've lost fifty-five marines. Our company's shattered. Find someone else."

"There isn't anyone else. Do you know what they do to prisoners? Do you?"

"They don't take prisoners."

"They do now. You got a visual feed? I'm sending you what I just saw. Watch it. Then tell me you can't come."

Prax transmitted the recording. Meanwhile, using my antigrav field, I rotated my bird ninety degrees up and one hundred and eighty degrees around. Settling my bird back down, I now faced away from Lori. Utilizing my antigrav field, I drifted down the street. I directed Prax to keep trying to locate the SARCOP as well as keeping tabs on Gorgon boxes and ground troops. Three hundred meters down the street from Lori, I stopped. My bird floated a meter above the rubble-strewn street.

"This is Gunnery Sergeant Wilson. We're on the way. Give us the location of your pilot. There's only ten of us left in my platoon so be careful where you point that bird of yours."

"Affirmative. Thanks."

"Keep it. I better not be gettin' into somethin' I can't get out of. I'm responsible for these kids."

"Understood. Watch your tails."

"You're damn right we will."

I had Prax darken my canopy. It protected me much better from radiation that way.

"Prax, display tactical location of the enemy ground unit."

"Affirmative." Several microprobes, unable to move, sent visual information from their locations. Three probes observed the enemy force moving up the street toward us. Prax directed four of the flying probes to keep discrete contact with the enemy. I ordered the fifth probe kept near Lori.

While we waited for the enemy to close, my mind dwelt on the horror I'd witnessed minutes before. While I'd heard of the savagery inflicted upon Eosian civilians and soldiers by the enemy, I'd placed it at the back of my mind. I had performed my job without animosity toward the Gorgons. I destroyed the enemy's gunboats without emotion in my heart, other than the pride I felt in my own accomplishes and those of my friends and fellow pilots.

But now, as the enemy crept up the street toward me, cold hatred filled my heart. I wanted them dead. I wanted the terror to cease.

Most of all, I wanted to kill the enemy.

"Three hundred meters," Prax announced.

I glanced at the left side of my canopy. Little red dots represented individual Gorgons, while red triangles represented tanks drifting on antigrav fields. I counted fifteen tanks and more than a hundred troops.

"How many wormheads in a tank?" I asked.

"Unknown. Perhaps six. Why do you inquire?"

"I want to know how many I'm going to kill."

"Hector?"

"What?"

"I am worried about the tone in your voice. And your body chemistry has changed."

"So?"

"You cannot let what you saw dominate you."

"Later." A grav tank had just popped into view. As I watched the tank drifting up the street, twin plasma cannons on each side of its bulbous turret wickedly aimed in my direction, I nudged my bird to the left, lining the tank up with my own cannon. Closer it crept, with a second tank, and then a third, creeping up behind the first. Seven Gorgons soldiers maneuvered amongst the rubble on the left side of the street, while fourteen more climbed over the debris to my right. Abruptly, the soldiers on my right stopped, staring straight at me.

I blasted the lead tank. Its pitiful energy screen flared purple. Then, as I fired a second time the tank's turret exploded in blue-white flames. Molten metal rained down upon a nearby Gorgon, incinerating him.

It. Not him.

I engaged my thrusters and popped my bird up as four bright blue plasma streams from the second tank spat beneath me. Two more shots and I destroyed a second tank.

"More tanks approaching," Prax warned.

"Got 'em," I acknowledged. I rotated onto my right side and slipped between two ruined office towers. Dropping down on the deck in the next street over, I roared along it at five hundred kph. Ten seconds later, my inertial dampers groaning, I boosted over a block of broken buildings and came down behind the enemy formation. My attack on the lead pair of tanks had surprised the Gorgons and they now proceeded with caution.

My sensors showed that three tanks abreast now moved up the street, with three more tanks fifty meters back and fifteen meters higher up. Behind them, at thirty meters, drifted a third set of tanks. Four more tanks drifted low along the street, with maybe fifty Gorgons milling about them.

If only I had missiles now.

"How far are they from Lori's position?" I asked.

"Two hundred seventy meters."

"And where's Sergeant Wilson's Marines?"

"Seven hundred meters behind Lieutenant Clark's position."

"Tell them to hurry."

"Affirmative."

I fired at the backs of the rear-guard tanks, aiming at the two on the left. The right tank split into four big pieces and several smaller fragments from my first shot. The second shot, half a second behind the first, vaporized one the four big pieces. Their energy screens seemed directed forward, expecting another assault from me, so I fired only once at the left most tank. It became a cloud of debris and white-hot plasma.

The enemy tanks began turning about in the street. As they maneuvered, I flew down the street at a meter and a half altitude. Two more shots and two more tanks became fireballs. My bird bounced as it struck a rock pile, but my antigrav field and energy screen protected me from damage.

The thirty or so Gorgons I flew into weren't so fortunate. My impacting screen killed them all.

"An enemy box is en route," Prax announced.

"Good." Just past the molten remains of the rear-guard tanks, I pulled into a sharp climb. I flew up, rotated my nose downward, my inertial dampers wailing, fired at another tank, then dived past the worms and boosted up the street at fifty meters up.

"Watch where you move that damn thing, skyboy!" Sergeant Wilson growled over the comm channel at me.

"Sarge, over here," a new voice said.

"They got Mulhare!" someone else said.

"Sonsabitches!" Wilson howled.

"We got her, Sarge," a female voice said.

"Get the hell outta here then," Wilson bellowed. "Ryan, Zhou, set up a cross fire. The skyboy'll cover you."

"I'm on it," I replied. Where was that damned SARCOP when you needed it?

"Box approaching from the southwest. Another is vectoring back from the skyport."

"Ice Maker to all GORCOPs. I need help. I'm out of missiles and have two boxes coming my way."

"Well, get out of there, stupid!" a pilot said.

"Can't. I'm covering Marines."

"Let them cover themselves."

"Can't. I promised."

"Well, we can't help you. GORCOP Seven out."

The two rear-guard Marines, Zhou and Ryan, had their hands full. Twenty Gorgons fired at them from different positions.

I dropped back into the canyon of broken buildings and ruined streets. My plasma cannon fired twice, sending rubble and enemy bodies flying every which way.

The two Marines, mounted on individual, circular grav discs, wearing ceramcarb armor and carrying heavy caliber plasma rifles, retreated up the street, crisscrossing back and forth, covering each other and picking off whatever Gorgons were foolish enough to follow them.

"Thanks, skyboy," one of them called. "We're clear."

"Just get Lieutenant Clark to safety."

"Aye, aye, skyboy!"

"Sure," I replied, unsure if the Marine was grateful or sarcastic. It really didn't matter. Lori was out of harm's way.

I, on the other hand, wasn't.

"Location of enemy boxes?" I asked Prax.

"Another formation has joined the first from the southwest. The second formation is approaching just over the city from due north."

"We might be dead soon," I told Prax.

"I have confidence in you, Hector."

"Your confidence might be misplaced," I replied. "Give me a vector to *Sahara*."

"Done."

I angled our bird skyward and applied full acceleration. Meanwhile, I tried contacting Ava.

"Racer, this is Ice Maker. Do you copy?"

"Ice Maker, Racer. I'm en route back to *Akagi*. The SARCOP has returned home after it's birddog suffered severe damage. Another SARCOP is on the way with two more birddogs. They'll reach your location in ten minutes."

"Not if I can help it they won't. I've got three boxes flying up my tail."

"I'm coming back."

"Negative. Diamond has been picked up by Marines and I'm maxing for home. Do the same."

"Affirmative. See you out there."

I hoped so.

"Enemy formations closing. The formation from the north has retired. The other two will be in firing range in forty seconds."

"Prax, shift what energy you need from life support for our energy screen. And give me all the acceleration you can."

"Affirmative. Thirty seconds until contact."

We climbed skyward, a white fireball as the atmosphere ignited against my screen. Not far away the two Gorgon boxes looked like small comets flying away from the surface, racing after me. Soon tongues of blue-white energy would lick at my screen as their plasma cannons opened fired.

My sensors showed our picket ships far ahead. But they also revealed two enemy destroyers vectoring in on me The Gorgons wanted me badly.

On my canopy's navigational display I saw that our destroyers were too far away to help me. I glanced at the enemy's vectors. They came at me like two sides of a vise. But the space in the middle remained open.

My inertial dampers screamed as I twisted my bird hard to the right. Pressure from escaping Gee forces slammed me into my acceleration couch. The wind was knocked out of me. For a few moments, stars amid a field of black danced before my eyes; but not the stars of space.

At forty thousand kph, my bird skipped along the edge of the atmosphere. Wherever my energy screen touched it, blue-white fire erupted from atmospheric friction.

The enemy destroyers, not as maneuverable as the gunboats, turned wide, following me. The gunboats pulled around tighter.

We flew far above Eos now, in the dark sky of space.

"Where the hell is everyone?" I cried out on the emergency channel.

"The destroyers are closing," Prax announced.

A high energy plasma beam struck my bird, knocking it sideways.

"Damage report."

"Minor damage to all systems," Prax replied. "Energy screen at full power. We cannot take many such shots."

"Hang on, stupido, we're on our way!"

"Vixen, is that you?"

"None other, Ice Maker. GORCOP Three coming in fast."

"Watch out. I've two big ones on my tail."

"We see them."

Roberta Vasquez and her GORCOP approached at a right angle to the Gorgon boxes following behind their destroyers. I watched the sensor display as the two boxes made a wide turn and ran for it. But GORCOP Three blasted through them. In moments, both Gorgon formations had disintegrated, individual gunboats diving for the surface, as their fellow gunboats disappeared from existence when missiles and plasma fire reached them.

Another shot rocked my bird. Then I felt a jerk. One of the enemy destroyers had grabbed my bird in a graviton beam.

I broke hard to my left, dislodging the beam's grip on my bird. Another jolt followed by another jerk. The second destroyer had fired upon me and then grabbed me with a beam.

"Seventy percent of our screen has failed," Prax announced.

I rotated my bird hard to the right. I found myself slammed into my couch, almost knocked senseless. I hadn't escaped from this second beam. My velocity dropped. A more mild jerk and I knew both destroyers had me.

And then they let go.

Without waiting, I accelerated forward, jerking left and right in hard, fast maneuvers. The Gorgons fired several shots from their heavy caliber plasma cannons at me. Then they stopped firing.

"Enemy ships are retreating," Prax announced.

"Why?"

"One of our heavy cruisers from the Bombardment Group is hailing us. It has come to assist us."

"Sky Command fighter, this is *Minsk*. Are you okay?"

"Affirmative, *Minsk*. Thanks for your help."

"Our pleasure. First fun we've had since arriving. Our captain asks if you'd like to lure them back?"

"No thanks."

"Then have a safe journey home."

"See you out there," I said.

CHAPTER FOURTEEN

As I returned to *Akagi*, conflicting emotions filled my heart. I'd just saved my best friend's lover from an unimaginably horrible death. I'd also just saved a valuable officer and pilot, not to mention a dear friend. And I'd discovered a new and horrific atrocity of the Gorgons.

But contrariwise, I'd disobeyed a direct order from a superior officer, while in combat. The last time I'd disobeyed a direct order I'd saved seventy lives, won a promotion and a medal, and been kicked out of the squadron I'd served in for seven years.

True, I'd racked up an impressive score of destroyed enemy sky craft today, but so had almost everyone else who flew today. And while I'd flown quite well, what would it matter against disobeying Captain Mboko's orders? I'd been forced to choose between my obedience to a superior officer and my duty to a fellow pilot.

Well, my duty to my fellow pilots out-weighed my duties and obligations to my superiors. But would my superiors agree?

Certainly not Captain Mboko, who so deeply resented me. Her feelings toward me out-weighed any logical assessment of the situation.

It all came down to feelings, and mine were extremely jumbled right now.

I felt elation over how well I'd performed today. I had out-flown and out-fought the enemy in every instance. I had destroyed so many gunboats that I'd lost count.

I also felt excitement over how well my peers, especially Pedro, had done. Pedro was the best pilot I'd ever flown with; I'd known this at the Academy and today my belief was confirmed in the sky over Eos.

Yet excited though I was at our sky victories, I was shocked over the atrocity I'd seen the Gorgons committing. And disgusted over the anger it had brought out in me, not to mention the sudden desire for revenge. I had thought of nothing but murdering the enemy, lusting after the death of each and every Gorgon I saw, while fighting to protect Lori and the Marines.

And it sickened me. I had become one of the enemy. Killing for the sake of killing, out of hatred and sickness. How could I judge them when I behaved like them?

These thoughts troubled me more than fear of what Captain Mboko intended for me. As the squadron's executive officer, she had power over me in all personnel matters. But the final judgement lay with Major Garacyk. And even he could be over-ruled by Colonel Wallis or General Devon.

The question was, would they support me over her? Or would they support her for the sake of discipline within the ranks and the good of the squadron?

"Are you okay, Hector?" Prax asked, interrupting my brooding.

"I'm tired."

"You performed quite well today. You should be proud."

"Thanks. I am. How far are we from *Akagi*?" I had let Prax fly us home, while I'd closed my eyes, letting bitterness wash over me. I found it hard to believe that our entire time spent in the skies over Eos, not to mention our departure from and return to *Akagi*, had consumed lest than four hours.

"We have clearance for landing. A graviton beam has connected with us and we are being guided onto the flight deck. There are several messages awaiting you."

"How many of them are good?" I asked.

"They are mixed. Search and Rescue wants you to know they've picked up Lieutenant Clark. They apologize for being late. Two of their birddogs suffered damage in the fighting today and the other SARCOP busied itself assisting the evacuation of trapped ground units."

"At least they finally made it. What else?"

"Lieutenant Alvarez seems quite joyful and wants you to meet him in forward upper lounge after you debrief. Admiral Greely congratulates you on a superb job of gathering intelligence concerning Gorgon atrocities. A Marine colonel named Duval thanks you for breaking apart a Gorgon thrust upon the remnants of one of his companies. And..."

"And what?"

"Captain Mboko wants you in her office five minutes ago. Why do humans make temporal demands they know others cannot achieve?" Prax inquired.

"It's a way of showing anger. Don't let it disturb you."

"I won't. I wish you well in your meeting with the captain."

I grunted, then touched a small button on my flight suit's left sleeve and my helmet folded away from my head, receding down my back. Removing my gloves, I wiped my face.

I needed a shower and some rest. But Captain Mboko had priority over me. My needs and wishes were secondary to her demands.

I asked Prax to morph my canopy transparent. As *Akagi*'s graviton beam guided us back aboard ship, I watched while eight other birds from our squadron maneuvered toward their gravitic catapults. Yet another GORCOP appeared headed into the hell of Atlatya.

Once aboard, the ship's beam cut out and Prax moved us into our hangar bay. Our engine had cooled outside the carrier and now, as our bay's doors closed and pressurization began, I wrote my after-action report.

"Prax, you'll send this along with yours?" I asked, as I finished my report.

"Affirmative, Hector."

Pressurization completed, Prax popped my canopy open.

"We might not be flying together for a while," I said. I avoided adding "if at all."

"We shall see," Prax replied.

"Yeah." While the bay had pressurized, Prax had directed the antigrav platform over and up beside my cockpit. I climbed on, directing it downward.

"You brought my bird back in good shape. Good for you," Sergeant Lincoln said as she and two of her techs, followed by four robots, entered my hangar bay.

"What d'you mean your bird?" I said, stepping off the platform as it settled to the deck.

"When it's here, it's mine. Out there, it's yours. Got that?"

I nodded.

"You look tired."

"I am."

"You should get some rest. I hear you blasted away a goodly share of the wormheads. Good for you."

"I'm not so sure it's all that good for me."

"Well," she said, "it's certainly not good for them. But it's good for our people down there. You did a good job. So go visit a lounge. Take a load off, relax, and get some rest."

"Affirmative."

"Good boy. Cortez! Run a diagnostic of the inertial dampers first. I swear, that guy's a good tech, but sometimes he lacks the brains for breathing."

"Right." I exited the bay and made my way to the men's changing room. After changing out of my flight suit and back into my day uniform, I dragged myself to Mboko's office. I felt worn out, both because of the battles I'd fought today, and because of the forth-coming battle with the captain.

Stopping in front of her office, I announced myself to her door. It slid open and a crisp, cold "enter" snapped out to me.

As I entered, I glanced at the walls around me, especially at the mural of red-coated men fighting nearly naked black men, sunlight gleaming off the metallic tips of the black warriors' spears. I felt a sudden kinship with the beleaguered men in red.

Entering the captain's inner office, I paused before her desk, coming to attention. She glared up at me. I waited for her to offer me a seat, but she didn't. Instead, she stood and marched around her desk, stopping a few centimeters before me.

"You consider yourself a perfect pilot. I'm right, am I not? An answer is expected, lieutenant!"

"I'm not sure how to answer, ma'am."

"Oh, come off it. You consider yourself superior to everyone else, don't you? And you are, aren't you? Only a superior person flagrantly disobeys orders. When one is superlative, one need not condescend to one's diminutive cohorts, even one of senior rank. Is that not so, lieutenant? I await your answer."

"I did what I felt was right, captain."

"Perfect words from a perfect pilot."

"I'm not perfect, ma'am."

"Oh, but you are," Captain Mboko hissed at me. "Only a paragon of perfection, a paladin such as yourself, would dare to flagrantly disregard the commands of others. Do not deny it, lieutenant. You recognize the truth in my statement. You consider yourself perfect, superior to all others, even those who are correctly your superiors.

"You have disregarded orders enough to realize the truth of my statements. But never again."

"I don't understand, ma'am."

"A reply was neither requested nor expected. However, I will endeavor to explain for your perfect brain. You are grounded, pending the convening of a court-martial board."

"Why?"

"What part did you fail to comprehend? You failed to obey my direct orders in a combat environment. That is a mutinous offense. And I will so prosecute you. Not once, but repeatedly today, when I recalled you to my location, you failed to comply. The last instant was extreme insubordination!"

"Listen, ma'am, I had to provide cover for Lieutenant Clark. The SARCOP was busy."

"There's always an alibi for you, isn't there? But why would a perfect person such as yourself need one?"

"I'm not a paladin and I'm not perfect."

She glared at me. For a moment, I thought she might hit me. Or at least spit in my face.

"Oh, but you are, lieutenant. You are. At least to your minuscule mind. You consider yourself above authority. You consider yourself superior to your seniors. You consider your concepts of right and wrong perfect and everyone else's concepts unbalanced.

"Someone such as yourself doesn't belong in Sky Command. And I shall see to it that you are expelled with alacrity."

"I don't know what you have against me, captain. But if I hadn't protected Lori Clark, she'd be dead now. Haven't you seen the images of the atrocity I discovered? She'd have been next."

The captain turned her back to me and waved her hand. "Dismissed."

"No."

She spun around, her eyes full of hatred. "Do you wish that I summon security? Exit my office at once!"

"Lori Clark would be dead now if it weren't for me. But this isn't about me. Or about Lori. It's about you. I don't know why you hate me, but there's no reason to. I'm not your enemy, ma'am. The enemy is the one down there exterminating human life on Eos."

"Get out!"

"As you wish, ma'am. But I'll fight you."

"Of course you will. Perfect people do that. Now, leave."

I turned my back on her and left. Out in the hall, as her door whooshed closed, I wanted to scream.

This was worse than what had happened to me when I was promoted off of *Soyuz*. At least then I still had the promise of a career.

But if Captain Mboko prosecuted me my career would be over; I might even be sentenced to prison. Mutiny and disobeying orders while in combat carried severe penalties.

Why was she doing this to me? She knew that downed pilots needed coverage until a SARCOP could arrive. And both SARCOPs had been too busy to rescue Lori right away. Tactically, I hadn't acted irresponsibly. So why persecute me?

Why did Captain Mboko hate me so much?

I stormed down the corridor. Minutes later, in my cabin, my door secured against intrusion, I sat down at my desk, shaking my head. This day had been such a roller coaster of emotions. My hands trembled from rage.

I got up and moved to my bed, lying down. I took several deep breaths, calming myself down. Then I closed my eyes, desiring but a few minutes of sleep. Thankfully, it came.

CHAPTER FIFTEEN

MY COMM UNIT BEEPED, awakening me. Sitting up, I spun around and faced my monitor. "Hello?"

Pedro's face appeared. "Amigo? What have you been doing? Didn't you get my message? Vector up to the lounge. I'll buy you a steak. I'll even name my first born after you."

"What?"

"Just vector in, mi hermano."

"Give me a few minutes to shower. I stink."

"You usually do."

"Thanks."

Pedro laughed. "What kind of steak do you want?"

"A big T-bone. Make it beef. And no pranks this time. I'll pound you if you sneak me another rubber steak, like you did t the Academy. Medium-well, with brown rice, and vegetables. Lots of vegetables. After this morning, I need them."

"Si, amigo."

"See you in fifteen."

Entering my bathroom, I stared into the mirror. I looked like hell. I felt like hell. All I wanted to do was sleep. I wanted to sleep a thousand years, until Mboko, Geys, and the Gorgons were long gone.

But I couldn't.

My shower felt great. Fifteen minutes later, clean, dressed, and feeling much better, I walked into the forward upper lounge. Glancing up through the dome, I saw a black sky full of stars. *Akagi* had rolled over again, orienting away from Eos.

As I crossed the lounge, I heard some opera in the background. From the History of Earth's Music course at the Academy, I recognized it as "The Barber of Seville." Full of life and energy, it uplifted my spirit.

Almost everyone sat at our usual table, even Lori.

She hurried over to me. Hugging me, she kissed my cheek. "Thank-you," she said. Then, taking my arm, she paraded me over to the table.

"The man o' the hour," Lyle quipped.

I chuckled, not knowing what to expect next.

"You're amazing," Ava said, almost in awe.

"No. You're the amazing one. I've never seen anyone shoot as well as you did."

She smiled at me.

"Where's Jacques and Lisa?" I asked.

"Jacko's on GORCOP. And Lisa just returned from a SARCOP. She'll be here soon, amigo," Pedro said.

"Himself admires what ya did today. Yer a better man than himself thought ya were."

"What's that supposed to mean?" I asked.

"Nothin' more or less than it means."

"Take it easy, amigo. We're all excited over being back together again. I don't know what I'd have done if mi corazon had been lost."

I looked at Pedro. "I wouldn't let that happen."

"I know, hermano."

"And you didn't let it happen," Lori said. "For the rest of today, you are my hero."

"Amigo, are you vectoring on my love?" Pedro asked.

I laughed. "No. My sights are set elsewere."

"Good. Because it would be bad form to vector on another man's beloved, wouldn't you say?"

"Not to mention fatal. I've seen how you fight."

"Very true."

Lori pushed me toward a seat. She sat next to me, with Pedro on her other side. Ava slid closer to me. Only Lyle sat across the table from me.

A moment later, my steak dinner arrived.

"What do you want to drink?" Pedro asked.

"Water. A big glass of it. My throat feels dry as dust."

"Combat does that to you," Ava said.

"It does," I agreed. "It dehydrates you."

"Why didn't ya sip from the water bottle attached to yer suit?" Lyle asked.

"I got caught up in what I was doing."

"If yer no' careful, it may be yer undoin'."

"You could be right."

"Himself's da says a man should always be right."

"And what does your 'da' say about a woman?" Lori demanded.

"That she should always be lovin' an' kind."

"It's hard to fault that kind of reasoning, eh, amigo?"

"Affirmative," I replied.

"So," Ava said, changing the subject, "how many gunboats did you get today? Everyone at this table became an ace today. And Pedro almost became a double ace."

"I don't know. I lost count."

"Your counterpart would know," Ava replied.

"I'm sure Prax would."

"I know," Pedro announced.

"Why am I not surprised," I said.

Pedro grinned at me. "Mi amigo got seven today. I checked with his counterpart as they returned. An exceptional score, wouldn't you all agree? I, myself, only got six."

"So, I'm still ahead of you," I said.

"Si, amigo, but only by two. I'll get ahead of you tomorrow. Or the day after, perhaps. It'll take an exceptional man to beat me and while you are that, you're not as exceptional as I am."

I laughed. "That's what I love about Pedro. His head's bigger than anyone else's, with the possible exception of Lyle's. But Pedro's not afraid to admit it."

Pedro smiled back, picking up the gauntlet I'd just thrown at his feet. "And why shouldn't I be, hermano? You've seen me fly. You're good, but you're not as good as I am. It's not your fault. How could you be?"

I grinned. "You're the best, Pedro. I've always known you were. All kidding aside, I'm glad you're out there."

"Himself is, too," Lyle agreed. "There'd be a lot more wormies ta worry about wi'out him."

"And I'm glad you're there too, amigo. You saved my soul today."

"The cost was worth it."

"What do you mean?" Pedro asked.

"Mboko's grounded me."

Pedro waved his hand as if brushing aside a fly. "That won't stick. You saved my love's life. The Command values initiative. And you're an exceptional pilot. You're almost as good as me."

"And two kills ahead of you."

"I'll soon be ahead of you."

"Without my competition, it won't be a problem."

"I said it won't stick. How can the Command keep one of its best pilots grounded when it needs everyone of them in combat? And you're certainly among the best or you wouldn't be here. So don't worry, amigo. You'll be fine."

"I hope so. But I doubt it."

"An' why is that, himself wonders?"

"Because Mboko is demanding that I be court-martialled."

"What?" my four friends exclaimed as one.

"That's right. She's charging me with gross insubordination during combat. She's right, too. I disobeyed her direct orders."

"But, if you hadn't, my love would have died. You did the right thing," Pedro said.

"I feel the same way. But she hates me. I don't know why. She just does. And she intends on blasting me anyway she can."

"I don't believe the major will stand for it," Lori said. "He knows you're a good pilot. He trusts you."

"He'll have to back his exec."

"Then we'll go to Colonel Wallis," Ava said. "He won't let one of his best pilots be vectored out of the Command."

"Himself disagrees. Himself thinks the colonel will back one of his squadron commanders."

"So what?" Ava snarled. "General Devon won't let it happen."

"He might," Lori replied.

"Are you insane?" Ava said. "He's already helped Hector once. He'll do it again. Even Admiral Greely will come to Hector's aid. Hector solved the problem with our missiles. And he's just brought back information about a Gorgon atrocity. One which you almost experienced! They'll both overturn the captain's request for a court-martial."

"I don't think so," I replied.

"And why not?" Ava demanded.

"Because, my dear," Lori interjected, "they might back the captain, for discipline's sake. If a field commander's authority can be challenged or cancelled out by either inferiors or superiors, what will happen to discipline? Hector's right, he's in a lot of trouble."

"But..." Ava began.

"But nothing," Pedro said, "When Jacques and Captain Jonkowski get back from their COP, we'll figure something out. We're not going to let Mboko crucify Hector. Mi amigo saved mi corazon's life. I'd be a fool to let him burn for performing such a miracle."

"Just don't ruin your careers over it. I don't want that, do you understand me?" I said.

"We understand, amigo. But what are friends for, if not to sacrifice themselves for one another?"

"I don't want that," I said.

"You've put everything you hold dear on the line for my safety's sake," Lori said. "I'd be quite an ungrateful creature if I didn't do the same for you."

"You hardly know me."

"I know enough about you. I know you're a good man who values his friends and human life above his own life. I know you value doing the right thing. And so I wish to return the favor. You've given your friendship freely. And you're willing to sacrifice everything you love for us, for myself and my dearest here. Don't you see, I can't do less for you than you're willing to do for me."

"I do see that," I said. "Thank-you."

"Your water's here, amigo. You should eat your steak, before I do!" Pedro stabbed at my steak with his fork, but I blocked it with mine.

"I'm glad you waited for me," a rude voice said. I glanced up to see Vladimir Geys standing beside our table, Lisa holding his arm. She smiled sweetly at me.

"Hello," I said to her.

"Hello yourself," Geys answered for her.

"Don't be rude, Vlad," she said.

"But he deserves it so much. Running away in combat. I suspected he was a coward."

"He didn't run away!" Ava snarled.

"Down, girl," Vlad chided. "Don't be his lap dog."

Ava started to stand, but Lori rose first. "If you cannot be polite, you're not welcome at this table."

"I wouldn't think of staying. What self-respecting pilot would want to sit with this coward?"

"Why are you with him?" I asked Lisa, ignoring Geys.

"I wasn't aware you were back. Vlad asked me to dinner and I agreed. I detest eating alone."

"You don't have to stay with him. You could eat with us."

"She's an honorable person," Geys said. "Not like some people."

I gave her a pleading look.

"I can't."

"See, Crossman. That's honor, something you're unfamiliar with."

I stood. Geys glared down at me. "You wouldn't know honor if it bit your ass."

He leaned over and whispered to me, "I know you won't be around much longer. Once you're out of my way, Lisa will be mine again."

"Not if she doesn't want to," I whispered back.

Vlad let go of Lisa's arm and shoved me into my seat. "Sit down, little man!"

"Get your hands off of him!" Ava snarled. Before anyone could stop her, she leaped across the table. She landed on Geys, slamming him backward onto to the deck. With one hand she pulled his uniform tight around his throat, choking him, while her other hand cocked back, fist tight and ready to strike.

But Lori grasped Ava's raised hand. "Let him go. He's not worth it. Besides, dear friend, everyone's watching."

Lori was right. Ava's attack had attracted the attention of almost everyone in the lounge.

Taking a deep breath, Ava backed away. Standing and straightening her uniform, she said, "You don't know how lucky you really are."

"I see you've started a harem. A coward's pride, I'd say," Geys snarled, standing. With one hand he brushed his blond hair back in place, while with the other he rubbed his throat.

"I don't know if my love can hold her back again," Pedro said. "I'd boost away if I were you."

"Let's go," Vlad said to Lisa.

"I don't think so," Lisa replied.

"You promised you'd have dinner with me."

"I didn't promise to let you insult my friends."

"Don't my feelings count, too?" Geys whined.

"They do."

He took hold of her arm. "Then let's go."

"Don't my feelings count?" Lisa retorted.

"Yes."

"Then I want to have dinner with my friends. You can join us, if you wish."

"They're not my friends. Not while he's present."

"I like Hector. Does that mean you don't like me?"

"You know I do."

"Then say that you'll join us. Say that you'll forgive whatever debt Hector owes you."

Geys shook his head. "I can't."

"This is where I want to eat, Vladimir."

"Can I see you tomorrow?" he asked.

"I don't know."

Geys stared at her. Since I didn't know what to expect from him next, I stood again and stepped beside Lisa.

"This isn't over yet," Geys growled at me.

"I think it is," I said.

"You won't always have your little guard dog around. We'll have words one of these days. If you're still here." He left.

"Thank-you, all of you, for standing up for me," I said.

"Everyone in both SAR squadrons knows what you did today."

"I'm a fighter pilot. That's what I do."

"I know," she said. We gazed at each other.

"Sit down before I get sick," Ava said.

I laughed. "Okay, my guardian angel."

"Oh, shut up."

I offered Lisa my seat, then sat beside her. I leaned past her and said to Ava: "I've never had anyone come to my rescue like that before. I'm glad you're on my side. You can fly with me anytime."

Ava smiled at me. "Thanks."

CHAPTER SIXTEEN

AS I SAT BESIDE Lisa, I asked, "How was your COP?"

She paled. "Difficult. Our birddog was damaged by a pair of Gorgon gunboats. For a few moments, I didn't think we were going to make it out alive. And then a pilot from Third Squadron came to our assistance. She vaporized one of the gunboats, chased the other away, and escorted us clear of Eos."

Lori reached across the table and clasped Lisa's hand. "I'm grateful you're okay."

"So am I," I said. "I'd like to thank this pilot. Did you get her name?"

"No. But her call sign was 'Vixen'. I liked the sound of her voice. It was strong, but still feminine."

"Vixen," Pedro mused. "I haven't heard of her before."

"Sounds to himself like a good name for the lass."

"I know her," I said. "She saved my life this morning, too. She was part of GORCOP Three. They drove off two boxes that pursued me after the Marines rescued Lori. Her name's Roberta Sanchez and she's tough. I served with her on Vasalyssa for several months before being transferred here. She grew up on Uno Mas, which she tells me is a tough place."

"She gets around, doesn't she, amigo?"

"Seems so. I'm glad she was there for you, Lisa."

"Thank you. I'm grateful she saved you, too."

"Seems like we've all had an exceptionally hard day," Pedro said. "And more's to come. For now, let's eat. Best to put it behind us, wouldn't you all agree?"

I nodded, then said to Lisa, "What would you care to eat?"

In response, she ordered a Caesar Salad and some tea. We waited for her food to come before continuing our meal.

While we waited we listened to the background music. It had changed from opera to jazz. The music seemed sporty, friendly, upbeat. It eased our tensions.

When Lisa's salad arrived, we returned with energy to our dinner, quickly finishing our food. Then we sipped at our drinks. I enjoyed just drinking water, while Lori and Pedro had coffee, Lisa had tea, Lyle had beer, and Ava had red wine.

I couldn't take my eyes off of Lisa. Though I saw the strain of the day's events in her face and eyes, I also saw her grace and beauty. I hoped she cared for me as much as I cared for her.

She caught my eyes on her and smiled at me. Then a shadow crossed her face.

"I wish you and Vlad could get along," she said. "He's really a good man. He likes sports. He loves to run and is quite an accomplished diver and swimmer. And I know he's a fine pilot. The two of you should be friends."

"I wish we could be, though I prefer swimming to running. The water's a lot more pleasant to move through and you never know when you'll see a beautiful woman beside you."

She smiled again. "He's also a good swimmer. The two of you should swim together sometime."

"I don't think that would work."

"Why not? Why can't you get along?"

"We have an irreconcilable difference."

"Which is?"

I looked at her.

"He means you, dear," Lori said.

Lisa glared at me. "I don't want to be fought over. I'm not an object and we're not animals. We're people and we don't fight over each other. I don't like people who fight over others like that."

"Ava fought for Hector," Lyle said. "Do ya no' like her anymore?"

"That was just the stress we've been under, I imagine," Lisa said. "Vlad feels it. I feel it. I'm sure the rest of you feel it, too. But it doesn't change my point. I don't want you to fight over me, Hector. Do you understand?"

I nodded.

"You might want to explain that to Vlad, too," Lori said. "It doesn't always take two to start a fight."

Lisa nodded.

"I'm sorry," Ava apologized to Lisa. "I don't know what came over me. I shouldn't have attacked Vlad like that. It's just that when he shoved Hector down, I couldn't believe it. All that crap about Hector running away. Hector saved Lori's life. Without Hector, Lori wouldn't be sitting with us now.

"I'm sorry. I now know that it offended you and I sure didn't mean to do that. I just got mad. And then I acted, without thinking."

"But that's what we have to avoid, isn't it?" Lisa said.

"Acting without thinking. People get hurt that way. People die that way. And everyone of you here is important to me. I don't want to lose any of you!"

"You won't," I said.

"You sound so certain. But we're in a war. People are dying every day. We bring downed pilots back, yes. But we also retrieve the wounded and dying. We bring them back for the medics and doctors to save. But some don't make it.

"Last week, we flew into Atlatya to rescue some Eosian soldiers whose transport was shot down. Before we arrived, Gorgon tanks killed them. Plasma streams from the tanks turned them into human torches. I didn't have to hear their screams, I could feel them. I could imagine their terror and agony."

"I know what you mean," I said, staring at the table top. "When I saw what those... things were doing to the Eosian soldiers, I lost control. I vaporized them all, even the mutilated bodies of their victims. All I wanted to do was kill the enemy. I just wanted to kill everyone all of them. I became like a machine, programmed for destruction."

I glanced up at my friends. "I didn't want it to be that way and I don't want to be that way, but I was that way. What they did, I couldn't believe it. I just couldn't believe it!"

Lisa put her hand on my arm. "It's okay. I understand. I think we all do. This is a war of hatred."

"All wars are about hatred," Lori said.

"But I don't want to lose control again," I said. "I don't know if I can stop hating the enemy. I feel like a little bit of me died today. I'm not even sure what I feel now, except anger. I've only been aboard ship a few days and already I've killed dozens of aliens and half the ship hates me."

"No, the whole ship does," Pedro joked.

"Thanks."

Pedro grinned. "Don't mention it."

"I won't."

"No one hates you," Lisa replied.

"Vlad does. So does Captain Mboko. And that craphead who flew with me today, Brattano. I don't even know what I've done to offend him."

"Why does Captain Mboko hate you?" Lisa asked.

"I don't know. She just does."

"The captain's grounded him," Lyle told Lisa.

"Why?"

"For disobeying orders," I said.

"When did you do that?" Lisa asked.

"When I went to Lori's aid. The captain felt that SAR could get to Lori in time."

"We couldn't have. We were too busy. She must have known that. It was broadcast over the tactical command net. She had to know that someone else had to provide cover for any downed pilots. All the SAR boats were engaged or damaged. No one could've reached Lori before the Gorgons did. Captain Mboko must have known that."

"Then why is she planning on court-martialling me?"

"I don't know. But there's no basis for it. The SAR commander over Atlatya informed all other commanders of our immediate situation. He informed them we couldn't reach any downed pilots for a while. He told them to provide cover until more SAR boats arrived. She had to know."

"That's it, amigo!" Pedro exclaimed. "Your vector out. The captain had to have known the situation. And even if she didn't, you were still covered. You acted responsibly. No one can claim you disobeyed orders."

"I'm not so sure."

"Be certain," Lori said.

I shook my head. "I just don't know."

"Lyle and I are scheduled for another COP soon," Pedro said. "I'd like to spend a little quality time with my love."

"Okay," I said.

Lisa, finished with her food, stood. "My birddog's down for repairs. I won't be going out for a day or two. But I've lots of other work to do. I'm the squadron's information officer. I've statements to write for the Eosian News Service, as well as news to gather from other squadrons and the Eosian military and then disseminate it amongst my squadron."

I stood, too, as did the rest of us. "D'you have to go so soon?" I said to Lisa.

"Not right away. But I wanted to take a walk through *Akagi*'s botanical gardens."

"Would you mind if I came along?" I asked.

"Not at all."

Pedro came around the table to me. He grasped me by both shoulders. "Thanks, amigo. I don't know what I'd have done if something had happened to Lori."

"I couldn't let that happen to you."

He pulled me into an embrace. "Gracias, hermano. I'm glad we're flying together again."

"So am I."

Pedro stepped back. He took Lori's hand and turned to go, then turned back around. "See you out there."

"I hope so."

"I know so."

As Lori and Pedro left, Ava and Lyle came over. They stood around for a moment, not knowing what to do.

"You want to come along?" I asked them.

"Himself's got nothin' better ta do."

"Sure he does," Ava said. "Himself's the assistant armament officer. Maybe he should see what our weapons status is, huh?"

Lyle's eyes narrowed. "Quiet, lass."

"But himself's such a good target," Ava retorted.

"That'd be enough from ya!" Lyle growled.

"I'm just getting warmed up," Ava replied, winking at me. She made a little pushing wave with her hand down by the side of her leg, motioning for Lisa and me to leave while we could. So I took Lisa's hand and guided her away.

"You know," I said, "I've never heard of gardens on a warship before."

"Didn't you have any plants on *Soyuz*?" Lisa asked as she preceded me down the circular stairwell out of the lounge.

I followed her down, enjoying the way her hair bounced on her shoulders. I wondered how soft it felt. "Some individuals had plants in their quarters. And we had hydroponic gardens. That's where we got some of our fresh fruit and vegetables, such as strawberries, cranberries, tomatoes, beans, and some other items. But nothing you might call a garden.

"*Soyuz* is a warship, designed for patrolling the frontier. It has a few amenities, but not like *Akagi*. I almost feel like I'm on a star liner rather than a carrier."

She turned and smiled at me when she reached the bottom of the stairs. Dozens of people milled around the lifts, waiting either to descend or for friends to arrive. "Escort carriers see a lot more action than attack carriers, I suppose. *Akagi*'s designed with more crew comforts. We spend a lot more time in port and less time on patrol. After all, who would dare challenge us? Other than the Gorgons, of course."

"You seem to know a lot about warships," I said.

The lift door opened. Several people came out and just as many entered. Lisa and I squeezed in among them. "It's crowded in here," she said.

"Do you want to wait for another lift?" I asked.

"No. I want to get going. I've other work to do today, but I want to spend some time with you."

I looked at her and she smiled again, warming my heart. "I want to spend time with you, too."

Her smiled brightened. "About your previous question. Vlad's told me a lot about *Akagi*. But from the very first day I boarded this ship, I began exploring it. I like exploring."

"Then why didn't you join the Navy and its Exploration Branch?"

"I might, someday. But I wanted a little more independence. And I wanted to give back to the Association some of what it's done for me."

"And what has the Association done for you?"

"It gave me a safe world to live on. It's provided technology, medicine, and security for my friends, for my family, and for humanity. I know, it all sounds so trite. But it's the way I feel. I just wanted to serve the Association for a while."

"And now?" I asked, a little nervous. Was she thinking she'd served the Association enough and was ready to leave Sky Command? What was it with these women from Gentry? Why did I fall in love with the ones that always wanted to leave?

"Now, I'm seeing what war is like and I don't want to be part of it. But I can't just leave, that wouldn't be right. I can do more good staying and saving lives than running away. But I dislike hatred. I dislike war. And I certainly dislike killing."

"You might run into all those things in the Explorers," I said. Our lift opened and the crowd herded us out.

"I might. But I'm not quite yet ready to join them. I'm not that interested in scientific exploration." We proceeded to the central travel tube and boarded, heading astern.

"They always need shuttle pilots."

"True. But thousands apply every year. And I'm more independent. I feel I'm in the right place for the moment. After this war ends, I'll see then. At any rate, I still have several months to serve before I'm free to make a decision."

We hopped out of the travel tube.

"We walk from here," Lisa explained.

"How far?"

"A little way."

"I can hardly wait."

"Are you being sarcastic?"

"No. I just don't know what to expect. What's it like, this garden? Is it like *Soyuz*'s hydroponic gardens?"

"*Akagi* has hydroponic gardens. But this is so much more than that. This is beautiful. It casts golden images upon the heart and mind, consoling and healing them."

"Nothing could cast a more golden image than you upon my heart."

"You're sweet." She took my hand and almost dragged me down a narrow corridor. We stopped beside a wide double door. She pressed a button beside it. The doors slid open.

"Old-fashioned, isn't it?" I said, pointing at the button.

"Perhaps."

The first thing I noticed was how much warmer it was inside the room. Then I noticed the smells, the scents of potted soil, dried animal manure, a thousand different sweet flowery smells, the tangy moist perfume of green plants and life. Then I noticed the room's size. It was huge, as big as First Squadron's flight deck. But the ceiling, the overhead in naval parlance, appeared higher. The garden's computer projected images upon the ceiling, images of blue sky, puffy white clouds, and a bright, warm sun.

In fact, as we entered the garden, I felt the simulated sunshine warming my face.

The garden seemed to stretch into the distance, but it was an illusion created by computer-generated images upon the walls. As we entered the room, we walked beneath a curving wooden arbor covered with climbing roses. Beyond the arbor and to either side of it stretched rows of bright tropical flowers, their yellow, orange, and red blossoms magnificent and dazzling. Yellow and orange streaks striped the dark green leaves of the tropical plants.

A wide path meandered from the arbor throughout the garden. Brightly colored stepping stones dotted the path, set amid tiny gravel pebbles. Some of the smoothed pebbles were a light pink, while others were gray or white, yellow, even blue.

The path wandered through the park-like setting. Tall trees dotted a soft and very green lawn. Across the vast lawn, on the far side from where Lisa and I walked, stood a gazebo, covered with green vines and white, yellow, purple and pink flowers. The trail curved around islands of flowers and mounds of bushes. We passed pink and red azaleas, tall white and blue rhododendrons, and dozens of rose bushes and rose trees.

We stopped and smelled the roses. Some had vibrant scents, while others had none. And quite a few of the roses considered themselves minimalists, possessing only a hint of fragrance.

I sighed. "Impressive."

"I'm happy you like it."

"I do. It's incredible. I can't believe I'm on a warship. What's that over there?" I'd seen something moving amongst the roses, creeping upon the dark soil beneath them.

"What do you see?" Lisa asked.

"Come on." Grasping her hand, we left the path, dodging around people lounging on the lawns, reading, eating, kissing, sleeping. I hurried over to the roses, Lisa in tow. As I walked, I noticed how thick the lawn felt beneath my boots. I wondered how it might feel beneath my bare toes. So I stopped in my quest, bent over, and brushed by hands across the grass.

"Nice, isn't it?" she said.

"Nice doesn't even begin to define it."

I continued toward the bushes. When I reached them, I knelt down, peering beneath them. A small, brown lizard stood motionless before me.

"Is this real?"

"It's a robot," Lisa explained. "There are hundreds of them, tending to the lawn, caring for the flowers, cleaning up fallen leaves. Most are shaped like toads and lizards. But some are the common machines we'd expect in such a place."

"I should've known."

"Does it spoil the effect, knowing there aren't any real woodland creatures here?" she asked.

I stood. "Somewhat. But this place, all of this, I just don't have the words for it right now. It's all you suggested it might be when you said it casts golden images upon the heart. Thanks for bringing me here."

"Your welcome." Lisa led me back to the path.

We followed the path to where a huge pool, surrounded by real boulders, lay. A small waterfall cascaded over a ledge, gurgling as it fell among the rocks at its feet. From there the water babbled over several smaller ledges, then flowed away in a small, winding, rock-strewn stream, disappearing beneath a wall. The Garden's computer projected woodland images upon the wall where the stream disappeared, as if it continued on forever rather than recirculating through pumps and piping to return to its artificial source just above the waterfall.

Listening to the bubbling waterfall, I glanced around at the trees, the flowers, the virtual sky, then asked Lisa, "Is this all there is?"

"Oh, no. There's much more. Parallel to this room are several rooms of hydroponic gardens. And beyond all this are fruit trees."

"Amazing. But why devote all this space to so much splendor? This is a warship, after all."

"For peace of mind," she explained. "For the softening of our souls. To remind us that we're human and what's important is maintaining our humanity. For beauty's sake. To ease our troubles."

"But why, when another fighter squadron or gunboat deck could fit in here? More fighters and gunboats are what Eos needs right now, not a place for people to roll in the grass while in high orbit."

"I wondered the same at first, too," Lisa replied. "But when I asked one of the gardeners here one day, who turned out to be one of *Akagi*'s medical officers, he said it was therapy."

"Therapy?"

"Yes. He said that the Navy and Sky Command have considered for a long time how to best help their personnel deal with the boredom of long journeys through deep space and with the stresses of combat. This seemed the most effective way, he said. By letting people relax in a simple and quiet environment, where they could do something with their hands."

"But what about art classes, music, even wood shops and gymnasiums and the pools? I know this ship has all those, not to mention the lounges. It seems to me that this ship has too much of everything."

"You might be right," Lisa agreed. "But after today's fighting and terror, this is the only place that I feel safe."

I understood what she meant. I felt safe here, too. "You mentioned that one of the gardeners was also one of *Akagi*'s medical officers. Do many people work here as gardeners? I assumed it was all automated."

"There is a lot of automation. But, yes, there are living gardeners. Crew members come here and work on their own time. I've seen dozens of people down here at various times, planting, watering, and even weeding."

"There are weeds?"

Lisa laughed, a cute little laugh that sang in my heart. "I think some of the robots plant them, just to give us something to do."

"You work down here, too?"

"Whenever I can. I like the feel of the soil around my fingers. It smells so good. If not for here, I think I'd have left long ago. Space travel is exciting and wonderful, but nothing is as beautiful as Gentry. You probably feel the same about Earth."

"Earth is beautiful."

"The world you grow up on is always the most beautiful and perfect world," she said.

"Vixen wouldn't agree with you."

"Why not?" Lisa asked.

"Her world is a hell-hole. According to her."

"Perhaps not all worlds are beautiful, then."

"Certainly not every part of them. There must be beautiful places on Uno Mas. Just as there are beautiful places down on Eos. But Atlatya isn't one of them anymore."

"I understand it was beautiful once," Lisa said. "Just a few months ago, before the war arrived."

"Let's not talk of such things right now. I just can't get over how beautiful this place is."

Lisa smiled. "It is that. It's almost as if I were home right now."

"Ever seen anyone you know down here?"

"Oh, yes. Many of my fellow squadron members, as well as some of the Marines from the gunboat squadrons. I've even seen Brigadier General Devon wandering among a grove of apple trees on the far side of the garden. When the fruit's in season, he likes to come and pick some of it."

"You've seen the general here?"

"Yes. And when the trees are dormant, I've seen him help many of the other volunteers prune them. I think he likes working with his hands."

"I can believe that. He has quite a collection of miniature antique tractors in his office. I wonder if he would've liked being a farmer more than a fighter pilot."

"Who knows?"

I wandered over to a wide and tall oak, then stared up at the ceiling-sky. A few wisps of white simulated clouds drifted across the artificial sky's bright blueness. Simulated sunshine cast long shadows across the lawn, the pool, the stream.

"Are you all right, Hector?" Lisa inquired.

I nodded again and sat down beside the oak. The soil beneath it, though covered with thick, soft grass, felt rough.

Grunting, I removed a small rock from beneath me. "They think of everything, don't they?"

"They do," she said, laughing and sitting beside me. "What were you thinking of just now?"

"Of home. Of my dad. And of my best friend when I was growing up, Raul Peres. When we were teens, Raul and I hiked a lot of mountain ranges. We even climbed some of the peaks in the Alps. That's a mountain range in Switzerland. But it's also in Italy, France, and a few other countries in Europe. I don't suppose you're familiar with the geography of Earth?"

"Just a little."

"Well, they're beautiful mountains. Steep, magnificent, green mountains. Worth hiking, worth climbing."

"What happened to your friend? Where's he now?"

I shrugged my shoulders. "I don't know. He wasn't interested in flying or serving the Association. He was always more interested in commerce. He thought I was insane, wanting to spend my life flying for Sky Command. So we eventually went our separate ways."

"Have you ever seen him again?"

"No."

"Not even when you return to Earth for a visit?"

"I haven't been back since graduating the Academy."

"Not even to visit your father?"

"He died when I was thirteen."

"I'm so sorry."

I nodded.

"What about your mother? Is she still alive?"

"As far as I know."

"Don't you ever visit her?"

"No."

"Why not?"

I sighed. "We were never close. In fact, she hardly ever showed any emotion toward me when my father was alive. And after his death, it was like living with a stranger. We never spoke. She never asked how I was doing. She never asked where I was going. She lived her life and left me to live mine.

"In fact, the only thing she did for me was endorse my application to the Academy. The day I left, all she said was, 'Goodbye'. I was so stunned that she actually spoke to me that I walked over to her and hugged her. She just stood there like a metal pole, her arms at her sides.

"She never wrote to me at the Academy. She never sent me any messages. The first summer, when I returned home for vacation from the Academy, she was gone. I spent two days there, not knowing if she was even alive. Then I contacted her office and found out that she lived there now. I sent several messages to her, but she never returned any of them. The next summer, I discovered our apartment had been rented to someone else.

"I haven't seen her since. She didn't even come to my graduation."

"Perhaps she never knew what to say," Lisa suggested. "Perhaps she feels a great deal for you, but doesn't know how to express herself. How sad that would be, caring deeply for someone and never able to say so."

"I never thought about that. She had plenty of opportunities. Years of them. But I can certainly relate to caring for someone and not being able to tell her."

"You mean the girl you left behind on *Soyuz*?"

I nodded. "And my mother, too."

"You've had a sad life."

"Don't we all, sometimes? But I've had a good life, too. My father was my best friend. Before he left me. He named me after a hero in Greek Mythology. People almost always assume I'm Spanish because we lived in Spain and because Hector is a common Spanish name. But we actually came from England. It's just that my mother always wanted to live in the Spanish mountains. And then there was Raul. And while attending the Sky Command Academy, Pedro. Pedro's family welcomed me in. I visited them often while attending the Academy. Without them, I don't know what I would've done. I had nowhere else to go."

I didn't tell her that while spending one summer visiting Pedro's family, I fell in love with Pedro's sister, Anna. We were lovers for more than a year, until she realized how much Sky Command meant to me. I still remembered the message she sent me after we broke up. She desired a future for herself, one outside of the Command. She didn't want to marry me and wait either on Earth or some other world for me to return from frequent patrols and missions. She needed more than I could give her then.

Pedro never knew about us. Even now I had no intention of telling him that I'd slept with his sister. Close friends that we were, he'd still feel betrayed.

We sat and stared at the mock sky, at the trees, and the flowers and shrubs. After a little while, Lisa took my hand in hers. She leaned her head against my shoulder. We stayed that way for a while.

"Lisa," I began, but she stood, letting go of my hand.

"I have to get back, Hector. I've duties to attend."

"So do I, I think," I said, standing. "All this has been wonderful. Thanks."

She caressed my face with her hand. "You're welcome."

We walked across the Garden, until we reached the far side and another arbor, with pink, yellow and white honeysuckles covering it. I stopped before passing beneath the flowered arch and glanced back.

"This place is so incredible," I said. "It makes me miss Earth. But I don't have a home there anymore. The Command's my home now. So I guess that means this ship is my new home. Already everyone here seems like family to me, even though I've only been here a few days. But there's a lot of people who don't seem to want me to be part of their family."

"I'm certain it will all change," Lisa said. "It just takes time. And a willingness to forgive."

"Well, I'm willing, because this is all the family I have. I have nowhere else to go."

"That might change, too," she said, smiling at me.

"I think I'm falling in love with you," I said.

"I know I'm in love with you, Hector."

"You are?"

"You sound amazed."

"I am."

"Don't you feel worthy of being loved?" she asked.

"Sometimes I wonder. Real love and real happiness have eluded me so much that I've wondered if I'm meant to be alone."

"No one's meant to be alone, Hector. We're a social species. We're meant to be together."

"Yet it seems easier for some more than others. Life is so fragile. One moment, you're happy and in love and the next, it's all gone."

"What do you mean?" she asked.

"Look at Lori and Pedro, how happy they are. They deserve each other."

"Don't you feel we deserve each other?"

"Yes. But life is so fragile. Look at all the people dying down on Eos. Lori would've died today if not for me. She still can. So can Pedro. This damned war can tear their lives apart forever. And the same could happen to us."

"Then we should be as happy as we can before that happens. Love is for now, not the future."

"I'm afraid. Both to care and not to care."

"Then let love wash that fear away. Love is strong enough for that."

We looked at each other for a long moment, then kissed. Afterward, holding hands, we walked beneath the arbor. Just beyond was another exit. Smiling, Lisa led me out. "Come, dear. The best is yet to be."

CHAPTER SEVENTEEN

LISA AND I KISSED again just outside the gardens, then we went our separate ways, she to her squadron further aft and me to mine farther forward. I walked but a few steps before I turned around to watch her disappear down the corridor, a sense of peace and pleasant anticipation filling my soul. After she was gone, I spun around and almost collided with Major Garacyk.

"Excuse me, sir, I didn't see you there."

"Evidently not. But it's my fault, too. I hurried too much. I'm glad I ran across you."

"Sir?"

"At ease. I'm not here officially. I was coming down to spend a little time in the gardens. I need a little peace."

"It's good place for that, sir."

"It is. I'm sorry about Captain Mboko's behavior. I read all the pertinent reports. She's asked for severe discipline against you. But the situation warrants otherwise."

"Sir, I had to protect Diamond. There weren't any SAR boats available."

"I know that, lieutenant. I don't intend to court-martial you. Neither does Colonel Wallis, nor General Devon. You acted properly. But I must support my exec somehow. So I'm restricting you to your cabin, the pilot's mess, and your official station. You will spend your time inspecting all the current sims that have arrived in the last few days. You will also program a new sim based on your experiences today attacking enemy ground units."

"Sir, my official station is aboard my fighter."

"Not as of this moment. Your official station is in Captain Jonkowski's office."

"But, sir, I belong out there. You need every pilot and every bird. My bird's in good shape. And so am I."

"I agree. But I have to support Captain Mboko. For today, you are grounded. Tomorrow, you'll fly again. But not for today. I'll hear nothing more about it."

"Affirmative, sir."

"Starting tomorrow, you will no longer fly in any COP with Captain Mboko."

"Affirmative, sir."

"You did a fine job today, Crossman. I've got your measure. I'm proud you're in my squadron. With luck we'll all survive this. See you out there. Tomorrow."

"Thank you, sir." I spent the next several hours sorting through and updating the sims in Captain Jonkowski's office. It'd been two days since I'd last worked there. Since then no less than fifteen sims had arrived from the other squadrons fighting over Eos, not including three new training sims that had arrived with the latest supply ships from Ilmatar. It took three hours to run through them.

Five of the sims, including the three training sims from the Command's regional training facility on Ilmatar, proved useful. But the other ten sims had serious flaws.

One sim had fighters destroying boxes without missiles, the fighters's plasma cannons burning through the enemy's shields without even a hint of difficulty. The author of that sim suggested that pilots needed practice penetrating enemy formations and that believability was less important than practice. That might be fine for a planetary sky force which never intended fighting a real enemy. But without a semblance of reality and acute attention to detail in a simulation, a pilot could die when thrust into real combat. Once the pilot was dead, it would be too late to blame the lazy author of a poorly constructed simulation.

Lack of attention to detail plagued all the remaining sims. Either the Gorgon gunboats were too slow or they were too fast; they were too good or they weren't good enough. In one sim there weren't enough plasma cannons on each enemy gunboat. In another, the pilot's fighter outperformed its capabilities.

It was as if the pilots had never flown fighters before designing these sims. It frustrated the hell out of me and after three hours of trying to correct the mistakes in each simulation, I discarded the whole lot. We'd received five good sims. That was enough. The others were garbage and into the electronic garbage can they disappeared. None of our pilots would ever fly these grotesque misrepresentations!

Done, I took a break. I visited the head, Navy talk for the men's room, then I went down to a snack booth and got a container of milk and a delicious chocolate brownie.

Returning to Jonkwoski's office, I noticed one of the simulators occupied. It was the first I'd seen anyone in here and I wondered who it was.

I didn't wonder long.

After a few minutes, during which I finished my brownie and milk and discarded the milk container in a recycling unit in Jonkowski's inner office, I saw the hatch to the simulator pop open. A tall, muscular man with short-cropped blond hair exited.

It was Vladimir Geys.

"So," he said, "that was your great Gargaphia adventure?"

I nodded.

"If that's all it was, you should go back to basic flying and learn how to pilot all over again. I almost fell asleep."

"I'm sorry it bored you."

"Not as sorry as I am."

"Don't you have a COP to fly? Gorgons to kill? Asses to kiss?"

"Listen, Piss Maker—"

"My call sign's Ice Maker."

"Piss Maker fits you better."

"Why don't you get out of here?"

Vlad stepped closer. With both hands, he shoved me into a wall. "You're not good enough for her. When I find a way, I'll prove it to her. Until then, stay away from her."

"Or what?" I growled. He towered above me, more muscular and powerful than me. I felt like a child threatening a giant.

"Or we're going to have words. And then you're going to spend a long time in *Akagi*'s sickbay."

"Is that how you're going to win Lisa, by beating me up? You think she'll be attracted to you for that?"

His jaw muscles tightened. "I'll do whatever it takes to keep you away from her."

"Vlad, she loves me. And I love her," I said, leaning away from the wall.

He grabbed me by the throat with both hands, choking me, slamming me into the wall again. I felt my eyes bulging. My tongue jutted out of my mouth. I struggled to breathe.

I kicked him hard in one of his shins. Howling, he let go of me, stumbling away, clasping his leg, rubbing it. "You fight like the coward you are, Piss Maker! Did you wet your pants?"

I slumped to the deck, rubbing my throat. "You're the coward," I croaked. "You can't accept reality. You're afraid to. Lisa loves me. It's true. It's real. Believe it. Accept it. She picked me, not you!"

Vladimir growled. Straightening, he advanced upon me, his fist raised to strike. I stood to meet him.

The door to the outer office whistled open. Captain Jonkowski entered. She glanced at Geys, then at me.

"Am I intruding?" she said, her voice cold as death.

Vladimir lowered his arm. "We're not through, Piss Maker."

"I think we are."

He started toward me, then stopped. Straightening his uniform, he spun around and lunged out of the room.

"Are you all right?" Rana asked me.

"I think so," I croaked.

"And what was that about?"

"Lisa Mauros told me she loves me."

"And he doesn't like that?"

"That's putting it mildly," I said, standing.

"So I noticed. Do you love her?"

"Yes."

Rana smiled. "Good! That is as it should be."

I straightened my uniform and brushed my hair back into place with my hands. "What should I do about Vlad?"

"Learn how to fight."

"I already know how to fight."

"Learn how to fight better."

"Thanks a lot."

"You are most welcome. How do you feel about your COP today?"

"How should I feel about it?"

"You seem very defensive. Considering what I witnessed between you and Lieutenant Geys, and Captain Mboko's mistreatment of you, it is understandable. But I am your friend, Hector. I only wish to help. You can relax with me."

"It's been a very difficult day. First I'm fighting for my life and the life of my best friend's lover. And then I'm accused of insubordination and threatened with a court-martial. Then I discover Lisa loves me. Then I come here and spend hours going over some of the worst simulations I've ever seen, only to be attacked by my rival for Lisa's affection. But he doesn't know he's not in the running anymore and he can't accept that.

"I've never had a day like this with so many ups and downs, with so much horror and so much joy. I don't know whether to laugh or cry, but I know I'm close to exhaustion."

"It's understandable," Rana said. "But we all have days like this. That's what war is about. Sorrow and joy and hatred and fear and loathing, all these emotions can come to us in one day. But we are safe in here, in this room, aboard *Akagi*, safer than those below on Eos. Men, women, soldiers, pilots, families, children are all dying down there.

"While we're aboard ship we can let go of the horror below. We not only can let go, but we must let go. Those below have to live through hell every minute of every day.

But we can relax and rest before exposing ourselves to those horrors again. We can live the life others have put on hold. It is not fair that they have had to place their lives on hold to survive a war while we can relax and live for a few hours aboard this ship, but war is never fair. Yet we must live our lives while we can, for that is what anyone, especially those fighting and dying on Eos, would do. They fight for us and we fight for them.

"So, love Lisa and worry about Vlad and the war another time. Relax. Rest. Now, what have you done about the simulation Anton has asked you to write?"

"I haven't had much chance to work on it yet."

"Then let us get to work. I think we may be flying many ground support missions in the future, until the Marines get more gunboats and crews to replace their losses against the enemy. That may be soon. Or not. Who can say?"

I nodded. "I thought I'd begin with the atrocity I witnessed today."

She sighed. "It is important knowledge, but don't let it consume you. It is not important for a training sim concerning ground attack missions. Let us begin with your detection of the enemy tanks and ground forces and then move from there."

I nodded.

"Good."

We spent the rest of the afternoon working on my sim. I discovered that Rana knew her stuff. Not only could she out-fly most pilots, but she knew better than anyone I'd ever met how to put her experiences into a simulation. She helped me remember details that had slipped past me during the heat of battle. We examined the sensor logs from the destroyer pickets, from the micro-probes, and from my fighter, and then began construction on a detailed, dynamic, suitable simulation.

We had just reached the halfway point in our sim when Rana suggested we quit for the day.

"We will finish it tomorrow," she said. "It will give us something to do between fighting and loving."

I gave her a questioning glance. She grinned back.

"Go to her, Hector. I am certain you have plans for the evening. But watch out for Vladimir."

"You bet I will," I replied. She escorted me from her office and into the corridor beyond. I glanced up and down it, checking for Vlad, and for anyone else.

"You know, it's ironic," I began.

"What is?"

"Just some months back, I was in Vlad's place."

"In what way?" Rana asked.

"Aboard *Soyuz*, I was in love with another woman from Gentry. Her name was Corinna Vernon and I can't tell you whether I loved her like Lisa or not, because I don't know."

"We never love anyone exactly the same. The intensity might be there. Or might not. But each person is different and the love we feel for them is different. We only need to know that we love someone. That should be enough."

I nodded. "Well, Corinna was interested in someone else. And I didn't think he was good enough for her. In fact, I know he wasn't. Once, on leave, he sought me out and assaulted me. He was somewhat like Vlad in that respect."

Rana nodded. "I see. Now you are on the other side of the equation. How did it turn out?"

"She wanted different things than he wanted, so she left him. She left me, too."

"It is just as well."

"Why? I suffered a lot of heartache over her."

"Letting go of loved ones is difficult. But if you hadn't let go of her, you wouldn't have room in your heart for Lisa."

"You're right."

"I am always right. Now find her. The two of you make a fine couple. Remember, let go of the past. And do not worry about Vladimir. He's strong. He, too, will let go."

"I hope he does soon."

Rana shrugged. "Who can say?"

CHAPTER EIGHTEEN

"How did it go today?" Lisa asked, snuggling beside me in bed. We were in my cabin this time. Last night we slept in her cabin. We alternated cabins every night, allowing us each an opportunity to be near our squadrons in case of an emergency.

I stared at my cabin's ceiling. Dim light from the stars of a pseudo-Earth sky glowed down upon us; in Lisa's cabin Gentry's night sparkled at us. "Ava's quite a pilot. Lori's lucky to have her for a wing mate. And I was lucky to fly with her yet again. That's four days in a row now, while Lori's been flying with Brattano. She's flown SARCOP and seen some action but I think it's been mostly to give her a chance to relax after being shot down and maybe regain some of her confidence. However, she and Ava will fly their next COP together. So I wonder who I'll fly with next. Hopefully, not Brattano."

"Hopefully not," Lisa agreed. "But you still haven't told me how your last COP went."

"Well, in the first box, Ava and I each destroyed three gunboats. I only used my missiles, but Ava used both her missiles and her cannon. In the next box, I got three more gunboats while she got the remaining four, none of them with missiles! She's an incredible shot. I wouldn't want her on my tail hunting me."

Lisa's soft hand stroked my bare chest. "There probably isn't much chance of that happening."

"Probably not. Anyway, that's the way our COP went. I expended all of my missiles and Ava expended ten of hers. She came back with six spares. We each killed fifteen gunboats, splitting apart five different boxes. She's only a few behind me now. Garacyk and Yakima each bagged twelve. The four of us combined shot down fifty-four gunboats.

"I can't say how everyone else is doing, but our squadron's shooting down several hundred gunboats every day. You'd think the wormheads would start to run out of them. But they just keep coming. They seem to have an endless supply."

"I sincerely hope not," Lisa said.

Turning onto my side, I looked at her. Dim as the ceiling's virtual starlight was, I could still see her lovely face and eyes. I wanted to tell her everything would be okay, but I didn't want it to be okay. I wanted to kill as many Gorgons as I could. I wanted to make them pay for what they did to that young woman and to make certain they didn't do it to any of my friends and especially not Lisa.

Instead, I asked: "Is something troubling you?"

"I might ask the same of you," she replied.

"What d'you mean?"

"You've been pensive all evening. Are you still thinking about what happened a few days ago?"

I caressed her hair. It felt like silk. "There's no place I'd rather be than right here, right now, with you. What you said about the Garden warming our hearts is true, but you warm my heart more than anything else ever could. I feel warm and comfortable and loved when I'm with you. I'm not alone in the universe. I'm not even alone in my own heart. No one has ever touched my soul like you."

"Are we friends?" she asked. "Or just lovers?"

"Both, I hope. I certainly love you as both."

She pushed me onto my back and kissed me, then rested her head on my chest. "I think of you as my friend, too. As my best friend. And I do love you, dearest."

We kissed some more.

Afterwards, she reminded me, "You still haven't answered my question."

"What question's that?"

"Is that atrocity still bothering you?"

"It'll always bother me. I just can't get that image out of my head. What they did to that poor woman, chopping her up like meat. And she was alive when they started, Lisa! She was still alive."

I took a deep breath to calm myself. "When I first flew against the Gorgons, I didn't feel anything toward them. They were the enemy and it was my job to stop them. But now I know they're evil. They kill for the pleasure of killing. Yes, we're told that our appearance and biochemistry drive them insane. But they enjoy killing us. It pleases them and they'll stop at nothing in butchering us in as many horrible ways as they can. I've seen burnt bodies on the streets. I've seen the visuals taken from probes behind enemy lines. They incinerate children, Lisa! They've no compassion for us, no empathy, no remorse. They desire our destruction and they seek it in the most horrible ways imaginable.

"I can't just be satisfied with shooting a few of them out of the sky. I've got to stop them. I've got to wipe them out.

Every single one of them, if I can. I've got to keep them from murdering anyone else."

Feeling Lisa trembling, I stopped. I forced myself to relax. "I didn't mean to scare you."

"You didn't. Well, maybe a little. Hector, I don't want you to become a monster. I believe that if we're not careful, this war will rob us of our souls. We have to hold onto what's good and true inside ourselves. We cannot let the war crush our spirits. We cannot give up hope that the hating and violence will eventually stop, that peace can and will return to us and to the people of Eos.

"I couldn't be with you if you turned into a vengeful monster, dearest. I couldn't live with a man like that."

"Would you stop loving me?" I asked.

"I'd try not to. But I couldn't remain with you."

"Then I'll try not to lose myself in this war."

Lisa held my hand. "I don't know if we can ever forget what we've seen here. I still see the images of shuttles full of innocent people being destroyed by the enemy. But I know we have to put it behind us. If we don't, I firmly believe it will consume us."

"I don't know how to do that yet."

"We'll find a way together, Hector. For our souls, we'll find a way."

While Lisa slept, I dressed. I had an early briefing to attend. I'd meet my new partner today. I hoped he wasn't another idiot like Brattano.

After dressing and freshening up in my bathroom, I returned to look at Lisa. She seemed so peaceful, so beautiful, so perfect. I wanted to say goodbye to her, but I couldn't bring myself to awaken her. I wanted her to have what peace existed for her, for any of us, while she slept.

Leaning over, I kissed her forehead. She slept on, undisturbed. I listened to her gentle breathing. I stroked her hair one more time. The gentle pre-dawn light of the ceiling's virtual sky bathed her face in a bluish glow.

I didn't want to leave her. I didn't want to go to the briefing. I didn't want to fly today, to fight today. I wanted to stay with her. I wanted to hold her in my arms. I wanted to be safe and secure and warm in her presence. I wanted happiness, peace, a future. I wanted to love Lisa all day and all night.

I wanted to shut the universe out.

But I had to go my briefing, because if I failed to fly today someone else would have to do it for me. Maybe one of my friends or another member of my squadron, would have to fly into harm's way, assuming the burden my cowardice gave them.

Yet I couldn't do that. I couldn't ask someone else to serve in my place.

So I proceeded toward war, toward destruction and death.

Where I journeyed, I need no soul. I needed no love, no future, no past. I only needed the now.

A now of destruction, death, ruin, and rampage. My fellow pilots and I would kill the enemy. We existed for one purpose: to erase our enemy from the memory of the universe.

And we would do it, because if we didn't, the Gorgons would do it to us. They would wipe humanity from this planet, eliminating all memory of the men, women, and children that had lived here.

So I left Lisa behind, to fly, to fight, to become that which she dreaded the most: a monster, a killer, a hater, a destroyer; but only for this moment, for this COP, and the next COP, and the one after that, and for every other COP after that. I would kill for my friends and for Lisa.

This was my dilemma. For how could I kill and destroy and return to Lisa not as the monster I was, but as the man she loved and wanted me to be?

How?

Suited up, I entered the gallery. I noticed six other pilots present. I spotted Jacques over by a corner, his head leaning against a wall. As I approached him, I heard him snore. I debated whether or not to awaken him, but Captain Inagaki solved the issue for me.

"Eyes front," Inagaki announced, entering at a march.

Jacques sighed and sat up. He rubbed his eyes. "Oh, hey, mon," he said to me. "How long you been here?"

"Less than a minute."

"Good. Did you sleep well?"

"Very much so."

"With Lisa?"

"None of your business."

Jacques laughed. "I'm glad you two are happy."

"Listen up!" Inagaki growled out. "We've got a lot of changes today. We'll get right to it."

"Hey, it's piss maker," Brattano said, noticing me.

"We've been covering the Eosian Army and our Marines as they've retreated out of Atlatya," Inagaki said. "Well, they're clear now. They've traveled a hundred kilometers north and have now crossed the Asopus River.

"While our forces fought for Atlatya, several Eosian Army engineering brigades built defensive positions on the northern bank of the river. These positions rival those built in the center of the continent south of Austeropolis.

There we've stopped and contained the Gorgons's central army. We hope to do the same thing here with the Asopus Line."

"Is that what they're calling it?" a young woman I had yet to meet, asked.

"Affirmative. It's forty kilometers deep and three hundred wide. It consists of shielded fortifications, each of which are covered by five other fortifications. These fortifications are set in rolling, tree-lined hills. Several streams flow through these hills."

"It must have been beautiful before the war," I commented.

"Probably," Inagaki replied.

"But it ain't gonna be anymore," Brattano said.

"That's right, mon. After the wormheads roll through it, it'll look like hell."

"Every place on Eos is starting to look like hell," Vlad said. "If we don't stop the Gorgons soon, it won't just look like hell, it'll be Hell!"

"Here's where we come in," Inagaki continued. "We have to help the Eosian Army keep the Gorgons from penetrating the Line."

"What do we have defending it?" Jacques asked.

"Six Eosian divisions, plus a scattering of border police and militia battalions. There's also a Colonial Guard division. And twenty-six sky defense battalions spread about the Line."

"What about the far side of the continent?" an unfamiliar pilot, tall, thin, and bald, asked. I wondered whether he or the female pilot, both strangers to me, would be my new wingmate.

"That's a good question," Captain Inagaki said. "The Gorgons have penetrated deeply on the eastern side of

Titanus. Though they've been contained in the middle of the continent at the foot of the Auster Mountains, and though we hope to contain them here, they're running wild along the eastern side. They've destroyed Napei and Misene. At defensive positions in the Morz Desert they fought a huge battle with the Eosian Army, with militia units, with the Marines, and with four Colonial Guard divisions."

"What happened?" the unfamiliar female pilot asked.

"We lost."

"How bad was it?" Vlad asked.

"Bad enough. More than twenty thousand dead."

"Oh, my god!" the female pilot exclaimed.

"How many did we kill?" Vlad asked.

"Possibly twice as many. There's no way to know."

"Mon, we cannot win a war of attrition," Jacques said. "They're like ants. They keep coming and coming and we cannot fight them all."

"Agreed," Inagaki said. "The enemy has broken into the vast Argolian Plain. The Gorgons have slaughtered the inhabitants of dozens of small farming villages and hundreds of farms. One column wiped out both Marpessa and Ajenor. Those two cities, the villages, and the farms bring the recent civilian casualties in the East to nearly a million dead. Defensive positions have been set up around D'Amato, Argus, and Dorman City. Their populations are being evacuated. Peterstown is far enough back that it's being used as a staging area.

"All Colonial Guard squadrons are now assigned to the Eastern theater. Three more are expected to arrive in a few days. What's left of the Eosian sky forces fight there, too. Additionally, one of *Resolute*'s fighter squadrons has been detailed there."

"With only three squadrons protecting the center?" I said.

"Oh, you can add, huh, piss maker?" Brattano said.

"Shut-up!" Captain Inagaki growled.

"Sorry, sir," Brattano replied.

My right hand covered my mouth to hide my smirk.

"You might like to know that another task force is en route to join us. The Navy's had some difficulties gathering together Task Force Thirty-three. They diverted forces from other regions to protect this region's frontier. As a result, five escort carriers are en route, along with more cruisers, destroyers, Colonial Guard units, and two more Marine brigades. The fighters and gunboats from these carriers will be assigned exclusively to the Eastern Theater."

"Why?" asked the dark-haired pilot named Amal, who I had briefly encountered the first time when I met Inagaki. "We need them here, too."

"Most of the refugees from Atlatya, Austeropolis, and all the cities on the eastern side of Titanus are located around Eospolis, Breckenridge, and Brickridge star port. If the Gorgons break out of the Argolian Plain, those refugees will be unprotected. We have to hold them to the plains."

"Understood," Amal replied.

"What about the Colonial Rangers?" Geys growled. "Those damned cowards have been hiding in orbit for a long time. They should be down here."

"They are down here," Inagaki replied.

"What?"

"We've had troubles lately getting supplies from Ilmatar. Either the Gorgons have broadened the war, or else Na pirates are responsible. Two days ago a transport carrying eighteen new gunboats and their crews was vaporized by raiders. A second transport was damaged a day later. It carried six hundred Marines, thirty of whom were killed. Fortunately, two destroyers were close behind and they arrived in time to run off the raiders."

"Sir, how does this apply to my question?" Vlad asked.

"I'm getting there," Inagaki replied. "Even with the increased risks beyond this system, the Colonial Rangers have managed to sneak in several battalions. More importantly, they've managed to land all their forces undetected by the enemy."

"Where are they?" the female pilot asked.

"Some are dug in behind the Asopus Line, waiting to strike. The rest are somewhere near Peterston. I believe they're planning a counter-strike. But where, when, and how is unknown to me. I don't have clearance for that. But I do know that more Rangers are coming with Task Force Thirty-three.

"None of that changes our assignment today. Each squadron is keeping a GORCOP over the battlefield. We will replace the present GORCOP. While deployed we'll be known as GORCOP One. Coming and going we'll be GORCOP One-A.

"Our job is to shoot down gunboats. We will concentrate on those gunboats causing the most havoc. If a ground unit calls for help, do all you can for them. But only against sky forces. Leave the ground to the grunts. Got it?"

"Affirmative!" we chimed.

"Good. We will carry maximum loads. Sixteen missiles. Watch your tails and good hunting. See you out there!"

As we stood, I wondered who was my new partner.

"Crossman," Captain Inagaki said, walking over to me. Behind him trailed Amal, his partner, and the two unfamiliar pilots. "This is your new partner. Take good care of him."

"Glad to meet ya," the bald pilot said, poking a hand toward me. "I'm Sherman Kent. You can call me Sherm. Everyone does."

"I'm Hector Crossman. Glad to meet you, too. Is Sherm your call sign?" I shook his hand. There was something about this guy that I liked right away. He had a twinkle in his eyes, the sort of twinkle that Pedro had.

"Nope. Boxer's my call sign. My nom de plume."

"Your what?"

"It's French. It means 'pen name'."

We went out the door and headed down the corridor toward my bird's bay. "Your bird this way, too?"

"Yep. Bay Twenty. What's your call sign?"

"Ice Maker."

"Sounds like a beverage," he quipped.

I laughed. "You're right, it does."

"I like it."

"Good." We walked along in silence for a moment, not knowing what next to say. We were new to each other, strangers who had to become the best of friends as soon as possible for survival's sake.

"So, compared to me, you're a cherry here?" I asked.

His face broke into a big, wide, pleasant grin. "You bet."

We descended the circular stairs leading our birds.

"I think you and I are gonna get along fine," he said.

"So do I. How long you been here?"

"I've been here a few days."

"Flown any COPs?"

"Every day. I was doubled up with Third Squadron. Twenty-six pilots instead of twenty-four."

"With that new female pilot?"

"Nope. She came in from a replacement pool just today. I heard she's scheduled to fly later today. The pilot I served with is Lieutenant Munk, who also transferred here me today. He was on the Academy's gymnastics team. Everyone said he was a regular monkey in gymnastics. So the flight instructors, when picking his call sign, said it was proper that the monkey's name should be Munk, which is also his real name."

"He told you all that?"

"Yep. Here's my bay. He told me something else, too. For a long time, he had trouble hearing his instructors when they called his training bird's comm. So, whenever they wanted to get his attention, they shouted 'Munk' real loud. He heard that."

"He doesn't have trouble recognizing call signs now, does he?" I asked.

"Nope. He's over that. See you out there."

"See you out there, Sherm."

Sherm smiled and entered his bay. A few moments later, I entered mine. I was surprised to find it empty except for my bird. Not even a robot lingered performing a last-minute task. I walked around my bird, inspecting it.

Climbing onto the grav platform, I floated up to my cockpit, climbed in, and settled into my acceleration couch. "Hello, Prax," I said. "Where is everybody?"

"Hello, Hector," Prax replied. "Sergeant Lincoln and her crew left a few minutes ago. She said don't break anything."

I laughed. "Are we pre-flighted?"

"Affirmative."

"Then send away the platform, close the canopy, and begin de-pressurization."

"Affirmative. You are in a good mood."

"As good as I can be under the circumstances."

"Understood."

With the canopy closed and sealed, and de-pressurization completed, Prax opened our bay door to the flight deck and maneuvered us out. To my left, I spotted Sherm's bird leaving its bay. Just to his left another bird emerged.

From across the flight deck five more fighters glided out, shifting into their gravitic launchers. The two fighters to my left drifted into their launchers.

I did the same.

"Ice Maker, Boxer. Hey buddy, you in there?"

"Affirmative, Boxer. Where else would I be?"

"Just checking. Say, what do you get when you cross a Gorgon with a Na?"

"I don't know." Most people considered the Gorgons as hideous creatures. And the Na, with their transparent bodies, were almost invisible. "What do you get?"

"A really ugly guy you can't see."

I laughed.

"Hey, buddy, that's the slowest laugh I ever heard. It's like you're standing still doing the speed of light downhill."

"Only if I lived in that black hole between your ears," I replied.

"Ouch! That's a good one. Mind if I use it sometime?"

"You have a mind? I thought it was just vacuum."

"Okay, okay, you win."

"Cut the noise, you two," Captain Inagaki called.

"Oops. Affirmative, Guardian," Sherm said.

"Affirmative," I added.

"GORCOP One-A, this is *Akagi* control. You're cleared for launch."

"Affirmative, *Akagi*," Inagaki replied. "One-A, launch!"

Each of our birds hurled from the carrier's side, two seconds apart. Once out, we turned and dived toward Eos, our vector designated by one of the picket destroyers watching over the Asopus River. In twelve minutes, we'd be there.

"Hector, may I inquire of your good spirits?" Prax asked.

"You may. I like this new wingman. He's comfortable to be around. He has a good, if strange, sense of humor. He reminds me of Pedro."

"I see. Are there any other reasons?"

"Not really. It's hard to keep a good moment while knowing we're being butchered down on Eos. You have to take the moments of happiness and joy when you can. But I'll have to put it behind me soon. Once we're past the pickets, Prax, then it's all business, understand? We have to burn as many gunboats as possible. There's a new line below and we have to stop the Gorgons down there. Got it?"

"Affirmative, Hector. I am sorry if I annoyed you."

"You didn't. You just reminded that I've a job to do. When someone loses their concentration, that's when accidents happen. Let's avoid accidents today."

"Affirmative."

"One-A, leader," Captain Inagaki called. "One of our picket destroyers suggests we watch out for marauding Gorgon corvettes. They're as large as our corvettes are and just as dangerous. It has spotted several just above and beyond the sky battle, trying to pick off our fighters. One corvette has already damaged two birddogs. Be alert."

We chorused "Affirmative."

As we descended, we received telemetry from various sources, including micro-probes released into the battle arena, Eosian ground units, Association Marine units, from the destroyers monitoring the fighting, even from the SAR boats and many of the fighters engaging the enemy. So much information arrived that at times even Prax had trouble sorting it out.

But I hardly cared how much information came in, or if none arrived at all. We had our own sensors and that'd be enough. All I wanted was to get down there and blast the enemy.

"Ice Maker, Boxer. Hey, buddy, you've been pretty silent over there the last few minutes. You okay?"

"Boxer, Ice Maker. Just waiting for the fighting to begin."

"I hear ya. Just don't let it get too personal, okay? We make mistakes when we get too involved."

"How can we not be involved? They're trying to kill us. And they're killing thousands of people down there, too."

"I know, buddy, I know. But step back a little, okay. My dad told me that when you fight, be angry. But control your anger, he said. Keep it cold. Then you won't lose control. Didn't your dad ever tell you something like that?"

"No. But it's good advice. Thanks."

As we continued our descent, I began paying attention to the telemetry information. Prax had darkened our canopy against the flaring atmospheric friction caused by our energy screen. He now projected imagery and technical graphics upon the canopy's interior curve. I saw scattered clouds, then flashing from energy discharges, then explosions on the ground, and then thousands of contrails made by fighters and gunboats racing through the moisture-enriched atmosphere.

The Gorgons fielded two hundred boxes over the Asopus Line, attacking everywhere. Thousands of laser beams, invisible to the naked eye but enhanced by Prax to appear as thin red lines, swept back and forth over the battlefield as the Eosian Army's sky defense batteries sought to down the enemy's gunboats.

Countering these deadly beams were the bluish-white plasma streams from the enemy's formations as they fought back. Defensive energy screens flared brightly as lasers touched gunboats, or as plasma cannons contacted the energy barriers surrounding ground fortifications. Wherever the enemy's plasma streams contacted unprotected surfaces, whether trees, rocks, structures, barren ground or even armored soldiers, flames erupted and explosions occurred.

And as the Gorgon gunboats swept across the sky, so too the enemy's ground forces swept into the Asopus Line. Thousands of tanks and hundreds of thousands of armor-suited troops stormed the line, crashing through barriers, vaporizing walls, slaughtering defenders.

The enemy rolled onward, a giant, multi-headed beast with dozens of sharp and bloody claws ripping and tearing at the men and women in its way. Yet the Eosian soldiers slashed at the monsters, chopping off heads, breaking limbs, smashing claws.

Plasma streams stretched from tanks, searing walls and flesh. In turn, plasma cannons buried deep behind ceramcarb walls flamed back, exploding tanks and roasting Gorgon soldiers.

The ground below appeared scorched, no tree, no plant, no native animal left breathing, let alone alive. Barren hills covered with blackened and grotesque shapes extended everywhere. Scattered around burned-out bunkers lay the charred remains of machines, of tanks, of gunboats, of various armored ground vehicles used by man and alien alike.

Smoke drifted over the battlefield. Black smoke. Greasy smoke. Bloody, evil, sickening smoke.

"Looks like hell," Boxer called.

"Affirmative," I replied.

"One-A, leader. Concentrate on the sky. We're holding them on the ground. Vector your eyes to the battle's fringes."

I did as Captain Inagaki suggested. There, out over the sea, and over the forested plains far east of the fighting flew large Gorgon gunboat formations.

Prax adjusted the resolution. Enemy corvettes flew in looser formations, also seeking prey.

"One-A, leader. Look high above the Line. The enemy's flying fifty formations there, engaging our GORCOPs. We have to penetrate their HICOP. We'll dive in pairs. Keep tight and accelerate as you dive. Pull out as close to the deck as possible. Engage as many boxes as you can. Then get out of there before the corvettes arrive. Questions?"

"What about friendly fire from the ground?" Brattano asked.

"Watch out for it," Inagaki replied.

"And if we're attacked as we dive?" I asked.

"Then piss your pants and run," Vlad said.

Brattano laughed.

"Shut up, Vampire. Avoid the enemy until on the deck. We have to penetrate their HICOP. Understood?"

"Affirmative," we all replied.

"We have officially relieved the last GORCOP," Captain Inagaki stated. "We are now GORCOP One."

Plowing through the atmosphere, we became eight fireballs diving for the hellish fighting far below.

Prax kept me informed of crucial enemy activity. He reported two corvettes flying far to the west of the Asopus Line. They harried fighters from Fifth and Seventh squadrons.

We tightened our formation as we approached the fighting. Captain Inagaki vectored us toward the eastern end of the Line, where enemy sky activity seemed the least concentrated.

"Leader to GORCOP One. Guardian and Saracen will dive first, followed by Vampire and Brat. Jacko and Swan follow next. Boxer and Ice Maker, you'll bring up the rear. Jacko, vector right when you reach the deck. Try to disrupt any attacks on the bunkers."

"Affirmative," Jacques replied.

Inagaki and Amal pulled ahead of us, flying so close that their energy screens almost touched. Static energy from atmospheric friction and the close proximity of their screens arced back and forth between them. They appeared as one large meteor falling from the sky, the energy arcs between their screens looking like lightning from the Greek god Zeus as he sent his holy warriors after the monsters attacking his heavenly world, Eos. They were avenging angels, descending from heaven, intent upon inflicting their holy wrath against the monsters desecrating the beautiful world below.

Guardian and Saracen screamed past the enemy's HICOP, catching them by surprise. Within moments they pulled up, barely clearing the ground as they vectored left, then right, then left again, avoiding both friendly and enemy fire, then vaporizing an entire box attacking a bunker.

Vampire and Brat followed but seconds behind Guardian and Saracen. They, too, caught the Gorgons off-guard. Five seconds after the first flaming pair dodged destruction over Eos, the second pair raced low over the Line, vaporizing four gunboats.

Jacko and Swan faired less well.

The enemy was ready now. As Jacques led his wingmate into a steep dive, two boxes followed them. The Gorgons accelerated, seeking to close with the divers. Abruptly, their formations split apart, shifting into four vics. Each vic consisted of three gunboats, one leading with two others on either side. They tightened their formations as they dived until they almost touched each other, their hulls barely a few meters apart, their energy screens overlapping. These tight formations allowed them to fly through the crowded sky much as our fighters did.

As each box split into vics, their center gunboats sped away, absorbed by other boxes and escorted from the battle zone. It was the first time we'd seen these tactics.

"Oh, shit, they're dead!" Boxer exclaimed.

"Negative. Keep close. We'll cover them."

"We're supposed to break through and kick Gorgon butts."

"We're supposed to wreck gunboats," I countered. "And that's what we'll be doing. Keep my tail clear. And keep close."

"I'm with you."

We dropped behind the vics, accelerating faster and faster. Jacko and Swan burst through a box, vaporizing a gunboat apiece and scattering the enemy. The vics followed them. One of the fleeing gunboats, seeking to avoid them, crashed into a different box, vaporizing itself and another gunboat.

"We're diving too fast!" Boxer called.

"Keep on my six."

"I'm here," he said.

We shot towards the surface, Jacko, Swan, and the vics preceding us. Jacko and Swan pulled up at the last moment, Swan's fighter tearing the sensor mast off the top of a bunker, barely clearing its roof. The Gorgons continued their pursuit, pulling out sooner in a more shallow arc.

And we followed them all.

The wormheads had not caught sight of our pursuit. Neither had any of their other fellow gunboats.

"Too fast! Too fast!" Boxer yelled.

He was right. "Pull up," I called, bringing my nose up as my inertial dampers and antigrav generator screeched. My bird vibrated wildly. I feared it might tear apart. But it held together. We avoided the ground. We also avoided a bunker right before us as I pulled up a little more and to the left, while Boxer vectored right. We rejoined almost immediately on the other side of the bunker.

"Locate Jacko and Swan," I told Prax.

"They are twenty-seven kilometers ahead, near the surface, with enemy formations in close pursuit. The enemy is vectoring them toward the ocean," Prax announced.

"And their waiting corvettes," I replied.

"Possibly."

"Boxer, Ice Maker. Keep on my six. We're covering Jacko and Swan."

"Hey, buddy, there are targets everywhere."

"Shoot anything in our way, but save something for the wormheads following Jacko."

"Affirmative."

As we pursued the enemy, we received frantic calls from fortifications needing help. Altering our course slightly, Boxer and I spread out.

Black smoke hung low over the battlefield. My sensors apprized me of it even as they penetrated it, revealing the world beyond.

Fires raged everywhere. Flames soared skyward. Molten metal glowed. Trees burned. People burned. Tanks exploded. Bunkers exploded. The ground exploded, tossing humans, aliens, machines, rocks and parts of fortresses everywhere.

Hell raged around us.

We continued onward.

We flew toward a box high over a bunker, its collective cannons burning through the ceramcarb barriers beneath it. We each released a missile, incinerating a gunboat apiece in the formation. The remaining five boats scattered every which way, expecting pursuit and death as we raced beyond them.

We vectored toward our right where a gunboat formation assisted several of their tanks as they hunted down and massacred Eosian soldiers fleeing from their ruined fortress. Boxer vaped two of the boats with missiles, while I blew two more out of the sky with my plasma cannon. Then I dropped tight to the deck and brushed two tanks, the energy from my screen and forward momentum flipping them over and tearing them apart.

"Boxer, loop around and clean out some more of those tanks. Then catch up with me."

"Gotcha. Watch your six."

"Always."

I resumed my pursuit. Jacko and Swan had managed to avoid fire from the wildly maneuvering vics while knocking two more boxes out of the sky, together destroying nine boats. Then they roared through an enemy troop column, killing dozens of armored soldiers.

The enemy, whether sky craft or grunts, deserved no more mercy than they gave us. They slaughtered us and we slaughtered them. But I wasn't going to let them drive Jacques and his wingmate into a trap.

"Guardian to Ice Maker. Pull out and attack a box on one of our bird dogs."

"Negative. I'm chasing four formations on Jacko's tail."

"Understood. Will advise Vampire and Brat."

"Ice Maker to Jacko."

"Jacko. Go ahead, mon."

"You've got four formations on your tail."

"Affirmative. We can't shake them, mon. And the sky's too full to maneuver."

"They're driving you toward the coast. It's a trap."

"I know. What do you suggest?"

"Split up over the water, vectoring left and right, respectively. Come around and cover Swan's tail. I'll cover yours."

"Affirmative."

"Watch for fat ones," I said, referring to the enemy's corvettes.

"Got it, mon."

"Ice Maker, Boxer. I'm on my way."

"Cover my tail when you get here."

"You got it, buddy."

We approached the coast. Before we reached it, we had to climb over a blackened ridge. Mangled tanks and broken bunkers littered its sides, attesting to fierce and grim fighting.

Jacques and his partner popped over it, hugging its surface. Jacques crashed through the burned-out hulk of a once-living gigantic tree. His energy screen held, but the tree burst into great blackened splinters.

As they climbed over the ridge, an enemy box tried to stop them. Jacko and Swan smashed four more gunboats and the remaining three darted out of the way.

They descended the far side, rocketing over the beach, twisting their birds' noses left and right, but holding their vectors, as they fired upon enemy tank columns gliding up the shore. A dozen tanks exploded as Jacko's and Swan's cannons tore into them.

I popped over the ridge seconds behind the vics. A sky defense battery firing upon the gunboats fired upon me as well.

"Tell Ground Defense Command to be careful!" I growled.

"Affirmative," Prax replied.

Over the beach, I fired half a dozen times, killing five tanks and their crews. The enemy had been busy regrouping after Jacques's attack. Now the tank crews abandoned their machines and ran for cover.

"Ice Maker, Jacko. We're vectoring, mon."

"Affirmative," I replied.

Jacko and Swan split up. Swan vectored to the right in a wide arc, with Jacko pulling tight around to the left. The Gorgon formations followed, two vics behind each of them.

White columns of water surged up beside the fighters and their gunboat pursuers as their passage through the atmosphere created vortices near the surface of the sea. The leading gunboats fired again and again, striking each fighter's energy screen. Their screens glowed red from the plasma streams hitting them. Soon their screens glowed orange, then blue, as the combined gunboats in the each pair of pursuing vics burned at them. When they glowed purple, their screens would fail.

"Enemy corvette vectoring in upon Jacko," Prax warned.

"Damn!" I broke from my pursuit of the vics and accelerated toward the corvette. My plasma cannon was as powerful as any of those carried on our destroyers. While our corvettes carried two such cannons, I knew that Gorgon corvettes carried four less powerful cannons. The disadvantage was that their combined plasma streams were more potent than my single cannon. And their energy screens outclassed mine by a factor of about five. But when flying combat, the more daring you are, the better your chances of success.

Usually.

As I climbed past the vics pursuing Jacko, I began firing at the closing corvette. My plasma streams licked at its energy barrier, without effect. I had fired few missiles since descending into Hades. The corvette was unaware I still carried nearly a full complement.

The corvette returned fire, its plasma cannons hammering me. My bird shook. My energy screen flared blue, with a few touches of purple.

"We cannot survive another such attack," Prax said.

"I know," I snarled. "Target five missiles at it."

"Affirmative."

A fighter carrying a full combat load of missiles has as good a chance as any warship in damaging and even killing a destroyer, providing the fighter fires its missiles before it is vaporized. And providing all the missiles survive to impact the destroyer's screen and hull.

I fired my cannon twice more, then rolled onto my side and dived as the corvette fired at me. One plasma stream struck my screen dead on. The screen flared blue. Another close call.

Dropping toward the sea, I pulled out centimeters above the surface as the air pressure from my passing twisted the water around me. White foam and water engulfed me, creating a tunnel that collapsed after my bird passed through it. The corvette's energy weapons vaporized the collapsing tunnel behind me. My bird leaped out of the tunnel, rocketing skyward, pulling straight up and then falling over, coming down and around behind the corvette, racing up its rear.

Of all the craft flown by the forces of the Interstellar Association, the TF5F sky fighter is the most agile. Nothing can out-maneuver it.

With the corvette's plasma weapons directed forward, I attacked it from behind, unthreatened and unimpeded. I released five missiles and then corkscrewed upward and away. The missiles hit. The corvette became a giant fireball.

"Locate Swan and Jacko," I ordered Prax.

"They are one hundred kilometers north-northeast of the Asopus Line. Lieutenant Duquesne has cleared four gunboats from Lieutenant Heinz's tail. She is at present clearing the gunboats from his tail. Lieutenant Kent assisted them and is now en route to assist us," Prax reported.

"Ice Maker to Boxer," I called to Sherm. "Meet me down on the deck over the beach."

"Hey, buddy, you got it. Say, how did you get away from that corvette?"

"I didn't."

"You shot it down?"

"I did."

"You couldn't have!"

"Why not? It took five missiles, fired all at once and from behind, but I did it."

"Holy shit!"

"I didn't consider it holy, but it was shit."

I dropped down low over the beach, searching for targets. But the wormheads kept their distance. I would, too, if someone had just vaporized one of my small starships.

Without any sky targets, I settled behind a sand dune, my bird's nose pointing down the beach. A column of enemy tanks and armored troops stretched away for kilometers. They sought to out-flank the Asopus Line by scurrying up the beach. Our little sky raid hadn't deterred them. So, as they worked along the shore, I began blasting their tanks apart Soon the beach was littered for kilometers with the smoldering hulks of tanks.

"Ice Maker to Boxer. Where are you?"

"I'm fifty-five kilometers northeast of you. There's two boxes in my way. I'm gonna blast one apart. Got 'im! Two less gunboats. Two more for my score. They oughta give you five kills for that corvette, but they won't. Hey, according to my records, I'm leading you."

"Still the old man," I replied.

"You got it, buddy. Say, what're you doin' so low in the sand?"

"Killing wormheads."

"Save some for the crabs."

"What?"

"Never mind. My dad always said that if you have to explain a joke it ain't funny anymore."

"You should listen to him more often."

"Funny. Hey, buddy, don't forget that Guardian said we're to destroy gunboats, not ground troops. You better get back to work. Oh, shit!"

"Boxer! What's wrong?"

No answer.

"Boxer's location?" I demanded.

"Thirty-three point five kilometers northeast."

Sand fountained into the air around me as I brought my engine to full power and boosted out from behind the sand dune. Pulling my bird's nose around, I turned in toward Boxer's location. Moments later, I found him dodging no less than eight pursuing vic formations. His screen glowed bright blue.

Not wasting time, I dived into the nearest vic, vaporizing two gunboats with missiles and the third with my cannon.

"Cannon reserve at fifteen percent," Prax announced.

"Impossible," I said.

"It needs time to recycle."

"Re-route energy. Take life support. Take whatever you need."

"The cannon's elements need to cool."

"Melt the damned thing."

"Sergeant Lincoln will not like it."

"Do it!"

"Affirmative."

The remaining seven vics continued swarming around Boxer, oblivious to my destruction of their eighth formation.

"Boxer, Ice Maker. One less vic on your tail."

"Get me out of here, buddy!"

"Remember to focus."

"Trying."

"Four more vic formations are closing upon us," Prax announced.

"Cannon reserve?"

"Eighteen percent."

"Even with transferring power?"

"Affirmative."

"Take more."

"Unable to comply. Nothing more is available, Hector, except for engine power."

"Damn! Ice Maker to Guardian. We're in trouble. We've seven formations attacking us, with four more on the way!"

"Leader to Ice Maker. Swan's been hit. Jacko's escorting her out. We're on our way."

"Affirmative." My bird shook as plasma streams from four formations struck me. My screen flared bright blue.

"Screen failure imminent. Cannon reserve at twenty-one percent."

I needed my cannon! But I needed my screen more.

"Transfer all available power to the screen."

"Affirmative."

I brought us hard around, my back shoved into my acceleration couch as four Gees escaped the inertial dampers. I raced into the nearest vic. Two missiles vaped the side gunboats. The lead gunboat broke off and boosted away. Another vic leaped upon me. Its three gunboats flew so close they appeared almost as one. I quickly twisted my bird around, so much so that six more Gees escaped my dampers, slamming me into my acceleration couch and tearing my breath from me. Through a red mist filled with shooting stars I stared at my canopy's images. Lining up the lead gunboat, I loosed a missile at it. The gunboat disappeared in a bright, white fireball. The fireball's energy damaged both flanking gunboats. I shot my cannon at the right one and it fell from the crowded sky, crashing near a bunker and bursting into a yellow fireball.

I scanned for the third boat, but it had disappeared.

"Cannon reserve at five percent."

Plasma streams from the other vics raked my screen, flaring it blue and purple.

"Screen failure imminent."

"I know! I know!"

"Ice Maker, where are you!"

"Coming!" I brought us back around. Boxer's screen flared purple now, empty patches in it. Plasma energy blazed through the emptiness. In spots, his hull glowed red.

I had two missiles left. I bolted into one of the formations on Boxer's back, banging against them, my energy screen protecting me, the blow tossing the gunboats away from me. The impact seemed to frighten them and they raced off in three different directions.

But the remaining vics held tight.

"Cannon reserve at eleven percent."

I fired another missile into a vic pressing at his back, vaporizing a gunboat. The vic's other two gunboats split off.

Too late!

A final burst from the remaining formations struck Boxer's bird, dissolving it into a white cloud of superheated particles.

Screaming, I launched my last missile into one the vics that killed Sherman Kent, disintegrating a gunboat. Then I pointed my nose spaceward and continued accelerating until well clear of the fighting. The Asopus Line shrank far beneath me.

"Guardian to Ice Maker, vector back to *Akagi*."

I said nothing. Slowing, I brought my bird around.

I had rained death and destruction upon my enemies today, slaughtering those who slaughtered us. But I hadn't been fast enough, smart enough, or careful enough. I had sent my partner off on his own. And he'd been ambushed.

Feeling superior, I had attacked those unable to defend against me. A killing machine, I'd forgotten my obligations to my partner and to my squadron. I'd lost my focus and an error in judgement had cost the life of a valued member of our squadron.

I'd won every battle, but the last.

I lost the last.

CHAPTER NINETEEN

IT WAS A LONG trip back to *Akagi*. On the way back I tried writing my after-action report. But I couldn't focus on it. Instead, I had Prax clear my canopy and I stared out at the blackness of space. It was cold and dark and empty. It was also quiet and accusing.

I had let my partner down. I had let him die. I had been busy ignoring orders, as I often did, while Sherman had flown into an ambush.

After vaping the corvette, I'd felt so superior. The Gorgon gunboats had avoided me, letting me slaughter their ground troops at my leisure. And while I toyed with the enemy, the sky fiends closed in on my partner with murderous intent.

I hated these creatures. They were monsters, beasts, murderers, devils: vile, evil, empty-hearted things. I wanted them dead. I wanted them all dead.

They were things, but they were intelligent. They planned and conspired, with murder in mind. When they acted, they destroyed everything. They tolerated neither anything human, nor anything touched by humanity.

We let them murder us anywhere, at any time, in any way they sought while we fought them in the skies and on the ground. We retreated and they advanced. We killed them and they killed us and yet we gave ground, losing lives by the thousands.

Why didn't we attack their continent? Why didn't we fly into their cities and villages, destroying their civilization?

Why did we only fight their soldiers and pilots over Eos, not even fighting them in space? We had the firepower to destroy their fleets. We had enough ships. So why didn't we use them?

Because, we were told, the Association didn't want the war to spread beyond the Thea system. The Association feared an interstellar war. The government could accept a few tens of millions brutally murdered, but it feared billions of deaths.

But we had enough ships, enough troops, enough fighters, enough weapons, enough technology to obliterate the Gorgon race from the universe. So why didn't we? Because our leaders were cowards. They would rather let the Gorgons obliterate us, killing us bit by bit, than risk a devastating war that we could and would win.

Cowards had kicked me out of my former squadron. Cowards had wanted me to abandon the lifeboat that had crashed on Gargaphia, letting seventy people die. Now other cowards watched while hundreds of thousands of brave men and women fought and died for a cause unsupported by those cowards.

These timid, fearful, spiritless leaders let us fight without hope of winning while they followed a course of containment. But how long before we turned on our leaders? How long before we lost control and destroyed the enemy?

How long before I lost control?

A strange tapping made me blink. The view outside my canopy appeared different. The emptiness of space was gone. Somehow, I had arrived within my fighter's bay. But how? And when?

Prax must've brought us back. He must've docked us and then pressurized the bay after its doors closed. But why hadn't I been aware of it? Had I been asleep?

With a tired movement, I turned my head to locate the source of the tapping. It was Sergeant Lincoln. She stood on the grav platform beside my bird, her red hair coiled into a tight bun on her head.

Her lips moved, but I heard nothing.

I opened my canopy.

"It's about time. I thought you were gonna sleep all day. Major Garacyk's waiting for you in his office. Best get going."

Nodding, I stood. My legs trembled. It was as if I were an invalid and couldn't walk. Sergeant Lincoln had to help me out of my cockpit. I almost fell off the grav platform.

"Watch it!" she snapped, grabbing me, keeping me steady. "What's your problem, anyways?"

"I lost my partner today."

"Everyone knows that. It happens. Get a hold of yourself. This is a war. People die. It can happen to any one of us.

"Is that your problem, Crossman? Has it hit you that you could get killed out there? Have you lost your nerve?"

The platform settled to the deck. Jerking free from her, I stumbled off the platform and stared at her. "Where d'you get off talking to me like that?"

She just stared at me.

Taking a deep breath, I slowly let it out. I shook my head, clearing it. "Where did you say I was to meet the major?"

"In his office. I think he expected you there several minutes ago. Better move your ass. Sir."

I marched to the door. Stopping at it, I turned back around. "Sergeant Lincoln."

She stood on the platform. "What now?" she snapped.

"Take good care of our bird."

She nodded. The platform rose from the deck and a moment later she climbed into my bird.

I entered the corridor and walked down it. My walk slowed as I passed Sherman Kent's hangar. He'd never visit that hangar again. It would remain empty until his replacement arrived, a man or a woman who would occupy it until he or she died.

Ascending the stairwell, I walked down the corridor past the gallery. In the men's dressing room, I ran into others. Captain Inagaki nodded at me, but said nothing. Geys and Amal kept quiet. Jacques wasn't in sight.

But Brattano was.

"So, the mighty warrior has returned. Been off pissing your pants again, huh? Playing with yourself, maybe, while others are doing the fighting? Where have you been, chickenshit?"

I stared at him.

Brattano turned to the others in room. Jacques came from behind a row of lockers, drying dripping water from his body with a bright white towel.

"You're back just in time, DuQuesne," Brattano said. "The coward's back. Piss Man himself."

Before anyone could say anything, Brattano spun around and walked right up to me. He was shorter than me, but with very muscular shoulders that bulged through his uniform. "You let your partner die. You would've done the same to me. You'll do it to all your partners. You hear that, everyone? No one's safe with him. He sends his partners off to fight pissing little battles and then he takes his own sweet time rejoining them. It's like he doesn't want anyone out there with him."

Brattano's eyes narrowed, just a bit. "That's it, isn't it? You don't want anyone to share in your glory. You want to win all the glory for your stinking self while everyone else dies for you. You're worse than a coward. You're puke!"

"Shut up," Vlad growled.

"What are you defending him for?" Brattano demanded.

"He did everything he could," Vlad said.

"He wasn't there when his partner needed him."

"He was there. He fought hard. But the Gorgons are learning. He did all he could do, which was more than you would've done. Leave him be."

"He deserves what he gets," Brattano replied. "Worse even. He doesn't even deserve the air he breathes, nor the woman he's sleeping with. He deserves nothing, nothing at all."

"I said leave him be," Vlad growled.

Brattano stared at Vlad, then he glared at me. He opened his mouth to say something more, glanced at Vlad, closed his mouth and left the dressing room.

"Thanks, Vlad," I said.

"This changes nothing," he replied, leaving.

"Get cleaned up," Inagaki said. "The major's waiting."

I nodded. I changed quickly, saving my shower for later.

"I'm sorry, mon," Jacques said, finishing toweling off.

"Brattano's right," I said. "I wasn't there for Sherm when I should've been. I should've kept my partner close in, rather than sending him off. Hell, I should've stayed close to him. But I didn't, did I? I should've been killing the wormheads in the sky, not on the ground."

"I can't argue with that, mon. But I can tell you this, that corvette would have had me. I would have been the fireball, not the corvette. And if I had been, then so would have been my wing mate.

"You did something incredible out there today, mon. You vaporized a corvette. And while you were doing so, your partner helped Kara and me clear our tails."

I stared at him.

"I'm sorry about your partner," he continued, "and about the way you feel. I'd feel the same way, mon. But it's just the way the universe is."

"I know," I grunted. "It's life."

"No, it's war. Try as we might to make all the wormheads die instead of us, it doesn't work that way. Because they're trying to make us all die. And some of us will, mon, some of us will."

"Not if I can help it."

"But you can't kill them all. No one can."

"I can try. I have to. I don't want anyone else that I care about to die. I can't and I won't let that happen."

"You can't stop it. The statistics are against you. And besides, you have your duty, mon. To us, to the squadron, to your orders, to humanity."

"I know what my duty is!" I exclaimed. "If I'd done my duty today, Sherm would be alive."

"Maybe. Or maybe not."

I finished dressing. I shoved Jacques out of my way. I washed my face and combed my hair.

"You can't change the universe, mon," Jacques said as I left the dressing room. "You have to learn to live with things the way they are."

"No, I don't," I said, as I walked away, not looking back.

Minutes later, at the major's door, I paused, not wanting to go inside. I dreaded seeing him. I dreaded explaining how I let my partner die. I dreaded the tongue lashing I knew he intended for me. Yet I deserved it.

I deserved anything and everything he said to me. I'd been derelict in my duty and it had cost the squadron a good pilot. Whatever happened after I entered his office, I deserved it.

The major's door whispered open. His outer office seemed dim, almost dark. The door to the inner office was open. Sad music emanated from within. As I walked toward the inner office, I noticed the lighting was set low in that room, too.

What went on?

Major Garacyk sat at his desk. Stepping up to it, I came to attention.

He ignored me. He just stared at a holoviewer on his desk. From my side, all I saw was the flickering of the viewer in the dim light. If not for that flickering, I wouldn't have known that he stared at anything at all.

He continued ignoring me. I cleared my throat.

Major Garacyk looked up. "What is it, Crossman?"

"You wanted to see me, sir?"

"Affirmative. You didn't file an after-action report."

I took a deep breath. "I didn't know what to say."

"Why not?" His voice, empty of emotion, made me nervous.

"I let my partner down," I blurted out, unable to stop myself. "I disobeyed orders. I went off on my own. I sent my partner off on his own. I let my partner get killed. It's all I've been able to think about, sir."

"Then think of something else."

"What?" I exclaimed.

"What didn't you understand? You shot down an enemy corvette today. No one's ever done that. How'd you do it?"

"It's all in my counterpart's report."

"That's not good enough, Crossman. I want to know what you did. I want to know what made you think of doing it. I want a report on that in two hours."

"Maybe I should just write a sim instead, sir."

"I don't want to hear that shit!" Garacyk growled at me, standing. He pressed a button and the lights came on, bright. His desk's holo imager flickered off. The music stopped.

"Sir?"

"If you haven't noticed, mister, we're fighting a goddam war here. People are dying all the time. There's no time for goddammed simulations! I want that report written and sent here. Got it, mister?"

"Affirmative, sir!"

Garacyk glared at me. His face seemed devoid of color. His eyes bulged at me. He looked like he was about to scream at me. His mouth twitched. He blinked a couple of times. Then he took a deep breath, calming himself. His eyes relaxed.

"Look, I understand how you feel. Maybe you've never lost a wing mate before," he said.

"I disobeyed orders, sir. I sent him off on his own while I vectored a different way."

"You showed initiative. I value that in a pilot."

"I let my partner down. I should've been there for him."

"He was a grown man, Crossman. He knew what he was getting into. We don't let children fly for the Command. He was a fighter pilot. He could handle himself.

"Grow up, Crossman. You can't carry the universe on your shoulders. People die out there and they're going to continue to die. And there's not a damned thing you can do about it, except learn to live with it and move on. And value what little time any of us have with our friends. We're all mortal. We're all going to die someday, sooner or later."

I stared at him.

"You don't want to accept that, do you?"

"No, sir."

"You better. If you don't, you'll crack. I need every pilot I have and I can't have any of them breaking now. You got that, Crossman?"

"Affirmative, sir."

"Then get out there and live your life. There's a lovely young woman waiting to see you. Worry about the war later."

"I'll try, sir."

"It wasn't your fault, Crossman. You did nothing wrong. In fact, you did everything right."

"It doesn't seem that way, sir."

"That's the way it is. Live with it. Now get to work on that report."

"Affirmative, sir." Coming to attention, I spun about and started out.

"Crossman."

I stopped and turned around. "Sir?"

"There's been a change in assignments. You're now in charge of training."

"What about Captain Jonkowski? She's the training officer."

"Not anymore."

"Why not, sir?"

The major's eyes grew sad. He sat down behind his desk again, staring at its surface. Tears formed in his eyes.

"Sir?"

"Rana died in action thirty minutes ago. She's gone."

"How?"

"How do you think?" he snarled, glaring up at me. "She died just like Kent did, by enemy action."

"I'm sorry, sir."

He looked away from me. "Just get out," he whispered.

Returning to my cabin, I couldn't believe that Rana was gone. I hadn't seen her for a couple of days, our schedules being so different. But I always counted on her being there when I went to her office.

Yet it wasn't her office anymore, but mine now. As I sat at my desk, in my cabin, writing my after-action report, I wondered how I'd get along without her.

She'd been my first friend in the squadron, encouraging me, believing in me. She was intelligent, strong, warm and kind-hearted. She trusted her fellow pilots. And she trusted me.

Everyone said she was the finest pilot the Command had ever known; the most graceful, the most talented. But I'd never seen her fly. Now I never would.

How many more things would I never know of my friends? How many more things would I never see them do, hear them say? How many more people that I loved were going to die in this war?

I finished my report. I copied it, stored it, sent copies to Major Garacyk, to Captain Mboko, to Colonel Wallis and to General Devon.

Stretching out on my bed, I stared up at the simulated night sky of the stars visible from Earth. No one had operated the simulators today. None had for days. Now two less pilots ever would. How many more would die before those similators saw use again?

How many pilots had to die before we stopped functioning as a squadron, becoming but a collection of spent warriors, too few to fight, too worn out, too beaten down, too angry, too empty, too lonely, too lost, too sad?

How many deaths before victory lost its meaning? How much suffering, how much sorrow, before peace became important again? How long before life, alien or human, became valuable again and the killing stopped? How long before the hating stopped?

That was the real question. The question I couldn't answer. Because I wasn't ready to stop hating.

I hated because I was afraid. I was afraid for my friends. I was afraid for the innocent lives on Eos. I was afraid for Lisa. Most of all, I was afraid for myself.

Not afraid of my own death, no. I was afraid of losing everyone that I loved.

I had lost my dad. And somehow my mother, too, for she was never really there. I lost Anna Alvarez. I lost my squadron aboard *Soyuz*. I lost Corinna. I couldn't lose Pedro or Lori, and especially not Lisa.

If I lost Lisa, I lost everything. It'd be the blow I couldn't survive. It'd be the end of me.

I couldn't let that happen. But what could I do to stop it? I couldn't be everywhere. I couldn't kill enough Gorgons to end the war.

I was just one man, one pilot. And no single man or woman, no single warrior, could end this war alone. It took all of us, every soldier, every spaceman, every pilot, every one of us, fighting and dying, to stop the Gorgons, to inflict enough death and destruction that they'd want to end the war.

Fighting and dying. Everyone. There was the terror. We all had to fight. And some of us, maybe most of us, had to die. There wasn't a dammed thing I could do about it, except kill as many of the enemy as I could.

I had become the monster Lisa feared. If she discovered my hidden sin, she'd leave me. She'd have to, for I was the antithesis of everything she believed in, everything she cared about. Living with me, loving me, would drag her into my horrible pit, into my sinful soul.

And if she left me, I'd lose the best part of me. I'd lose my hope. I'd lose my future. But if she died, I'd lose not only my heart, I'd lose my center, my circumference, my soul.

How I wished I could leave the war, and the monsters out there and inside me, behind. But only death would bring me release. Only death would bring me freedom.

Rising from my bed, I shaved and showered, enjoying the water's warm wetness washing over me. Then I dressed and left. I needed companionship now. I needed not solitude, but life. I needed warmth, laughter, joy.

I needed my friends, my family.

I needed love, joy, peace, to forget.

I needed life.

CHAPTER TWENTY

I LEFT MY CABIN, SEEKING release from my torment.

I wanted Lisa's companionship, but I couldn't have it now. I needed her gentle caresses, her beautiful smile, her laughter, the softness of her hand in mine, the sweetness of her voice in my ears. But I couldn't turn to her now, I couldn't find release and redemption in her presence, for if she knew the horrible hatred that burned within me, that lusted for the enemy's destruction, she'd turn from me, frightened by the monster buried deep down inside me, seeping through the walls that my love for Lisa had constructed around it, seeking to consume the enemy, consume my soul, consume those that I loved.

No, I couldn't turn to Lisa; I couldn't let her see my inner self. Of all my friends, of all my family aboard *Akagi*, there was only one I could turn to with safe assurance, the best friend that I'd ever had, the man who was more brother than friend.

I'd never had a brother before I met Pedro. I'd had close friends, yes, but no brother. Pedro's family had adopted me, cared for me, respected me, even as he had.

After the death of my father, I had doubted I'd ever again have as close a friend as my dad had been to me. And for many years, I hadn't. Then I met Pedro at the Academy. We'd had Historical Dynamics together. We became friends.

During our years at the Academy, we helped each other whenever necessary. Without Pedro, I'd never have passed Close Tactics. Without me, he'd never have passed Quantum Calculus; not only did he pass it, he achieved the second highest grade in the Academy's history.

When Pedro's grandmother died, I was there for him. His Grand Mom, he called her. He was closer to her than to anyone else in his family, as close as I'd been to my dad.

I remember that day. I found him in his dorm room. He'd missed Physical Ed, his second most favorite subject, after flying.

He just sat there, staring out the window, watching the snow fall across the campus. We never spoke. I knew how he felt. A big hole had opened up in his life, one than no one could ever fill. He would always remember his Grand Mom, just as I would always remember my dad. And he would always miss her, just as I always missed my dad.

I might not miss Sherman Kent as much as I missed others, but I'd always know that I should have been there for him. If I hadn't indulged my hatred for the enemy over the beach, slaughtering them as they had slaughtered us, I could've saved Sherman.

I should've saved him.

Pedro's door informed me that he was in the forward, upper lounge. And that's where I found him. He sat in the outermost ring of tables, against the great curving surface of the dome. His table was small, designed for two occupants. He held a glass of wine in one hand, and stared out the dome into the pure blackness of space, looking, as far as I could tell, beyond Eos, beyond the Thea system, beyond space and time itself. But whether he gazed into his past or his future, I couldn't say.

He looked up as I approached. "Hector! I've just been thinking about you."

"And why is that?" I asked, sitting down across the table from him. "Trying to come up with some new practical joke to pull on me, maybe embarrassing me in front of our friends?"

He smiled deviously. "Perhaps."

"I don't like the sound of that."

He laughed. "Easy, hermano. We all have more than enough misery to deal with today, wouldn't you say?"

"I would."

"I'm sorry about your partner. But you did all you could."

"No, I didn't."

"What more could you have done, amigo?"

"I could've saved him."

"How? The wormheads have changed their tactics. They're learning from us. How, exactly, could you have stopped them?"

"I could've done something," I said. "He'd be alive now if not for me. It's my fault."

"How?"

I glanced out the dome, at the blackness, the emptiness, at the accusing stars.

He sighed. "You've had a bad day. Have some wine. Get drunk. It'll help."

"What makes you think so?"

He shrugged. "When mi corazon is away, it helps. I know others are watching out for her, just as you did a few days ago, thank you again! But I still worry about her. How can I not? She's everything to me, as Lisa is everything to you.

"And yet, I don't want her to fly without me. I want to be there for her. I want to protect her. But she's independent. She doesn't want to be protected. She's as exceptional as any of us. She made it into the Black Birds on her own, didn't she?"

He glanced at me, his eyes red from exhaustion, a trace of fear in them. "If anything happens to her, Hector, what will I do? How will I breathe? She's my life, my heart!"

"You live to remember her."

"You sound like my father."

I smiled. "I like your dad."

"And he likes you. He wants you to come home and raise many sons and daughters and be part of our family again, as before."

I laughed. "I didn't know he had such plans for me."

Pedro leaned across the table. "He was quite disappointed when you and Anna stopped sleeping together. He envisioned the two of you marrying and giving him many fine grandchildren. We were all disappointed that the two of you broke up."

I felt the color drain from my face. "How did you know?"

"I didn't, until just now, amigo. A guilty conscience is so easy to manipulate, wouldn't you agree?"

"But how'd you know? Tell me."

"By the way Anna looked at you."

"You knew I was sleeping with your sister by the way she looked at me? And you didn't want to kill me? You always said you'd kill anyone who touched your sister. You said it long after we broke up."

Pedro grinned at me.

"D'you know how long I've been afraid you'd find out?" His grin widened.

"How could you torture me all these years?"

He spread his hands apart. "You touched my sister. I couldn't kill my best friend. So I did the next best thing."

"Damn you."

Pedro laughed, loud enough to draw the attention of others in the lounge.

"You've been planning this for a long time, haven't you?" He nodded.

"I don't know if I can ever trust you again."

"I trust you," he said.

"Shut-up."

"Okay, mi hermano."

"So you knew all these years and you never told me. Until today. Why now?"

"Why not?"

"That's not an answer."

"One time is as good as another."

I shook my head. "If you tortured me all these years, what'd you do to Anna?"

"Nothing."

"Why not?"

"Because she would've killed me. You know what she's like, amigo. Body by Satan, temper by God."

I laughed. "She's that way, all right. Just like Lori. Maybe you picked Lori because she's so similar to your sister."

"Similar, yes, but Lori's every bit as different from Anna as she is the same. Much more independent. Much more charming. Much more loving."

"And more trusting," I said. "She hardly knew me, yet she stood beside me against Mboko and Garacyk. Even against Colonel Wallis. And she did it because she loves and believes in you."

"She's exceptional, won't you agree?"

"She is. I hope she gives your father several fine grandchildren."

"That pee on Uncle Hector's knees."

"Such a wonderful friend you are."

"What're amigos for, except to wish each other fine futures? And that would be a fine future, wouldn't it, amigo?"

"It would. Except for the peeing part."

Pedro ordered a glass of wine for me and more for himself. Then we spent the better part of an hour reliving the past. We talked about the Academy. We talked about mutual friends. We talked about his family. We talked about Anna.

Eventually, our conversation returned to the present.

"You know, amigo, these new tactics that the wormheads are using seem familiar."

"How so?" I asked.

Pedro shrugged. "They just do."

"Well, they're very much like the tactics men in various Earth air forces used in the Twentieth and Twenty-first centuries. We studied them in Major Mahura's Ancient Aerial Tactics class."

"Si. But this is different. There's something familiar about these moves. They're not how the Gorgons fly or fight."

"They do now," I reminded him.

"But they shouldn't. They don't think that way."

"And you're an expert on Gorgon psychology?"

"Fighting them every day makes us experts on how they fight, amigo. It makes every pilot an expert."

"Agreed. But how is this different?"

"Because this is not the way they would figure out how to fight us. They face us every day, yet they fight the same. On the ground, they face new tactics from us, yet they throw more and more strength at us until they overwhelm us. They're doing that in the sky, too.

"Look at how their destroyers try to pick us off. And now they've committed corvettes to the sky dueling.

"No, Hector, they're getting help from the outside. Someone is giving them expert advice on how to fight us."

"Then we better hope that we figure out who that is, before more of us die," I said.

"Affirmative. And that's exactly why you couldn't have saved Kent. You went out to fight the wormheads and their tactics. But instead you fought someone else's tactics. You did all you could. It just wasn't enough."

"But it should've been enough, Pedro. It should've been."

"Why, amigo? What could you have done differently?"

"I could've stayed off the beach. I could've taken my hatred for them out in the sky."

"That wouldn't have changed anything."

"It could have."

"Why?"

"Why?" I retorted. "You have the same feelings and affections for Lori as I have for Lisa and you ask me that? You have the same fears for her, too. What happens the next time one's shot down? How do we save them if the tactics keep changing?"

"They caught you off guard, amigo. You won't be off guard next time. Neither will I. It'll be different. You'll see."

"It should've been different today."

"What's wrong with you, Hector? Why are you so focused on what happened today?"

"I should've been there for him."

"You were there for him!" Pedro exclaimed.

"How so? He's gone. He was my responsibility and I let him down. It's my fault he's dead. But I won't let that happen again. I won't let anyone else die."

"That's loco talk, amigo. You're not omnipotent. Only God is omnipotent and none of us are God. We can only do what we can do and pray that it's His will that we live. Who can know the mind of God, after all?"

"God's will! You talk like you believe in that crap. If god exists, he doesn't care about any of us. You think he'd have let creatures like the Gorgons exist, knowing how they hate humanity and what they'd do to people?

"I can't believe in a god like that. Besides, when did you find god? I thought you swore god off long ago. What was it you told me at the Academy, that you couldn't believe in god when you considered how religion had caused most of the wars on Earth? You said there was no god, especially one that would let your grandmother die!"

Pedro stared at me. And I hated myself. I knew how much he loved his grandmother and how much she believed in god. What a cruel fool I was, insulting my best friend, hurting him so, just because I hurt.

"Remember, amigo, there aren't any atheists on a battlefield. I was raised believing in God, Hector. I need to believe in Him. I need to know someone greater than myself, greater than the enemy, greater than any of us, is watching out for those that I love. I need to believe, mi hermano, that God exists and that He's watching out for Lori. It's the only way I can climb into my fighter day after day, COP after COP. It's the only way I can fight.

"After all, we're fighting evil, aren't we? Well, God is on the side of good. And if He weren't on the side of good, then we're on the wrong side, wouldn't you agree, amigo?"

"I can't accept a god that let my dad die. That gave me a mother incapable of loving me."

Pedro stood. "Then I pity you, amigo. If anything happens to us, you'll be all alone in the universe."

I jumped up, spilling what was left of my wine across the table, its blood-colored burgundy running onto the carpeted deck. "Don't you think I know that! Don't you think I think about that every day? Since I saw what those evil bastards did to that poor young woman down there, what they could've done to Lori, it's all I've been able to think about. I don't want Lisa to die, or you, or Lori, or anyone else. Not even Vlad, believe it or not. Not even that screwed up sonofabitch Brattano!

"But how can I stop it? How can I protect you? How can I protect anyone? I can't. Not even if I were to kill every onr of those monsters. But I've gotta try. I've gotta do something, or I'll go mad. I'm almost mad now!"

"I don't know what to say."

"It doesn't matter what you say. I know what I've got to do. I know my vector."

"You frighten me, Hector. You need to talk to someone. Have you talked to Lisa?"

"Are you crazy? If I told her about all this, she'd leave me. She couldn't live with the monster I've become. And I wouldn't want her to, either."

"She's stronger than you think, Hector. She won't abandon you while you're in trouble."

"And what about afterwards? Can you guarantee me she'll always be there? Can you?"

"Of course not. But I can guarantee you that she loves you. She's exceptional, like Lori. She won't leave you."

"I can't change my vector. Those things killed Sherman Kent and Rana Jonkowski. I've got to punish them for it."

"You can't kill them all."

"Maybe not, but I can kill enough." I marched past Pedro, across the lounge to the stairwell, turned and glanced at him. He stared at me in disbelief. I glared back and then left the lounge.

CHAPTER TWENTY-ONE

THE NEXT SEVERAL WEEKS became a blur of pain, frustration, fear, and hatred. We flew more missions now: three, four, sometimes five or six, each and every day. The Gorgons threw everything possible against the Asopus Line, thousands of tanks and gunboats, hundreds of thousands of troops, and dozens of corvettes, all desiring the mass murder of the Eosian defenders.

More and more Gorgon gunboats flew in vic formations, as did their corvettes. Hundreds of box formations filled the skies.

Thousands of Eosian soldiers, Association marines and Colonial Guardsmen from various worlds, died holding the Line. They suffered through hell, watching as friends and fellow soldiers were vaporized or became human fireballs.

And as they suffered, so suffered we. They fought and died on the ground while we fought and died in the sky. What kept them going kept us going: fear of the enemy winning.

I cannot say what days upon days of unrelenting combat, of terror, of agony and anger, did to the men and women on the ground. I only knew what it did to us; to me.

In seven weeks we lost sixteen pilots from all four of *Akagi*'s fighter squadrons. We also lost six SAR crews aboard as many birddogs. Five of the dead fighter pilots belonged to the Black Birds.

First Squadron was no longer immortal, no longer perfect. We fell from our pedestals as fast as we fell from the sky. Yes, we still led our peers in other squadrons with impressive kill numbers, but we weren't the divine beings we had been. We were no longer the squadron that guaranteed a pilot's career, but rather the squadron of death: death to our enemies, death to ourselves.

First Squadron became a cursed squadron.

I hated the enemy. I still vaporized unprotected Gorgon ground troops. I still fried their tanks. Their gunboats ran from me. Their corvettes hunted me. But every gunboat I destroyed, I killed it in Sherman Kent's memory. With every corvette I vaporized, I vanquished it for Rana. And every enemy soldier, every enemy tank, died for my fellow pilots.

I became vengeance incarnate on the battlefield, my rage giving me the strength and power to consume my enemy, as my rage consumed me.

My relationships became strained. Lisa and I still slept together, but we grew apart. An invisible barrier separated us.

I loved Lisa more than life itself, but I had stopped loving myself. And when you stop loving yourself, then loving others becomes first difficult, and then impossible.

I grew to resent Lisa. I resented her for the fear I felt for her safety every time she flew. I resented her strength, her joy, her spirituality, when all inside me was dying, crushed under the weight of my fear and hatred. I resented her presence, her existence, for it kept my hatred for the enemy bottled up inside me, hidden beneath an ever thinning layer of humanity.

But most of all, I resented Lisa for still loving me when I no longer loved myself.

And yet, Lisa's love was all that kept my slipping sanity together. I awakened every night beside her, panic consuming me. What if she died tomorrow on her latest SARCOP? How could I protect her when I was never near?

And what of Pedro and Lori, of Lyle, Ava, and Jacques? How could I protect my friends? How could I save them and still kill the enemy? How could I be a guardian angel when I had become the devil's disciple?

Lying beside Lisa every night, frightened and panicked, I felt trapped. I wanted to awaken her, talk to her, reveal the monster I'd become and ask for absolution. But how could I tell her? How could I release the poison within me, even as it seeped through and poisoned our love?

So I let her sleep each night, loving her, hating her, fearing for her. And hating myself for my feelings.

As my relationship with Lisa grew strained, so did my relationships with my other friends. I never talked to them anymore. We hardly saw each other, as we were always flying and fighting. Whenever our paths crossed, I managed to avoid them, saying at most that I had to get to a briefing or get some rest.

Nor did I tell them about my new wing mate. His call sign was Bishop; his name, Raulo Polano. That's all I knew about him, all I wanted to know about him.

He was good. He kept close to me when fighting. And I kept him safe. No monsters murdered him.

Bishop saved me several times. But he couldn't save my soul. Who could? I didn't know. But I wanted to be saved.

I wanted to love myself again. I wanted to stop hating. I wanted Lisa and Lori and Pedro and all the others safe. Most of all, I wanted to be at peace.

But, how?

Lisa and I still switched cabins back and forth, though this last night seemed strange and unnatural. We hadn't talked. We hadn't made love. We ate our dinner in silence, not looking at each other, not daring to, but rather staring at our food. Afterward we kissed, a passionless and empty meeting of the lips. Then we climbed into bed together. We were two bodies, cold and afraid, each needing the other, each desiring the loving caresses now long lost.

The night was long and empty. I awakened several times. I wanted to touch her, but I couldn't.

In the morning we dressed, ate a quick meal together, and said goodbye. No kisses, no embraces, no desperately needed love. As I stood in my open door and watched her walk down the corridor, I felt the fear crushing my heart.

I wanted to run to her, hold her, kiss her, plead for her forgiveness. But fear and hatred entombed my soul.

As Lisa walked away, she stopped to chat with Vlad for a moment. He stood at his door, exhausted, back from yet another grueling COP. He touched her arm. She embraced him and continued onward, never looking back.

I hated him.

He came over to me. Stopping a hand's width from my face, he said: "You have some nerve."

"I like to think so," I said.

He trembled, hatred in his eyes. I felt it, too.

"With everyone dying around us," he began, "you torture the best woman around. She needs you and I know she loves you. I wish to God she loved me. But she doesn't.

I accept that. I have to, else I'd go insane. But she doesn't deserve you; you're not good enough for her."

"So?"

His hands balled into huge fists, his knuckles turning white.

"I could kill you," he hissed.

"Why don't you? It'd end all of our misery. Go ahead. Be a man. Kill me. Prove to Lisa that you're just what she needs. Do it."

His face turned red. I tensed, ready for the assault. I knew he could kill me. But I knew I could kill him, too. That was what I was, after all, a killer.

He cried out in rage, then lunged. Not for me, but for the display panel along the wall beside my cabin. He slammed his fists into the panel, blow after blow, shattering it, crying out in anger and grief. Tears streamed from his eyes; blood poured from his torn knuckles. He punched and punched and punched, his blows battering the panel, battering the wall, battering his soul, battering my soul.

His rage brought others from their cabins. People stared at him, at me, at the bloody and broken panels, at his bloody fists, and wondered what hell had been unleashed upon Vlad that he cried out in such anger. Abruptly, Captain Mboko and Captain Inagaki rushed down the corridor.

"Vlad! Stop it!" Inagaki cried out. He grasped Vlad from behind, his arms not quite reaching around Geys's broad frame. He struggled with Vladimir, but Vlad shook him off and continued pounding the wall.

"You did this!" Captain Mboko snarled at me. "Your self-righteousness did this. You've injured a fine pilot and officer. And all because you couldn't contain your wicked ambition."

"Sanura, help me!" Inagaki cried.

But Mboko couldn't hear him. She wanted to take her own rage out on me.

"You escaped a court-martial. With subterfuge you convinced Major Garacyk to abandon the charges against you. But you will pay for your depravities, your malignancies, your heinous transgressions against this squadron and against me."

"Sanura! Help me. Vlad, stop it. Stop it," Inagaki cried.

"What's going on here!" Major Garacyk bellowed, hurrying down the corridor.

The major's voice awakened Vlad from his rage. Breathing hard from his exertions, he stared at his bloody knuckles. He glanced at me, the hatred still in his eyes.

"I asked what's going on here. Someone tell me. Now!" The major glared at his captains, at the people in the corridor, at Vlad, and finally, at me.

"It appears that Lieutenant Crossman has grievously insulted Lieutenant Geys," Captain Mboko announced.

"And so he beat the wall? Is that what you're telling me?" the major asked.

"What other course could he follow? How could he strike a fellow officer, even one so dishonorable as Lieutenant Crossman?"

"I see. Captain Inagaki, take the lieutenant to Sickbay."

"I believe we should confine Crossman to his quarters, pending a court-martial," Mboko said.

"Oh, give it a rest, Sanura," Garacyk said. "It's me you hate, not him. You just can't admit it to yourself, so you take it out on him. He's never done anything to you."

Captain Mboko stared at him.

"Just admit it," the major said.

"You've prevented me from commanding the squadron I rightfully deserve. I should be your equal, not your inferior."

"You're more than my equal," the major replied.

"Liar!" Mboko screamed, glaring at us, then turned and left.

The major and I watched her leave. The corridor was empty now. With the show over the others had retreated into their cabins. They needed rest before their next COP, before their next opportunity to die.

He turned back to me. "You all right?"

"Affirmative, sir."

"This all about that girl?"

"Afraid so, sir."

"I see." The major let out a heavy sigh. He stared at the broken and bloodied display panel, shook his head, and left.

I re-entered my cabin. The door sighed closed behind me.

My hands trembled. Not from fear, nor from rage, but from exhaustion. How much more of this could I take?

I couldn't avoid my friends forever, especially after the incident with Vlad. After returning from my first COP of the day, I ran across Lori and Ava outside the changing rooms as they headed for the domed forward lounge. They asked me to join them.

I made excuses.

"Come on, we haven't seen you in weeks. Quit being such a hermit," Ava said.

"Yes," Lori agreed. "I wish to have lunch with my hero."

"I'd rather not. I'm very tired."

"Spending time with two beautiful women is too much for you?" Ava asked. Then, more firmly, she said: "You do think we're beautiful, don't you?"

I started to say no, but wisdom intervened. "Yes."

"Was that yes to 'beautiful' or yes to 'come'?" Lori asked, a twinkle in her eyes.

"Yes."

They each took one of my arms and escorted me toward a lift.

"Which question were you answering just now?" Ava asked, pain crawling up my arm from her grip.

"I think that he answered both questions," Lori said.

"Yes," I said. "Yes."

I rode the lift in silence, listening to them chatter. How did they do it? How could they so easily set the war aside, while it consumed me?

We transferred from the lift to the central travel tube. It was filled with *Akagi*'s crew members, chittering on about daily activities and down time, ignoring the death and destruction beneath us.

I wondered at their callousness. People died on Eos, while they went about their business, oblivious to the hell below.

I wanted to denounce them, to reveal their cold-heartedness, to bitterly chastise their self-interest. But I kept quiet.

We reached our landing, exited the tube, and entered a lift.

"It's been a long time since we've seen you," Lori said. "You've been avoiding us."

"After what Vlad did this morning, I can see why," Ava said.

"You were there?" I asked.

"Who wasn't?" Ava retorted.

"Everyone knows?"

"If they didn't, they learned soon enough from someone else. Gossip travels fast aboard ship," Ava said.

I sighed. "Faster than light."

"That's what Pedro always says," Lori agreed. "What exactly happened?"

"He loves Lisa," I replied.

"Things seem strained between you and Lisa," Ava said.

"Between all of us," Lori said.

I nodded.

The lift opened. We exited and began climbing the spiral stairs into the lounge. Happy, jazzy music echoed from above.

"Is Pedro here?" I asked.

"He's over the Line right now," Ava said. "We won't talk about that."

"Why not?"

"We just don't talk about him when he's in harm's way."

"Got it."

"I hope our table's free," Ava said as Lori climbed the stairs ahead of us.

"It is," Lori said, exiting into the lounge. Ava followed. As did I.

Glancing at the dome, I paused. The ship had rotated again, the dome oriented toward Eos. But instead of showing Titanus, which revealed constant fighting, even in daylight, the dome revealed the dark blue oceans.

Those oceans reflected the blueness of the sky and I stood, transfixed, drawn into that blue, wishing I flew in those blue skies. I missed that blueness. I missed its peacefulness, its strength, its joy.

I missed its solitude.

A few puffy white clouds cast shadows upon the ocean, visible even from orbit. I missed a sky devoid of death and destruction, filled with nothing but my bird and white, clean clouds.

I shivered. Moisture filled my eyes. I swallowed.

I couldn't remain. I hurt too much.

I turned to leave. Ava grabbed my arm. "Where are you going?"

"I've gotta go. I can't stay."

"Why not?" Ava asked me.

I shook free. "I just can't."

"You don't even want to hear the good news?" she asked.

"What news?"

"There's a rumor that we're going to be pulled out."

"What d'you mean?" I didn't want to be pulled out. I had a job to do, monsters to murder.

Lori had gone to the table; she returned as Ava spoke. "She means that someone's suggesting that *Akagi* will be withdrawn from the Thea system," she explained.

"Why?"

"Because we're worn out," Ava snapped. "Because Fifth Squadron only has eleven pilots left. Because we deserve a rest."

"Easy, dear," Lori said. "I don't know how true it is. They're just rumors. But if we're removed, then we're safe."

"It's something to celebrate," Ava said, smiling.

"Yes." I glanced at the dome again. That blue hurt too much. Rumors meant nothing. Only facts mattered. "I have to go. I'm sorry."

"Your loss," Ava chided.

I nodded.

"See you out there," Lori said. She gave me a quick, strong hug, then she and Ava headed for their table.

I avoided glancing at the dome. I wiped my eyes and turned back to the stairwell's entrance. I started for it, and stopped.

Lisa came up. She saw me.

"Hello," I said.

"Hello." She looked away and went past me. I watched her go. She glanced back, saw my attention, stopped, and turned to me.

"I won't be by tonight," she said.

"Okay."

"I won't be by any other night, either. I don't think we should see each other anymore."

"Why not?"

"Hector, I need more than you seem able to give me. I need your strength and your love, but it's just not there. I think our relationship was a mistake. You're just not the man I thought you were. I'm sorry."

What could I say? She was right.

For a long moment, we looked at each other. Then, tears in her eyes, she turned, glanced around the room, saw Ava and Lori waving at her, and headed for them.

I entered the stairwell. As I descended, I wept.

CHAPTER TWENTY-TWO

ANOTHER WEEK PASSED; A **week without** Lisa.

My life contained a void now, a void so vast and empty, so sad and deep that I thought I'd be swallowed up in it, forever lost. It was worst than when I said goodbye to Corinna Varney, sadder than when I broke up with Anna Alvarez, and deeper and darker than when my father died. I felt lost and alone. I wanted to cry all the time, but I couldn't.

I had no tears left.

Our squadron lost two more pilots. The fighting grew worse.

But there was hope.

Six new Marine brigades and three fresh Colonial Guard divisions, launched a counter-attack on the eastern side of Titanus. They surrounded and destroyed a hundred thousand Gorgon troops.

The enemy asked no quarter and none was given. They refused to surrender, fighting to the very last creature.

A new task force had arrived and with it came the new Marine brigades and five escort carriers with five fresh fighter squadrons and fifteen Marine gunboat squadrons.

The enemy threw everything they could against our new squadrons, against the Marines, and against the defenders of the Asopus Line. But our forces not only held, they pushed the wormheads back.

The defensive line in the center of Titanus, at the base of the Auster Mountains, also held. It was the strongest of all our positions and so the enemy dug in before it, transferring a third of its central force eastward and another third westward.

Then exciting news came down from Brigadier General Devon. A new task group was en route from the heart of the Association, with two more attack carriers and two support carriers, which would replace *Akagi*, *Resolute*, and *Yorktown*. Our task group would return to Ilmatar, minus some of its warships. Sky Command wasn't about to throw away all our lives, not to mention all the experience we'd gained fighting the Gorgons.

The general also told us that many members of the fighter and SAR squadrons, as well as members of the surviving Marine gunboat squadrons, would be transferred to other squadrons throughout the Association. Our experience needed to be spread around. For many of us, he said, that meant promotions.

But where would we go? Where would we end up? What would happen to my friends? Provided they all survived until the new task group arrived, then they'd be safe. As safe as anyone could be, flying for Sky Command.

And where would Lisa end up? Would she return to Gentry, as had Corinna? Would she be transferred to one of the frontier worlds where SAR crews were so needed? How would I find her? How could I reconcile with her, if she were posted thousands of light years away?

I desperately desired reconciliation with her. I realized that, without Lisa, life no longer had meaning for me. But how could I reconcile with her, how could I be the man she needed me to be, when I was a monster?

I hated what I'd become. But I wanted to stop hating myself. I wanted freedom from fear, freedom from hatred, freedom from the monster within me.

I wanted to love again; to live again.

But living proved problematic. Along with the Marines and five escort carriers that arrived with the new task force came three Colonial Guard divisions. They landed near the Asopus Line and after gathering themselves together launched an attack against the Gorgon forces traversing westward from the Auster Line. For three days, these troops fought and bled and died, until they threw back the enemy.

And while our ground forces fought, we covered them in the skies, where the enemy butchered us. The Gorgons had moved gunboats from the center of the continent, doubling their numbers against us.

Then the Gorgons did the same thing to our western forces as we had done to their eastern forces. They cut off part of our ground forces, surrounding them, seeking their demise.

Then the Gorgons attacked the main part of the Asopus Line.

I had just returned from a COP forty minutes before, had turned in my after action report, had showered and dressed, and headed for the pilots' mess, and had just started to eat my food when general quarters sounded aboard *Akagi*. Minutes later, again in my flight suit, I wandered into the squadron gallery.

Everyone was present. Everyone still alive.

"Attention!" Colonel Wallis bellowed, entering the gallery.

"We have a serious situation on our hands."

Of late, all our situations were serious.

"Enemy forces have broken through the Asopus Line. They have also cut off a Marine company two hundred kilometers east of the Line. The Marines are committing their reserves to plugging the breakthrough. They're too heavily engaged at this time to rescue their trapped company. That's where we come in.

"First Squadron will fly LOWCOP over the trapped company, keeping enemy sky forcs off of them and driving back ground assaults."

"We can do it, colonel!" Major Garacyk exclaimed.

Colonel Wallis nodded. "I know you can. Now the bad news. You're all aware of how the Gorgons have been adjusting their tactics against us. What you may not know is that our psychologists believe the enemy is incapable of such rapid changes in their tactics. We know that they are slow, methodical-thinking creatures. It took them ten times as many centuries as it did humanity to achieve star travel. We believe they've been receiving outside assistance. In fact, we know they are."

"An' what's the source o' this help they've been gettin'?"

Lyle asked. "We knew they used O technology against us. But from who'd they git it?"

"From the Na."

"It figures," someone said.

Colonel Wallis continued. "They not only bought O technology for the Gorgons, the Na have also given them tactical support."

"An' what would that be?"

"They've trained the Gorgons in new tactics against us. However, they've gone beyond that now."

"In what way?" Pedro asked.

"They've inserted their own ground troops into the fighting," Wallis said.

"That's how they penetrated the Line?" Jacques asked.

The colonel nodded. "Affirmative. Six Na battalions crashed through the Line's center, followed by fifty thousand Gorgons with hundreds of tanks. More Na battalions fight on the East Coast. And the Na seem to have taken command back there."

"And there's worse news to come, sir?" Pedro asked.

"There is. Na fighters now fly on the East Coast."

"Those lucky bastards!" Brattano exclaimed. "We fight stinking gunboats while those guys fly against real pilots."

"Don't be too hasty to fight against them, Brattano," Major Garacyk said. "The Na fly in vics of three, and they're deadly as hell. Their birds look like bright, multi-faceted, giant diamonds. They're fast and nasty. They're as good as we are, maybe even better."

"That's right," Colonel Wallis added. "They rotate constantly while fighting, never presenting the same side to an opponent at any moment. They also jig and jag every which way. They carry two plasma cannon, each as powerful as ours. And they carry a dozen missiles. If you survive a fight against one of them, you should feel lucky."

"Do they fight individually?" Lori asked.

"They always attack in threes. A vic will fly like a single entity. If you can break them apart, you and your wing mate have a chance, though maybe only a slim one."

"Do you think they'll fight against us?" Lori asked.

"Affirmative. Now, this is how it stands, you'll be fighting Gorgon gunboats. You'll attack their ground forces. You'll respond to any and all requests for help from the trapped Marines. And watch out for Na vics. If they jump you, your chances for survival nose dive. Remember that.

"I'm giving the rest of this briefing over to Major Garacyk. Keep your seats. I can find my own way out."

As Colonel Wallis made his way out, Major Garacyk moved forward. "First off, the colonel failed to mention that we won't be alone. Third Squadron will be flying HICOP and SARCOP. They'll keep our backs covered while we're on the deck.

"Second, because of the seriousness of this situation, *Akagi*'s presently descending to a lower orbit so we can get back sooner for resting and re-arming. And third, we'll be flying in three COPs, launching ever forty minutes. This will allow us to keep at least one COP over the trapped troops at all times.

"Now we'll fly a standard four-bird COP. Because there are only fifteen of us left, after the third COP flies, we'll rotate three pilots out of the first COP so they can rest. Those three will rotate with three from the second COP, and so on. This way everyone will receive extra rest.

"We're going to fly continuously, with the first COP launching in twenty minutes. At the moment, Marine gunboats are providing ground support for the displaced company.

"When you need to contact them, call the Marines on the emergency channel. Their company belongs to the Third Battalion, Eighteenth Brigade."

"Lieutenant Clark will now fill you in on the various weapon systems the Na use. Lieutenant?"

Lori walked up front. "We've a variety of weapons confronting us today. Some are friendly. The Marines, as always, use armored space suits powered by minature fusion power plants. Their suits can deflect several shots from the Gorgons's own plasma rifles. But fire from Gorgon tanks or even gunboats is beyond the capabilities of the Marines's personal shields."

"What does that mean?" I asked.

"It means that we are their only defense against Gorgon tanks and gunboats, and Na fighters."

"Understood," I replied.

"As for the Na, you heard Colonel Wallis mention that they carry plasma cannons as powerful as ours. What that means is if both weapons from a single Na fighter strike your energy screen, they'll damage your systems, maybe even penetrate your shielding. If all three fighters in a vic hit you at once, you're dead. Also, their missiles are as good as ours and just as deadly.

"Major Garacyk has informed me that our weapons will be somewhat different. Everyone will still utilize plasma cannons. But instead of a full missile complement, one bay will be devoted to two canisters carrying fusion and neutron bomblets. Don't forget that both sorts of bomblets utilize plutonium to create their respective yields. So don't release them too close to friendly forces. And make certain you don't linger over ground zero when you drop them.

"They are low yield, capable of killing hundreds of enemy troops in a three-hundred meter radius. But even with the further Gorgon troops from the center, the chances their shields will deflect the radiation and blast effects is still minimal.

"Finally, all other weapons, friendly and unfriendly alike, are just as we've encountered every day."

After a brief pause, allowing for questions, of which there were none, Lori sat down. The major stood.

"If you haven't figured it out, things are getting worse down there and even more worse all the time. And if you haven't also figured it out, with our rotation system, some of you will be flying with different wing mates on different COPs. Get used to it.

"I'll lead the first COP. Captain Inagaki has the second. Captain Mboko, the third. Yakima, Alvarez and Lem are in the first. The rest of you will receive your assignments shortly. Dismissed."

"Heinz, Crossman, Polano," Captain Inagaki announced, "you're with me." The captain's previous wing mate, Second Lieutenant Khaled Amal, had been killed five days before.

"Clark, Farley, Munk, with me," Captain Mboko announced.

That left Jacques, Vlad, and Brattano in reserve.

Pedro met me at the exit, a grim smile covering his face. "Well, amigo, more opportunities for me to out-score you today. Fortunate for me, wouldn't you agree?"

"Be careful out there. You're irreplaceable, you know."

"You be cautious too, amigo. See you out there."

"See you out there."

Ten minutes later, the first LOWCOP launched. I watched it leave from the gallery.

"I hate this," a soft voice said.

I turned around. "I didn't know you were here, Lori."

She nodded. "I've always watched his launches. At least, whenever I wasn't on a COP with him. You see, when we were first seeing each other, I watched because I felt closer to him that way. And then we arrived here and I watched because I didn't know if it might be the last time I saw him."

She turned from the gallery's windows. The LOWCOP's fighters had departed. She seemed tired, her eyes darker than I remembered them.

"I love him, Hector."

"I know."

"I love him more than anyone I've ever loved. I don't want to lose him. I die a little every time he flies into combat. And I'm reborn every time he returns. I pray for him while he's out there."

"I worry about him, too," I said. "He's the only brother I've ever really had."

She placed a hand on my shoulder, squeezed it. Then her hand dropped away. "You're a dear friend. He loves you, too. You'll always be welcome at our home."

"Thank-you. And you'll always be welcome at mine."

She nodded again, then smiled.

"Are you hungry?" I asked.

"Tired, mostly."

"Me, too. I fly in about twenty-five minutes."

"I should eat, too. But I'm not really in the mood for the dome," she replied.

"I just came from the pilots's mess."

"I haven't been there for such a long time."

I waved my hand toward the door. She smiled. We left.

In the pilots's mess, I watched her eat. Though I'd only eaten a little of my meal before, now I was no longer hungry.

Partway through her food she glanced up at me. "I know it must hurt, but I really need to ask," she said.

"About Lisa?" I asked.

"Yes."

"I don't know if I can explain it," I said.

"She told me that you had grown distant and cold. She told me she felt unsafe around you."

"I didn't mean for her to feel that way."

"Do you love her still?"

"Yes."

"What happened? I hope I'm not prying too much."

"You're not. I'm just not the right man for her."

"I think you are. In fact, I know you are. And she felt the same way, too."

"Does she still?"

Lori glanced at her food. "It's not my place to say. You'll have to ask her."

"I don't know if I can. I want to, but so much has passed between us."

"What has passed? Tell me."

"I can't."

Reaching a hand across the table, she clasped one of my hands. "You can, if you want to."

"Look, Lori, it's…I just can't say. It's too personal."

"Try."

I glanced around the room, panicked. "D'you have family? Back home, wherever home is?"

"I do," she said.

"I don't. Pedro's my only family. And you. And Lyle and Ava. And Lisa. Rana was.

"You worry for Pedro every time he flies. He's your future, your family."

"I worry for you and everyone else, too," Lori said.

"But it's not the same, is it?"

"No."

"If Pedro dies, and Lisa, and the rest of you, I'm all alone in the universe."

"Until you make other friends."

"Do you realize how patronizing, how trite and callus, that sounds?" I snapped.

"I'm sorry. It's my mother talking."

"Are you close to your mother?"

"Very much so."

"It was that way with my father and me. But then he died. My mother was as cold as they came. She didn't want me. I haven't seen her in more than a decade."

"You should."

"That's what Lisa said. But I can't do it without her, and that'll never happen now."

"Why not?"

"Because I'm a monster, that's why. Because I'm just like those things down there that we're fighting. Because Lisa doesn't want to love a monster. She can't love what I've become and I don't love what I am, either.

"I hate those things. I want to kill them all. If I don't they're going to kill you and Pedro and Lisa and I can't let that happen. I can't live if that happens. I've got to stop them."

"Why?"

"They're monsters!" I exclaimed. "More like unintelligent machines. They're cold-blood killers and I have to kill them before they kill everybody and everything on Eos. They're evil."

"What makes you think they're evil?" she asked.

"How can you ask me that? Haven't you seen what they're doing down there?"

"I have. They almost got me, remember?" she reminded me.

"Then how can you ask me these things?"

"I've been thinking about them. The Gorgons, I mean. I'm not so certain they're like you say they are."

"Are you insane? They're like bugs, like the mindless ants on Earth. They mindlessly march to battle. They fight, they kill, they exterminate us like we are so many worthless bugs, and they march on and kill some more."

"We march on," she said to me.

"We don't march, we fly."

"Same difference."

"How so?" I demanded. I was quite agitated by the shift in the conversation. "What are you getting at?"

"They must have families. They must think for themselves."

"They're mindless machines, robots, killers."

"Our robots aren't killers," she pointed out.

"That's because they evoled differently. They became sentient. They chose not to be killers."

"Fear leads you to judge them, to hate them. You already said you're just like them."

"I'm nothing like them."

"Exactly. You are nothing like them. But if you were, would you be the way they seem to be? What if they do have families? What if they love their children? What if they kill because they're afraid of us, of you? What if they're just like us?"

"I don't know what the hell you're talking about!"

"What if they are pulled away from their loved ones so they can wipe us out before we wipe them out?"

"That does't make any sense."

"But it does. What if the Gorgons are afraid that we will kill their loved ones and want to stop us before we do so?"

"That doesn't make any sense at all," I said. "I pulled away from Lisa because I don't know what I'll do if she dies. I can't face it. I'm not afraid of my own death, I'm afraid of hers. And yours. And Pedro's."

"But don't you see, Hector," Lori said, "none of us can know when we're going to die. We'll all die someday. We're born, we live, and we die. It's the order of the universe. Planets, stars, galaxies all are born and all die.

"I'm certain the Gorgons are the same way. They're fighting because they afraid of us. Maybe, probably because they don't want to lose the ones they love, either. We know so little of them. Maybe their armies are made of male and female soldiers like our military is. Maybe they're fighting for each other, like we are."

"So what if they're fighting for the same reasons we are? What's that got to do with anything?"

"They probably see us as monsters, as we see them as monsters. But we're not monsters and neither are they."

"I still don't understand."

"You're not a monster. You're just afraid. Well, we're all afraid. Don't let fear drive you. Don't let it keep you from loving Lisa."

"I am a monster," I said.

"No, you're not. You're just afraid. Not all the courses at the Academy were mandatory. Some were electives. I took a psychology course."

"I took a classics of literature course," I said, grateful for a change of subject. "I took it because it was one of my dad's favorite subjects. Everyone thinks my name comes from Spain, that my family's Spanish, like Pedro's family. But we're not. I'm not."

"Really?" Lori asked. "How so?"

"My dad loved the classics, especially the story of the Greeks' war with Troy. Hector was one of the heroes of Troy, so dad named me after him."

"But you lived in Spain."

"So? Lisa's from Gentry, but she never met Corinna Vernon, even though they both became SAR pilots and are both from Gentry."

"Gentry's a big world," Lori said.

"So's Earth," I replied.

"Got it," she said. "So, the reason I mentioned taking a psych class is because I learned from it that there are only two basic human emotions."

"And you're going to compare them to Gorgon emotions."

"No at all. The two emotions are love and fear. From love comes compassion and kindness. From fear comes anger and hate. Your fear breeds your hate."

"So?"

"That doesn't make you a monster."

"I feel like a monster."

"But you're not. You're human. Focus on love. Love for Lisa. Love for all of us, your friends. Love for yourself."

"We're in a war, facing a crucial battle, and you're talking about love?" I asked, amazed and puzzled.

"Love frees us. Fear traps us. Be free."

"Then why d'you pray for Pedro's safety? If you're afraid for him, aren't you working against the universe? Aren't you working against love?"

"No, because I believe that life has a purpose. I believe that a perfect principle governs the universe and everyone in it. I believe that principle to be love, not human love, but the love that is of God. I also believe that regardless of what evil exists in the universe, that the perfect principle that is God, that is love, is greater than any evil. I believe that this principle listens to our prayers and grants them. So I pray for Pedro's safety. Just as I pray that we won't die until we're old and have had a long and warm life together."

I shook my head. "I don't know anything about any perfect principle, Lori. All I know is what I see happening and what's happening is death. Rana died. Sherman died. My dad died."

"You have to let it go, Hector."

"I don't know how."

"You have to focus on life, on living, on loving. Let go of hatred before it consumes you."

"It's too late." I stood. So did she.

"You have to let it go," Lori said. "Trust in us, Hector. We can take care of ourselves."

"I trust in you. I don't trust the enemy."

She wrapped her arms around my shoulders and embraced me. "Be careful out there, Hector."

I said nothing.

After leaving Lori, I returned to my cabin. I used my bathroom, then dropped onto my bed, trying for a few more minutes of rest. But I couldn't rest. I couldn't stop thinking about my conversation with Lori. She had said to trust that they could take care of themselves. But how was I do that?

How could I let my friends go off and die? And what of Lisa? I couldn't live without her, yet that's just what I was doing now, living without her. I had pushed her away, so I didn't have to say goodbye and maybe watch her die.

Yet life without Lisa was almost like death, only worst, for I still felt pain. The pain of loneliness.

Death was just sleep without sensation, without dreams, without feeling, without existence, without excuses.

I went over to my desk and activated my comm panel.

I called Lisa's quarters, but she was out. So I left a message.

"Lisa," I said. "It's Hector. I need to talk to you, but I don't know what to say. I don't know if you can forgive what I've become, but I need your help. Call me when you can."

It was time. I left, headed toward the dressing room, where I climbed into my flight suit.

I met Captain Inagaki and the others in the gallery. His briefing was short. Stay close together, he said, and stay low.

Then we went to our fighters.

Polano's fighter was on the forward side of the hangar deck, as were Heinz's and Inagaki's. As they descended the forward stairwell, I wondered which of them might not return after today's COP. The more I flew and fought, the more morbid my thoughts became.

I walked alone to my fighter bay. As the door opened, I saw one tech, Sergeant Lincoln, busy beneath my bird. I crossed over to her.

"Everything set?" I asked.

She crawled from beneath my fighter. "Yeah. I wanted to double check part of your defensive screen. We had a little trouble with some of the projectors. But they're fine now."

"Good." I stepped onto the platform and rose toward my cockpit.

"Lieutenant," Sergeant Lincoln said.

I stopped the platform and lowered it down. "Yeah?"

"You're a hell of a pilot. I'm proud to know you."

"Thanks."

"Kick the shit out of them."

I smiled. "See you out there."

"Not me," she said. "I work for a living."

She left the bay. The platform carried me to the cockpit. I climbed inside.

"Hello, Hector," Prax said.

"Hello, Prax." I settled in. "Close up. Begin depressurizing the bay. Pre-flight completed?"

"Affirmative."

"Anything wrong with our projectors? Or the generators?"

"Negative. All systems nominal."

"Good. Sergeant Lincoln said she'd had trouble with them some of them earlier."

"I am unaware of any previous problems, Hector."

"She was just outside working on them."

"Perhaps she was trying to say goodbye."

"Are things that bad?" I asked.

"The latest reports say two fighters from Third Squadron flying SARCOP were destroyed, along with the two birddogs they escorted. Eleven wounded Marines died on those birddogs."

Fear squeezed my heart. "Was Lisa on either birddog?"

"Inquiring. Negative."

I relaxed.

"Have you worked things out with her?"

"Not yet."

"You should."

"I know."

"Atmosphere cycled out. Opening hangar deck."

"Take us to our catapult."

"Affirmative."

We floated over beside Polano's fighter.

"Bishop to Ice Maker."

"Ice Maker here. Go ahead," I replied.

"All systems nominal. See you out there."

"See you out there. Watch my six. I'll watch yours."

"Affirmative."

"Guardian to Ice Maker," Captain Inagaki called.

"Ice Maker."

"If anything should happen to me, you're the lead. Complete the COP. Those Marines need us. Copy?"

"Copy, Guardian."

"No hot-shotting, Hector. Too many lives are at stake."

"Affirmative."

"LOWCOP One-B, you are cleared for launch," one of *Akagi*'s flight controllers announced.

Prax cut our antigrav field as the catapult began building negative gravs. We settled a little, then floated up as the catapult caught us in its field.

Inagaki launched, followed by Heinz, then Polano. Then us. We exited the brightly lit bay into the darkness of space. Our fighters dived beneath *Akagi* toward the big blue ball of Eos.

"LOWCOP One-B, Lead. Keep tight. Maintain comm silence."

Though our flight took half the normal time, it seemed like an eternity. More than ever now, I worried about my friends and what was happening to them, and about what could happen to them. To keep my mind from wandering,

I checked and rechecked all my systems. I had to focus on this COP. On helping the trapped Marines. On killing the enemy.

Descending toward Eos, our screen snapped on as we punched into the atmosphere, turning us into a fireball. We vectored east of the Asopus Line. Our sensors picked up the intense fighting over the Line, revealing numerous explosions as sky defense lasers knifed into gunboats, as gunboats and fighters destroyed each other, as tanks and troops burned, butchered, and bled each other.

Black rain clouds covered the region, turning daytime into night. Brilliant flashes of lightning and even more brilliant explosive flashes from the combat bleached the darkness white.

As we dived into that black hell, screaming low over friend and foe alike, Prax projected upon my darkened canopy the horrid landscape below. Trees, hills, tanks, bunkers, and bodies burned. The world was shattered, polluted by radioactive debris, by unnatural chemicals, by hatred, fear, insanity, destruction.

"LOWCOP One-B,this One-A. We are engaging gunboats over the Asopus line. Support the lone Marine company. Gorgon gunboats are attacking them. A single platoon is separated from the company. Support it, too. Watch for friendly forces. LOWCOP One-C has launched early and will arrive in twenty minutes."

The call hadn't come from Major Garacyk but rather from his wing mate, Lieutenant Yakima. It was the most I'd ever heard him say. According to Prax, the major still flew with us, but was too busy fighting to update us.

The Marine company spread out over a kilometer, its two remaining platoons surrounding the company's headquarters. The Marines were dug in at various points forming two defensive circles around a central location that consisted of a landing zone for birddogs, the team's headquarters, supplies, and whatever else they had down there.

Crossing over their lines, we climbed up to two thousand meters. We decreased our velocity to six hundred kph. We didn't want to overshoot them.

Wondering what Pedro was up to, I checked my sensors for his recognition signal. He and Lyle dueled with four vics. They were only sixty kilometers off our present course. Polano and I could pop over, blast a vic or two, and pop back in just a few minutes. I started to vector away, Polano keeping up with me.

"Ice Maker, Guardian. Rejoin the formation. Black Angel can take care of himself. Those Marines need us."

Inagaki was right. I hated it, but he was. I wanted to protect my friends. Yet Lori had said that I should trust in their ability to take care of themselves. I knew Pedro was a better pilot than I could ever be, but was the rest of the squadron good enough?

So, though I wanted to go to Pedro's aid, I vectored back behind Guardian.

We approached the separated platoon. The Marines formed a defensive position scattered in an area of about one hundred meters in diameter. Situated on the edge of a small portion of woodlands, the Marines fired across a wide, grassy plain dotted with scattered trees. Explosions erupted all around them as they held back a considerable force of infantry.

A Gorgon box orbited high above the platoon, looking for available shots. They found none. Gorgon gunboats are designed for widespread destruction, not precision shots. Though they could destroy the whole platoon in minutes, they were unable to do so. Their own troops were too close.

"Ice Maker, Guardian. Swan and I will take care of the box. Provide ground support for the Marines."

"Affirmative. Ice Maker to Bishop, we're going down on the deck. Watch yourself."

"Affirmative, Ice Maker."

"Prax, contact the Marines. Let them know what we're up to."

"Affirmative."

Polano and I circled around the platoon, slowing to five hundred kph. About a kilometer from the platoon's outermost positions sat twenty tanks. Scattered around the terrain were groups of Gorgons. Some groups numbered as many as one hundred members, while others appeared composed of no more than eight or ten. All closed on the platoon from various directions. And the closer they got to the Marines, the more fire the Marines received.

"Bishop," I called to Polano, "Ice Maker. Try to hit some of those ground units further back. Use your neutron bomblets. I'll do the same. Take the west side. I'll go east."

"Affirmative."

"Prax, any incoming enemy formations?"

"Negative, Hector."

"Where's Guardian and Swan?"

"Fifty kilometers west of our location. They are engaging two enemy boxes attacking the main body of the Marine company."

"Keep me posted."

"Affirmative."

Flying wide and low, I circled around the enemy. Pockets of Gorgon troops were everywhere. Because my energy shield was down and I drifted slowly on my antigrav field, the Gorgons failed to detect me. Thirty kilometers east of the platoon, I found a column of fifty Gorgon tanks moving around behind the Marines. Trailing them marched a thousand enemy troops. The column stretched out five kilometers.

"Prax, open bay four. Select five neutron bomblets and twelve fusion bomblets. We're going to break-up this column."

"Affirmative, Hector. Weapons selected."

Accelerating back to five hundred kph and climbing two thousand meters, I spread my neutron bomblets along the column. Every kilometer a brilliant-white micro-flash created by a plutonium detonation, released a five-hundred-meter circle of lethal neutron radiation. Only the area of the small explosion suffered blast damage and lingering radiation. The neutron radiation quickly dissipated.

Most of the Gorgons died.

Dropping back down to one thousand meters, I released my fusion bomblets among the tanks. These functioned like the neutron bomblets, but instead of just showering the enemy with lethal radiation, their tiny plutonium blasts also threw out a kiloton of shockwaves, million-degree heat, and death.

My bomblets destroyed twenty tanks and damaged twenty more. The remaining tanks split into pairs and skittered away.

I pursued them.

Dropping down to near the ground, I slowed considerably as I hunted them down. There were small pockets of Gorgons everywhere. I ignored them. None were larger than thirty troops. The Marines could easily deal with them.

Closing on the platoon's location, I found a long, low ridgeline toward which the Gorgon tanks maneuvered. Upon the ridge sat fifteen more tanks. My sensors indicated that these tanks could fire directly at the Marine platoon. Since they hadn't fired yet, I assumed they were waiting for their numbers to increase so the bombardment would devastate the Marines, if not outright wipe them out.

Pulling my bird's nose up, I climbed straight up above the ridge. Upon my request, Prax selected three more fusion bomblets. At five thousand meters, I released the bomblets. Blinding light and tremendous explosions, with a tremendous shockwave depressing the ridge turned the tanks into so much radioactive debris. All fifteen tanks were destroyed, along with four other tanks which had joined them.

Scanning the area, I spotted the six surviving tanks from the troop column retreating. Dropping back down, I eliminated them all by blasting each from behind with my plasma cannon.

"Ice Maker, Guardian. Rejoin."

"Affirmative."

My sensors indicated Polano covered the Marine platoon. Reconnecting with him, we shot up a few of the larger groups of Gorgon soldiers and then, climbing to thirty kilometers, we raced to regroup with Inagaki and Heinz, who covered the main body of the Marine company.

As we approached them, we saw they were engaged with two Gorgon boxes and two vics. The three Gorgon gunboats in each vic, flying tight, tried distracting Inagaki and Heinz as they blew apart a box. Together Guardian and Swan destroyed four gunboats, while the box's other three gunboats fled.

"Bishop, Ice Maker, let's get those vics off of us."

"Affirmative."

Polano drew tighter to me. Almost as one, we bounced a vic hot on Swan's tail. We each loosed a missile. Two bright fireballs. Two gunboats gone. Polano blew apart the third gunboat with his plasma cannon.

"Guardian and Zulu, Kingslayer, watch for Na fighters. We have engaged one vic. Hawkeye is down. SARCOP is picking him up now. Watch yourselves."

The other Gorgon vic cleared the area, escorting a box missing two gunboats as we vectored west. Polano and I each had most of our missiles, and plasma and neutron bomblets. Our plasma cannons were at full capacity.

"Ice Maker, you and Bishop will cover our tails," Inagaki said. "Swan and I will fly over the enemy troops, releasing our neutron bomblets. Follow our vector. Target all tanks."

"Affirmative," I replied.

"LOWCOP One-B, Kingslayer. One-C will attack the southern front. One-A will provide cover."

"Affirmative, Kingslayer," Captain Inagaki replied. "Ice Maker, we're beginning our attack."

The wormheads were throwing everything against the Marines. They attacked from too many directions while there were too few of us to handle everything.

"Ice Maker, Kingslayer. Help that platoon. We'll cover Guardian and Swan."

It was too late. We had already begun our run. As we dived on the eastern force, brilliant white flashes revealed the detonations of Guardian's and Swan's neutron bomblets. The surviving Gorgons scattered.

We flew tight behind them. I fired five times, destroying five tanks. Polano dropped six more fusion bomblets, destroying two dozen tanks. Then we pulled up and came around, vectoring back towards the separated platoon.

"Na fighters! Na fighters!" Lyle called. He sounded scared.

"Prax, where are they?"

"Two Na vics are engaging Kingslayer's COP. Another Na vic is attacking Zulu's COP."

"Kingslayer's hit! Kingslayer's hit!" Lyle exclaimed.

I brought us around again, vectoring for Pedro's COP. Without Major Garacyk, Pedro and Lyle didn't stand a chance against two Na vics.

"Ice Maker, Guardian. Those Marines need you."

"We're no good to them if we're wiped out," I said.

"Are two lives more important than hundreds?"

"They're my friends!"

"Do your duty. Let your friends do theirs."

Someone in the isolated platoon contacted us. "Where the hell are you? We need your help. We're being overrun!"

"Na fighters, Na fighters, Na fighters," Ava Farley cried out. "Is there anyone out there to help us? Three vics are attacking us. We need help!"

"Sky boys, we need your help…" another voice from the Marine platoon cried out. "You damned bastards are never here when we need you."

Everyone needed help all at once Pedro needed help. Lori and Ava needed help. The Marines needed help.

My friends were dying, my family being murdered. If I helped them, hundreds might die. If I helped the hundreds, my friends would die.

It was all too much, happening too fast, and it was the damned Gorgons' fault. They had brought in the Na. They were trying to obliterate humanity from Eos. They sought the destruction of our forces, of my friends. I wanted to kill all the Gorgons and all the Na alike. I wanted them all dead. But I also wanted the fighting and killing to stop. I wanted my friends alive. I wanted peace. I wanted Lisa's love again.

As we orbited the battlefield, lightning brightened the landscape below, revealing thousands of Gorgons rampaging through the Marines. Flashes from Gorgon plasma rifles mingled with bright plasma streams fired by the Marines. The Gorgons were close enough to strike with their strange axes, while the Marines fought back with everything they had, even their hands.

I hated the enemy. I hated them because I had to choose between saving my friends or saving the Marines. I hated the Gorgons because there were too many of them, because they planned well, throwing everything at us when we couldn't reach everyone. I hated them because I couldn't stop them.

Whatever choice I made, I knew I wouldn't be able to live with it. If I saved my friends and the enemy broke through, they'd slaughter the Marines. If I saved the Marines, the enemy would murder my friends.

"You skyboy sonsabitches are useless," some Marine called. "We're dying down here, you bloody cowards."

The hating wasn't going to stop. I was never going to have freedom. I was never going to have Lisa's love again.

I made my decision, the only one I could make, the one I had to make. The one that left me hating myself more than the enemy.

"Ice Maker, Bishop. What're we going to do?"

"Our duty."

"Which duty?"

"Help the Marines. The others will have to take care of themselves."

"What?"

"You heard me. Keep close. We're helping that platoon down there. If anyone's left to help."

"Affirmative."

I led Polano back down. As we sped along, I fried a couple of Gorgon tanks, blowing them apart. I dropped a neutron bomblet on a cluster of enemy troops pursuing five Marines caught out in the open. The Marines were well out of range of the bomblet.

I might not be able to save my friends, or even the Marines, but I could kill the enemy.

We reached theisolated platoon's position. Twenty enemy tanks sat in the middle of it, in a circle, their plasma cannon firing every which way, their energy screens forming a protective blanket around them.

Hovering over the circle of enemy tanks, I fired my plasma cannon four times at a single tank, my first three shots shattering its screen, my fourth shot turning it into molten metal. I dropped two fusion bomblets into the circle. Two more tanks exploded.

Polano orbited around me, guarding me from enemy sky craft and occasionally taking pot shots at the tanks, destroying two of them.

The remaining tanks scurried away, unable to fire at us, unable to defend themselves.

A blast shook my bird, skidding me sideways.

"Damage report?" I asked Prax.

"Negative damage. A Gorgon sky defense vehicle fired at us."

"Range?"

"Two kilometers due east. On a low hill."

"Got it. Bishop, Ice Maker. Can you engage that skydef tank?"

"On it."

"Watch yourself."

"You better believe I will," he replied.

"We're under attack," Kara Heinz, Guardian's wingmate, called. "We need help. Ice Maker, can you help us?"

"Negative," I replied, my throat tight.

Prax alerted me to three columns of enemy troops running toward the platoon from different directions. According to my sensors, each column was a thousand troops strong. No tanks were with them.

Contacting Polano, who had obliterated the skydef vehicle, he vectored after me. We spotted the enemy about a kilometer away.

"Weapon's load?" I asked Prax.

"Seven missiles left. Plasma cannon at eighty percent and recycling. Twenty plasma bomblets and twelve neutron bomblets left."

"Ready the neutron bomblets. Bishop, use only your neutron bomblets. Take out the nearest column. Vaporize anything you want."

"Affirmative, Ice Maker. Suggest we climb to two thousand meters."

"Agreed."

We dropped our bomblets, the radiation slicing through the enemy. Those that didn't die right away soon would, while others would be sick for a long time. We came back right on the deck, just meters above the ground, our cannons firing, the turbulence from our passing shockwave flattening the enemy. When we left minutes later, the enemy force had scattered.

"Situation?" I asked Prax, climbing, looking for targets.

"Contact has been lost with Guardian, Swan, Diamond, Racer, Kingslayer, Zulu, BS, Munk, and Black Angel. The SARCOP is under attack by Na fighters."

"Bishop, we're going to help the SARCOP."

"Affirmative." There was a hardness to his voice I'd never heard before.

Contact had been lost with everyone. Were they all dead? How could that be? Had I lost them all?

We accelerated to four thousand kilometers per hour and reached the SARCOP in less than sixty seconds. Four fighters protected two birddogs from three Na vics. We matched velocities with the fighters.

"SARCOP, Ice Maker and Bishop from what's left of First Squadron."

"Ice Maker, Vixen. Good to hear your voice, Hector. Your friend, Alvarez, saved my life a little while ago."

"When was that, Roberta?"

"Five minutes ago. Could you get that vic off my tail?"

"Affirmative. Where's Black Angel at?"

"Black Angel went to aide SARCOP Two. We lost two pilots over there."

"Affirmative." Pedro might still be alive.

Polano and I dropped behind the vic, concentrating our cannons on the left fighter. But the vic kept rotating, our plasma streams glancing against first the left and then the right fighters, their energy screens momentarily flaring red.

"Ice Maker, Bishop. This isn't any good."

"Affirmative. Lock onto the center fighter. Loose a missile at it and keep firing."

"Affirmative."

"Plasma cannon at seventy percent," Prax announced.

"Boost it anyway you can, Prax," I said.

We began firing on the central Na fighter. The vic dropped away from Vixen and her wing mate, breaking hard right. We followed, slow in response. The vic continued rotating and began jinking left, right, up, down. Just as we got a lock on the center fighter, the vic broke hard right again.

Six missiles dropped away from the Na fighters, following us.

"Break left," I called to Polano. He pulled hard left, I pulled hard right. Four missiles followed him, two followed me.

"Oh, shit!" Polano screamed. There was a bright flash behind me. Polano was gone.

The two remaining missiles followed me.

I dropped down on the deck, near the ground, the missiles hot on my tail. I punched to maximum acceleration and climbed straight up. The missiles followed, closing.

At fifteen thousand kph and accelerating, it took only minutes to clear Eos's atmosphere. The two missiles closed on me. They were only twenty kilometers behind.

"Get ready to release all the remaining fusion bomblets in their path. Lock two missiles on them."

"Affirmative," Prax replied.

I stopped accelerating at twenty-five thousand kph. The pursuing missiles closed. Prax released the bomblets. As he did so, I brought us hard around. Several Gees escaped the inertial dampers, slamming me into my seat. I almost blacked out.

The fusion bomblets detonated. One missile exploded. A single missile leaped from one of our bays and destroyed the other missile.

Now I knew why so many of us had gone down. These bastards were good.

"Vixen is down. Vixen is down," a pilot called.

I dived for the deck, maintaining my twenty-five thousand kph velocity. Prax located the vic that had killed Polano and almost us. Hurling toward it, my screens aflame with atmospheric fire, I blasted through the vic as it chased a climbing birddog.

My bird shuddered as I struck the center fighter. Prax informed me that all our systems still functioned.

The Na fighters split three different ways. I had them. Cutting my velocity as I swung around in a long arc, I bounced the furthest fighter. He jerked every which way, rotating as fast as he could. I pumped plasma streams at him and let loose a missile. He died as Polano had died.

My bird shook from an explosion. A Na missile had detonated close by, just missing. My screen power dropped thirty percent.

"Damage to right side screen projectors. Plasma cannon malfunctioning," Prax announced.

"Shit! Anything else?"

"Number three bay will not open."

"Load?"

"Three missiles."

"Fix it."

"Unable to comply."

"Then jettison the door."

"Affirmative."

I came back around as the other two fighters closed with me.

I blasted through them again, but my screen failed on the right side. A collision with one of the Na fighters gouged my hull.

Turning quickly, slowing to less than five thousand kph, a few Gees smashing me down, I let loose the missiles from bay three, its jettisoned door fluttering downward and away. The fighter I'd rammed became a white fireball of superheated metallic particles as my missiles vaporized it.

The last fighter looped around, settling behind me. His twin plasma cannons fired and what was left of my energy screen collapsed.

I cut my velocity and he pulled alongside me, still rotating. I kept even so he couldn't fire either his cannons or his missiles. With great effort, I matched his rotations, drifting so close that my hull glanced against his screen. Where my bird touched his energy field, my hull reddened while his screen flared yellow.

He jerked left and I jerked left. He jinked up and down and I jinked up and down. He dived. I dived. He climbed.

And I dropped back, firing my remaining missiles. He became a cloud of expanding plasma.

More plasma streams hit my bird and my engine died.

"Send out the call," I told Prax. I activated the controls releasing the cockpit from our bird. We jettisoned just before a missile vaporized it.

"Ice Maker's down," Prax called.

"No, he's not," came the reply. A graviton beam caught us.

Our cockpit, the canopy no longer darkened, was pulled inside a birddog's retrieval bay.

Minutes later, free of the atmosphere, we returned toward *Akagi*. What was left of Vixen's SARCOP escorted us.

CHAPTER TWENTY-THREE

MY RETURN FLIGHT TO *Akagi* aboard the birddog was the darkest moment of my life, darker even than when I'd learned that my dad had died. For all I knew, most of my squadron, and maybe all of my friends, had been killed.

I remained in my cockpit rather than exiting into the birddog's retrieval bay. I wrote my after action report, made certain Prax had downloaded himself into his memory canister and waited for the SAR boat to dock in *Akagi*'s belly.

Once the birddog had settled inside its bay, and the bay had re-pressurized, the birddog's tail ramp lowered. Sergeant Lincoln, followed by two medical technicians, entered. Only then did I open my cockpit.

Lincoln helped me out. "You did good."

"What's the squadron's situation like?"

"Bad."

"How bad?" I asked.

"Bad. But you might like to know that Colonel Wallis led lieutenants Brattano, DuQuesne, and Geys out in a NaCOP forty minutes ago. They should be back anytime."

"I didn't know the colonel had a bird."

"During normal times General Devon and Colonel Wallis fly as often as they can."

"I didn't know that. But don't they just borrow birds from the different squadrons?"

Sergeant Lincoln shook her head. "They keep their birds in one of *Akagi*'s shuttle bays. The colonel moved his bird up to the nearest flight deck, which belonged to Fifth Squadron, where it was armed and readied and he launched from there, joining up with the remainder of First Squadron."

The remainder of First Squadron. That phrase frightened me. Who was left besides me?

"D'you know anything else? Who's been saved, who've we lost? If you know, tell me."

"I don't know, lieutenant," Sergeant Lincoln said. "I'm sorry."

"How'd the colonel's NaCOP do?"

"They got a couple of vics, that's all I know. And that they're all okay."

I nodded.

The robot medtechs led me out of the birddog. Just down the ramp, I turned and called back to Sergeant Lincoln. "Take good care of Prax. I'm going to want him for my next bird."

"Count on it, lieutenant."

The medtechs took me to Sickbay, where they helped me out my flight suit. They then examined me for injuries and radiation exposure. Finding that I was okay, they released me.

I returned to my cabin, removed the temporary clothes the medtechs had given me, showered, got dressed in a fresh uniform, and then lay down on my bed, ordering the lights out. I stared at my ceiling as my computer projected Spain's night sky on it.

I felt drained of life.

Unable to rest, I got up and hurried to the squadron's gallery.

I needed to know if anyone had survived or if I was all alone. I needed to know if Pedro still lived. Most of all, I needed to know if Lisa lived.

The gallery was empty. I walked over to the viewing ports and stared at the hangar deck below.

"They're not back yet, son," General Devon said.

I turned around. I hadn't heard him enter. He looked as tired and as empty as me.

"I need to know."

"I know. They'll be back soon. You did well today."

We stood in silence for a few moments. Then I asked: "How soon do I go back out?"

"You don't."

"Why not?"

"Your squadron's decimated. So's Third and Fifth squadrons. I've only enough pilots for two COPs in Seventh Squadron. And both SAR squadrons are so badly beat up that they can't fly anymore.

"How many..." I tried asking. I stopped, afraid.

"Not many."

I turned back to window. "It's odd."

"What is?"

"How this day began. A few hours ago, I stood here with one my friends, Lieutenant Lori Clark, as we watched Pedro leave on his COP."

"I'm sorry about Lieutenant Clark, son. She was a good officer and pilot."

"Then she's dead?"

"And her wingmate, Lieutenant Farley. Like you, they fulfilled their mission. They bombed the Gorgons until the Na killed them."

"And Pedro? He and Lori were lovers."

"He fought until he ran out of missiles. Then he fought until his cannon burned out. He got two Na vics before that happened. When a third Na vic bounced him, he rammed one of its fighters, wrecking it and his own fighter. I wonder where he got that idea?" he said, glancing at me.

"Then he's gone, too?"

"He survived. The Marines got to him before the Gorgons did. He'll be back soon."

"Does he know about Lori?"

"He knows."

"Who else did we lose?"

"Lieutenant Lem. Captain Inagaki. Major Garacyk. Lieutenant Heinz. Lieutenant Polano. Lieutenant Munk."

"So many."

"Too many. I sent lots of good people out to die today. And I will remember them all."

We stared out the window. "I shouldn't have let Colonel Wallis go out. But how could I stop him? Every CSG is allowed to fly with his or her pilots when they're in danger. But CSFs aren't. The Command doesn't like losing generals."

"Why didn't you want the colonel to go out, sir?"

"Because I'd already lost enough good people today. But Brad's the only pilot under my command who'd had any experience against Na fighters. Of the twenty kills to his credit, fifteen were against the Na, including six today. With Brad's kills, as well as yours, Major Garacyk's, and

Lieutenant Alvarez, almost two thirds of all the Na fighters over Eos have been destroyed. That's why I said that we hurt the enemy bad.

"But this is what commanding is all about, Hector. It's more than organization. It's more than making sure the right people are in the right slots. It's about making the hard choices. It's about ordering people to their deaths, praying that they don't die, but knowing that some, maybe most, will.

"It's the greatest burden of all, because among all those people with promising futures, with loved ones and families, you often have friends. It's a helluva thing, ordering your friends out to die so that others might live, but you have to do it. You have to choose between the greater good and what you want.

"It's what I do every day."

"I made that choice today," I said.

"I know," he said.

"I let my friends die so I could help the Marines."

"You did what you had to do."

"But what about my friends?"

"You did your duty to them."

"I let them die."

"You let them choose for themselves. You let them sacrifice themselves for what they believed in. You did your job, while they did theirs. You honored them by doing your duty. Now honor them by not blaming yourself for what you couldn't do."

"But they're dead. I could've saved them."

"How? Look at the facts, son. You lost your wing mate and your fighter engaging one Na vic. Had you gone to rescue your friends the outcome wouldn't have been any different, except a lot more Marines would've died. You did all you could. Don't blame yourself for something that you couldn't change."

"Maybe you're right, sir."

"I know I am. You know, Hector, you're a lot like Claude Daggett. After a particular mission against the Shh'Uruu fifteen years ago, he felt like you did. He decided that he'd had enough killing and after that conflict ended he transferred to SAR. Maybe you should consider the same move."

"I'm where I belong, sir."

"I think so, too. Looks like your squadron's home."

I glanced into the hangar. Five fighters drifted in on graviton beams, Colonel Wallis's among them. There were plenty of empty bays for him to dock in.

"What's going to happen to us?"

"*Akagi*'s being pulled out. The new task group will be here in a few hours. Then I'll transfer my command to one of the carriers coming with it.

"As for you, you have choices to make."

"Sir?"

"A few days ago, Sky Command decided it wanted to pull First Squadron back to Earth. Good thing, too, since the squadron needs rebuilding. And its gonna take a long time. I've three captaincies available. If you want one, it's yours."

"What about Captain Mboko?" I asked.

"I'm giving her the squadron. If you can work out your differences with her, then you should stay. The squadron needs you. But if you can't, I'm sure I can find another captaincy somewhere for you."

"I'll talk to her. What about the others?"

"I can't make any promises. But, between you and me, I think Lieutenant Alvarez would make a good captain. And personally, I think he's gonna need a lotta therapy and time with his family on Earth. And with his best friend."

"Thank you, sir."

"I'm sorry about your friends, Hector."

"Thank you, sir."

He started to go.

"Sir?"

"Yes?"

"Did a SAR lieutenant named Lisa Mauros make it?"

"She did. Her birddog should dock soon."

"Thanks."

"By the way, son, you'll be gettin' some medals soon."

"Medals aren't worth much, sir."

"You're wrong, son. Medals are important. They represent who we are, what we sacrificed, and what others sacrificed for us. Medals don't hurt you, people do. Remember that."

"I will."

"See you out there, Hector."

"You, too, sir."

I hurried down to the men's dressing room. Jacques, Vlad, and Brattano were just climbing out of their flight suits.

"You shit!" Brattano spat at me. "You let everyone die."

I wasn't going to take this from him anymore. Before he could say another word, I shoved him away.

Even with his flight suit around his ankles, Brattano was ready to fight me. He swung at my face, a blow that certainly would've loosened most of my teeth. But I ducked and drove my shoulder into his chest, knocking the wind out of him. Tripping over his pants, he fell to the deck.

"You. You," he gasped. He shook his head, clearing it. He kicked his flight suit free. Standing, he lunged at me again.

But he never reached me. Geys grabbed him, spun him around, and threw him back down.

"What're you doing?" Geys yelled at him.

"He let everyone die. He ran away."

"He did what he had to do," Geys replied.

"You hate him as much as I do!"

"I hate that Lisa loves him, not me. He fought with courage and honor and I don't hate that. He's more of a man than you are. Get out of here before I beat the hell outta you."

"But..." Brattano stammered, getting to his feet.

"I'd do what he said," Jacques said. "Because if he doesn't pound you, I will."

Brattano stared at Jacques, then at Vlad. He cursed and started for the showers. He stopped in front of me.

"If you say it, I'll vector every last tooth of yours down your throat," Vlad said.

Brattano glared at Vlad, then left.

"Thanks," I said to Vlad.

"You flew well today. I'm proud of you."

"You, too," I said.

"Go to Lisa. If you break her heart, I'll break your neck." With that, Vlad walked behind the lockers, toward the showers.

I turned to thank Jacques. His eyes were sad.

"You heard?" I said.

"I did. See you later."

"Sure."

Outside the dressing room, I let out a deep sigh. Then I glanced around to make certain Brattano wasn't following me.

He wasn't.

"Crossman." I turned as Captain Mboko strode down the corridor, still in her suit, her helmet folded down her back.

"Captain."

"You mean major."

"Affirmative, major."

"Good. I just completed a conversation with Brigadier General Devon. Crossman... Hector, I made an error concerning you. If you can forgive me, I'd appreciate your assistance in rebuilding the Black Birds. I consider you the best officer for the job. Will you assist me?"

"I'll think about it, major."

"My name's Sanura, Hector. We lost a lot of beloved comrades today. Let's not lose any others."

"Yes, ma'am."

"See you out there, Hector."

"See you out there," I replied.

I spent the next few hours in my office, going over the simulations, updating some, reworking others. Most of the time, I waited with impatience for Lisa and Pedro to return. I frequently checked the information net, searching for the arrival times of the various SAR boats coming back from Eos. Neither Lisa's boat, nor the one carrying Pedro, had yet returned.

I continued working and waiting, waiting, waiting, until I couldn't take it anymore. So I went for a walk. I headed aft, toward the SAR squadron hangars. When I reached

Lisa's squadron hangar, I found out that she had already arrived and gone. She'd attended her debriefing, then returned to her quarters.

So I went to her quarters, but her door informed me she had come and gone. I asked around, but no one seemed to know where she went.

Akagi was a big ship. Lisa could be anywhere. My head told me to be patient. My heart couldn't wait.

I wandered about, seeking her. I checked the ship's gardens, the pools, the lounges, and down numerous corridors.

What, if she just didn't want me anymore?

After more than hour, I returned to my cabin. The door was open. Was Lisa inside?

It was Pedro.

"Amigo," he whispered.

"Are you okay?"

"No."

He sat on my couch. I sat on my bed, across from him. "I don't know if this will help you any, but Lori's prayers were answered today."

"How would you know?" he snapped at me.

I forgave him. His pain struck at me, not him. "Lori and I watched you leave today. She told me she always prayed for your safe return. She wanted you to survive. She loved you and wanted a life with you."

"What will I do without her, amigo?"

"I don't know. I guess all you can do is hold onto her love for as long as you can. And see to it that her prayers for you are always answered."

Pedro stared at the deck. Then he took a deep breath and looked at me. "What about Lisa?"

"She survived. Other than that, I don't know."

"Lori and Lisa were close friends, like us. Find her. Say anything, do anything, but keep her."

I stood. "But where should I go?"

"Keep looking until you find her."

As I left my cabin, Pedro said, "See you out there, amigo."

"And you."

I searched everywhere again, I finally found her in the forward lounge. She sat at a table along the dome's rim, staring out into space. She heard me as a I came up and turned around. Her eyes were wet.

"I've been wandering around, searching for you. I finally came here because I was too exhausted and saddened to search anymore and now you walk right in," she said.

I sat across from her. "I looked for you, too. Everywhere."

She reached across the table and took my hands in hers. "I spent a lot of time thinking about us while I sought you. I want to tell you that I'm sorry."

Here it came. Lisa didn't want me. It was over and she wanted to tell me so. Months back, when Corinna told me she loved me only as a friend, my heart had cracked. Now, as Lisa rejected me, I wished the Na had killed me.

Tears filled my eyes. "You're going to tell me you can't love the monster that I've become. That there's nothing left. And you're right. You're right."

"No, no, no, I would never say that," she said, her eyes tearing up as well.

"I don't understand."

"I told you that I couldn't be with someone filled with hate. That I didn't want this war to consume you, to consume us. But today I lost almost every friend I have.

And I find myself at the brink. You see, I hate the enemy too. I hate them for what they did to us today. But most of all I hate them for coming between us."

"So do I," I said. "But hating took me away from you and I don't want to hate anymore. I want to live, to love, to be with you. I want peace, if there's any to be found."

She nodded, removing her hands from me and lifting them to wipe the tears from her eyes. "I want to be with you, too, dearest. I want love and peace, too. But I need you to understand, to know, what happened.

"When you pulled away from me, my heart crumbled. I knew your fear. I knew you couldn't tell about it. It was my fault. I made conditions you couldn't meet. I couldn't meet them, either"

"It wasn't your fault."

"But it was," she replied. "My grandmother once told me that for love to work it has to be unconditional."

"I should've told you what was happening to me, but I couldn't. And today, out there, I almost lost you."

"And I almost lost you!"

We stood. We held each other close.

"What do we do now?" I whispered.

"We start over," she said.

"How?"

"Without conditions," she replied.

"Anything else?"

"We find peace. Together."

THE END

www.ingramcontent.com/pod-product-compliance
Lightning Source LLC
Chambersburg PA
CBHW071226300726
48975CB00002B/308